Acknowledgments

Thanks to the many people
that made this book possible:
Ann Cecil, Nancy Janda, Laurel Jamieson,
Susan Petroulas, Hope Erica Ring, M.D.,
June Drexler Robertson

Special thanks to Lisa Janice Cohen
for "Stone Clan Lullaby," "Forge,"
and "We Are Pittsburgh."

In Loving Memory of Ann Cecil

1: TUNNEL TO NOWHERE

Life was so much simpler when Tinker didn't have a horde of heavily armed elves following her everywhere, all ready to kill anyone that triggered their paranoia. It didn't help that she was still recovering from hairline fractures to her right ulna and radius. Her shiny new status as a *domana*-caste elf princess meant she was expected to cast spells triggered by complex finger positions and vocal commands. So, yes, breaking her arm was a very bad thing. It didn't mean she was helpless. With an IQ over one-eighty, and standing only five feet tall, she always considered her wits to be her greatest weapon.

Her Hand (the military unit of five *sekasha*-caste bodyguards, not the appendage attached to her arm) had spent the week acting like there were evil ninjas hiding in every shadow. With her Hand in protective overdrive, the last thing Tinker needed was a pushy stranger trying to talk to her. Not that Chloe Polanski technically was a stranger; the woman was one of

Pittsburgh's most popular television reporters. Elves, though, don't watch TV. The tall *sekasha* towered between Tinker and Chloe like trees. Dangerous trees with magically sharp wooden swords that could cut through solid steel.

"Good morning, Vicereine." Chloe greeted Tinker from the other side of the forest of warriors. "You're looking—well-protected. How are you today?"

"Oh, just peachy." Tinker sighed at the scale-armored back blocking her view of the reporter. Tinker loved her *sekasha*, especially her First, Pony, but in the last few days she just wanted to whack them all with a big stick. She suspected if she asked, they'd find her a suitable club. They might even stand still and let her smack them. She would feel guilty, however, since she had nearly gotten them killed the week before last. Cloudwalker and Little Egret still sported an impressive set of bruises, and Rainlily had a slight wheeze from smoke inhalation.

"Elves have these nifty spells that focuses magic into their—our natural regenerative abilities." Tinker put a hand on the center of Pony's armored back and pushed him out of the way. Or at least, she tried; it was like trying to move a tree. "It sends our healing into overdrive. Compressing eight weeks of healing into one, though, hurts like—shit!" She made the mistake of using both hands and pushing harder. She hissed as pain flashed through her right arm.

"*Domi!*" Pony's hand went to his sword as Tinker curled into a ball around her arm. "Are you hurt?"

"No, I'm fine," Tinker growled as she straightened up, forcing herself to ignore the pain. She'd learned the hard way that any sign of weakness on her part made her bodyguards extremely antsy. Nervous *sekasha* were deadly *sekasha*. She didn't want them mowing down Chloe just because Tinker had been stupid.

"Are you sure, *domi*?" Pony looked down at her, his dark eyes full of concern.

"My arm is still bruised." Tinker gave a few more futile pushes against his armor, careful to only use her left hand. "Can you give me space? I'm trying to have a conversation here."

Pony gave her a worried look but shifted aside.

They were on the bridge that led into the Squirrel Hill Tunnels. It was the beginning of September, but heat blasted off the sun-baked concrete, scented with ancient gas fumes. They had been out of the air-conditioning of the gray Rolls-Royce for all of three minutes, but there was already sweat trickling down Tinker's back. The only good thing about Tinker's dress of jewel-green fairy silk was the breeze she could generate by flapping the skirt.

Despite the heat, Chloe Polanski wore her beauty like an impenetrable shield. Every hair of her pale blond bob was in place. Her makeup was so flawless that only the black eyeliner around her pale blue eyes and the glint of lipstick on her full lips betrayed the fact that she was wearing any. Her tortoise blouse and black slacks managed to be elf flamboyant and yet human formal at the same time. Chloe seemed completely at ease; only her perfectly manicured fingertips, nervously fidgeting with her amber necklace, betrayed her awareness of how dangerous the *sekasha* could be.

"What are you doing here?" Tinker really didn't want to do an interview. It had been a weird summer, even by Tinker's standards. So far she had accidentally changed from human to elf, unknowingly gotten married, ripped a hole in the fabric of reality, fallen off the planet, crashed a spaceship into Turtle Creek, and fought a dragon. If that wasn't enough to set some kind of record for weirdness, there were twenty days left of summer to go. Trying to explain everything would take half the afternoon, a large whiteboard, and a great deal of advanced physics.

"I have a couple of questions that I wanted to ask you." The corners of Chloe's mouth tightened as she kept a predatory smile in check. Chloe didn't cover the hoverbike circuit, so Tinker had been spared Chloe's cat-and-mouse tactics. "You're a bigger prize now that you're vicereine."

Tinker fought the temptation to stick her tongue out at Chloe. The reporter was wearing her signature face-to-face camera eyepiece, allowing her to film both herself and her interview subject without a cameraman. In a fabled remote and secure place, often sought out by those she interviewed but never found, everything Chloe saw was recorded. Only part of Chloe's success was based on her eyepiece. None of the other Pittsburgh reporters had the eyepiece since much of Pittsburgh's technology was stuck in the last century. The rest of her success was due to her vindictiveness: if someone tried to play hardball with her, she took a hatchet to their reputation. She had the "impossible to look away" quality of a train wreck.

It would behoove Tinker to play nice for her first official interview as the elf princess, even if the experience were akin to waterboarding. "So, what do you want to know?"

Chloe's mouth curled up into her cat smile. "Everything," she purred.

Tinker laughed. "Here? Now? You do realize we're in a war zone?"

"As I stated before, you're now very well-protected. You're a very difficult woman—I mean female, since 'woman' doesn't apply to you anymore—to nail."

Judging by Stormsong's soft growl, Tinker wasn't the only one feeling like that statement had been loaded with subtle insults.

"This isn't a safe place or time for an interview." Tinker started to walk in hopes of scraping Chloe off somehow—perhaps against a wall or something. How had Chloe gotten to the stretch of abandoned highway in front of Squirrel Hill Tunnels? Had she walked? "Call Director Maynard of the Earth Interdimensional Agency and he'll set up an interview for some other time. I've got tons of shit to do." For her own subtle insult, she added. "Mind-boggling complex shit."

Chloe began walking backward, keeping just a few feet in front of Tinker. "This is Chloe Polanski. I'm here with our own little Cinderella, Princess Tinker."

"Do I need to use smaller words for you to understand me?" Tinker held up her fingers to indicate tiny words. "Call Maynard."

Displaying what years of practice could achieve, Chloe sidestepped a pothole without glancing down. "Princess, please, the people of Pittsburgh could do with some reassurance in this time of uncertainty."

Annoyingly, Chloe was right. Tinker stopped with a sigh. "Prince True Flame and Windwolf and Director Maynard are working closely together to protect everyone in the city from the oni."

"You don't add yourself to that triumvirate of power? Or is this a male-only club?"

"It isn't male-only. Jewel Tear on Stone is currently the head of the Stone Clan. She and Forest Moss on Stone are also working with the prince and the viceroy. They're all out right now looking for oni."

"And you aren't?"

"I'm still recovering from a broken arm." Tinker pulled up her sleeve to show off the impressive bruising. It made for an easy excuse.

"Surely there were things you could have done while you were recovering."

"No." Because that felt too rude, Tinker added, "The healing spells forced me to sleep through most of last week. Today is the first day I've felt awake enough to leave the enclave. I'm certainly not up to running all over Pittsburgh to fight oni."

Not that it had even occurred to her to join in the combat. It wasn't the best use of her abilities.

Chloe changed tactics. "Each Stone Clan *domana* was given a hundred thousand *sen* of land as remuneration for their help in fighting the oni. Earth Son was killed by his own people within a week of arriving. What happens to his share? Will the Wind Clan still be giving up that land? Is it true that they will also receive part of the city?"

"I haven't been paying strict attention to what's going on" would be a truthful answer but would also made Tinker look stupid. She'd spent the last month or so either held captive or unconscious or busy trying to save the world or not even *on* the planet. She settled for "Jewel Tear has sent word of Earth Son's death to the head of her clan in the Easternlands.

Until the Stone Clan responds, all negotiations have been put on hold."

"Are you really going to let your husband give away part of Pittsburgh for one week's worth of work?"

It was tempting and terrifying at the same time to know that the *sekasha* could stop this interview cold. Tempting because Tinker really didn't want to talk about all the mistakes she'd made that summer. Terrifying because one slip on her part, and all of Pittsburgh could experience a digital recording of Chloe's beheading. It would be one more mistake that Tinker wouldn't want to have to explain.

"My husband and I only care for the safety of our people," Tinker said carefully. "We will do whatever it takes to guard them."

"The hundred thousand *sen* of land is to be all virgin forest beyond the Rim." Stormsong was the only one of Tinker's Hand that was fluent in English. The female *sekasha* had spent decades living in Pittsburgh, reveling in the human culture. Stormsong probably recognized Chloe, but judging by the look on her face, she also knew of the reporter's venomous reputation.

Chloc's hand went nervously to her necklace. Her perfect white-tipped fingernails tapped the dark honey-colored stones. The pendant had an insect trapped within the fossilized resin. Did it represent her interview subjects, trapped for Chloe's inspection?

"I see." Chloe retreated on the subject and looked for a safer battlefield. She scanned the *sekasha*. Those working as Blades had spread out to secure the area while Pony and Stormsong continued to flank Tinker, working as Shields. "You've taken two full Hands now?"

Good, a subject Tinker didn't mind talking about.

"I only have five Beholden." Tinker gave Pony and Stormsong's Elvish names as her First and Second and then added Cloudwalker, Rainlily, and Little Egret as the rest of her Hand. She wasn't sure if the warriors continued counting out their positions; if they did, that would be her Third, Fourth, and Fifth. They'd become officially hers after she nearly killed them the third or fourth time. "The other five with me actually belong to Windwolf."

"And Blue Sky Montana?" Chloe had spotted the boy among the adult *sekasha*. Blue Sky was just one of the many bastard half-elves in Pittsburgh, most of whom were born to human women with a sexual obsession with elves. Blue, though, was the only one with a *sekasha* father: Lightning Strike. Blue Sky drifted among the adult *sekasha*, dressed in a miniature version of the wyvern-scale armor. The little half-elf lacked the spell tattoos that scrolled down the arms of the adults and the magically sharp wooden *ejae* sword but had a bow and quiver of spell arrows slung across his back. At a distance, the only noticeably human thing about him was his short hair, gelled into spikes.

Chloe's predator smile flashed. "Whom does Blue Sky belong to?"

Stormsong's hand went to her hilt. Tinker caught Stormsong's wrist before she could draw her sword. The *sekasha* were a close-knit group, and they were all fiercely protective of the boy for his father's sake.

"Leave Blue Sky out of this." Tinker fought to keep her voice level. She'd never met Lightning Strike, but she had grown up with Blue Sky. He was one of her best friends.

"It was reported," Chloe pressed on, "that the

Wyverns forcibly removed Blue Sky from his brother's home in McKees Rocks. Their neighbors are afraid that the Wyverns had executed Blue Sky."

Chloe was obviously in full reporter mode. Tinker was surprised that she didn't manage to work in the fact that Blue Sky rode for Team Big Sky, which was Team Tinker's main competition in the hoverbike races. It reminded Tinker, though, that thousands of humans were going to witness the conversation. Things were rocky enough in Pittsburgh without Chloe stirring up resentment against the royal forces.

"Blue Sky was not forcibly removed." Technically, he wasn't, since that implied that he had been dragged physically out of his home. John Montana, though, had been given little choice in giving up his baby brother. "Blue Sky is half-elf; he inherited his father's life span."

Blue actually inherited the entire *sekasha*'s package down to temperament: he liked to fight. He was a good, sweet kid, but in a race he was pure steel. According to Tinker's Hand, as Blue got older, his urge to fight would spill out into his day-to-day life. Despite being tiny for his age, he was also very good at fighting. Tinker didn't want all of Pittsburgh thinking that Blue Sky was going to turn homicidal.

"Blue Sky will be a child for another eighty years," Tinker said instead. "John Montana is already in his thirties, and they have no other family in Pittsburgh. John asked me as a close personal friend to take Blue Sky into my household and see that he learns everything he needs to know to live among elves for the next ten thousand years."

All true and innocuous, although not the complete truth. It left out the fact that Blue Sky didn't like elves very much and was still very resistant to Tinker "adopting" him. The fight training, though, was slowly winning him over.

Chloe considered the partial truth with narrowed eyes, obviously looking for holes in Tinker's version of events. "It is my understanding that only *sekasha*-caste can wear the armor made of wyvern's scales. Does this mean that Blue Sky's father is one of your *sekasha*?"

"He was one of Windwolf's Beholden."

"Was?"

"He was killed by a saurus." Tinker had witnessed his death. Since the Montana brothers had kept the identity of Blue Sky's father secret even to Tinker, she had seen him die without realizing who he was.

"Oh, so his father was Lightning Strike?" Chloe said.

Tinker nodded, surprised that Chloe could put a name to a male that been dead for five years. Then again, elves were immortal; the traitorous Sparrow was the only other elf that Tinker had ever heard of being killed.

Blue Sky drifted across the pavement to stop beside Tinker. He didn't bump shoulders with her as he normally did. Blue was seventeen to her eighteen; he considered himself as almost adult despite all physical proof that he wasn't. Tinker had hit five foot tall—and then stopped growing—at thirteen. Blue Sky continued to be child-short; only recently had he'd caught up to her height-wise. Of course, one day he'd be as tall as the other Wind Clan *sekasha* and tower over her, but that was decades into the future. It was a point of pride with him that he was tall enough *now* to be shoulder to shoulder with her and he usually took every opportunity to prove it.

Tinker glanced at Blue to see why he'd restrained himself. Apparently there been some unspoken *sekasha* consensus that Chloe was dangerous. Blue Sky had picked up the adult's hard look and was trying to edge himself between Tinker and the reporter. Tinker bumped shoulders with him to get his attention and then scowled hard at him. The last thing she wanted was Blue throwing himself between her and the type of danger that came looking for her. She'd promised John to keep his baby brother safe, not use him as a shield.

Blue Sky gave her a look that started as a seventeen-year-old's rebellion but ended as a ten-year-old's pouting hurt.

Chloe watched the interaction with interest. "Rumor has it that the hoverbike races will be starting back up now that martial law is being lifted. Will the two of you be riding against each other once that happens?"

"Yes," Blue Sky said without thinking through the ramifications.

"No." Tinker earned another hurt look from Blue Sky. "I'm going to be too busy. My cousin Oilcan will be riding for my team."

"Will Blue Sky be allowed to race?" Chloe asked.

"Of course," Tinker and Blue Sky said at the same time. "It's not like Blue Sky is under house arrest." Tinker put her arm around his shoulders and felt the tension in his small, wiry body. She gave him a little shake to try and get him to relax. "He's always been like my little brother; now he's officially family."

Blue Sky gave her a shy smile and relaxed slightly.

"Now, if you don't mind..." Tinker started again for the tunnel openings. "I have a lot to do."

"Mind-boggling complex stuff." Chloe echoed back her earlier comment. "Like build a gate? Do you really think that's wise, considering what happened with the last one?"

"I'm not building a gate," Tinker said. "But in my defense, the gate I built for the oni did exactly what I designed it to do. It stopped the main oni army from invading Elfhome."

"By destroying the gate in orbit?"

"Yes."

"So how do you explain Pittsburgh still on Elfhome?" Chloe said. "Shouldn't the city have returned to Earth after the orbital gate failed?"

Tinker really didn't want to answer the question. In layman terms, Pittsburgh had been on a giant elastic band and held down on Elfhome by a simple on/off switch. Every Shutdown—with the flip of that switch—the city rebounded back to Earth. Chloe was right; Pittsburgh should have returned to Earth. It hadn't because Tinker had managed to also mess up the fundamental nature of the cosmos—not a feat that she was proud of. "There were unexpected—complications—which is why I'm not building another gate."

"What exactly are you going to be building?"

"Nothing." Tinker held up her hands in an attempt to look innocent. Both Stormsong and Blue Sky gave her a look that spoke volumes—she was coming too close to lying for their comfort—so she added in, "I will be acting as project manager for work beyond the Squirrel Hill Tunnels." Beyond as in another world beyond. "I probably will have no technical input on the undertaking. I'm just one of the few people that can easily supervise a large work force that includes human, elves and tengu." And the dragon, Impatience, but Chloe didn't need to know that. There, that was vague enough without lying. Tinker poured on more information in hopes to distract Chloe from important details. "I'm here today to inspect the tunnels for any defects. The tunnels are almost a hundred years old. They've been spottily maintained since Pittsburgh started to bounce between Earth and Elfhome. The discontinuity in Turtle Creek might have led to tremendous stress in all neighboring areas. The tunnels might not be safe to use."

Chloe nodded through Tinker's rambling and then launched a counterattack on her unprotected flank. "Tinker *ze domi*, I'm sure I don't have to tell you how nervous all of our viewers are about the current situation. There are sixty thousand humans in Pittsburgh. The city doesn't have the infrastructure to adequately take care of our needs. During Shutdown, everything from warm clothing to medical supplies was shipped in from Earth. The last Shutdown was mid-July. What is going to be done to address the fact that we're facing winter without supplies from Earth?"

"I'm fully aware of the facts." And scared silly by them. The number was actually closer to a hundred thousand once you added in tengu and elves and half-oni that were allied to the humans. As the Wind Clan *domi* and vicereine of the Westernlands, Tinker was responsible for them all. "We won't starve; the elves are shipping in keva beans from the Easternlands. The first shipments arrived by train yesterday. Martial law is being lifted later today so people can go to distribution centers that the EIA will be setting up for their share of the keva."

Giving away the first shipment had been her idea since she knew that the big chain food stores with corporate offices on Earth only stocked a thirty-day supply that became ridiculously low just before Shutdown. By now, only the little stores with ties to local farmers would have food. Those stores were holding steady because most Pittsburghers had small gardens and currently were up to their armpits in zucchini and tomatoes. In a few days, the first frost could kill off the gardens and the little stores would have to support all of Pittsburgh. Hopefully, handing out a supply of keva beans would keep those stores from collapsing and panic setting in. "We expect a second shipment within a week. That will go to food stores for resale."

"That's really just sticking your finger in the dike." Chloe smiled brightly as she refused to be distracted. "Shouldn't you be focusing on reconnecting Pittsburgh with Earth?"

That's exactly what Tinker was doing, but she didn't want everyone in Pittsburgh knowing that. Tinker sighed at Chloe's predatory smile. "You really like your job?"

"Love it." Chloe's smile broadened. "I get to corner people, ask them all sorts of embarrassing questions and watch them squirm."

Tinker tried to keep her temper but it was fraying fast. "If you keep pushing people's buttons, someone is bound to push back."

Chloe laughed. "It wouldn't be good for morale if Pittsburgh's favorite field reporter was chopped into little bits while reporting live. So, be a dear, and smile and tell Aunty Chloe everything."

Completely the wrong thing for Chloe to say. It triggered all sorts of other things that Tinker didn't want to be thinking about. How her previously anonymous mother had nearly driven her insane. How her pseudo-mother had turned out to be her real aunt. How Tinker had totally lost it all on a dark road and gotten an old friend killed.

"You are not my aunt," Tinker growled, suddenly too frustrated to be nice. "And this conversation is over."

And all the *sekasha* kicked into overdrive, spearheaded by Stormsong. One moment the warriors were flanking Tinker, ignoring the conversation to give her the illusion of privacy. The next, they were between Tinker and Chloe with swords out.

"Don't kill her!" Tinker ordered in Elvish, afraid that they would do just that.

Stormsong snatched the headset off Chloe. "I know how irreplaceable this is." Stormsong held it out of Chloe's reach. "Either you take yourself and it away from here, or I'll grind it into pieces."

"Fine. I'll go." Chloe tucked away the headset after Stormsong handed it back. "My boss has been texting me for the last five minutes to go cover the keva handouts."

Chloe had a hoverbike tucked into the shadows of the inbound tunnel. The mystery of how Chloe reached the abandoned highway was solved. She raced the motor, making it roar defiantly before taking off.

"I have never liked that woman." Stormsong watched Chloe speed off, her hand still on her hilt.

"Neither have I," Tinker said.

The "us versus her" lasted mere minutes after the sound of Chloe's engines died in the distances. Then everything clicked back to normal. Tinker's right arm ached dully, her temper was frayed, the *sekasha* scattered out to find hidden evil ninjas, and Blue went back to pouting. When they were growing up together, Blue always looked like his brother John to Tinker. Now she could only see the Wind Clan *sekasha* stamp on him—the black hair, the blue eyes, and the tendency to glower.

"They won't come out and say it." Blue glared at her borrowed Hand as they checked the ironwood trees growing beside the bridge for strangle vines and steel spinners. "But they don't want me to be a Blade. They're all scared something will jump out and eat me."

"It's entirely possible something could," Tinker said. "We're at the Rim."

Blue Sky huffed like he was going to argue the point. At one time, "the Rim" meant only the line of destruction where the transfer between worlds shattered everything at the edge down to elementary particles. On one side of the line was Pittsburgh urban sprawl and on the other was virgin Elfhome forest. Over time, though, Elfhome's deadly flora and fauna had pushed inward, sometimes by several miles. Pittsburghers now considered the Rim to be where the dangerous Elfhome vegetation started.

"So what am I supposed to do?" Blue scuffed the pavement with his boot. "It's not like I can be a Shield; I don't have spells or a sword and my bow is useless at close range. Besides, you have the great wall of kick butt."

Tinker understood completely. She could outthink just about anyone in Pittsburgh, but she was vulnerable to brute psychical force, especially when applied rapidly. It was always annoying to know that ninety percent of her enemies could simply pick her up and carry her off. The current record of being "carried off" stood at four if you counted the black willow tree, which hadn't so much carried her off as flung her halfway across the city.

Dealing with Chloe had at least made it easy to think of something Blue Sky could do. "You know your way around tech though." She led him back to the Roll Royce and dug through the backseat that had become the catchall for her toys. "You can help me take measurements and stuff."

"Measuring what?" Blue took her camera and flicked it on and checked the battery power.

"The tunnels." Tinker waved a hand toward the absolute black of the twin tunnel entrances. The black holes created eyes for a skull-like building abutting the foot of the steep hillside. Between the two tunnels, a tall garage door completed the skeleton grin; a steel grate broke the white door into rows of teeth.

"Okay." Blue took three steps toward the inbound tunnel before she managed to catch him by the collar and haul him back.

"After we get the lights on," Tinker said.

Once upon a time, "Skull Mountain" wouldn't have fazed Tinker. She would have plunged into the tunnels without a second thought. Sure, she would have known that the solid darkness within the nearly mile-long tunnels could hide virtually anything: collapsed ceilings, rifts in time and space, man-eating trees, frost-breathing wargs, or even just machine gun wielding oni. She would have naively assumed that her intelligence would carry the day. After tearing a rift in the fabric of space and time as a side effect of single-handedly thwarting an army of oni, falling off the planet, and other odd and painful misadventures, Tinker was starting to be a little more cautious. Her life wasn't the only one on the line; wherever she went, her Hand would be bound and determined to follow. Worse now Blue would be caught up in the danger.

Blue obviously knew he was part of the reason she was being cautious and he didn't like it. "I'm not afraid of the dark."

"I want to get the lights before I start anything." Assuming they could get Impatience to cooperate. To be completely fair, it wasn't clear if the little dragon knew that she needed his help. So far she hadn't been able to pin him down with translator in tow. He'd spent the last week drifting unfettered about Pittsburgh, walking through walls and whatnot, scaring everyone from Ralph at Eide's Entertainment to the counter help at Jenny's bakery.

She got a headache every time she just thought about the upcoming work. "I need to get a hyperactive dragon—that only tengu can communicate with—to build a pathway to Earth using work crews of elves that don't speak English and humans that barely speak Elvish. I'm not going to do that in the dark."

Speaking of language barriers, they were still speaking English which only Stormsong understood, although Pony had been working hard to learn. Tinker switched to Elvish. "I thought the tunnels would be lit. There are lights in Fort Pitt and Liberty Tunnels."

Blue sighed, obviously wishing they'd stayed in English, but spoke Elvish in reply. "Those tunnels go someplace."

"Technically, Squirrel Hill does too." When Pittsburgh used to return to Earth for one day each month—before she stranded the city permanently on Elfhome—I-376 was routinely reattached to its severed half so that it once again lead to Monroeville. There was only a sliver of actual city beyond the steep hill, though, and it had been largely abandoned over the years. Man-eating trees, frost-breathing wargs and machine gun wielding oni had that effect on suburban life.

The there-but-not-there status of the largely unused tunnel made it perfect for the project.

"Why don't we use the cars to light them up?" Blue pointed the camera at the three big gray luxury sedans.

There seemed to be a rule that when her Hand was working, only her First was allowed to talk freely. "*Domi* wouldn't be able to call her shields inside the Rolls," Pony explained. "Cars are easy to disable. You must always consider them as a possible trap, especially in confined spaces like the tunnels."

Blue Sky nodded his understanding, now eyeing the tunnel warily. "So, how do we get the lights on?"

"Trial and error," Tinker said. Hopefully "error" didn't involve death and mayhem.

"Are you sure this is okay?" Blue Sky asked while he filmed her picking the lock on the access door. Someone had been serious about keeping people out; there were two deadbolts on the heavy steel door. "Shouldn't we call someone first?"

"I'm the Wind Clan *domi*. I can do whatever needs to be done." At least, that was what being *domi* seemed to entail. She was still trying to figure out the limits of her power. So far, it was easier to plow on ahead instead of trying to track down someone that could verify if she had authority or not.

"But—but this belongs to the city, not the Wind Clan." Blue tapped the faded words stenciled on the steel door that read AUTHORIZED PERSONNEL ONLY in English. "We should call . . . someone."

Blue was always such a morally straight arrow. When they were kids together, he was the one that kept her out of trouble. She could talk her cousin Oilcan into anything, no matter how crazy dangerous, but Blue was an immovable rock, sticking firmly to the rules his older brother had laid down. The elves thought of the *sekasha* as holy because they had been created perfect in every way. The warriors were considered above flawed laws made by flawed elves. It was weird to think that Blue's moral compass was genetically based.

"It was the city's," Tinker said. "According to the treaty, though, anything left on Elfhome after the gate failed would become the Wind Clan's."

Blue Sky made a face at the news. Raised by his human brother, Blue thought of himself as a Pittsburgher first and foremost. "Does that include people?"

"Humans are considered neutral at the moment," Pony said. "Clan alliance cannot be assigned, it must be chosen. It is the only way you can pledge your loyalty and be true to it."

The cylinders of the second lock clicked into place and the door unlocked.

Stormsong stepped past Tinker and pushed the door open. It swung open to reveal a cavernous garage. Tinker noticed for the first time that Stormsong was wearing button-fly blue jeans instead of black leather pants. The rivets and buttons were done with ironwood instead of steel that would have messed up the *sekasha*'s protective spells. They were very much the female warrior's style, matching her blue dyed short hair.

"I could have gotten it," Tinker grumbled.

"I'm just doing my job." Stormsong tucked Tinker's right arm into the sling that Tinker had been ignoring. "You're going to have to be careful or you'll break it again."

"I'm not made of glass," Tinker complained.

Stormsong laughed. "I think you've proven that but for the next few weeks, it would be better if you pretended that you were. The bone has healed but it's still bruised and fragile."

Pony put a hand on Tinker's shoulder. "*Domi*, let the Blades go first."

What did they think was going to be locked inside the garage? Then again, this was Elfhome. She stepped aside to let the *sekasha* search.

The tunnels had a surprisingly complex and extensive control room for two cement-lined holes nearly a century old. Beyond the switches for nearly a mile of lights, there were also controls for a massive ventilation system and a fairly new monitoring array. Tinker flicked on the lights, powered on the cameras and scanned the screens.

A 1953 Pennsylvania Department of Highways report stated that the tunnels were driven through "poor ground" as they were being dug and that extensive reinforcements were put into place to make them safe. Between what happened to Turtle Creek and the war with the invading oni, it was possible that the tunnels were no longer safe to navigate. Before they started fiddling with the fundamental nature of reality, Tinker wanted to test the tunnels' support beams for stress fractures.

At first glance, the passages seemed undamaged. Then she noticed the small lumps on the pavement near the halfway point in both tunnels.

"What are those? Did part of the ceiling collapse?" Tinker played with the video controls. She found the zoom feature and panned over the objects. They were obviously not part of the tunnel. They were some kind of device, fairly simple in design—seemingly nothing more than a stack of bricks with wires sticking out of them—but she couldn't recognize any of the individual pieces accept an obvious tripwire that stretched across both lanes of the tunnels. "What the hell are they?"

"Something bad," Stormsong said.

Tinker turned to look at the female when nothing more was forthcoming.

Stormsong shook her head. "I don't know what they are, but my talent says that they're very dangerous."

Elves described magic as the power to render things down to possibilities and reshape them. The *intanyai seyosa* was an entire caste who had been bioengineered to take "educated guess" to scary levels. Stormsong's mother was the queen's oracle and the female *sekasha* had inherited some of her mother's talent. If Stormsong said the objects were dangerous, then they were.

Tinker studied the twin machines. The tripwires were connected to a cylindrical object about three inches long that was inserted into what looked like blocks of white molding clay. Tripwire. Clay. Tinker suddenly realized what she was looking at.

"Shit! They're bombs." Tinker pushed the elves toward the door. The tunnels would direct most of the force of the explosion laterally, but there was no telling what would happen once the tunnels collapsed. "Everyone out. Out!"

"Our shields are not strong enough to protect us from bombs." Stormsong caught Tinker by the good arm and made sure Tinker followed them out.

"I figured that," Tinker said. The spells tattooed onto the *sekasha* were meant to counteract other *sekasha*'s attacks; their protective shields could only deal with swords, normal arrows, and to a limited extent, bullets. Tinker's *domana* shielding spell was nearly impenetrable, but penetrating was only the start of the forces at play.

"Your shield won't keep you from being buried if the roof comes down," Stormsong continued.

"I fully understand the physics involved," Tinker snapped. "I'm not going to do something stupid."

They did an odd mutual herding back to the cars, and then they milled about at the—possibly—safe distance.

"So what do we do?" Blue Sky asked.

Tinker took out her phone. "Find someone that knows about bombs."

The director of the EIA answered his phone with a barked, "Maynard."

"I have bombs in the Squirrel Hill Tunnels," Tinker told him.

There was a long pause, and then Maynard asked in overly polite High Elvish, "Tinker *ze domi*, why are you going to blow up the tunnels?"

"What? Me? No! Someone else put them there; I've just found the stupid things."

"Oh, okay," and then Maynard leapt to the same conclusion as Stormsong. "Oh please God, tell me you're not trying to disarm them."

Tinker sighed. Why did everyone think she'd try? The only things she knew about bombs came from movies—which boiled down to cutting colored wire before a timer ran out—and a few childhood experiments with ANFO. Her experiments had been very educational on the destructive nature of explosives and how they could go wrong. "I'm not! I need someone to come get rid of them."

"I'll send my bomb squad," Maynard said.

"You have a bomb squad?"

"Yes. So when we find bombs, someone knows how to disarm them. Give me your word that you'll wait for the bomb squad to make the tunnels safe."

Tinker sighed, recognizing the verbal snare that Maynard just put out. If she promised him, she'd have to keep her word, no matter how long it took to dispose of the bombs. On the other hand, there was no way she could attempt disarming the bomb without getting all the elves and Blue Sky involved. The bombs looked simple, but they could be booby trapped. "Yeah, sure. I promise."

Apparently after living over a hundred years, standing idle for a few hours was no big deal. While her Hand were perfectly fine with doing nothing while they waited for the bomb squad, Tinker didn't have that kind of patience. There were ironwoods growing beside the bridge into the tunnels, their trunks far below in the valley underneath the highway. After the *sekasha* triple checked the trees for strangle vines and steel spinners, Tinker settled in their shade to work on her datapad.

Inspecting the tunnels was just the start of the work needed to reconnect Pittsburgh to Earth. Next step would be pin down Impatience to work out the spell. Considering the fact that her Hand was in protective overdrive, it might be saner to put that conversation on hold. The dragon had the attention span of a five-year-old on a sugar rush. Having the small hyperactive dragon and the jumpy *sekasha* in one room together would be like doing cigarette tricks in a fireworks factory.

She leaned her head back against the concrete barrier. Life was so much simpler before she became an elf princess. The *sekasha* were just the tip of the iceberg. Almost everything on the continent was "hers" and she had no clue what the hell she was supposed to do with it all. She was a mad scientist. A hoverbike racer. A junkyard dog. What the hell did she know about being a princess? Did Cinderella have this problem once the prince tracked her down with the glass slipper? Was this the real reason she took off halfway through the ball? Did Cinderella see all the *sekasha* and *laedin* and *nivasa* and realize that all those people would expect her to be a princess?

What Tinker really needed were the technical specifications on "princess," not fairytales.

An odd vibration suddenly thrummed against her awareness, like an invisible guitar string had been plucked. Windwolf was tapping the power of the Wind Clan Spell Stone. A moment later a flash of lightning tore down from the clear sky, a jagged dancing column of brilliance. It struck southwest of where they were standing. Thunder boomed out instantly, confirming the strike insanely close.

"Oh crap." Tinker scrambled to her feet. She felt another thrum of power, slightly different, and flame blossomed above the trees.

"Wow!" Blue Sky pulled out the camera. "What the hell is that?"

"Windwolf and Prince True Flame. Okay people we have to move!"

The flame strike had been close to the nearest on-ramp, less than a quarter mile away. The road elevated after that point; it was close to fifty feet off the ground when the highway entered the tunnels. With the bombs in the tunnel, the only way to safety was toward the battlefront.

Tinker hurried toward the cars, the *sekasha* flanking her.

Blue Sky trotted backwards, still filming, as lightning struck again—closer. "Coolness!"

"Blue!" Tinker felt a third thrum of magic; the Stone Clan had casted a scrying spell. In a weird other sense, like an invisible eye opened, Tinker could suddenly "see" the tight knot of *domana*-caste elves with their *sekasha*-caste at the on-ramp, and an unruly swarm of something racing toward her on the highway.

"We've got incoming—lots of them. They're big and they're moving fast. I think they're wargs." At one time wargs had been Elfhome cousins to wolves, but then, in some ancient war, were turned into oversized bio-weapons. "They're going to cut us off."

"Away from the cars." Pony ordered. "*Domi*, shields."

Tinker cocked her fingers and brought her hand to

her mouth. Her *domana* shields were generated by the Wind Clan Spell Stones which sat astride a massive spring of magic. In theory, her shields could protect them from anything but it depended on her getting them up and keeping them up.

She spoke the trigger word that set up the resonance between her and the Spell Stones. It was if a giant engine just as kicked to life; magic growled deep within her bones. The vibration rumbled through her bruised bones. She barely kept from whimpering in pain. Power was blooming around her in a rush of heat; the wrong sound could be deadly. She pressed her lips tight, changed her hand position, and triggered her shield. The power shifted and changed and the wind wrapped her and the *sekasha*.

"Shitshitshitshit." She hissed now that it was safe to talk. The pain continued to burn bright as the power flowed across the resonance between her and the Spell Stones. "Feels like someone is arc welding my bones."

"Wolf is coming." Pony wrapped his arms around her, keeping her steady against the onslaught of pain.

She focused hard on keeping her fingers locked into position even though she could barely feel them beyond the searing. If she moved her fingers, the spell would collapse. "He'd better hurry."

Lightning struck closer and closer.

"That is so cool!" Blue filmed the sudden wild storm of lightning. "Can you do that?"

"Not yet." If she could sense Windwolf, then he must feel her and was trying to stop the beasts before they could reach her.

The pack of wargs raced toward them, too many to count. They made a ragged wall of fur, taller than she was. The first one slammed into her shield hard enough to rebound a dozen feet, tumbling off its feet.

The next warg learned from the mistake of its pack mate. The beast stopped, braced itself, and roared out white frost. The wave of magical cold struck her shield and wrapped around them, instantly encasing them in thick ice.

"Shit!" Tinker's breath came out in a plume of mist. She hated that she could only stand there, hoping her shields held. She hated that if she flinched even once, they instantly become vulnerable to attack. The highway was lost behind the ice wall, an opaque haze, marking the range of her shield. She couldn't see the road, or how many more wargs were between her and Windwolf. "Oh, Windwolf, hurry."

Fire blasted down on them, making her flinch.

"Nothing can breach your shield, *domi*." Pony sounded so calm and confident.

The ice wall cracked under the heat of the flame strike and rained down in thick pieces to the pavement. One of the wargs was dead on the pavement, a smoldering corpse, and the rest were retreating into the tunnels.

At one time she had thought that the *sekasha* were the greatest weapons of the clans, but then she discovered the truth. The warriors were mere escort for the heavy artillery that the *domana*-caste represented. That fact was clear as the royal troops moved down the highway in a wash of Fire Clan red. Prince True Flame was walking in the lead, all regal elf splendor in white and gold, the hot shimmer of his protective shield running before him. His Wyverns were behind him and a horde of *laedin*-caste troops were bringing up the rearguard.

True Flame summoned another strike with a quick series of hand motions and hard utterances and the roar of fire was deafening as it flared past her shields. It struck one of the trailing wargs, igniting the beast instantly. The rest, however, made it to the safety of the tunnels.

True Flame moved forward until she was behind his protective shield. "Are you hurt?"

Tinker knew he meant hurt by the wargs, so she said, "No."

She was about to release her shields when Pony tightened his hold on her and murmured, "Wait for Wolf, *domi*." Stormsong had shifted between Tinker and the Prince and a heartbeat later, Cloudwalker followed suit. Why were they leery of True Flame? She thought she could trust Windwolf's older cousin.

Then she realized that Forest Moss of the Stone Clan stood beside the prince. The one-eyed and quite mad *domana* had come to Pittsburgh without *sekasha* or a household. Wyverns guarded Forest Moss; Tinker had missed Forest Moss in the wash of Fire Clan red because he had no Stone Clan black to mark his movement. The male watched her intently with his one good eye. His pure white hair was unbound and flowing in the heat that True Flame's shield gave off. The left side of his face was an unreadable mask of scars radiating around the sewn shut lids of his eye. The right side showed hard, cold anger. Last time she'd seen him, he'd tried to kill her; no wonder her Hand was jumpy. Forest Moss was insane, but surely even he wasn't crazy enough to attack her in front of True Flame and the Wyverns.

Where was Windwolf? She wasn't sure how much

longer she could maintain her shield. She was getting all weirdly lightheaded which usually meant she was about to go facedown.

A small knot of Wind Clan blue pushed through the royal red as Windwolf made his way to her with his two Hands of *sekasha*. He stopped at the edge of Tinker's shield. His face was full of concern for her, making him look impossibly young. There had been a time where she thought of him as "lots older" and was only lately realizing that he was as much a teenager as she was. Tinker dropped her shield and he swept her up into his arms.

"All is well. You're safe." He murmured, and she realized it was to calm himself as much as to soothe her.

It did weird scary things to her heart to see him so vulnerable. It reminded her that he was out all day, fighting oni forces, with the Stone Clan at his back.

"Wolf," Prince True Flame started toward the tunnel. "Send her home where she'll be safe and come."

"Wait!" Tinker tightened her hold on Windwolf as he moved to set her on the ground. "There are bombs in the tunnels. A blast could collapse the whole hillside. I called Maynard; he's sending someone to disarm them."

True Flame laughed at her. "The wargs split up; they went through both tunnels. They would have set off any bombs."

"Cousin, wait." Windwolf put out his hand to stop True Flame. "The oni could be using the wargs to bait us into a trap. The beasts know this area. They could have scattered into the woods, but instead they chose to funnel us in this direction."

"The wargs are smart enough to avoid a simple

tripwire," Tinker said even though she wasn't totally sure that was true. It was as close to lying as she could get to keep Windwolf out of the tunnels. "Maynard's people should be here soon."

True Flame glanced to his First, who gave a slight nod in agreement with Tinker. The prince growled slightly in annoyance. "There's no need for us to waste time waiting. Forest Moss," True Flame waved the Stone Clan *domana* to him. "Jewel Tear."

A Hand of *sekasha* with black chest armor and spell tattoos shifted forward. They belonged to Jewel Tear. Like Tinker, the short female was hidden behind a wall of tall warriors. Jewel's First, Tiger Eye, stepped to the side to reveal his *domana*.

What was it about elves? They were out hunting oni and yet all of them looked ready for the red carpet. Jewel was wearing a forest green silk full length gown with a shimmering overdress of fairy silk patterned with leaves. Her hair was the same dark brown as Tinker's, but instead of Tinker's jagged spikes of a haircut, Jewel's flowed down to her ankles. It was braided with a glorious complication of pearls, ribbons and flowers. Two small stone orbs whirled about her head like she was the sun. The elf female was radiant and Tinker felt rough and unkempt in comparison.

It didn't help to know that once upon a time, over a hundred years ago, Windwolf had asked Jewel Tear to marry him. Apparently he had a type: short, dark haired and dusky skin. Tinker's only consolation was that Windwolf married her and not Jewel Tear. It was small comfort, though, since technically Jewel Tear had ended the engagement.

True Flame explained the bombs in the tunnel.

"Can you contain the blast so it doesn't damage the tunnel?"

"Easily," Forest Moss said.

Jewel Tear eyed the tunnel more warily. She cast a scrying spell but the magic hit upon the steel reinforcements in the tunnel and tangled into useless noise. "Forest Moss is correct. We could easily contain the blast, but if there are other traps . . ."

"Pft, we are Stone Clan." Forest Moss waved away her objections. "We have nothing to fear; we have the strongest protection shields of all the clans."

Forest Moss activated his protection shield and marched fearlessly into the right-hand tunnel. There was a moment of hesitation among his borrowed Wyvern Hand; they were clearly not happy at having to follow the mad *domana* into danger. Jewel Tear was even more unhappy. She went up on tiptoe to whisper something into her First's ear.

Tiger Eye shook his head, took Jewel's hand and kissed her fingers. "I will not let you go into danger alone. My place is beside you."

Jewel Tear sighed and smacked him lightly. "*Sekasha* fool."

Tiger Eye grinned down at his *domi*. "Always."

Her Hand gathered close to Jewel Tear as she activated her shield, and they went determinedly into the left tunnel.

True Flame waited until Jewel Tear was out of sight before turning again to Tinker. "Go home."

It felt a lot like being sent to her room so the grownups could talk. Worse, it probably was how True Flame and his Wyverns saw it too. Even with her arm feeling like someone had beat on it with a baseball bat, Tinker opened her mouth to protest. Her mind was blank but she was positive she'd think up some intelligent point—eventually.

Windwolf kissed her. "Beloved, I'm proud you protected our people, but your arm is still weak. Anything could break it."

"Damn it, I'm not a child," she whispered to him in English.

"I'm fully aware of that." Windwolf kissed her again. "There will be another day, after your arm is fully healed, when you'll fight beside me. Today, though, you are hurt. If you break your arm again, the damage would probably be worse."

There was a thrum of magic against her senses as one of the Stone Clan *domana* cast a spell. News that Forest Moss had cleared his tunnels was shouted from the entrance. She hugged Windwolf fiercely with her good arm, not wanting to let him go. She hated that she couldn't do anything to protect him.

"I don't need two Hands at the enclave." Tinker offered up the only help she could give him. "I'll take my Hand with me but the others can stay with you."

Windwolf nodded to her logic. Despite their innocuous appearance, the enclaves were fortresses complete with guards and magical barriers.

"Wolf!" True Flame called from the tunnel entrance.

"Keep yourself safe," she said and let him go.

Knowing he'd wait until she was in the cars and gone, she left as quickly as she could.

She needed to know how to do the scry spell so she could see danger coming. She needed attack spells so she could stop it instead of just stand there and hope that her shields didn't fail. She had the genome keys needed to tap both the Wind Clan and Stone Clan Spell Stones, and possibly even the Fire Clan's too. What she needed was to learn how to use them.

Ironically, it all came down to having time. It would be one thing if she could study them on her own, but someone had to sit down and teach her.

"That was so cool." Blue Sky murmured beside her in the back of the Rolls.

She glanced over and saw that he was replaying the footage of the warg encasing her protection shield in ice. She grunted slightly; it was incredible that the beast could generate so much coldness, but she didn't think it was "cool."

"How does it work? You're not drawing spells on paper with grease pencils! He just—just—" For lack of words, Blue waved his hands in mad parody of the *domana* casting. "Whoosh! And boom!" He held out the camera, giving her pleading eyes for an explanation. On the display, he'd paused on Prince True Flame cocking his hand up to his lips to trigger the flame strike.

"I'm not sure," Tinker said slowly, taking the camera, and stepped through the frames showing True Flame casting. It looked so simple. "But I think I can figure it out."

2: ECHOING OF MERRIMENT

It was the elf's tunic that caught his eye, a sun-ripe splash of yellow, like a daffodil in a raw spring morning. A female elf stood just outside the train station at the edge of Pittsburgh's bleak Strip District. She was staring at a Coke machine as if it were the most amazing thing in the world. Her thick braid of walnut-brown hair swung back and forth as she swayed hip to hip, nearly dancing to music only she heard. She drummed her silent melody with a pair of *olianuni* mallets, complete with exuberant flourishes of victory.

Oilcan found himself slowing down as he drove past the station, watching her. There was something joyous about her that made him smile.

She was impossibly slender and surprisingly short. It made him think that she was an adolescent—she probably wasn't over a hundred years old. A small mountain of brightly colored travel sacks and the distinctive bulk of an *olianuni* sat at her feet. As he rolled past her, she paused in her drumming to reach out cautiously and touch the selection buttons on the Coke machine—clearly mystified. The train aside, it could be the first machine that she'd ever seen.

He reached the light at the corner before he realized that it was odd that she was just standing there, alone. Usually one of the elves at the train station would be herding a newcomer to safety, especially a child. He sat through the red light, studying her in his rearview mirror. It took him a minute to realize why she was alone—there wasn't a speck of Wind Clan blue on her. Her loose tunic shirt was yellow, and her leather pants and slouch boots were black. Even the ribbons and flowers threaded through her braid were yellow and black. She was Stone Clan.

The elf clans weren't allowing a common enemy to deter them from feuding. Since the train station was Wind Clan territory, none of the elves there would help the female.

He sighed, put his pickup in reverse, and backed up to pull even with her.

"Hoi!" He called to her in Elvish. "Do you have someplace safe to go to? Is there someone who knows you've arrived here?"

She startled, looked behind her as if suspecting he was talking to someone else, and then came down to the curb to look in his pickup window. "Forgiveness, are you talking to me?"

"Yes. The streets aren't safe after dark. The oni have been raiding at night. Do you have someplace safe to go to tonight?"

Her eyes went wide at the news. "I—I'm coming to my majority." He was right; she wasn't an adult. "I've heard so much about Pittsburgh. I've heard the music they play here—it's so raw and wonderful—and—and with the war and everything, the Stone Clan is receiving remuneration . . ."

Oilcan sighed as she trailed off. "Do you know anyone that lives in Pittsburgh?"

"I—I have a letter of recommendation to the *domana* Earth Son—is that bad?"

His dismay must have shown on his face. "Earth Son is dead."

She gave a quiet "oh" of hurt as her plans unraveled. She frowned at the ground, worrying her lower lip with her teeth. "Majority" for an elf was a hundred, which made them physically equal to an eighteen-year-old human. Elves, though, sheltered their children so much that the extra years did little to prepare them for Pittsburgh.

"My name is *Nahala kaesae-tiki waehae lou*." There was a reason most elves in Pittsburgh picked up short English nicknames. Literally her name was "echoing of merriment in stone" but truly meant "laughter echoing through a cave," with the implication that it was the innocent laughter of children. The focus of sound in her name meant that her family were most likely musicians. If he had to pick an English name for her, he'd probably choose Merry.

Merry gave him a hopeful little smile.

"I'm Oilcan."

"Oilcan." She repeated the English word, clearly puzzled by it but undaunted. "There, we know each other now. I know someone that lives in Pittsburgh." She paused, losing courage, but then rallied to finish with "Can—can I stay with you tonight?"

Why were the human runaways so much more streetwise than the elves who were nearly five times their age? She clearly had no idea what kind of danger she could be stumbling into.

Maybe it was the color of her hair, the hesitancy of her smile, or the open sweetness of her face, but she reminded him of his mother. Having recognized that, he couldn't just drive away, but she was a minor female and he was an adult male, albeit still nearly eighty years her junior.

"I'm not sure I can just take you home with me," Oilcan said.

Merry nodded as if she expected the answer. "Your household wouldn't allow you—"

"No, no, I don't have a household. I live alone."

"That's horrible. What happened to your household? Oh! Did the oni kill them?"

Oilcan laughed, shaking his head. "It's something humans do when they reach majority. They live alone until they find someone to love."

Clearly the idea was so completely foreign to her that she couldn't quite grasp it. "But—isn't that lonely?"

Months ago he would have said no. He had a comfortable rhythm to his life. He shared his work day with his cousin Tinker and split the weekends between hovercycle racing and the local rock scene. He actually had to work hard to create his time alone. But then the oni invaded and everything changed. "Sometimes it is lonely."

"Let us be lovers," Merry suddenly said in English, stunning him. "We'll marry our fortunes together."

He laughed after a moment, recognizing the lyrics, keenly aware that they were across the street from the old Greyhound bus station in Pittsburgh. He sang the next line of lyrics back to her. "I've got some real estate here in my bag."

Her smile was radiant with delight. "You know the song!" she cried in Elvish and dived into one of her travel sacks to pull out a hand-bound journal. "An *olianuni* apprentice that I know let me copy his songbook." She flipped through pages of carefully hand-drawn musical scores to find the Simon and Garfunkel song. Below the English lyrics were Elvish translations. His eyes caught on the line: "I'm empty and aching and I don't know why."

Yes, that's the way I've been feeling.

The first line had been horribly mangled in translation. "Lovers" had been mistranslated to an Elvish word that meant members of the same household and "marry our fortunes" to "face a common enemy."

Oilcan laughed, shaking his head at the discrepancy between the two. "Get in." He'd take her out to the enclaves and make sure the Stone Clan wouldn't try to kill him for taking her home. "We'll see what we can work out."

The closest thing that the Stone Clan had to an embassy was Ginger Wine's enclave out at the Rim. While the gates to the enclaves on either side stood open, the heavy doors to Ginger Wine's were shut and barred. He rapped on the door, and the spyhole opened to reveal a pair of Wind Clan blue eyes.

"Forgiveness," said a male voice that went with the blue eyes. "We are not able to take customers."

"May I speak with someone from the Stone Clan?"

A slight shake of the head indicated that he couldn't.

"The Stone Clan *domana* are not here. They are out with Wolf Who Rules Wind *ze domou ani*."

The door guard was one of Ginger Wine's staff, since the title he used for Windwolf was the ultra-formal "our lord."

"Anyone would do," Oilcan assured him. "Someone from their household? I merely have a question on propriety."

"Earth Son's *sekasha* are here," the door guard said hesitantly, as if he wasn't sure he should be telling Oilcan the information. "They—they would be well-versed on propriety."

"May I speak with one of them?"

"*Nagarou*!" The male gasped. He obviously knew who Oilcan was. For some reason, the Wind Clan elves had adopted his relationship to Tinker as his nickname. He was never sure if he should be flattered or offended. Did they call him that because they couldn't remember his name, or because they'd adopted their *domi*'s cousin as their own? "They are *sekasha*! And they are Stone Clan." The male glanced at Merry behind Oilcan and then whispered in English, "The Stone Clan are arrogant and conceited, and they eat and eat and eat as if they're hollow. Everyone is frightened. We're tripping over each other in our fear. It might be too dangerous for you to speak with their *sekasha*."

Recent history made clear how deadly the *sekasha* could be. "Do you really think they would hurt me?"

The door guard obviously wanted to say "Yes," but elves have a thing about telling the truth. Finally he admitted, "I do not know, but if they wanted to, they could. It is their right."

As holy warriors, *sekasha* had the divine right to do whatever they wished to whomever they wanted. They were considered above the law. From what he understood, though, the very nature that made them above the law also meant that they didn't run amuck, randomly killing people—only people that deserved it. For his own sanity's sake, he had accepted their role as judge and executor.

"It will be all right," he said. "I have a few simple questions and then I will go."

The door guard considered him for a minute and then unbarred the door. "Please, *nagarou*, be careful."

Merry refused to face the *sekasha*, even though the warrior was of her own clan. She cowered in the front garden, too afraid to go deeper into the enclave. Oilcan couldn't understand why the lower-caste elves were so terrified by the higher caste they claimed to be perfection embodied. He knew from personal experience that anyone could become a killer. Wasn't it better that the *sekasha* were so righteous that their violence was controlled and not random?

The door guard summoned Ginger Wine, the elegant, red-haired owner of the enclave. She also tried to convince Oilcan that talking with the Stone Clan *sekasha* would be unwise.

"Everyone is on edge here," Ginger Wine murmured in English. None of the Stone Clan must be fluent in the human language. "It's as if suddenly we all have two left feet."

"I will be careful," Oilcan promised.

The female elf sighed and nodded. "I'll take you to Earth Son's First."

Ginger Wine led Oilcan through the sprawling public dining rooms of the front building to the inner courtyard. Apple trees heavy with ripening fruit filled the square acre protected on all four sides by the enclave's other buildings. It was an area that normally no human would ever see.

From the kitchens to the right of them, there was a crash as if dozens of metal pots had been dropped, and High Elvish quickly devolved into shouted Low Elvish.

Ginger Wine sighed and bowed an apology. "Forgiveness, I must attend to that. Thorne Scratch on Stone is over there."

Oilcan wandered through the acre of apple trees until he found the female *sekasha*.

Thorne Scratch was undeniably Stone Clan, with the brown hair and dusty skin that marked the clan. Her wyvern armor was iridescent black, shimmering like an oil slick in the dappled sun as she moved through her sword practice. Tattooed down her arms were the spells that triggered her protective shields, done in stone black.

"Forgiveness." Oilcan bowed slightly.

Her eyes flicked to him, checking his position, and then her focus returned to her practice. "Well?" She had a smoky rasp to her voice like Janice Joplin. "What is it?"

"A young female of the Stone Clan arrived today by train. She came with letter of introduction for *domana* Earth Son, but he is dead."

"I know," she snapped. "I killed him."

"Condolences on your loss."

She whirled, and her sword's point was suddenly at

his throat, a strangely small prick of pain considering the danger it posed. "Do you mock me?"

"No." And seeing the doubt in her eyes, he held out his own hard-won truth. "My father killed my mother in a drunken rage. Afterward, he was so grief-stricken by what he had done that he tried to kill himself. I imagine you must regret what happened—even if you thought it was necessary."

Tears glittered in her eyes, and she turned away from him. "That is not the same," she growled after a moment. "Your mother's death is tragic. Earth Son's death was inevitable."

"It doesn't lessen your pain."

She glanced at him, and surprise flowed across her face. "You—you're human?"

"Yes."

She sheathed her sword. "I thought you were one of Jewel Tear's household. You have the Stone Clan coloring. What are you doing here?"

"A young female of the Stone Clan arrived—"

"Yes, yes, you said that. Your point being?"

"The city is not safe for a child to be wandering around alone."

"Child?"

"She is very young."

"A double?"

Oilcan nodded. It meant that the elf only needed two numbers to represent their age, not three or four. It was the Elvish equivalent to "teenager." Since majority came at a hundred, Merry was definitely a double.

"Gods save us from idiots," Thorne Scratch growled in her raspy voice. He wondered what she'd sound like if she sang something slow and tragic. "What is a double doing traveling alone to this oni-infested hellhole?"

He could only spread his hands in ignorance. "I wish no harm to come to her, so I've taken her into my protection."

"You?"

"Is there someone else that will? Would Jewel Tear take her?"

Thorne Scratch looked away, fighting to keep anger off her face. "Jewel Tear could not, even if she wanted to. She came here destitute. She has pushed herself to her limit, and perhaps beyond it, taking in Earth Son's household. She is trusting beyond reason that the clan will compensate her for Earth Son's failure. Jewel Tear cannot do anything for your double."

"What of the other *domana*? Forest Moss?"

"Bite your tongue!" Thorne Scratch snapped. "Do not even suggest such a thing. He is mad. I would not give monkeys to him, let alone a child. And do not breathe a word to her of the possibility that he would happily take her, because she cannot imagine the pain he would put her through. Doubles think of now and tomorrow and maybe the day after that—they do not think in hundreds of years."

Oilcan nodded. "Is it acceptable then that I continue to take care of her?"

She studied him a moment before asking, "Why are you doing this?"

"Because it's the right thing to do. There are the oni and wild animals and—I'm ashamed to say—some humans—"

She cut off his honesty with a huff of impatience. "And there are some elves that would see a child of another clan as prey. We are kin at even our baser nature."

He'd suspected as much.

"What is your name, human?"

"I'm Oilcan." He held out his hand without thinking. Normally elves didn't shake hands, so he was surprised when she took hold of his hand with both of hers. Her fingers were strong as steel and rough with calluses. They were a good match to his own rough hands. "I'm *nagarou* to the Wind Clan *domi*, Beloved Tinker of Wind."

"I see." Thorne Scratch scanned the courtyard. "And where is this double?"

"She's waiting in the front garden."

Thorne released his hand and sent off with a long, purposeful stride.

Oilcan hurried after her. "Go soft with her. She's in the front garden because she is afraid—"

"Yes, yes, they always are."

Merry squeaked when she saw the *sekasha* bearing down on her. As Thorne silently studied her, Merry edged slowly sideways until she was tucked up against Oilcan, looking very much like she wanted to hide behind him.

"Where are you from?" Thorne Scratch broke her silence to ask quietly.

"Summer Court." The city was named for the fact that the queen held court in the city during the summer. It was located in Elfhome's version of England, approximately where London stood on Earth. Merry had come across half the world by herself. "The Stone quarter by the ninth bridge. My household is small, beholden to Crystal Vein of Stone, who is beholden to the clan head, Diamond. I studied under Bright Melody of Fire."

Thorne nodded. "Did you sever ties?"

Merry's lip trembled and she whispered, "I severed ties."

"Why?" Thorne snapped.

"I had to." Merry flinched in the face of the *seka-sha*'s anger. "It was the only way they'd let me go." Merry caught hold of Oilcan's shirt and twisted the fabric around with her fingers. It was as if she soaked up courage through the touch. She raised her chin to meet Thorne Scratch's eyes. "If I'd stayed, I'd have had to play everything the way it's always been played, because only the 'gifted,' the ones that play like gods walking the earth, can change anything. You have no idea what it's like to see your whole future laid out for you, and it's nothing but fitting into a neat little box they've designed for you. And all of a sudden, there's this place across the ocean where you won't be locked in because you're—you're just acceptable."

Thorne shook her head and looked away. "I'd tell you at length what an idiot you're being for coming here—but I was just as stupid at your age, so I have no right to criticize. What is done is done. Try to be a little more wise. You are in a city full of enemies. And terrifying as I might be, I am the only one that you can trust fully. Anytime you think you're in danger, day or night, come to me, and I will keep you safe."

Merry gave a tiny, wide-eyed nod.

Thorne turned to glare at Oilcan. "I am trusting you. Betray me, and I'll have your head."

Merry squeaked again in alarm.

"I won't betray you." Oilcan bowed to the *sekasha.*

Then Merry all but dragged him from the enclave by the tail of his shirt.

There—permission granted. Oilcan melted on the hot leather of the pickup's seat in the late August heat. He still wasn't sure how he was going to work Merry into his life, but at least he knew that he wouldn't have holy warriors chopping off his head for shacking up with an underage female.

Snow Patrol had come up on the random play of his ancient iPod, and Merry had her eyes closed, air-drumming in accompaniment. She seemed sublimely happy.

". . . there's this place just across the ocean where you won't be locked in a box just because you're—you're acceptable."

Windchime used to wave away praise, embarrassed, saying that his amazing skills were just passable. Oilcan always thought modesty was part of the elf psyche; every elf artist he'd ever met, from glassblower to weaver, would denounce their skill. It never occurred to him that the elves were comparing themselves to masters still alive in Easternlands. It would be as if Mozart and Beethoven and Elvis had never died and you were constantly being compared to them.

Hell, even Elvis wouldn't have been "acceptable" for a world still locked on to Mozart's standard. Elvis in a powdered wig trying out for the role of Figaro? Oilcan shuddered for the poor elf soulmates to the rock-and-roll king.

Oilcan wrote songs for local bands, but they were a hybrid blend of rock and roll and traditional elf music.

No one compared his music to past masters, because there weren't any. Not many people understood both cultures well enough to create a fusion of the two. A few years ago, before the first generation of humans grew up on Elfhome, there wasn't even an audience to appreciate it. His art was embraced and celebrated because it was new.

The artistic freedom of Pittsburgh would explain why most of the elves that came to the city were artists. Weavers. Potters. Painters. Musicians. They settled close to the enclaves and sold their wares to humans. They were all young, and they all had been Wind Clan. But that was most likely about to change. Merry was probably just the first of the Stone Clan artists to arrive.

The next Snow Patrol song cued up on the iPod.

"Oh, I don't know this one!" Merry waved her mallets in agitation. "He didn't have this song."

"He?"

"Chiming of Metal in Wind." Merry gave Windchime's proper name in Elvish.

The songbook with the mangled Simon and Garfunkel lyrics clicked into place. Windchime had been called back to Easternlands last spring by his family. He had left with a solar-battery recharger, two MP3 players, and promises to return within a decade or two. His leaving had seriously crippled the band he played with, since all their sets were built around his *olianuni*.

"If you know Windchime, you could have gone to Moser."

Merry made a raspberry. "I asked for a reference letter, but Chiming of Metal said I was too young to travel alone. He wasn't sure if Briar Rose on Wind would let Rustle of Leaves above Stone stay. He was sure, though, that she would refuse someone else from the Stone Clan, since they only needed one *olianuni* player."

Yeah, that sounded like Briar. Carl Moser technically owned the artist commune, but his elfin lover had ultimate veto power. Oilcan hadn't heard anything about a new *olianuni* player in town, but then again, elves operated on a different time sense than humans.

"When was Rustle of Leaves coming to Pittsburgh?"

"He left ahead of me."

Pittsburgh and its outlying suburbs had been home to two million humans before the first Startup. Only sixty thousand remained. It meant whole sections of the city were nearly abandoned. Finding housing was easy—making it safe and livable was the trick.

Carl Moser was leading vocalist and bass guitar for his band *Naekanain*, Elvish for "I don't understand," which was usually the first thing humans learned to say. Moser had laid claim to an entire block of porch-front row houses on the edge of the Strip District. He was in a constant state of renovation as he merged the individual houses into a commune for artists. The place confused most humans since it presented twelve front doors to visitors. Since only the middle seven of the twelve houses had so far been merged into "main house," it was sort of an intelligence test. The "front" door was the one painted Wind Clan blue with Moser's name written out phonetically in Elvish on the lintel.

Moser threw open the door a few minutes after Oilcan rang the bell a third time. "Freaking hell, I'm going to take this damn thing off its hinges if no one else answers the frigging door."

"*Naeso sae kailani,*" Briar barked somewhere in the back of the rambling house. The High Elvish was an extremely polite way to say "No way in hell."

"Then answer the damn door!" Moser shouted back in English.

"It's not my job," Briar called back.

"Not my job, not my job," Moser muttered in falsetto and then shouted, "Then freaking tell someone else to answer the door!"

"Floss Flower!" Briar shouted in Elvish.

"*Shya.*" The reply from the newest resident, a weaver, came from somewhere far to the right.

"You're door guard from now on!" Briar shouted.

There was a pause in the clacking of a loom and then a slightly defeated "*Shya.*"

"Elves," Moser growled quietly in English. "Always 'who answers to whom.' Who freaking cares as long as it gets done?"

"Anarchist," Oilcan said.

Moser pumped his hand over his head. "Freedom!"

"You've gotta give for what you take." Oilcan sang the George Michaels tune.

Moser launched into song. "Freedom! Freedom!" He jerked his head to indicate that Oilcan was to come in as he continued to sing, his fingers picking out chords on an air guitar. "You've gotta give for what you take!"

Merry eyed the Frankenstein monster of a room beyond the front door. Originally it was the living room with a large archway to the dining room and a staircase to the second floor. The stairs were completely walled off with plywood, and a steel garage door had been installed in the archway so the foyer could act as a barbican. All the enclaves out on the rim had similar fortified entrances, but usually more elegantly decorated. Oilcan tugged Merry gently inside and made sure the door was locked behind her.

The two houses to the right and four to the left of the building they entered had been merged into the great "main" residence. The load-bearing walls between the houses had been carefully breached so the dining rooms merged into one long room. Moscr had paid someone that could cut ironwood to make him a twenty-foot-long table with nearly two dozen mismatched chairs around it. Platters of food were laid out for dinner.

"We've got meat!" Moser cried as Oilcan guided Merry into the dining room. Moser hit the automatic door opener on the wall, and the steel garage door rattled down into place. "You're staying for dinner."

"We won't have meat if you invite all of Pittsburgh." Briar came out of the nearest kitchen carrying another platter. She was wearing daisy-duke cutoff shorts and a halter top. She gave Oilcan a slight smile that vanished instantly as she glanced past him at Merry. "We're not feeding her."

"What?" Moser said.

"She's Stone Clan." Briar folded her arms. "We're not wasting food on her."

"Hey, hey, hey," Moser said. "I caught the damn river shark. I bought the damn groceries. We're feeding who I say we feed. Someone has to witness that I'm a mighty provider."

"I'm not feeding a filthy Stone Clan bitch," Briar snarled.

Oilcan was glad that the conversation was in English.

By the way Merry was ducking behind him, she could still understand the tone of Briar's voice.

"She's Oilcan's friend," Moser said.

"I don't care . . . ," Briar started to protest.

Moser played his trump card. "*Nagarou*'s guest."

Briar went still except for a muscle in her jaw that jerked with her irritation. "Fine," she finally snapped. "But he's not leaving her afterward."

"No, she's staying with me," Oilcan said.

Briar stormed into the kitchen to crash pots and pans together.

Moser leaned close to whisper, "She's so proud of Tinker saving us from a Stone Clan *domi*, you'd think Briar had given birth to her."

Oilcan winced and whispered, "Please, never repeat that to Tinker. She'd freak."

"I am not a stupid man," Moser whispered.

"Yes, you are," Briar grumbled as she came back out of the kitchen with two bowls of salad. "Sit. Eat." She thumped the two bowls down and shouted "Food!" to gather the troops.

Moser had added to his "family" since Oilcan had eaten here last. The count was now fourteen adults, equally divided between human and elf. As always, the conversation slipped and slided in and out of English and Low Elvish, often changing from one to the other in mid-sentence. The food was mostly produce out of the commune's walled-in garden, cooked into elfin dishes. The star of the meal was fillet of river shark grilled to flakey perfection.

"It was just little baby river shark." Moser stretched out his hands as wide as they would go. "Boy, it put up a fight."

"You're lucky it didn't pull you in and eat you," Briar growled.

"Or the jump fish didn't nail you," Oilcan said.

"I told you I'm not a stupid man." Moser served Oilcan another fillet. "I was fishing from the Sixteenth Street Bridge. It's too high up for jump fish." Because Moser loved to entertain, he grinned at Merry, trying to make her more comfortable. "Do you like it?"

"Yes, it's very good." Merry's smile was incandescent. "I like Wind Clan cooking. So many flavors in every bite. There's a lot of human food I want to try. Chiming of Metal said I have to have peanut butter."

There was laughter from the humans and a chorus of "Peanut butter is wonderful!" from the elves.

"Wait, you know Windchime?" Moser asked.

"We studied together under Bright Melody of Fire."

"You play an *olianuni*?" Moser shouted and slipped into English in his excitement. "You're fucking shitting me!"

"No!" Briar snapped.

"We need an *olianuni*," Moser said to Briar.

"Never!" Briar stood up.

Moser stood up, too. "We need an *olianuni*!"

"No, no, no!" Briar thumped on the table, making all the dishes around her jump and rattle.

"This is Pittsburgh." Moser put his hands on the table and leaned toward Briar. "We are Pittsburgh. We don't let the chains of tradition bind us."

"I will not work with a lying Stone Clan bitch!" Briar cried and stormed from the room.

Moser sighed and sat down.

"Shouldn't you go after her?" Oilcan asked.

Moser shook his head and picked up his fork. "Nah, she'll just throw things at me and be ashamed about it later. I'll give her time to cool down. Since the war broke out, the elves are the only ones with money to burn, and elves want the fucking works—the drums and guitars and the *olianuni*. The other bands are booking gigs, but not us. We have too many mouths to feed not to work."

"So, you haven't heard from another *olianuni* player? A male called Rustle of Leaves?" Oilcan shifted the conversation back to Elvish for Merry's sake.

Moser shook his head. "Never heard of him. Why?"

"Windchime gave him a letter of recommendation," Oilcan said. "Merry says he should have arrived already."

Merry nodded. "At Aum Renau, they said he took the train to Pittsburgh almost a month ago."

"A month ago?" Moser's voice echoed the dismay Oilcan felt. "If there was a new player in town, we should have heard about it. You know how people talk."

Merry's hand stole into Oilcan's. "Do you—do you think something bad happened to Rustle of Leaves?"

Oilcan thought of Merry standing alone on the street, where any stranger could have picked her up. She would have gone with anyone. "Rustle of Leaves? Is he a double, too?"

Merry nodded. "Windchime said it would be safer for him to make the trip, since he was male and older than me. He said that Moser was a good person and would keep him safe."

"Ah, shit," Moser swore. "We've got to find this kid, Oilcan."

✧ ✧ ✧

The NSA agent, Corg Durrack, answered his phone with "Well, if it's not the other Bobbsey Twin."

"I need some help," Oilcan said.

"What? Is it Find Novel Ways to Kill Durrack and Briggs Day? Fucking hell!" Gunshots rang loud over the phone.

"What the hell was that?" Then Oilcan realized what Durrack meant by Bobbsey Twin. "Is Tinker with you? Is she okay?"

"Oh, the fairy princess went home hours ago! God forbid she gets hurt! Let the NSA deal with fucking spiders from hell!" Another gunshot. "I've seen dogs smaller than these things!"

"Stop whining, Durrack," his partner, Hannah Briggs, growled. "And ask the kid the best way to deal with spiders."

Judging by the sound, they'd found a nest of steel spinners. "Flamethrower is the only way to clean out a nest safely."

"Ha! Told you! Flamethrower!" Durrack said.

"Fine, let's get out of here and find some flamethrowers." There was another gunshot.

"Hold on." There was noise of the two NSA agents running with occasional gunshots and a good deal of cursing on Durrack's part. Finally he put the phone back to his ear. "Okay, so how do you want to kill us?"

"I need help finding a kid." Oilcan explained how Rustle of Leaves had left the train station on the east coast but hadn't arrived at Moser's.

"Wait, the kid you're looking for is an elf?"

The NSA agents had just arrived in Pittsburgh in June. While they obviously learned fast, there was much they didn't know about elves. "An elf child. He's like sixteen or seventeen."

"Like?" Durrack laughed. "But really sixty years older than me?"

"Elves are still basically eight years old when they're your age. Rustle of Leaves might be ninety, but he'll look and act like a seventeen-year-old human—only he's going to be a hell of lot more naïve. Elves are extremely sheltered while they're growing up. He would have walked off with anyone that offered him a ride to Moser's without realizing the danger he was getting into."

"If Pittsburgh supported video on their cell-phone network, you could see me playing the world's smallest violin."

"He's just a child," Oilcan said.

"He's an elf. Let them look for him."

"I can call Tinker, and she'll call Maynard, and Maynard will call you and tell you to do it. Or I can owe you a favor."

Durrack was silent for a minute and then breathed out a sigh. "Oh fucking hell, I hate this planet. Fine. I'll help you find this kid."

3: PROTECTION MONEY

Tommy Chang had no sympathy for the humans of Pittsburgh. Every time he heard someone complaining about how dangerous the city had become with the war between the elves and the oni, he wanted to punch the speaker in the face. Pittsburgh had never been safe—not for his half-oni kind. He'd grown up a slave to his brutal oni father; his money controlled, his family held hostage for his good behavior, and his every action watched.

Tommy had wanted freedom, so he had thrown in with the elves during the last big battle. Somehow everything had changed, yet stayed the same. The city was under martial law, so the elves were controlling his cash flow. His family had to register as known oni dependents. And the arrival of a summons from the viceroy meant that the elves were keeping track of his moves.

If Tommy was currently free, then somehow he'd confused freedom with starvation. He didn't want to go talk with the viceroy at his enclave, but the elf owed him money that he desperately needed. At his knock at the enclave gate, a slot opened and elfin eyes studied him with suspicion.

"I'm Tommy Chang. The viceroy sent for me."

The slot closed. When the gate opened a few minutes later, armed elves filled the courtyard beyond. Most of them were common garden-variety *laedin*-caste soldiers, but sprinkled among them were *sekasha* with spells tattooed down their arms in Wind Clan blue.

Tommy figured it would go like this, but it was still hard to ignore the fear racing through him and calmly step through the gate. He raised his hands carefully as the gate clanged shut behind him.

"I'm a half-oni." They were going to find out one way or another, and he didn't want to give them an excuse for killing him. "The viceroy ordered me here."

"Weapons?" One of the *sekasha*-caste warriors asked.

Tommy surrendered over his pistol and knife. They searched him for more. He hadn't been stupid, so there was nothing for them to find. As a final humiliation, they had him take off his bandana and reveal his cat-like ears. Tommy locked his jaw on anger; he'd vent his annoyance when he knew he was safe.

Windwolf waited in a luxurious meeting room. With cool elegance, the elf noble wore a white silk shirt, a damask cobalt-blue vest, and black suede pants. That was elves for you—everything had to be done with polished style. Windwolf acknowledged Tommy with a nod.

"This wasn't necessary," Tommy said. "You could have mailed me a check."

"I wanted to talk to you. Sit."

Tommy considered Windwolf and his bodyguards. While the *sekasha* bristled with swords, guns, and knives, the viceroy seemed unarmed. Tommy had seen the elf blast down buildings and set oni troops on fire with a flick of his fingers; Windwolf didn't need knives or guns—he was a living weapon.

Tommy took a chair. "So talk."

Windwolf laid an envelope onto the table.

Tommy studied the thick, white envelope as if it was a trap. He couldn't see the strings attached, but he was sure they were there.

"That is for the damage I did to your family's restaurant," Windwolf said.

Tommy's great uncle started Chang's at a time when Pittsburgh existed solely on Earth. After the first Startup, the oni sought out Chinese families who had family members in Pittsburgh and used them to gain a foothold in the city. While his grandfather, his mother's husband, and Tommy's half-brother were held hostage for good behavior, his mother and her three younger sisters escorted Lord Tomtom and his people to Pittsburgh and the sanctuary of the restaurant. Once Lord Tomtom was safely in Pittsburgh, all three hostages were killed. His mother and aunts became useless except for whatever pleasure they could give the oni.

Tommy was the oldest of the half-breed children that survived. For twenty-eight years, Tommy had done mostly what he was told, and dreamed of somehow killing every last oni, starting with his father, Lord Tomtom. A week ago, he risked everything to save Windwolf's life. The stupid elf fuck picked a fight with oni warriors, blowing out the restaurant's front wall and structurally weakening the building to the point that it collapsed.

But it worked as Tommy hoped. The oni strangle-hold on him was broken, and Windwolf crossed the half-oni off the elves' "kill on sight" list.

"This is not stake money." Windwolf tapped the envelope between them. "But a repayment of what I owe you."

"Which makes us even." Tommy wanted that clear even though he wasn't sure if it was a good thing or not. There was some degree of security inherent in having Windwolf in his debt, but the elves were making it clear that their protection came at a cost.

"The question is now, what does the half-oni intend?"

"My family wants to rebuild." Tommy left the envelope on the table, waiting for the outcome of the conversation. "We have a good reputation in Oakland, so we would stay in the same place."

He used "want" to indicate desire, not concrete plans, as lying to elves was a dangerous thing to do. He wasn't sure, however, if the elves approved of his more lucrative but illegal operations.

"We hope to have a way back to Earth opened before winter. I have spoken with Director Maynard, and the Earth Interdimensional Agency will help you move to Earth, if that is what you want. Through the EIA, the UN has set up extensive programs to help the humans dislocated by Pittsburgh's move to Elfhome. Those programs can apply to the half-oni."

Tommy shook his head, locking down on a flare of anger. *Remember the* sekasha. "Moving to Earth would be a serious step down for my people. We don't know shit about Earth. The only people that know us over there are oni. And I know Earth history enough to know that the UN could completely dick us over—'relocating' us to whatever hellhole no one else wants."

"I see."

"There's no golden promised land for us. Let someone else chase that shit. We know the score here."

"Very well. Here you will stay."

When Windwolf said it that way, it sounded ominous.

"Are we done here?" Tommy asked.

"We elves had our own cruel masters, the Skin Clan, whom we turned against. We know that good can come from evil, which is why we're allowing the half-oni to live, but not without conditions."

Here it comes, Tommy thought. "Those being?"

"*All* of the half-oni must allow themselves to be known to us, so we can weed them from the oni. We are still set on our course to eliminate the oni from our world. The EIA are urging us to detain them and have them deported to Earth. Whatever is decided, the half-oni will be spared only if they reveal themselves."

"And have a Star of David sown onto their sleeves?"

"The oni invaded our world. If we are not ruthless in our actions, the oni will take Elfhome from us by merely breeding like mice and overrunning us. We are sparing the half-oni because we believe you have inherited compassion and the capability of honor from your mothers."

Tommy flinched, as always, at the thought of his mother. His father had murdered her when he'd grown tired of her. "You don't have to convince me that oni are filthy pigs."

"The half-oni will also have to conform to elfin

culture. You will form households under the Wind Clan."

"Why not the Stone Clan or the Fire Clan?"

Windwolf raised his eyebrows in surprise. "Has the Stone Clan offered?"

So Prince True Flame of the Fire Clan was so unlikely that it wasn't even a question. "Not yet, but rumor has it that Forest Moss on Stone is quite insane, and capable of anything."

"Yes, I suppose that's the truth. I would not recommend him."

"Because he's insane?"

Windwolf shook his head. "I don't know if he is as insane as he makes out to be; it might be a ploy he's found useful. I believe, however, that the Stone Clan sent Forest Moss here because they saw him as expendable. If that's true, he does not have firm backing by his clan. Nor does he have *sekasha*, which leaves any household he builds vulnerable."

"Ah." Tommy fought a flash of respect for Windwolf. The elf was shrewd. Unfortunately, that could work to Tommy's disadvantage.

"This is repayment." Windwolf tapped the money on the table. "If you wish to establish a household under me, I will advance you stake money. You would be under my protection."

Tommy had lived under the oni "protection" long enough to know that was a two-edged sword. "I'll need time to think about it."

Windwolf nodded. "We're lifting martial law today. Do what you will, but know that the offer is still on the table."

✧ ✧ ✧

Tommy collected the money, his bandana, his knife, his pistol, and his freedom, in that order. With the money stuffed into his jeans' pocket, he rode his hoverbike up to Mount Washington. There he sat, smoking a cigarette, looking down at the city. He had spent years taking calculated risks trying to free himself from his father, Lord Tomtom, leader of the oni. Looking back, it was odd which ones had led to this moment.

The most unlikely was staying silent when his father started looking for a man by the name of Alexander Graham Bell. Tommy knew Bell was really a teenage girl genius who went by the name of Tinker and ran a metal salvage company in McKees Rocks. He saw her and her cousin, Oilcan, every week at the hoverbike races. Knowing what his father would do to Tinker if he found her, Tommy went to her scrap yard to kill her. He told himself it was the merciful thing to do.

Tinker had been working on an engine but greeted him with a smile, a cold beer, and a blithe assumption that he cared about the inner workings of big machines. She was so small and trusting. He'd waited until she leaned back over the engine and wrapped his hand around her slender neck. . . .

And realized he was rock hard with excitement. He was getting off on the idea of killing someone who, with her pulse pounding under his thumb, only looked at him with mild confusion. It was like the monster that was his father suddenly woke inside him and stretched against the limits of Tommy's skin. It wanted out to fuck with something that had been beaten to bleeding and then kill it. Like Lord Tomtom had done to his mother. Like his father had tried to do to him.

Tommy jerked his hand back off Tinker's neck and wiped it against his pants, wanting it clean. He wasn't his father. He refused to be.

Three months after he'd fled his heritage and Tinker's scrap yard, she killed Lord Tomtom, blocked the oni invasion, and kept Tommy from being beheaded. Of all his little rebellions, he would have never guessed that the most important had been wrapped around that small life. Knowing how close he came to killing her made him worry about what he should do next. It was so easy to misstep.

He took out the cash and counted it. The insurance adjustors had been generous. His family could rebuild the restaurant and still have a small nest egg. But it did nothing for the other families that looked to him for protection. He employed all the half-oni that couldn't pass as human, making sure they could make ends meet without risking being discovered. His father's warriors had always controlled his cash flow; his oni watchdogs had stripped Tommy bare before they fled. Then the elves locked down the city, shutting down his businesses. What little he had hidden away had been drained just keeping everyone fed.

If he took care of just his family, he lost the ability to do anything for the other half-oni. With the loss of that power base, he would be less able to defend his family. It was a self-defeating loop. The more he tried to protect his family alone, the less he would be able to do it. Any disaster would put them at the elves' mercy. They'd go from being owned by the rabid oni to being controlled by the rigid elves. Slavery, no matter who was the master, held unknown terrors of helplessness.

But if he used the money to restart his businesses,

then it was more than enough to keep them free of elfin entanglements. The most profitable was running numbers on the hoverbike races. Now that martial law had been lifted, racing could start again. Carefully managed, he could grow the seed money.

And money meant freedom.

John Montana ran a repair shop and makeshift gas station out of the old McKees Rocks Firehall. He also captained Team Big Sky, which had ruled the racing season until the elves locked the city down. The fire-hall's three tall garage doors were open to the summer night as Tommy pulled up on his hoverbike. John had a car up on the end rack. Surprisingly, his younger half-elf brother, Blue Sky, was with him. The boy was practicing drawing a wooden sword and bringing it up into a guard position. It confirmed the rumors that the elves had discovered that the boy's father had been a Wind Clan *sekasha* and taken custody of him. Apparently they'd given John visitation rights to the brother he had raised like a son. How good of them.

John came out from under the car and greeted Tommy with a cautious look and a nod. "Blue, I'm getting hungry. Can you heat up the food you brought home from the enclave?"

Being a good kid, Blue immediately put away his sword. Blue was seventeen years old, but because of his elf heritage, he was as small and naïve as a ten-year-old. "Is Tommy staying for dinner?"

"No, he's not." John mussed Blue's hair and then gave him a little push to get him moving. He waited until the boy had left before asking, "What do you want?"

Did John know that Tommy was half-oni? Of all

the people in Pittsburgh, he might know, since Blue was coming and going from the viceroy's enclave. It was hard to tell, as John had always been protective of his little brother around Tommy.

"Elves lifted martial law," Tommy said.

"I heard."

"I'm setting odds for this weekend." Tommy leaned on his handlebars, keeping to his bike out of grudging respect for John. The man had always done right by his brother, even though he wasn't much more than a kid when they'd lost their mother. "Is Blue riding?"

John nodded. "The *sekasha* figured out fast that taking everything from him would only break him."

Was it good of the elves to be worried about breaking their possessions? The oni never did. Did it make the elves more compassionate, or just more careful with what belonged to them? "Letting him come back here is also to keep him from breaking?"

John pressed his mouth into a tight line, as if he'd said more on the matter than he wanted to.

"If I was you, it would piss me off." Tommy pressed for more information, wanting to know what is was like to have elves control your life. "Them taking him like that."

"Didn't say I was happy about it." John lowered the rack, dropping the car down to the garage floor. "But some of it makes sense. He likes to fight. It's why he likes to ride. And since we don't have any family here on Elfhome, they'll take care of him if something happens to me. He's going to be a kid for a long time—probably longer than I'm going to be alive."

Trust John to still be thinking of what would be best for Blue Sky even while the elves were rubbing his nose in shit. What made humans so damn noble and oni so monstrous? Was it because the oni greater bloods had bred the lesser bloods with animals? Tommy didn't like to think what that made him, but he couldn't deny the catlike ears hidden under his bandana. And did those ears mean he could recognize nobility, admire it, but never attain it?

Tommy distracted himself by starting up his hoverbike. He had dozens of teams to visit. "Still think it sucks."

Since Windwolf had reduced their warren to rubble, Tommy had hidden his family away at an industrial park on the South Side. The building was large enough to hold them all, had running water and toilets, and was easily defended by a handful of people. After the luxury of the enclave, it was also very dirty and ugly. His cousin Bingo guarded the main door. He slid the massive door aside to let Tommy ride his hoverbike into the cavernous warehouse.

"Glad you're back." Bingo pulled the door shut and threw the locking bar. "I've been getting calls all day. People are asking if we're taking bets."

"I've been out to the teams." Tommy fished out his datapad and handed it to Bingo. "Call Mason at the *Post-Gazette* and give him the list of teams that will be racing. Tell him we'll be starting to take bets tomorrow morning."

There was a brittle crystalline crash from the back of the warehouse. Tommy reached for his pistol then stopped as he realized Bingo looked only mildly disgusted by the noise.

"What's that?" Tommy asked.

Bingo shouldered his rifle. "Numbnuts got Aunt Flo knocked up last time he boinked her—just before Windwolf turned him into an oni candle."

"Shit, again?"

His cousins were all mildly terrified of Aunt Flo, even though their oni blood made most of them nearly two feet taller than her. The more the oni humbled her, the more she would rage at his cousins. Tommy suspected her fury was the main reason she'd survived where his mother hadn't. If he didn't stop her, she was capable of breaking all their dishware. Sighing, he headed to the back of the warehouse.

They had salvaged what they could from the restaurant, including the dishes. They had nailed up shelves to the back wall and stacked the survivors there. Aunt Flo had worked through rice bowls and was now throwing bread plates.

"Stop that," Tommy snapped. "We'll need those to start up the restaurant again."

She flinched away from him, shielding herself with the plate.

"I'm not going to hit you." Tommy wanted to, though, just for thinking he might. She read the anger on his face and continued to quail. "Throw the last one, and then clean up the mess."

Reassured that he wouldn't act, she let loose her anger again. "I didn't want another baby!" She flung the plate against the wall. It shattered, its pieces raining down to a pile of broken china. "I'm sick of babies! You could have stopped him!" She turned to flail harmlessly at him. "You stood there and let him finish and then you killed him! You should have just killed him when he first walked in!"

He caught her wrist and controlled himself so he didn't hurt her, despite his growing anger. "He had his warriors with him. Did you want us all dead just to save you from . . . what? Doing what he'd done a hundred times before? We're free of oni now. This time, you can go to the human doctors and have an abortion."

The fight went out of her and she started to cry, which only made him angrier, because he'd been helpless to protect her in the first place. It had been Windwolf that killed the oni, not him. She clenched the front of his shirt with both hands, seeking comfort from him as she sobbed. The herd of his younger cousins thundered past, all shrieking loud enough to wake the dead, the one in the lead with some treasured toy that all the rest wanted.

God, he needed a drink.

4: THREE ESVA SHY OF A FULL DECK

Tinker had spent the evening studying the recording that Blue Sky had made of the warg fight. She ran it through a video editor so she could isolate the *domana* and analyze every frame as they cast their spells. Blue Sky had caught Prince True Flame doing the fire strike, Jewel Tear doing the scrying spell, and both the Stone Clan putting up their shields. The fire strike scared her slightly. It looked so simple she barely could keep from trying it out; her curiosity, though, was often deadly to those around her. The problem was she wasn't completely positive how the prince was directing and limiting the power of his attack. She'd gone to bed wondering how she could practice the spell without worrying about setting things on fire.

She dreamed that she was back at the archery range at Aum Renau. She'd bolted marshmallows on sticks to the mechanical targets that the *sekasha* used for archery practice. Once on fire, though, the warg-shaped targets had somehow run amok, like crazed flaming sheep. Afraid that the entire palace would go up in flames, she'd wandered around lost, trying to find the Spell Stones in order to call a rainstorm to put out the wargs.

She woke slowly in a warm nest of sheets that smelled of Windwolf with the images tumbling in her mind. She thought of elaborate traps to catch and contain the flaming wargs until she woke up a little more and realized how silly the whole dream had been.

It did remind her, though, that during the three weeks at Aum Renau, she had visited the Spell Stones only once. From the air they had looked like giant slabs of black granite, but up close, it turned out they were layers of stone, each layer inscribed with spells, connected by jumpers just like integrated circuit boards. Why hadn't she taken the time to study them closer?

"Nothing for you," Sparrow stated the first time Tinker saw the Spell Stones from the airship.

Oh, yes, that was right, Sparrow had kept detouring her away from the massive granite slabs. Strange how in retrospect it was easy to see that Sparrow wanted Tinker helpless when the oni kidnapped her. Things would have gone so much differently if Tinker could have called her *domana* shields. Even now, though, it was still hard for Tinker to wrap her mind around why Sparrow had betrayed her.

"I'm using the oni to fix what is wrong," Sparrow said. *"I'm going to take things back to the way they should be."*

Like that would have worked. How would flooding Elfhome with oni do anything other than just wipe out the elfin race? By the oni's count, there were billions of them to the few million of the elves. The oni apparently bred like rabbits. The elves were killing all the oni they found in fear even two would eventually reproduce enough to outnumber them. How did Sparrow think she was going to get rid of the oni after the world suited her?

There was the murmur of male voices as Pony greeted Windwolf with "Brother Wolf."

"Little Horse," Windwolf said fondly. "She is still asleep."

"Hmm," Tinker said to indicate she was really awake.

Windwolf came to kiss her. "Go back to sleep. Your body is still healing."

She moaned since him saying that would get Pony all protective. Almost on cue, the bed dipped and Pony slid in beside her to wrap his arms around her. He slept only in loose cotton pants, so she found herself snuggled into warm skin over hard muscle. Assured that she was pinned in bed by her First, Windwolf went back to getting dressed. She groaned in protest, one that they were ganging up on her, and two that Pony was there, being sexy and available, and Windwolf approved. It was a little facet of elf culture that still freaked her out. Elves operated on an equation that read:

If Wolf Who Rules then (Tinker + Wolf Who Rules) Else (Tinker + Pony).

Everyone (except her) understood that when she took Pony as her bodyguard, it also made him the go-to guy for sex if her husband wasn't handy. The elves reasoned that immortality and basic nature would eventually lead you to want more than one sexual partner, that you'd naturally want to screw with your sexy bodyguard, and besides, said bodyguard was safe, where someone outside the household wouldn't be. Everyone (except her) would be fine if she made love to Pony. She felt guilty just being curled up in his arms and tempted to snuggle closer. Nor did it help that he nuzzled into her hair and brushed his lips against the tips of her ears. It felt sinfully good.

She groaned again and pulled herself out of Pony's arms to sit up. "No fair ganging up on me."

Windwolf grinned at her as he sat on the edge of their bed and pulled on boots. "I could call Discord in, too."

Discord was his nickname for Stormsong. Gods, she'd never get out of bed if both Pony and Stormsong decided that it would be better if she stayed in it. She smacked Windwolf—unfortunately with her right hand. Pain lanced up her arm. She curled around it, hissing in pain as both males moved to comfort her.

"I'm sorry, beloved." Windwolf let Pony scoop her into his arms, a sure sign that he needed to be somewhere else soon.

"I'm fine," Tinker growled. "Where are you going?"

Windwolf sighed. "We're still trying to figure out where the main oni forces are hiding. That there are nearly twenty thousand tengu in Pittsburgh is proof that there are more oni than we first thought. Pittsburgh is so large and has so many abandoned buildings, they could be anywhere. It has been like fighting shadows."

"Be careful." She had planned on working on casting spells, so there was no need for him to leave two Hands with her. "Take all three Hands. If I leave the enclave, I'll stay where there's cops and EIA."

He kissed her forehead. "I will be careful, my

little savage." He nodded to Pony. "Keep her safe, Little Horse."

Poppymeadow's was the oldest and largest of the enclaves in Pittsburgh. Its outer wall was fifteen feet high and had a defense shield that could be triggered to make the enclave nearly impenetrable. On staff were a score of *laedin*-caste guards that patrolled the grounds. The various wings and outbuildings formed a second line of defense around the inner courtyard filled with peach trees. All the buildings presented blind walls to the outer world; their only windows faced inward. The small orchard was the safest place in Pittsburgh.

For her Hand's sake, Tinker settled in a spot where she was in full view of the practice hall when its great double doors stood open to the courtyard. Spared the need to be endlessly vigilant, her Hand took the opportunity to spar with each other.

If she was going to safely cast the fire strike and find other spells she could learn on her own, she needed to widen her search. She went crawling into Pittsburgh's Internet. It was a stunted stepchild of the one on Earth, but it had its uses. First contact with the elves had been nearly thirty years ago. She had expected a lot more footage of Windwolf using magic, but apparently there hadn't been a whole lot of need for him to break out the big guns.

There was only one recording of him fighting; it was taken during the first Startup. She had seen the video dozens of times but never realized it was about Windwolf, mostly because he never actually appeared on camera. The clip was most commonly known as

"WTF" because the human military officer kept repeating "What the fuck?" as tanks pinwheeled down the street and Hummers were reduced to molten lava. Because of the refrain, it was actually pretty funny, especially with the right music added.

There was a lot of footage of Windwolf being handsome and princely without throwing around tanks. She loved watching him move effortlessly through the political dance, endlessly patient and yet unbending. He knew what he wanted, knew how to get it, and would not stop until he had it. He was the only person she had ever met that could match her in imagining huge and making it real. He felt like her other half. That he was handsome, rich, powerful, sexy as hell, gentle and patient, and loved her without reserve didn't hurt, either.

Realizing she'd been sidetracked for nearly an hour, she dropped Windwolf from her search words and added Prince True Flame. She found a mother lode of recordings from the black willow fight on the North Side. Apparently her failed attempt to stop the black willow had given people time to get into position with cameras. From the various recordings, she was able to assemble a composite of the fight. Annoyingly, the black willow (which had tried to eat her) instantly seemed to recognize it was outpowered and retreated as the prince blasted it into cinders. The increasing distance between the tree and the *domana* gave Tinker the vectors she needed to determine how the prince controlled the fire-strike spell. None of the cameras, however, had caught the prince putting up his very cool fire shield.

She flopped back onto the blanket and held her

hands up to the sky, studying her splayed fingers. So much potential locked away from her. So far she had only figured out the Stone Clan shield spell and one Fire Clan attack spell—in theory—and she wasn't even sure she could tap the Fire Clan Spell Stones.

"The Fire Clan *esva* is combined with the Wind's at Aum Renau?" she asked the sky.

"Yes, they are." Pony's voice was level and calm despite the fact that he was fending off Little Egret, Rainlily, and Cloudwalker. "Cover!"

Tinker glanced over and watched as Pony whirled back as Stormsong slid into his place, graceful and strong, blocking attacks with her practice sword. They were as beautiful to watch as dancers. They were all smiling widely; they loved to fight, even just each other.

Stormsong took up the discussion. "The first thing we did when we arrived in the Westernlands was set up the stones for both *esva* at Aum Renau. We slept that winter among the stones, warmed by their heat and protected by their shields."

The stones generated a constant shield that could shrug off a nuclear bomb. From what she understood, the shield not only protected the stones but also acted as a safety valve on the massive pool of magic under the stones, bleeding off excess power when the stones weren't being tapped.

"And the Fire *esva* is keyed to Fire Clan, not Wind?"

"Windwolf can use both *esva*," Stormsong said. "Since he used himself as a blueprint when he transformed you from human to elf, you will most likely be able to use the Fire *esva* once you've been trained."

Tinker considered her hands again.

Windwolf's mother was Fire Clan and his father

was Wind Clan. Of their ten children, Windwolf was the only one that could use both *esva*. Tinker knew enough about genetics to know that nature flipped a coin when a child was conceived. Heads, the child had the Fire Clan blond hair. Tails, the child had the Wind Clan black. How did Windwolf get both *esva*? Was this like blood type, where you could have AB blood from an A blood-type mother and a B blood-type father? That didn't seem right, though, since if that were the case, statistically half of Windwolf's siblings would have had both *esva*.

It wasn't simply that the gene was recessive. There was no way that it could be and Tinker still have access to the Stone Clan *esva*. It had been half a dozen generations since her elfin ancestor was trapped on Earth and married a human. If the key was recessive, it would have been bred out along with the immortal lifespan, pointed ears, and almond-shaped eyes.

She was aware of movement, and suddenly she was bracketed by Pony and Stormsong in full Shield mode. "What's wrong?"

Lemonseed was Windwolf's majordomo and thus head of the housekeeping staff (embarrassingly enough, Tinker had thought she was just a very bossy cook for the longest time.) Nine thousand years had made her infinitely patient. She waited a few feet away, hands folded over her stomach in a manner that Tinker had learned meant that someone was here on official business. "Ginger Wine would like to speak with you."

"Sure." Tinker sat up.

Only recently had Tinker started to learn how to identify castes on sight. What she always considered as "high caste" was actually *nivasa*-caste. They had been bred by the Skin Clan to be elegant, beautiful, and empathic in nature; they used their gifts to run the enclaves as long-stay hotels. Unlike most of the other Wind Clan members, they weren't uniformly black-haired and blue-eyed. Ginger Wine had glorious auburn hair and eyes like emeralds, though she compensated by drenching herself in Wind Clan blue silk.

The enclave owner bowed in greeting and said tentatively, "I—I'm worried about cousin."

Judging by the way Pony went tense, this was bad news. Tinker couldn't remember, though, who Ginger Wine's cousin was. "Why? What's wrong?"

"He brought a Stone Clan female to my enclave yesterday. None of the *domana* were available, so he spoke with Earth Son's First. Not only did Thorne Scratch refuse responsibility for the female, she forced cousin to accept it, and then she threatened cousin."

"Did Thorne Scratch hurt Oilcan?" Pony asked.

"Oilcan?" It felt like Tinker had grabbed hold of a live 220 line. "What did Thorne Scratch do to Oilcan?"

"She did not hurt him," Ginger Wine said. "But this Stone Clan bitch—she clearly has no sense. Who knows what trouble she will cause, and the holy one will blame cousin for it."

What the hell had Oilcan gotten himself into? Tinker had to see him, make sure for herself that he was fine. She headed for the coach house where the Rolls were stored, trusting that her Hand would follow.

5: TRAIN SPOTTING

Even when Oilcan was young, he always knew his tiny cousin would eventually find something large enough to express her soul. He'd assumed that it would take the form of a sixty-foot-tall robot that she could ride around in, smashing cars underfoot like Godzilla. It was somewhat of a relief that she settled on a collection of warriors. She was better off with flesh and blood that loved her than a thousand tons of quasi-intelligent metal. Still, it was a little bit startling to open the door to her "shave and haircut" knock and be face-to-face with *sekasha* first thing in the morning.

Pony filled the doorway, right hand on his *ejae*, scanning the apartment behind Oilcan with eyes cold and hard. When no danger was found, the warrior abandoned the death mask and smiled bashfully, revealing his gentle spirit. "Good morning, cousin."

"Hi, Pony." Oilcan had learned the drill well enough that he stepped sideways without being nudged. Pony and Stormsong brushed past him to search for spear traps and hidden ninjas. Oilcan lived in a three-bedroom loft in a high-rise apartment building on Mount Washington. It always seemed ridiculously huge until Tinker visited; even before she picked up her elves, she overflowed the condo. With the *sekasha*, however, the space became claustrophobic.

Tinker was on Stormsong's heels. She poked Oilcan in the ribs. "You have a female move in with you, and I have to hear about it from Ginger Wine?"

"I was busy!" Oilcan said.

"Obviously," Tinker said.

Cloudwalker grinned in greeting, handed Oilcan a basket smelling of breakfast, and closed the door. Because his condo could only handle so many warriors comfortably, the rest of Tinker's Hand would stand guard in the hall, frightening his neighbors to either side.

A slight squeak from Merry reminded Oilcan that his new roommate was terrified of *sekasha*. Pony had moved into the bedrooms, accidentally herding Merry out of her room. The little female scurried into the hall and careened off Stormsong with another frightened squeak.

"Is that her?" Tinker's surprise made Oilcan realize that she was expecting someone older.

"Yes." Oilcan sighed as Merry took cover behind him. "Merry, this is my cousin, Beloved Tinker of Wind, her First, Galloping Storm Horse on Wind and her Second, Singing Storm Wind. They brought breakfast."

Merry made little meeping sounds.

"Gods, finally, someone smaller than me!" Tinker drifted back, giving Merry space, but was studying the little female intently.

"For about a decade." Stormsong took up guard against sliding-glass doors out onto his balcony, which was the farthest point from Merry that the room would allow. "How old are you? Sixty winters?"

Merry pressed closer to Oilcan under the scrutiny of all the adults. "I'm seventy."

"Oh—geez." Oilcan barely kept from swearing. Seventy meant Merry was only about thirteen. No wonder she was so small.

"If she's only seventy," Oilcan said quietly in English, "shouldn't we send her home?"

Stormsong shook her head. "She probably can't go back if she severed ties."

Pony was frowning as he struggled to follow the conversation. The young warrior had been studying English but wasn't fluent. He understood enough to add in Elvish, "Between seventy and their majority, a child is allowed to sever ties with their parents' household to make new alliances. At seventy, I chose to join Brother Wolf here in Westernlands."

Pony's mother was a *sekasha* beholden to Windwolf's father, Longwind. If Oilcan understood correctly, Pony normally would have been part of Longwind's household for the rest of his life.

"You're *sekasha*." Stormsong pointed out that the normal rules didn't apply to Pony. "And you went with blessings. Wolf is your blade brother, and he'd just been named viceroy of the Westernlands, bringing honor to the clan. He needed support from the clan to keep his position. Most households see a child leaving as a betrayal."

Oilcan sighed as he remembered Merry's conversation with Thorne Scratch. "She severed ties."

Merry rested her forehead against the middle of Oilcan's back and said, "My mother—she—she called me a liar."

Lying was an unforgiveable sin to elves. To call someone a liar was to deal the ultimate insult. Oilcan wanted to tell her that everything would be fine, but they were empty words against the weight of the insult.

"But—I thought children were so precious," Tinker murmured in English. "They really won't take her back?"

"It's complicated," Stormsong said. "It's the head of household's decision to take her back, not her parents'. If her *sama* is old enough to have lived through the worst of the Skin Clan's reign—which they're probably are—then they would see any shift in alliance as treasonous to the entire clan. The punishment used to be stoning."

Tinker eyed Merry with pity and then gave Oilcan a wry grin. "Congratulations. You're a dad."

And that was why he loved his cousin so much. The fact that Merry was an elf and part of the Stone Clan didn't enter into Tinker's equations; she saw simply a child in need.

"There's a double missing, too." Oilcan told them about Rustle of Leaves. "I went to the train station and talked to the elves there. They confirmed that he arrived, but he was Stone Clan, so they ignored him. I have the NSA, the EIA, and the police looking for him, but they keep harping about how the kid is close to a hundred years old."

Stormsong growled in anger.

"Even Maynard?" Tinker asked.

Oilcan shook his head. "I didn't talk to Maynard himself. I didn't realize the kid was missing until after dinner. I talked to someone on the night shift.

I wanted to go out looking for the kid myself, but I had Merry to think of."

"I'll call Maynard," Tinker said. "And I'll get the Wyverns looking—"

"Let us deal with the Wyverns," Pony said.

"Fine." Tinker tapped on Oilcan's chest. "You don't go out alone looking for him. There's oni and shit everywhere. And Merry does not count as backup. You call me or you take someone that can kick ass with you."

"I won't," Oilcan promised, knowing that once he did, he would have to keep his promise.

As usual, the condo seemed huge after Tinker and her Hand left. Oilcan distracted himself from the sudden quiet by investigating the baskets of food that Tinker had brought from Poppymeadow's. Apparently the enclave had decided Oilcan was in danger of starving to death. Considering the state of his pantry, they weren't that far from wrong. He better spend some time laying in food before things got really sparse.

It seemed wrong, though, to be going through the normal motions of living when there was a child missing. He'd promised Tinker not to look mostly because he couldn't even start to imagine where to search. So much time had passed since Rustle of Leaves had left the train station. The male could have reached any point in the city within a day. How far had he gotten? The train station lay in the triangle formed by the confluence of the Allegheny and Monongahela rivers. The male could have only gone less than a mile in three directions without having to cross a river. What kind of directions did Windchime give to Moser's place? Did they include "If you come to a river, turn around quickly"? The river's edge was a dangerous place. That section of the Allegheny was thick with jump fish.

He had a sudden and awful vision of a pile of travel sacks sitting next to the water. Maybe he should check the river's edge.

"Beloved Tinker of Wind is nothing like I expected." Merry broke the silence. "She's so . . . so . . . so much like the sky."

Oilcan laughed. "The sky?"

"She's the only thing that Summer Court is talking about—the Wind Clan's new *domi* this and the new *domi* that. We hounded Chiming of Metal to tell us about her. He said he didn't know any words that would truly describe her, and anything short of the proper words would be a betrayal to his *domi*."

Poor Windchime. He was probably the only person in the Easternlands that had ever met Tinker. When Windchime had left, Tinker was a human hoverbike racer who occasionally acted as a roadie for *Naekanain*. During the summer, a chance encounter with Windwolf had catapulted her to the status of *domi* of the Westernlands.

"Chiming of Metal played this song and said it captured her essence." Merry hummed a tune that Oilcan recognized. He had written the song for Tinker but had never told anyone that it was about her. He'd called it "Godzilla of Pittsburgh." Apparently Windchime had recognized Tinker in the oversized melody.

"When he played me the song, all I could imagine was the sky. How it's big and unlimited, and sometimes it takes your breath away when you watch it, but you can't hold it and make it yours. You can only watch and be amazed."

"Yeah, that's her," Oilcan said.

"Do you think she'll find Rustle of Leaves?"

"If anyone can, she will," Oilcan said.

"What will happen to the others?"

"Others?"

"They said Earth Son needed clan members to build our presence in the Westernlands. Most people wouldn't dream of coming so far into the wilderness, but Earth Son was going to sponsor anyone that made their way to Pittsburgh. It was a chance in a lifetime for anyone that wanted to set up their own enclave."

"I don't know," Oilcan said. "That will be up to the Stone Clan."

Thorne Scratch had said that Jewel Tear couldn't take in any more people, and that Forest Moss couldn't be trusted. What did the Stone Clan think was going to happen to the people they were sending to Pittsburgh? Were they actually just dropping them into the city and hoping they would survive?

"Come on," he said.

"Where are we going?"

"To the train station."

Oilcan always loved watching the train coming into the station. The big diesel train rumbled up to the buffers with a growl that could be felt the whole way into his bones. The brakes hissed and cars lurched to a stop. For a moment, he was back in Boston, holding his mother's hand, waiting to go on some special adventure. Down to the harbor to watch the tall ships unfurl their bright sails. To Boston Commons to feed the mallards gliding beside the swan boats. Out to the windswept bay islands to fly kites. Anywhere his father wasn't drinking himself into a murderous rage.

Sometimes, his mother talked about getting on the train and just keeping on going. She kept their immigration papers for Elfhome in the zippered compartment of her purse, just in case they would ever need to flee to another world to be safe. Their ancestor had come from Elfhome, once upon a time, and they could always run back. They were both fluent in Elvish; it had been handed down through the family for generations. They used it as their secret language as they tiptoed around his drunken father. She'd get work translating, and they'd live with the grandfather he'd never met.

But they always went back home. Despite all his father's weaknesses, she loved him, and that love killed her. Only after she was dead did Oilcan take the train to Elfhome.

And it was Merry holding his hand tightly. "It makes the most marvelous sounds." She was nearly vibrating in place with her excitement over all the sights and sounds of the city. Her hands twitched as if she wanted to translate it all to music on her *olianuni*.

Laedin-caste royal marines in scarlet uniforms spilled out of the passenger cars like schoolkids on a field trip. They pointed up through the glass ceiling at the buildings that towered over Pittsburgh. They pointed out onto the street, where a hoverbike was passing a slow-moving van. They pointed at him.

"It's a human. Look, Blaze, your first human."

The soldiers gathered around Oilcan, creating a tall wall of red, to study him closely. In amazed exclamations, innocent of any contempt, they made comments on his short hair, his rounded eyes and ears, his T-shirt and blue jeans, and his obvious lack of any weapons. Perhaps because of their schoolchildren-like exuberance, Merry showed no signs of being afraid of the *laedin*-caste warriors.

"I thought they would all have guns." A female lifted her shoulder to indicate the rifle slung over it. The rifles were fairly standard issue, not the magic-insulated ones that the *sekasha* carried.

"Are you sure it's not an oni?" asked a male that seemed barely out of his doubles. "They said that the oni are disguising themselves as humans."

"He is not an oni!" Merry gave the young soldier a slight shove, which made all the soldiers laugh and push the soldier themselves.

"Oni are tall, Blaze," one of the officers stated. "And they tend to smell of vinegar."

"I didn't realize humans were so small," Blaze said.

"Forgiveness, I'm considered fairly short for a human male," Oilcan said in High Elvish. He didn't want the incoming troops to think all tall humans were oni. He raised a hand over his head to indicate several inches taller. "Most human males are taller. Some are as tall as you are."

"I'm still growing," Blaze snarled in Low Elvish.

The young elf male got smacked in the back of his head by his officer.

"You speak the high tongue very well, child." The officer gave Oilcan a slight bow that begged forgiveness.

Oilcan ignored the mistake about his maturity. He knew from experience that his height misled elves, but his true age would only reinforce the impression. "Thank you. Were there any Stone Clan on the train?"

There was a rattle of a drum toward the back of the train.

"Fall in!" the officer shouted, and the troops dutifully shuffled into formation. "No, child, there were no Stone Clan with us."

The drum rattled again, and they marched out, shouting excitedly and pointing at the new wonders of the human city.

Until the war broke out, the trains had been run by Americans, mostly by necessity since the freight cars would roll directly off Earth onto Elfhome and back during Shutdown. The tight schedules, the hundreds of freight cars that needed to be linked into one long train, and the necessity to match up rails to the exact inch meant humans well familiar with technology ran the system while elves worked in apprentice-like positions.

Oni had infiltrated most of the human organizations in Pittsburgh, and the train was no exception. In the name of security, the elves had taken over the rail lines.

The station didn't have a ticket booth, since tickets weren't required to ride the train. It did have a staff of three elves in Wind Clan blue who looked seriously overworked.

Oilcan bowed to the eldest looking of the three. "Forgiveness, but can you tell me if any of the Stone Clan arrived in the last few weeks?"

The elf male shot a look at Merry and pursed his lips as if he'd tasted something sour. "It is not my duty to pay attention to the comings and goings of the Stone Clan."

Oilcan locked down on his anger. All this bigotry was starting to really make him mad. "Just yes or no, did any other Stone Clan get off the train?"

"I don't have to answer you, human."

A black-tattooed arm suddenly flashed past Oilcan's head with the speed of a striking snake. Thorne Scratch caught the male elf by the collar and slammed him hard up against the wall. "Yes," Thorne Scratch rasped in her rough, scratchy voice. "You do have to answer him."

Merry squeaked and backpedaled from the female *sekasha*.

"Holy one!" The elf cried, eyes going wide with fear.

"Answer him," Thorne snapped.

"Yes! Yes, some Stone Clan arrived. They got off the train and left the station."

"How many? When?" Thorne said.

"I don't know," the elf said. "One every few days for the last three weeks. Six or seven total."

"Which was it?" Thorne snapped. "Six or seven?"

"I'm not sure. Let me think. There were the two *olianuni* players. The *taunrotiki* came first and a *taunlitiki* came just yesterday." He meant Rustle of Leaves and Merry. "There were three *taunrotiki*. One *nivasa* with his soup pots all clanging and two other—I don't know what they were. There were two—no—three *taunlitiki* before the *olianuni* player yesterday. One was in court fashion; I think she was a seamstress. One had the hands of a potter—she was the first to arrive. I'm not sure what the smallest *taunlitiki* was."

Oilcan felt sick. The Wind Clan male was using the gender words for children instead of adults.

"They were all children?" Thorne cried.

"They looked young," the male said. "Either doubles or just hit their triple."

"And you let them walk out into a war zone?" Thorne said.

"They were Stone Clan," the male said it as if it explained and forgave everything.

"No!" Oilcan cried as Thorne pulled her sword. "Holy one! Please don't! You will only make things worse. Please."

"He as good as gave those children to the oni," Thorne growled.

"Killing him will only turn the others against the Stone Clan more," Oilcan said. "This is for Wolf Who Rules. As viceroy, the protection of all the elves in Westernlands is his duty, not just those of the Wind Clan. Let him punish his own."

She glared at him for a long minute before sheathing her *ejae*.

Oilcan turned to the nearest elf, making him step backward when Oilcan pointed at him and said, "You."

"Me, *domana*?"

"Yes, you." Oilcan ignored Thorne's bitter laugh. "Do you know how to use a phone?"

"Yes, *domana*."

Oilcan took out the tablet he kept for making lists, tore off a sheet of paper, and wrote his phone number on it. "This is my phone number. Every day, without fail, watch for Stone Clan getting off the train. If any get off, ask them to wait here at the station and call me."

It was a poor temporary fix. Hopefully either news of Earth Son's death would stop the masses from traveling to Pittsburgh, or another Stone Clan *domana* would arrive that could sponsor the incoming. The damage, however, was already done. Seven children had disappeared into the city.

"Are you out looking?" Tinker cried when he told her about the other missing children. By the sound of it, she was still in the Rolls. "You promised not to!"

"I'm at the train station, not the river's edge," Oilcan said. "And I have Thorne Scratch here with me—she qualifies as someone who can kick ass."

There was a long silence, to the point he thought the connection had died, and then Tinker said in English, "Be careful with Thorne Scratch. Just because I sleep in the nest of dragons, doesn't make them less dangerous."

He sighed. "I know. She nearly killed the elves that work at the station because they let the kids wander off to be kidnapped. I told her that Windwolf would do something about it. He's the viceroy."

"Windwolf, hell. I'm coming down and kicking butt myself," Tinker promised.

He suspected Windwolf would have been gentler than Tinker.

Thorne was studying him with a look of mild annoyance, as if it bothered her to not understand him. "Why do you care about these children?"

"I was ten years old when my mother was killed. Humans don't have clans. My only kin lived here on Elfhome. Since news could only be passed during Shutdown, it was weeks before they learned of my mother's death, and then my grandfather needed to wait for the next Shutdown to come get me. I was alone on Earth for nearly three months, in the care of strangers, not knowing if anyone was coming for me."

"So you understand what these doubles are facing by leaving everything behind and coming here."

He nodded. "My grandfather was too wrapped up in his own grief at first to really take care of me. My baby cousin, Beloved Tinker of Wind, was only six." Oilcan measured off how tall Tinker was at the time. "But she understood that she was all I had. By day she taught me what I needed to know to be safe and at night she let me grieve without judgment."

Something that could have been envy flickered across her face before being banished. "You were kin. Why does she care for these children who are not her blood and not her clan?"

"Because that's the way she is," Oilcan said. "She cares about people. When she was basically the same age as Merry—" He was going to use Merry as a demonstration of size for when Tinker fought a saurus to save Windwolf's life. The little female, though, was nowhere in sight. "Where's Merry?"

Thorne scanned the room and then clicked her tongue in an elfin shrug. "I think I scared her away."

That was entirely possible. Merry probably retreated to the safety of the pickup. Still, with all the kids going missing, it worried him to have her out of his sight. He walked to the entrance to check his pickup. Merry wasn't in the cab.

"Merry?" he called.

The area was amazingly empty for an entire troop of marines having just unloaded from the train. Neither the soldiers nor Merry were in sight. The only thing moving was a dark van that was just pulling away from the curb.

He realized suddenly that he'd seen the van half

a dozen times since arriving at the station, always slowly trolling past. "Merry!"

Five running steps and he caught the van and jerked open its back door. There were four big men crouched in the back. They looked up as the door opened, surprised but unafraid. They had Merry pinned to the floor, a hand clamped over her mouth.

"No!" he growled and scrambled into the moving van. He needed to stop the van; he needed to get to the driver.

He ducked a backhanded blow from the nearest male, jerked sideways from a grab, caught the driver's head by the hair and slammed it into the steering wheel. The van jumped forward and bucked as the horn blared loud in protest. Oilcan grabbed the spindle and jerked the van into park. It shuddered to a halt, throwing him hard against the dashboard. It was an old van, and keys dangled in the ignition.

He reached for the keys, but hands caught him from behind and flung him through the front window. Merry was screaming as he hit the pavement in front of the van. He heard the unmistakable clacking of a shell being chambered in a pump-action shotgun.

He looked up into the barrel of the gun as it fired.

The pellets rained to the ground inches from Thorne Scratch as she stood over him, her *sekasha* shields protecting them both. "Idiot! You're not a *domana*!"

The van's rear lights flashed, indicating that the driver was shifting back into drive.

"Cut the wheels!" Oilcan pointed at the van's front tire.

Thorne caught Oilcan by the collar and spun like a matador before an enraged bull. The front bumper just missed Oilcan. She struck with her *ejae* as the van roared past, driving the blade through the driver's door and cutting a long gash down the side. The van careened as it leapt forward, jumped the curb, and slammed into the streetlamp on the corner. The horn stuck on, blaring loudly.

"That works, too," Oilcan said.

The back door was flung open and the males inside leveled machine guns at them. Thorne growled a curse and shifted in front of Oilcan as bullets chewed a path toward them. The first handful pinged off her shield, but then Thorne grunted as one plowed through her weakened defenses and hit her.

"Thorne!" Oilcan shouted.

The air around them suddenly changed, and the gunfire muted oddly as bullets ricocheted harmlessly to either side.

Pony pulled Oilcan up and back, eyes cold with fury. Oilcan blinked at him in surprise and relief. The Wind Clan *sekasha* ignored the oni, though, to square off to Thorne Scratch. "Peace?"

"We have peace until we agree to war." Thorne gave a slight bow.

Pony matched the bow. "Peace it is until we agree otherwise."

"Do we have to do this now?" Tinker was trembling with effort, right hand outstretched, finger cocked into odd positions. She was maintaining the shield that was protecting them. She must have raced to the train station after Oilcan called her.

"Yes," both Pony and Thorne Scratch said. The rest of Tinker's Hand nodded silently in agreement.

"Are you hurt?" Tinker asked Oilcan.

Oilcan shook his head. "They have Merry."

"We will get her back." Pony unsheathed his *ejae.*

"Don't kill them!" Oilcan cried, getting a surprised look from all the *sekasha*. "We need to find out where they took the other children."

Pony sheathed his *ejae* and pulled out two knives. "We'll take them prisoner. Ready, *domi*?"

"Yeah, fine, whatever," Tinker growled.

In one fast and violent motion, the *sekasha* attacked. Tinker had shifted forward, maintaining her shield spell to protect her Hand as they dove into the back of the van. Merry screamed as Thorne slammed into the oni holding her, knives flashing. Oilcan's heart hammered in his chest at the sound. Rainlily grabbed Merry and jerked her back, out of the fray. She was drenched with blood, and her yellow tunic hung in tatters. Oilcan tried to move toward her, and only then realized Cloudwalker had hold of him and was shielding him from stray bullets.

Just as suddenly as it started, it was over. The *sekasha* had the disguised oni pinned and bound. They used a spell to reveal the oni's true appearance.

"It is not her blood, cousin." Rainlily rocked Merry as the little female clung sobbing to her.

Oilcan breathed out relief. When Thorne slashed through the driver's door, he realized, she had cut the driver in half, spraying the inside of the van with his blood. The smell hung thick in the hot air.

"Where are the other children?" Thorne kicked the oni that been holding Merry. "Where did you take them? Are they still alive?"

Oilcan repeated the question in English, and then tried the little Mandarin that he knew. The oni gazed up at him blankly. "I don't think they speak anything but Oni."

Judging by the looks on the faces of the *sekasha*, none of them spoke Oni.

"I'll call Jin." Tinker rubbed her arm, grimacing in pain. "The tengu will be able to talk to them."

Tinker's Rolls-Royce sat abandoned twenty feet down Liberty Avenue, all doors open and engine still running. As Tinker climbed into the Rolls to find her cell phone, Thorne staggered to the low planter in the center of the street and sat down. Blood streamed down Thorne's arm from a slice in her shoulder.

Oilcan got the first-aid kit from his truck and bound the wound. "You'll have to have the hospice staff look at this."

"After we find the children," Thorne said.

Oilcan nodded and then hugged her carefully. "Thank you. I couldn't have stopped them. They would have just driven away with Merry, and I wouldn't have been able to do anything to save her."

She hugged him tightly, burying her face into his shoulder. There was something desperate in her hold, like he was the only safe handhold in a flood. She breathed deep, with only the dampness of his shirt to tell him that she was crying.

"Idiot," she growled after several minutes. "You don't have shields. You don't have a weapon. Next time, just stay out of my way and let me deal with it."

He opened his mouth to say that he sincerely hoped there wouldn't be a next time, but then, that would mean there would be no reason for her to stay close. "Okay, next time I'll stay out of your way."

6: WHELPING PENS

Tinker expected Jin to come with bodyguards. He was, after all, the tengu's spiritual leader. He came alone, apparently trusting her to keep him safe. He glided down out of the summer sky on great black wings. With one easy backstroke, a muffled clap of glossy feathers, he landed on the far side of the train station's parking lot. He stood there, bare-chested and panting, letting the *sekasha* grow used to his presence. His wings were solid illusions, called into existence by the spell tattooed on his back, real down to their vanes and quills and hooks. He dismissed them with a word, making them vanish back to the nothingness from which they came.

Tinker really had to figure out how they worked.

Jin had a white button-down shirt tied to his waist that he pulled on, buttoned, and tucked into his blue jeans like a priest donning his vestments. When he crossed the parking lot, he seemed nothing more than an Asian man out for a summer walk. He wasn't even wearing fighting spurs on his birdlike feet; he wore a pair of tennis shoes. The only things that marked him as the spiritual leader of all the tengu was the air of calmness that he seemed to radiate and the dragon birthmark of the Chosen faintly showing under the fine linen of his shirt.

"Thank you for coming," Tinker said as he bowed to her.

"You needed me, of course I would come." Even though she had greeted him in English, he'd answered in fluent Elvish. "You're our *domi*. It is our duty to serve as it yours to protect."

It was weird having elf pledges coming out of a tengu's mouth, but the tengu were safe only because they were her Beholden.

Jin tilted his head and then stepped closer to hug her. "Are you all right, *domi*?"

"No." She had nearly lost Oilcan. If she had been a minute longer reaching the train station. If Oilcan hadn't called her. If Thorne hadn't been there to protect Oilcan. It had been so very, very close. "I'd say 'give me time,' but we don't have it."

"Was he hurt?" Jin asked after Tinker explained how Oilcan had discovered that Stone Clan children were arriving in Pittsburgh and being kidnapped at the train station by oni.

"He got a couple of impressive bruises. I had him take Merry to the hospice; she'd been fairly roughed up by the oni." It had taken Tinker twenty minutes of bullying to get Oilcan to agree to stay at the hospice and wait for Tinker to find the children. After seeing Oilcan nearly killed, Tinker wanted him a safe distance from the fighting. He agreed only after Tinker had ruthlessly pointed out that the hospice staff were all Wind Clan elves and might not treat Merry without Oilcan there to force the healers into it.

As soon as he left, though, Thorne Scratch started to restlessly pace like a big cat in a cage. *Sekasha* apparently were calmer when they had someone to protect.

"It's unlikely the children are still alive," Jin said. "Lord Tomtom was very careful with you because he needed you well and functioning. Obviously the oni wanted the children for some reason, but still, they're rarely careful with their prisoners."

Tinker shivered and nodded. She had seen how the oni tortured their own; she didn't want to think of the horrors that the missing children were suffering.

Jin crouched down beside the first oni prisoner and spoke at length in the coarse oni language.

After several minutes, Thorne Scratch growled with impatience. "What are you telling him? Your life story?"

"No." Jin shook his head. "He knows he's going to die. He knows that the elves don't take oni prisoners. He also knows that the elves are too noble to torture prisoners."

"I'll show him noble," Thorne growled.

"You don't have enough experience in inflicting pain to impress him," Jin said gently. "I've reminded him that we tengu have lived as slaves to the oni for a thousand years. We had every excruciating torture that our masters know inflicted on us. We tengu are known to be clever and quick to learn. I have reminded him that we tengu have a bone to pick, so to speak."

The memory of sharp knives and white bone flashed through Tinker's mind. She wrapped her arms tight around herself. "Gods, Jin, I know what oni do—"

"So does he," Jin said. "You would give him a quick, clean death. It would be merciful compared being turned over to those who hold a thousand years of misery against his kind." He spoke again to the oni, and this time the oni glanced at the other tied-up oni and started to talk. Jin listened intently, nodding.

"They were told to come to the train station every day, that there would be elves traveling alone. They were to grab them quietly and take them to a warren on the North Side. Humans think that it's a dog kennel. There's a greater blood called Yutakajodo who wanted them for a project."

"Dog kennel? Shit, I know where that is." Tinker even knew people who had bought dogs from the kennel. Big ugly mutt dogs. She thought of Chiyo and the warg and shuddered. "What project?"

Jin asked the oni questions, but it was obvious that no more information was forthcoming—much to the oni's distress. "He doesn't know. I didn't expect him to. Greater bloods rarely explain themselves to the lesser bloods. All they knew was they were to keep the elves alive until Yutakajodo dealt with them."

"How did you get him to talk so much?" Stormsong asked.

"I promised that the first to speak would earn a clean death. I pointed out that you needed only one of them to talk. I told him once you had the information that you wanted, you'd turn your focus to the missing elves."

Jin had implied that the remaining oni would be left to the tengu.

"I'm not giving you them to torture," Tinker said.

Jin gave Tinker a smile that came straight from

his heart. "I know, and I'm glad. I want my people to make your nobility theirs. We've learned too much cruelty from the oni. It's time to learn a new way."

Tinker didn't want to go after the children with just her Hand, not with the oni armed with automatic assault rifles that could chew through the *sekasha*'s protective spells. Her people needed someone that could fling tanks around and reduce cars to molten lava—not someone that could barely maintain one shield spell. Judging by the very faint tingling against her magic sense, though, Windwolf was someplace very far away, fighting the oni. She couldn't wait for him to finish his battle and return to Poppymeadow's. The oni were so elusive because they scattered anytime one of their number was captured. As soon as it became apparent that the oni in the van weren't returning, the oni with the children would abandon their hideout, either taking the children or killing them.

"You need more than six *sekasha* to take out a warren," Jin said. "I'll call some of my warriors."

"Thank you." Tinker felt uneasy at the idea of leading her Hand and the tengu into danger. "I hate risking lives to save lives."

He smiled at the worry. "This is our war, too. If the elves lose, we'll fall under the oni's control again."

She supposed no one understood the dangers facing Pittsburgh better than the tengu.

Jin turned to face northeast and let out a crow call that resonated across her magic-sense like a spell being cast.

"What the hell was that?" Tinker asked.

"It's a power of the Chosen to be able to call the Flock," Jin said.

"You called the entire Flock?" Tinker said. "All twenty thousand?"

Jin laughed and shook his head. "I have warriors I know I can trust and are fluent in Elvish. I've called them."

"So, it's like calling out for Chinese? An order of Sum Yung Gai with wings?"

Jin laughed again.

Who else could she highjack into the effort? Remembering that Oilcan had mentioned a troop of royal marines, she sent Rainlily to track them down and then called Maynard.

"Durrack and Briggs are still clearing out the steel spinners," Maynard said when she identified herself. "There's a huge nest up in the air ducts."

She frowned at the phone for a moment. Which air ducts, and why did Maynard think she cared? Maynard made it clear when he finished with "Until we have the steel spinners cleared out, the highway engineers can't do safety checks on the tunnels."

"No, I'm not calling about that. I need backup on the North Side. The oni are holding some elf children prisoner. I'm going in to rescue them."

"Just you?"

She laughed at the question. "Just five-foot-tall me with the badly bruised right arm? No!"

"I'm at Shippensport with Windwolf, Prince True Flame, and both Stone Clan *domana*." In other words, all the heavy hitters were tied up protecting the nuclear power plant.

"I'll have my Hand—plus one—and some tengu—and

some royal marines if Rainlily can find them between now and then."

There was a moment of silence, and then, "I'll send you backup."

The royal marines turned out to be a small regiment that specialized in warg hunting. Her Hand claimed that they were a crack commando team, but they were like an unruly group of teenage boys, laughing and joking about the upcoming fight. She had the commanding officer repeat the information that "the tengu were allies and not to be shot at when they showed up" many, many times and loudly.

Maynard's assault team of thirty men seemed more like the steely-eye soldiers she would expect out of "crack commandos." They too were warned of the incoming tengu.

The warnings turned out to be a good thing, as the tengu looked dangerously feral when they showed up. They landed on the roofs of the buildings around the parking lot. Unlike Jin, they wore fighting spurs and war paint and not much else—it was like they'd pared clothing down to offset the weight of knives and guns. The lack of shirts really showed off the fact that flying was great for upper body strength. Jin's nephew Riki Shoji was the first to arrive.

Riki winged down and landed beside his uncle. "You called."

"The oni have taken some elfin children," Jin said. "*Domi* needs us to help rescue them."

Dismay and anger flashed over Riki's face. Tinker thought for a moment that he was upset at her for asking tengu to save elves, but then he said, "Oh, *domi*, nothing will give us more pleasure than to kill these monsters, but the children are most likely dead already."

Jin put a hand to his nephew's shoulder. "A greater blood wants them alive."

"Then there's a chance," Riki admitted.

"The greater blood is named Yutakajodo," Tinker said. "Do you know him?"

Riki shook his head. "I only dealt with Tomwaritomo. The oni don't play nice even with each other. Yutakajodo is a true greater blood and automatically outranked Lord Tomtom, but Lord Tomtom had clawed his way up from the lesser bloods, and he didn't see it that way. If Lord Tomtom could have gotten the upper hand, he would have killed Yutakajodo long ago. Yutakajodo, though, was always three steps ahead of Lord Tomtom. True to form, Kajo killed all his tengu a few hours before you returned Jin to the Flock."

"Kajo?"

"It's oni for snake. Yutakajodo is the name of the most poisonous snake on Onihida."

Fear skittered through Tinker as they drove across the city toward the dog kennel. Thanks to her elf regeneration abilities, the pain had been more bearable when she cast her shield to save Oilcan, but this wasn't going to be a short skirmish. She thought of Prince True Flame leading the royal forces, his shields protecting all his people. She was going to have to do that, but she wasn't sure she could withstand the pain for hours.

They stopped a mile from the base, and the tengu scouted ahead. The Rolls proved to have a small arsenal in its trunk. Thorne Scratch geared herself along with Tinker's Hand. With ninja-like stealth, Riki suddenly appeared overhead and dropped down with a quiet rustle of feathers. Since her protection of the tengu was through Jin alone, she had asked him to stay behind and give command to Riki.

"This is not going to be easy." Riki spread a map out on the hood of the Rolls.

"The warren is tucked between the river and this cliff. The oni know that they can't run, so they'll dig in and fight. The only way in is down this street"—Riki slid his finger along a road through several blocks of empty lots, void of any cover—"and through this reinforced gate. There's netting over this area here, so my people can't drop in and eliminate any guards quickly."

The netting and reinforced gate were new additions. The one time she'd been down this street, years ago, the compound had looked and sounded like just a dog kennel.

"So we go straight in." Tinker's stomach was doing flip-flops at the thought, but if they went in fast and hard, the fight would be over quicker. "I'll lead, and my Hand will take out the gate while I protect them."

Pony pointed to various areas on the roof. "Put your people here with rifles. Use the cover to stay safe but protect the others as they follow *domi* in."

Riki nodded his understanding. The marine commander took it for granted that the *domana* would lead the assault, but the EIA commando leader looked slightly alarmed that she would be first one into the fight.

"Get into positions," Tinker ordered, ignoring him. Actions would speak louder than any words.

She spent the next few minutes bracing herself for what was about to follow. She was going to lead a hundred of her people into a fight to the death for the lives of seven children—and it was going to hurt like bitch in more ways than one.

"We're ready, *domi*." Pony took his place slightly behind her and unsheathed his *ejae*.

Tinker took a deep breath and set up resonance with the Spell Stones and quickly called her shields. Her right arm throbbed with dull, bearable pain. "Okay, let's do this."

She walked as quickly as she could straight up to the gate. The EIA commandos might have been dubious, but the oni knew trouble when they saw it coming. They unleashed a thunderstorm of gunfire onto her. At the gate, her Hand slashed through the tall steel door. When it crashed to the ground, the marines charged with a roar up the street, and there was no turning back.

The first part of the complex was a wide roadway with small buildings to either side, which at one time housed security guards and office workers.

"We'll keep them pinned. Search the side buildings," Pony ordered the commandos and marines. He sheathed his *ejae* and unslung the bow from his back and nocked a spell arrow. The rest of the *sekasha* followed his lead.

The spell arrows screamed away. The sound of their flight triggered the spell inscribed on their shafts. The arrows flashed to laser-intense light and punched through the ranks of oni. Pony led the others slowly forward as they carefully picked out targets for their arrows, trusting Tinker to keep them safe. Tinker gritted her teeth against the pain throbbing in her arm and followed in their wake.

With Tinker pushing her shield forward, the oni had no choice but to retreat. The other fighting units fanned out to search the smaller buildings. Tinker tried to ignore the gunfire behind her to stay focused on maintaining her spells. She hated that she couldn't protect all her people. Until they found the children, she couldn't even use her one attack spell.

The narrow street ended at a loading dock with a dozen bays facing the road. All the doors were closed, the oni retreating in through a man-sized side door on the far right.

"Hold here." Pony stopped short of the loading dock. "Advise me, *domi*. What would lie behind those large doors?"

"It's a warehouse," Tinker said. "All those doors, including the small one, will lead to the same large room. If we hit the leftmost door, we can clear the room left to right."

Of course, there was the slight matter of getting onto the nearly five-foot-tall loading dock. The stairs were barricaded. It had posed no problem to the tall oni, but she wouldn't be able to use her hands to climb.

Pony backed up, slinging the bow across his back. "Cloud, assist *domi*."

The *sekasha* charged forward and leapt up onto the loading dock.

"Assist? What do you mean by—" Tinker yelped in surprise as Cloudwalker lifted her up and deposited her onto the loading dock. Somehow she managed to keep her shields up. "Oh for the love of God, I wish people would stop doing that to me."

"Forgiveness." Cloudwalker vaulted up beside her.

Her Hand and Thorne Scratch slashed through the bay door like it was tissue paper.

Apparently when you bred for animal size, strength, and brutality, you lost housekeeping somewhere along the way. The football field–sized room looked like someone had backed garbage trucks up to the loading dock and dumped the contents into the warehouse. Oni warriors had a weakness for Twinkies and Milk-bones, judging by the multitude of the empty boxes. There were walkways kicked through the litter. There were odd little semi-cleared areas—containing only filthy blankets, chewed pillows, and worn clothes. Oni of all shapes and sizes were bolting for more fortified positions.

The tengu came winging down and cut through the netting stretched across the street.

"Find anything?" Tinker called to Riki as he landed on the dock.

"No sign of the kids yet." Riki shifted so he was still protected by her shield and shot at a small oni that was struggling to reposition a tripod-mounted machine gun. "Most of the outbuildings were lightly guarded dog kennels and pigsties."

"This whole place looks like a pigsty." Tinker picked her way slowly through the garbage. The pain made it hard to keep her footing while maintaining her shield. She was losing track of the fight around her. "What's the deal with this mess?"

"This is a sleeping nest." Riki watched her nervously. "I've never seen one this disgusting before."

"If the kids are tied up somewhere in here, they'll be difficult to spot," Tinker said.

"Gods forbid." Riki fired off more shots. "The only reason they'd be in here is the greater blood had no more use of them."

The other teams came spilling into the sleeping nest. They spread out, weaving through the litter, looking for oni. Tinker started toward the only visible door on the warehouse's back wall. A dozen steps forward and she nearly tripped over a small body half hidden in an avalanche of trash.

She recoiled with fear, seeing only a snarling face. Riki shot it twice before either of them realized it was already dead.

"What is it?" Tinker asked. The creature was smaller than any oni she had seen before. It had a piglike snout, sharp tusks, and was covered with coarse hair. It was wearing only a loincloth and a bandolier filled with fat shells for the grenade launcher lying beside it.

"Oni." Riki reloaded his rifle. "Lesser blood. Very lesser."

She kicked it for scaring her. "How did this even get to Elfhome? Did the oni put it in a dog crate to get it halfway across Earth and through EIA checkpoints?"

"It was born here." Riki stripped off the bandolier and picked up the grenade launcher. "This is a whelping pen. The Greater Bloods brought females that could pass as human to Elfhome via Chinese visas. The father of that thing was probably one of the wild boars locked up outside."

She'd been so focused on getting through the trash while keeping up her shields that she hadn't thought about why the oni would have animals kenneled in the middle of the city. She shuddered. "For what logical reason would you mate a female to a wild boar?"

Riki passed the piglet's weapon and ammo to one of his warriors. "These hybrids reach maturity faster than humans. Think of Chiyo. Her pregnancy will run less than two months, not the nine months of a human. Within a decade, her puppies would be ready to breed."

Tinker flinched at Riki using the word "puppies" for Chiyo's children, but she'd seen the mating: the warg father had been pure animal. Chiyo already had fox ears and a tail—how human could her offspring possibly be?

"This is why the oni are hiding instead of fighting," Riki said. "They're immortal like the elves—they can afford to play the waiting game. The longer they wait, the stronger they become. Within a few decades, they'll easily outnumber the elves in this area. In thirty or forty years, they could have several million of their kind in Pittsburgh."

"Millions?" Tinker scoffed. "Even with a generation a decade, do they really have the numbers to hit that mark?"

"Do you think that the humans will be left out of their plans forever?" Riki asked. "There are sixty thousand humans in Pittsburgh, but with the exception of these EIA soldiers, they're sitting on the sidelines, watching. The Greater Bloods know that if the humans took up arms, it could tip the scales in the elves' favor, so they're leaving the humans alone. When the time is right—maybe as long as a decade from now—they'll kill all the men and turn all the women into breeders."

Tinker stared at him in horror. "You can't be serious."

"This is a war to the bitter end," Riki said. "The only ones that don't know this are the humans. If the elves lose, then the humans will end up like the tengu." He lifted his foot and flexed his birdlike toes. "Remember, we were once human."

She knew the oni well enough to recognize the truth in what he was saying, but she didn't want to believe it. "So—we're going to find oni children in here?"

"That is one of the oni children." Riki pointed at the dead tusked oni. "It's about nine years old. Don't worry—all the other oni 'children' will do their damnedest to kill us, too."

She had just reached the door when a shout went up from the other corner of the sleeping nest. One of the marines waved and flashed a series hand signals that Tinker didn't recognize.

"*Domi*, no." Pony blocked her from moving closer to the discovery. "You do not need to see this."

"What is it?" she asked.

"The oni killed one of the children," he said. "A female."

Tinker wavered, not wanting to see the dead female but feeling like she should force herself to look. She looked down at her arm. The only thing she'd done the entire fight was keep it locked in one position. It hurt so bad she felt like crying. "I feel so useless."

Stormsong breathed out a laugh. "If you were useless, there would not be nearly a hundred warriors in this filthy hole. We would still be trying to beat the information out of the oni and failing."

Pony hugged her. "Beloved, there is nothing you can do for this child. Focus on the ones that might be still alive."

✧ ✧ ✧

Beyond the back door was a maze of halls and small rooms. Tinker pushed the oni down the hallways with her shield and the *sekasha*. The other teams fanned out behind her, searching the rooms. Reports came back of weapon lockers, food caches, another animal kennel, and a "breeding room" that she so did not want to see. Arguments started to flare up as the tengu looted anything valuable.

"Damn thieving crows," the marine commander muttered to her at one point, apparently unaware that they were her Beholden.

Shouts in Elvish dragged Tinker back a dozen feet, where Riki was blocking the door to a large outdoor courtyard. Wood smoke drifted in through the open door, scented with roasting meat. Smoke and heat rolled up from crude fire pits of cinder block, rebar, and corrugated metal. Clear of burnable trash, the courtyard was strewn with broken pallets, split wood, full logs, and well-gnawed bones.

"What's wrong?" Tinker asked.

"My people will search this area," Riki said.

"Why yours?" the marine commander demanded. "Why can't mine do it?"

Riki looked to Tinker for appeal. "It's the kitchen. The oni eat—the oni consider children a delicacy. It would be kinder, if they butchered one of the children, for us to recover the body."

The looks on elves' face were enough for Tinker to say, "Yes, do it."

Deep in the maze, the constant pain of maintaining her shields caught up with her. One moment she was on her feet, and then she was in Pony's arms, face pressed against the strong column on his neck. Fear jolted through her as she realized she had dropped her shields. Luckily, all the oni in the immediate area seemed dead.

"You need to rest, *domi*."

She swore. "We don't have time for this."

"We need to let our rear guard to catch up with us. We're spread too thin."

Only then did she realize that there were only a handful of the royal marines with them. The rest were scattered somewhere behind them. She couldn't argue with his logic. With the marines covering their retreat, he carried her back to a smaller room they'd already passed. The room had been so obviously void of both oni and children that they had only given it a quick scan. He settled on a tufted leather bench so she could rest in his arms, safe within his shields.

"We're going to need to be deloused after this," Tinker grumbled, frustrated by her weakness. Bad enough to be wading through the trash; sitting down was making her skin crawl. She eyed the bench suspiciously and realized that it was surprisingly clean. In fact, now that she looked closely, they weren't surrounded by the normal oni filth. The litter here was entirely different; it was expensive, luxury clutter. There was good solid ironwood furniture buried under heaps of furs, bags of United States bills and Elfhome coins, and cascades of jewelry. The floor was scrubbed clean, covered with oriental rugs, and then stacked high with weavings, paintings, and electronics. If anything, the room looked like a warehouse of loot.

"Huh, what is this? A treasure room?"

"I am not certain, *domi*."

The tengu were going to be overjoyed, probably much to the annoyance of the elves and the humans. Much as she hated the thought, she should assign someone the job of cataloging the loot so it could be divided among the three groups. Perhaps the EIA could send an accountant over.

The shadows stirred and suddenly moved.

Pony jerked to his feet, moving back even as the others surged forward, swords ready.

"Put me down! Put me down!" Tinker squirmed out of his hold. She had her hand to her mouth when she recognized the lean body that snaked *through* the wall. "Impatience!"

"*Yanananam* Tinker." The oni dragon seemed large in the room, but after fighting his near cousin, Malice, Tinker knew he was actually quite small. Still, ten feet of scaled, muscled body was nothing to sneeze at.

"Can we trust him?" Pony was between her and the dragon, ready for an attack. They had fought the little dragon once when Impatience was "unconscious" and lost horribly. The only reason they weren't all killed was that Impatience had come to his senses before he actually did lasting harm.

"He's talking, so he's sentient." Tinker still backed up as Impatience came bounding through the clutter toward them. She would have thought, though, that Impatience would have stayed far away from the oni. What was he doing at the oni whelping pens?

"*Radadada aaaaah huuu ha—*" Impatience leapt back suddenly. His mane rose, triggering his impenetrable shield moments before Maynard's commandos spilled into the room.

"Hold! Hold!" Tinker shouted even as her Hand

shifted to protect her from possible attack from both the dragon and the commandos.

"Tinker *radadada pooookaaa aaaaah huuuuu* Yutakajodo *haaaaa ramaaaaanan.*"

What in the world was Impatience trying to tell her?

"You!" She pointed at the nearest commando. "Do you have a phone?"

"Yes." He handed it over.

"Hello?" Jin answered on the first ring.

"It's Tinker. Here, listen to this."

She held out the phone to Impatience.

"*Naadaaan pookuu.*" He reached out with his great five-clawed paw and plucked the phone out of her hand.

"No! No, don't take it apart! God damn, how can someone that's so smart be so stupid?" Tinker grabbed his paw and pried the phone free. "Talk! Talk!"

"*Yanananan?*" Jin's tiny voice came over the phone.

Impatience cocked his head and then gave a dragon laugh of "*Huuhuuhuuhuuhuu.*"

"Tinker *radadada pookaa,*" Jin said.

Impatience launched into a long discussion and then, after a minute, stopped and looked expectantly at Tinker.

Tinker put the phone back to her ear. "What did he say?"

"There is a box near you. It holds something that belongs to the Greater Blood Yutakajodo. You alone should take possession of it, but do so carefully."

"Why carefully?" Tinker asked.

"I'm not certain," Jin said. "He's speaking very quickly and seems to be using . . . slang?"

"Dragon slang?"

"Yes. Maybe. I'm getting the impression that the box might harm you if you're not careful."

Tinker eyed the collection of boxes piled high about the room. "How do I ask him which box?"

"*Huunaaaahaaaa.*"

Tinker carefully repeated the word.

At the far end of the room, under a pile of furs, there was a large ironwood chest. The thick lid was spell-locked.

Once Tinker focused on it intently, she realized the chest buzzed against her magic sense with contained power. It felt much like getting too close to a hornet's nest. There had to be an active spell inlaid on the back of the lid. Logically, keying open the locking spell would deactivate the hidden spell. Most likely if the lid was forced, then the active spell would trigger some kind of trap. The question was, what kind of trap? A simple alarm? Or something more deadly? She spent time playing with spell-locks. She thought she might be able to pick the lock, but it might be her ego talking. She wasn't sure how much she actually knew about magic compared to the elves themselves. . . .

She blinked at the lock. "This is elf magic."

Pony and Stormsong eyed the lock and nodded in confirmation.

"Transmuting wood and metal are Stone Clan magic," Pony murmured, glancing to Thorne Scratch. "They create such chests for other clans at a steep price. The owner chooses the key when it's made."

It seemed unlikely that the oni would have stolen it and not tried to open it. Unblemished as it was, it seemed more likely that the elf that owned it worked with the oni.

"Could it be Sparrow's?" Tinker asked.

Stormsong clicked her tongue in an elfin shrug. "She

took advantage of the fact that none of us *sekasha* liked her to keep her activities hidden. I was with her most, but I don't remember her having a chest like this."

They would have to deal with the chest later; they needed to find the missing children. She assigned Little Egret, a half dozen of the marines, and one of the tengu the chore of getting the chest to Poppymeadow's, and then pushed deeper into the whelping pens.

She was losing hope of finding any of the children alive. They reached the back of the maze to find another large courtyard with pits dug into hard-packed dirt. The holes were filled with garbage, urine, and feces.

"Are these their latrines?" Tinker asked. The holes seemed too big for latrines but too small for anything else.

"They're holding pens," one of the tengu said.

"Oh gods," Tinker whispered as something stirred in the nearest hole and started to whimper. "Get them out!"

One of the Fire Clan marines slid down into the hole and lifted the whimpering child out. It was a male, small in comparison to the *laedin*-caste marine. He started to keen inconsolably once he realized he'd been rescued and was safe to finally react to his torture.

"This one needs a healer!" a female marine shouted as a limp male body was passed up from the second pit to the waiting adults. His left arm had been broken so many times it barely seemed like an arm. One of the marines produced a healing spell on a strip of paper and pressed it to the child's barely moving chest.

"Here's another one!" an EIA commando called from a pit near the back.

A tiny naked female was lifted, wide-eyed and desperately squirming, by the humans. She saw Tinker and lunged toward her, arms outstretched.

"It's all right!" Tinker cried even as Thorne Scratch caught hold of Pony's sword hand. "It's fine! She's just scared."

The tiny female was a patchwork of bruises ranging from violet to sickening green to pale yellow. She wrapped arms tight around Tinker and wouldn't let go.

"She probably thinks you're Stone Clan *domana*," Stormsong murmured in English, nodding toward Thorne Scratch, who had grown angry and silent.

"*Quiee*," the little female said. "*Quiee. Quiee.*"

"What is she saying?" Tinker asked Stormsong.

Stormsong listened to a moment and then said with great uncertainty. "*Quiee*?"

"What does it mean?"

"It's what baby ducks say," Pony said.

"Ducks say quack," Tinker said.

"Adult ducks say quack," Pony said. "Baby ducks say *quiee*."

The little female nodded solemnly. "*Quiee*."

"We're going to have to make sure she's not with child," Stormsong murmured in English.

"She's just a baby!" Tinker protested. She didn't think elves could get pregnant until they were out of their doubles.

"If she's over fifty, she can get pregnant," Stormsong said gently. "Just like an eleven-year-old human girl could if raped."

Searching other pits, they found a female hiding in a mound of garbage, armed with an animal leg bone. As they were convincing the female to give up her grisly club for one of the commando's nightsticks, Riki slipped in beside Tinker. His wings and war paint were gone, and he seemed nearly human.

"I don't want to frighten the children," Riki said quietly in English. "If any of my people knew about this and didn't report it, I'll wring their necks."

"What did you find?" Tinker asked.

"There were two children in the kitchen," Riki said. "One had already been butchered down to roast."

Tinker clamped down on a whimper and tightened her hold on the little female in her arms. Seven children subjected to this merely because they weren't Wind Clan? "Someone is going to pay."

Two Hands of Wyverns and a swarm of royal *laedin*-caste marines arrived to secure the area, apparently sent by Prince True Flame, via Maynard. After making sure that the children would be delivered to the hospice and properly treated by the Wind Clan healers, Tinker headed for the train station. Thorne Scratch was reluctant to leave the children, but once she understood Tinker's mission, she agreed to help.

Tinker held her cold fury close as they drove back to the train station in the Rolls, the smell of the pits clinging to her dress. She stalked into the building, wishing for the thousandth time that day that she could fling tanks around with a word and a gesture.

The handful of elves that ran the station came to a halt of the sight of her and the *sekasha*.

"Which one did my cousin talk to?" Tinker growled.

"This one." Thorne Scratch pointed out one of the male Wind Clan elves.

The male flinched back as Tinker bore down on him.

"You saw children get off the train and you did nothing to help them?" Tinker asked.

"*Domi*, they were not of my clan." He said it as if it were a reasonable answer.

"They were children! You knew they were children—didn't you?"

"Yes, *domi*," the male said quietly, apparently still missing the point.

"You know that we're at war with the oni. That the oni will kill and torture anyone they find unprotected."

The light finally went on; it lit up a sign that read She's Angry About Something. He started to look worried. "Yes, *domi*."

"And you just let them go?"

If she weren't so angry it would almost funny to watch him realize that telling the truth was going to screw him over, and yet, as an elf, he was unable to lie. "*Domi*—I—I—I did not care what happened to them."

The last person that gotten her this angry, she'd beaten with a crowbar. She clenched her hands tight on the desire to beat the elf to a pulp. "Get out."

"*Domi*?" The male glanced at the various doors, unsure which direction she wanted him to go.

"Go home, pack your bags, and get out of Pittsburgh," Tinker snapped. "I won't have you in the Westernlands. I don't want your kind—so blind in your petty hate that you bring down poison on a child that you don't even know."

"*Domi*! Please. My household is here."

"I don't care!" She thrust her hand in the direction of the whelping pens and the ironwood forest beyond it. "Be glad that I don't stake you out in the forest for whatever finds you! Be glad I don't let you be raped by the oni, beaten senseless, and then eaten! Be glad that I have more morals than you!"

The elf had gone completely ashen. "Yes, *domi*."

"Get out! Now!" Tinker shouted.

He bowed and fled.

She turned toward the other Wind Clan elves that were standing, listening, mouths open. "If anyone allows harm to come to another child—be it human or Stone Clan or tengu—I don't care what it is—if anyone allows harm to come to another child, I'll see them gone!"

She was still shaking in anger as she stormed out of the train station. It wasn't until she reached the Rolls that she realized that she just assumed she had the power to kick an elf out of Westernlands.

"I can do that—can't I?" she asked Pony. "I can tell him to go?"

"Yes, *domi*, you can, and considering we are at war with the oni, it was wise that you made an example of him."

7: LULLABY OF STONE

Oilcan heard the wailing first. It was a thin, horrible sound. He followed it back through the hospice to where a Wyvern stood staring at a small quivering heap of filthy rags on the floor. It took him a minute to realize that the thing was an elf crying hysterically.

"Why isn't he being taken care of?" Oilcan asked the Wyvern.

"The hospice staff is busy with the others," the royal *sekasha* said. "This male is not badly hurt."

The Wyvern used the male gender that indicated a child. Was this Rustle of Leaves? Or was it another child, and the musician was one of the ones that died? Either way, the child would stay hysterical until cleaned, fed, and comforted. The Wyvern stood looking at the child, dismayed but seemingly helpless.

"There's a bathing room in the other wing," Oilcan said.

The Wyvern gave him the closest thing to a "deer in the headlights" look he'd ever seen on a *sekasha*.

Apparently childcare was not part of the warrior's training.

"Can you take responsibility for him?" the *sekasha* asked.

Saying "yes" might mean something beyond just bathing the child. Oilcan glanced to Merry, who was clinging to the doorframe as if it were the only thing that kept her from bolting. This is what could have happened to her—or worse—if Oilcan hadn't spotted her at the train station and taken her into his protection.

What was one more kid? He did have another spare bedroom in his condo.

"Yes," Oilcan said. "I can."

The *sekasha* bowed slightly but then asked doubtfully, "Will you be able to carry him?"

Oilcan checked an automatic "Yes" to consider. He'd have to get the double halfway across the hospice, through several sets of doors. The double was smaller than him, but not by much. "Could you please carry him to the bathing room?"

The child started to keen louder the moment the *sekasha* lifted him up. The *sekasha* stoically ignored the wailing and followed Oilcan down the hall.

At the start of the summer, the hospice had been a strange, unknown place. Oilcan had barely known where it even lay beyond the enclaves. Since delivering a wounded Windwolf to the hospice just before Mid-Summer's Eve, Oilcan had been back many times, visiting Tinker as she recovered from one mishap after another. By now, he knew the hospice well. The bathing room was huge, tiled in soothing shades of blue. There were hand showers to scrub off dirt before climbing—already clean—into a soaking tub large enough to fit a football team.

The *sekasha* settled the double onto the floor and backed off.

"Hush, hush." Oilcan carefully stripped the remains of clothes ripped into shreds and soaked with dirt, blood, urine, and feces. Under the filthy rags were massive bruises and dirt-crusted wounds. The oni had cropped the double's hair so short there were nicks from the knife they'd used. Excrement had been ground into the stubble as added insult. The boy's nose been broken, and both his eyes were swollen shut. Blood leaked from his nose as he cried.

"You're safe now. You're safe." Oilcan felt so helpless. What could he possibly do to make things right? The poor thing had merely walked out of the train station and into a nightmare.

. . . his mother lay so still on the kitchen floor, his father slowly crumbled down, arms outstretched, wailing in denial of what he'd done . . .

There were things that nothing could make right. They stayed hidden as black holes inside of you. You went on the best you could, pretending everything was fine.

"Gold is the light that scythes the hay, dusk softens the edge of day." Oilcan crooned softly the Elvish song his mother used to sing to him. "Lavender and lilly sweeten the sky, nightingale warbles a lullaby."

The little male leaned against him and went silent. Singing softly, Oilcan worked at washing away the filth. A river of muddy water ran from the child to the drain. It was difficult to keep singing and scrub. He was aware that the Wyvern had left and felt weirdly abandoned.

Merry came to sit beside him and sing. "Quicksilver shadows pierce the dark, starflash fireflies blaze and spark. Moonbeams soothe the fractured night. Sleep and dream, close your eyes."

So they sang and washed the double. When the water finally ran clean, Oilcan lifted the male into the soaking tub. Merry surprised him by suddenly stripping down and climbing into the tub, too. He supposed that the point of a swimming pool–sized tub was joint bathing, but he hadn't totally considered the implication.

Once in, Merry turned pleading eyes on him. "*Sama*?"

Oilcan sighed. In for a penny, in for a pound. Since much of the double's filth had rubbed off on him, he could use a bath. He stripped down, sluiced the dirt off, and climbed in.

8: ON THE NOSE

There were a million things that needed Tommy's attention if the races were to happen. He worked out how much of the seed money had to go to operating expenses and how much could be risked in betting. He would need to pay wages, stock the food concessions, and put aside tax money. True, he'd double his amount with the admission fees, but the money had to be spent up front first. Lastly, some cash had to be spent immediately so that various families didn't starve before race day. The entrance fees more than covered the purse money for the winners, so that money didn't need to be held in reserve. He set the starting odds, downloaded the spreadsheet to his datapad, and made sure his cousins' phones all worked.

"Remember, your cap is five hundred." Tommy paced the room. "Anything above that, call me first. We have to watch our bottom line closely on this one, so call in after every bet. The elves are jumpy; keep your guns out of sight. Watch your back. Remember that the oni are still out there loose."

"Danny. Yoyo. Zippo. Quinn." He tapped the chests of the teenagers as he passed them. "You're to guard the warren. If the elves know where we are, the oni might too. They might raid us for food, money, and sex. Call Bingo if you see anyone suspicious. He'll be stationed closest to the warren. If you're raided, don't give them any reason to kill you.

"This is just like before—only this time, we're doing it for ourselves."

All day his phone rang, giving Tommy a constant barometer of Pittsburgh to be entered into his spreadsheets. True, there were some names he recognized as die-hard gamblers. They carefully weighed the odds, dispassionate in their choices. The rest of the city, however, bet with their hearts.

The elves bet on Blue Sky without exception. They believed the holy *sekasha*-caste were perfection made flesh, and having seen the half-elf race, Tommy wasn't sure if he'd quibble with that.

The human population splintered into a multitude of factions. The younger crowd that thought of Elfhome as their world bet on Team Tinker or Team Big Sky. John's team had the most recent wins, their custom-modified Delta hoverbike, and their "perfect" rider. Team Tinker was still a strong contender even though Oilcan wasn't as aggressive a rider as Tinker used to be. Team Tinker had the experience and the only other Delta. While the team was all humans, Tinker had been magically transformed into an elf and was now married to Windwolf, which tainted the team through association.

The older humans didn't bet on either of the top

two teams. They saw Pittsburgh as still a city of Earth and men. They supported the underdogs. Then under that, came bets on teams connected to certain political ideology, or someone just had a lucky feeling for, but those were usually only to place, not to win.

He was out at the racetrack when he realized that his phone had stopped ringing. He took it out and checked on the signal strength. "Trixie, is your phone working?" he asked the half-oni in charge of the food concessions.

She took hers out and glanced at it. "Huh, no signal."

He went up to the track office and picked up the landline. It was dead, too.

Trixie had followed him. "What do you think it is?"

"The oni might be attacking town." He swore. "Last thing we need is to have the elves slap martial law back on."

"Well, we'll be eating hotdogs for the next two weeks."

He picked up the microphone to the racetrack's PA system. "I'm heading into town. Do we need anything out here?"

There was a call from somewhere near the concession booths.

"What was that?" Trixie's hearing was as human as her ears appeared.

"Toilet paper." Tommy tied his bandana back into place and headed out to his hoverbike.

"I've been trying to call you." Babe held out a list of bets.

"All the phones are down." Tommy entered the information into his spreadsheet. Babe had only taken four bets, one at the five hundred dollar cap for Team Providence to win. It was a fairly new team made up of tengu, having only run a half-dozen races and never even placed. None of Tommy's information suggested that they could pull a win off. They were such a long shot that the large bet required an immediate adjustment to the odds. "Shit, what a hell of a time for the phones to go down."

He didn't recognize the name: Kenji Toshihiko. Most the Japanese in town, though, were part of the tengu. "I don't like this taking bets blind. Spread the word: I'm closing the books."

Doug had a five hundred bet for Team Providence. And Syn, too. Tommy swore and ran numbers right there. If all of his cousins had taken bets at their cap, locking in the same long-shot odds, and Team Providence won, then he and his family were going to be royally screwed. Not only did it take out all the money they'd set aside to cover the bets, it would also eat up all the money that the race would bring in with admissions.

He checked his phone. It was still dead.

"Fuck, fuck, fuck, fuck." Tommy punched Syn in fury.

"We'll just call the bets off." Syn scrambled out of the way of a kick.

"We can't!" Tommy shouted. "The fucking anal elves and their frigging honor! A bet is a promise to them! If we welshed on the bets, they'd be all over our asses because they know we're half-oni!"

"Someone is suckering us!"

"Don't you think that I know that? I'm going to fucking find them and kill them. Spread the word. No more bets!"

✧ ✧ ✧

Whoever planned the strike against them had done it with great precision. It had only taken an hour to close down the books, but the damage had already been done. Twenty bets, all at cap, all made within minutes of the phones going dead. Ten thousand dollars, with a payoff of half a million dollars.

"The bets are to win," Bingo pointed out as they gathered at the warren.

"Because to show and place gave lower odds," Tommy snapped.

"How the hell do they expect Team Providence to win?" Bingo said. "Team Big Sky was creaming everyone before the elves locked the city down. And there's Team Tinker and Team Banzai and Team Eh?"

Tommy had talked to all the teams. They assured him that they were all racing. Some of them might have been lying, in on the scam, but not Team Tinker or Team Big Sky. They were tied too closely to the *honorable* elves to cheat, and they were the favorites to win. "Whoever the hell *they* are, they've got something else planned, then. They're going to cheat somehow. We've got to find out how."

9: THORNE SCRATCH

Oilcan had washed four battered souls, seen that they were dressed in simple gowns, fed, drugged, and put to bed. He was trying to determine his obligations to them when Thorne Scratch found him.

"Take the children and go home," she said.

Her command was fairly clear, but still he said, "I don't understand."

"The children cannot stay here. Take them and go."

"Why can't they stay? Is the staff trying to throw them out? Tinker won't allow—"

"The Wind Clan is not the problem," Thorne said. "Forest Moss has learned of the children. He will be here shortly to claim them. He cannot be allowed to take them. Take the children and go."

He sat down mostly because his knees suddenly didn't want to support him. "I—I don't know—all of them?"

Thorne went to her knees in front of him and caught his hands tightly. "Please. He is mad. If the oni did not drive him mad with their torture, then nearly three hundred years of isolation has. He is desperate for physical contact. The prince has given Forest Moss only male Wyverns to guard him, and he has pressed his suit on them. None of Ginger Wine's staff will be in a room with him with good cause—his actions are as close to rape as they can come and not be worthy of charges. Within an hour of Earth Son's death, he tried to corner even me. These children cannot be given over to him, not after what they've been through."

"Can't we just tell him no?"

"He's *domana*. If he comes prepared for a fight, then only Wolf Who Rules and Prince True Flame could stop him. The viceroy has no grounds to deny Forest Moss access to the children, since they are Stone Clan and the prince would sacrifice them to keep the peace."

What the hell was he going to do with five children, four of which had just been dragged through hell? But she was right—he couldn't give them to Forest Moss. They were more than a head count to him now. They were the emotionally fragile Fields of Barley, little Baby Duck, who no longer knew her real name and nervously quacked, Rustle of Leaves, who only cared that Merry hadn't been captured despite the fact the oni shattered the young musician's left arm, and stoic Cattail Reeds. Oilcan knew their names and faces, had seen the breadth and width of their strengths and weaknesses. Even Fields of Barley, once he stopped crying, had shown incredible resiliency, but none of them would be able to deal with an adult male demanding intimacy from them.

"Okay. I'll take them home." It was a big city. It was

unlikely Forest Moss would be able to find him—but the elf did have magic. "How long do I need to keep the kids hidden from Forest Moss?"

"Once they wake and have the situation explained to them, they can choose what to do. If they decide to stay with you, they'll be safe from him. The Wyverns will not allow a holding to be broken by an outsider."

"Even if I'm human?"

"A precedent must be set and protected if humans are to be part of our society."

Knowing that she wasn't lying to him didn't help; he also knew that people often deceived themselves into believing they were telling the truth.

Moving the children was surreal. They had been dosed with *saijin*, so all but Merry were asleep beyond waking. The staff lined the back of his pickup truck with mattresses and then tucked the sleeping children in like a litter of kittens. Thorne rode in the back to his condo and then helped him move both children and mattresses into the spare bedrooms. While he knew that he was doing it for the good of the children, it felt horribly wrong to snatch them out of the hospice and take them unawares to his home.

Luckily Oilcan had put Merry in the larger guest bedroom, so there was room for Cattail Reeds and Baby Duck. Rustle of Leaves and Fields of Barley went into the other bedroom, which was more of an oversized closet. He needed to get bunk beds so the kids didn't have to walk on each others' mattresses. The hospice had sent only sheets, so he also needed to track down five sets of blankets before it started to get cold. Tomorrow, he would have to find them clothes and shoes. He only had four sets of dishes. His pantry was half bare.

His new responsibilities loomed larger and larger before him like an iceberg sliding out of the mist. It made him want a drink so bad that it scared him. He opened the fridge and stared at the beer bottles gleaming inside. It was his father's answer to all life's little problems. This wasn't, however, a little problem.

Thorne Scratch shifted in the darkness that was gathering inside his apartment, reminding him that she was still there. There to stay, since if he drove her back to the Rim, it would leave the kids alone. Helpless as they were in their drugged sleep, he couldn't do that. Newly arrived, Thorne probably didn't know the city well enough to walk the six miles out to the enclaves. Hell, he would have to guide her through using the incline just to get down off Mount Washington.

The need for a drink became impossible to resist.

"Would you like something to drink?" At least he shouldn't sink to drinking alone. "I've got ouzo, apricot wine, mead." He'd been collecting things that Tinker might enjoy drinking since her transformation had made beer unpalatable. "Water?"

"Ouzo," Thorne said in her raspy voice. "Please."

He poured an inch or so of the clear, anise-flavored liquor into one of the canning jars that he used for glasses. Opening a bottle of cold beer, he carried her glass to her and then kept walking out to his balcony that overlooked downtown Pittsburgh, distancing him from the temptation in the refrigerator.

She came to lean against the railing with him and drank in silence.

Usually when someone visited him, they stared at the

forest, ignoring the city for the vast carpet of green. As night fell, and the lights of Pittsburgh came on until the city was a bright island of circus brightness, visitors would continue to stare at the will-'o-the-wisps faintly dancing over the ironwoods. It was like they were blind to the city below.

As Thorne Scratch studied Pittsburgh, Oilcan realized that all his visitors, with the exception of Tinker, had been humans from Earth. They were on Elfhome because they wanted something strange and new in their life.

"What do you think?" he asked Thorne.

"I remember being these children's age. You are so certain you know all that is to be known." She shook her head. "I was raised at Cold Mountain Temple." She laughed bitterly at herself. "At this point you're supposed to be amazed and impressed."

"Snow falls on Cold Mountain Temple, hewed from living stone, rock solid, rock strong." He sang the chorus of the Harvest epic. "Even here in Pittsburgh, we know of Tempered Steel. I am amazed and impressed."

She laughed again, this time at him. "The song does not do justice to the isolation of Cold Mountain Temple. It's a day's walk to the nearest holding, which is nothing more than a collection of pigsties. By nature of its location, Cold Mountain Temple is a complete but small world in and of itself. We had to grow all our own food, so every day we trained and tended to our crops. I hated the crops. The dirt. The bugs. That you worked and worked, then winter would come, and you would have to start all over again. Then one day, Otter Dance came to visit her father. She heard me cursing the same damn weeds I had to pull up for the thousandth time, and she laughed and started to help me, saying it had been *nae hae* since she last had to weed. And I was amazed. How was it that she hadn't been weeding? Even her great and famous father, Tempered Steel, weeded."

Oilcan closed his eyes as a feeling something akin to vertigo hit him. *Nae hae* was short for *kaetat nae hae*, which meant "count no years." It meant the person didn't want to sit and figure out how long ago an event actually happened. It could mean anywhere from a decade to a thousand years. The elves switched to *nae hou*, or "count no millennia." The puppet shows of Tempered Steel saving the world from starvation always started "*Nae hou*, a great famine swept the world." He'd always assumed that Tempered Steel was as dead as the pilgrims of Plymouth Rock. Yet, here, this female had weeded gardens alongside the famous warrior monk.

"Otter Dance had become First to Longwind, head of the Wind Clan," Thorne continued, most likely unaware of the disorientation she'd caused. "She told me about her life at court, how she spent her day protecting her *domou* or training and had nothing to do with weeds. It sounded like heaven to me."

He could see why the children had her thinking of her own youth. "So you left everything you knew behind to go to court."

"The day after I earned my sword, I left Cold Mountain Temple and never went back." She went to sip her drink and found her glass empty. She held it out to him. "May I have more?"

Surely someone as old and trained as Thorne Scratch knew how to handle her drinking. After long consideration of his own condition, he got a second beer. By the time he returned to the balcony, he remembered how she started the conversation: *you are so certain you know all that is to be known.* Was she implying that she had discovered the hard way that she didn't?

"So life at court blindsided you?"

She considered the question with the cant of her head. "Blindsided implies a quick awareness that things have gone horribly wrong. Everyone at Cold Mountain was brutally honest, keeping true to the belief that lying is a sin. At court, everyone carefully wove lies out of truths and wore them as masks. It was years before I saw enough of the true Earth Son to know I had made mistake in offering to him. If I had left him, I would have destroyed what little credibility he had at court."

"So you stayed."

"It was a mistake," she whispered. "We could tolerate him being a pompous ass at court, but he had been cowardly on the field of battle, had undermined the defense of Elfhome for his own personal gain, and nearly plunged us into a bigoted genocide of a useful ally." By "we" she meant all five *sekasha* of Earth Son's Hand. "I was his First. It was my duty to put him down."

"I'm sorry."

She reached out and caught him by the front of his shirt and pulled him to her and kissed him hard. She smelled of leather and anise. She kissed him like she was drowning and he was air.

"From the moment I struck him down, it's been like I suddenly went invisible. No one will look at me.

I—I know they don't think I was wrong—they would have killed me right there if they did—but they're scared of what will happen to us, and they don't want to look like they're afraid—so—so . . ."

"I see you," Oilcan murmured. "You're right here with me, and you're beautiful."

She tugged at his clothing, kissing him hard and desperate. Inhaling him.

Where was this going? He'd never been with a female elf, but if she were human, it would certainly seem as if they were careening toward sex. She was a *sekasha*, a deadly holy warrior; surely they weren't about to go at it like rabbits.

Then her hands were on his bare skin, just as needy as her kisses, suggesting that he was wrong to dismiss the possibility of sex.

She had grown up in a monastery. Maybe she wasn't used to drinking. Maybe she was drunk and he was taking advantage of her.

She pushed him up against the wall and pinned him there. Yeah, sure, who was taking advantage of whom? The angle of their bodies made it clear that she was inches taller than him.

"*Naekanain*?" Which was the politest way he could think of to say "What the hell?"

She pulled back, hurt on her face.

"Are you sure—" He fumbled for something safe to say. "Is this really a good place for this?" Whatever this was. "Maybe my bedroom?"

"Your bedroom." Her husky voice was full of need and promise.

He led the way through his condo, emotions in a tumbling freefall. He wanted her—had always wanted her—had wanted to hear her raspy voice make needful sounds since the first time she spoke. The sane, reasoning part of him was nearly lost under the want, but it was there, whispering ice-cold points of logic. He had an apartment full of kids. She was a *sekasha*; she could kill him if he pissed her off, and things like this tended to end messily for him.

Then they were in his bedroom with the door safely shut, and the reasoning part of him went silent as Thorne pushed him onto his bed. Somewhere between the balcony and his bedroom, she had shimmied out of her wyvern-scale armor. Underneath she wore a pale camisole that was taut over surprisingly full breasts, considering how lean she looked in armor. As she peeled off her leather pants, he realized he better work at getting naked, too. He kicked off his tennis shoes, stripped off his shirt, and undid his pants. She caught hold of his jeans and pulled them off him. His boxers followed. She moaned softly as she saw how ready he was for her. He reached for her, and, graceful as a dancer, she moved onto the bed, kissed him, and lowered herself onto him. They hummed delight into each other's mouths as they fit together as if they were made for each other. Each movement of her hips was sweetness and fire.

Afterward they lay, still joined, sharing the same breath. Her braid had come undone at some point, her hair flowing wantonly down across her face and shoulders. She smiled and traced his grin with her fingertips. Slowly the whisper of logic started up in him again, murmuring how this wasn't sane, but she felt too right in his arms to listen.

10: PANTY RAID

No one was happy about the unopened oni mystery box being at the enclave. To make everyone happier, Tinker allowed herself to be bullied into a bath. She still reeked of the pens. It made her skin crawl thinking of the fleas, ticks, or whatever else she might have picked up wading through the filth. After everything she'd seen today, she could use a deep cleansing of the body and a couple of stiff drinks. She hated, though, to take the time.

"An hour will not change anything now." Stormsong scrubbed Tinker's back for her after checking her hair for bugs. Tinker still wasn't comfortable with the elf mixed-gender communal bathing stuff, but there was no way she could feel totally clean without help. At least with Stormsong, there was no weird "I'm cheating on my husband" vibe that being washed by Pony would have triggered.

"If we'd gotten to the station just minutes later this morning—ow!"

Stormsong had smacked her lightly on the top of her head. "Don't drive yourself crazy with 'might have beens.' We were there in time to save cousin."

"But—"

"But nothing. We were there in time." Stormsong wrapped her arms around Tinker and kissed her on the temple. "And an hour will not change anything now. You need to take care of yourself before you can take care of others."

Tinker leaned back against Stormsong and made herself trust in her Beholden's instincts. Stormsong had an annoying way of being right all the time. Now, if she could only ignore the feeling that Stormsong was right because they were days too late already.

Tinker suspected that Windwolf's household staff had burned her dress. There was no sign of it. She was really starting to hate the way her clothes vanished behind her back. All her human clothes had gotten left behind when the Wyverns all but kidnapped her to Aum Renau. The missing dress had the sleeves removed, the skirt shortened, and pockets added. It was the second or third modified gown that she'd trashed to the point that the staff had made it disappear. They'd laid out two new unaltered dresses as possible replacements. Tinker really loathed trying to work in the long flowing gowns of fairy silk, especially in the nearly hundred-degree heat.

It was time to beg, borrow, or steal some better clothes.

All the *sekasha* had shuffled bedrooms the last few weeks as she picked out the rest of her Hand. As Tinker's Second, Stormsong was now just two doors down. Tinker wasn't sure exactly what the whole etiquette was for entering a *sekasha*'s bedroom. Everyone seemed to pop in and out of her and Windwolf's bedroom unannounced. The warriors, though, were always armed; they even bathed with their *ejae* within reach. It seemed unwise to walk into Stormsong's room unannounced.

"Come in, *domi*," Stormsong called as Tinker raised her hand to knock.

"You're scary sometimes," Tinker grumbled as she entered.

"I know the sound of your footsteps." Stormsong was still only dressed in her tattoos. For Tinker's sake, she pulled on black silk boy shorts. "We learn everyone's so we can tell who is moving around."

The bedroom was very much Stormsong despite the recent move. Weapons dominated the room, from a stand that displayed her wyvern-scale armor and *ejae* to wall racks that held various bows, guns, and knives. Sprinkled in were human mementos: a bookcase crammed with paperbacks and manga, stacks of vintage CDs, a set of skateboards, and an amazing number of Goth Hello Kitty stuffed toys. Most startling was the hoverbike poster that featured Tinker coming around the turn just before the grandstands, head to toe in mud, just inches off the ground, trying to slide under the leader of the race, who was taking the curve high. It was a great shot. What it didn't show was seconds later, the stupid jerk had dropped down to cut her off and hit her, destroying both their hoverbikes and nearly getting them both killed.

"I can't believe you have that." Tinker gestured to the poster. "Roach just started to sell those before—you know—everything." Before Windwolf. Before the oni. Before her and Stormsong.

Stormsong grinned smugly. "Print number four."

"You're shitting me." Tinker leaned close to check. Roach was part of her pit crew, but he functioned mostly as the business manager. The master of merchandising, he numbered the posters and sold them as "limited prints." In the corner, in Roach's careful printing, was "4/50." She knew for a fact that Roach always kept number one, and she and Oilcan had two and three. "Okay, you're now officially very scary."

Stormsong laughed and pulled on a silk camisole top that matched the boy shorts. She looked like a lingerie model in the outfit: lush, leggy, and perfectly fit. "I saw him take the picture and asked for a copy. He told me he'd make posters of the shot."

With Stormsong's love of all things human, it made sense that she'd been at the races, but it still felt odd. Her entire life, Tinker had seen the *sekasha* moving through the city on unknown missions, but she had always given them a wide berth. Until the queen summoned her to Aum Renau, they'd remained faceless strangers. Now that their lives were explicitly tied together, it seemed impossible that they had always been so close, and yet never interacted. After the picture had been taken, the race ended in a brawl between pit crews. Stormsong had been standing close enough to reach out and touch—and Tinker never noticed her. How did she miss a blue-haired elf? Then again, Tinker had been busy trying to kick in the teeth of the other rider.

Stormsong put her hand on the glass covering the poster. "I'd seen you race dozens of times before, but that day, that moment, I suddenly knew."

"Knew what?"

Stormsong gave a dry laugh. "That's the shitty thing. My talent is good for knowing 'duck now or die.' Every now and then it hits me with a sledgehammer that's simply labeled 'this is important.' I knew I would love you, but I had no idea how you would come into my life."

Tinker eyed her and then the poster. "I was right there."

"I was a *sekasha* bound to Windwolf, and you were human. I could not imagine how our lives would intertwine. Even if I had taken you as a lover, I was only in Pittsburgh when Sparrow came to the city."

Not to mention Tinker would have been totally freaked out if a female *sekasha* had asked her out on a date. Scratch that. To be perfectly honest, Tinker would have been curious enough to agree. It probably wouldn't have ended any worse than her date with Nathan.

That thought took her down a dark road to an intersection where Nathan lay headless.

Tinker distracted herself to safer things by randomly opening up drawers and rifling their contents. "What was that with Thorne Scratch? The peace and war thing? And why did we need to do that in the middle of fighting?"

"She was inside your shield. If we had engaged the oni, she could have easily killed you. That is why we needed to agree to a truce immediately. You have to remember—always—that the Stone Clan has tried to kill you twice."

"Idiots. We're at war with the oni. That's what they should be focusing on, not killing me. Is Windwolf safe with them?"

"They would not dare do anything while Prince True Flame is there with the Wyverns in force."

That made her feel only marginally better. How insane Forest Moss was was open to debate. Was he crazy enough to ignore the royal forces?

Stormsong apparently had a mild lingerie fetish for silk boy shorts and camisoles; two of the deep drawers were filled with every imaginable color and pattern. Stormsong pulled out cheetah-print done in Wind Clan blue and offered it to Tinker.

"Cheetah print?" Tinker asked.

"They'll look cute on you."

Tinker dropped her towel and pulled on the camisole first and then the boy shorts. As always, Stormsong was right; they were cute on her.

Stormsong comforted Tinker by adding, "His First Hand protected Wolf's grandfather Howling for thousands of years while he fought against the Skin Clan and during the Clan Wars. And Wolf spent half a century at court. They know the dangers well."

Better than Tinker did—it hadn't even occurred to her that Thorne Scratch might attack her instead of the oni.

The rest of the dresser was T-shirts. In this heat, did she need a T-shirt? No.

"Do we have to do the truce thing every time we see her?" With Oilcan taking care of Merry, it seemed likely that they might be tripping over Thorne Scratch a lot in the future. It was odd, though; she was the only one from Earth Son's Hand who had shown up at the train station.

"She has given her word. You are safe from her until we mutually agree on an end to our truce."

"Really?"

"Thorne Scratch is of the perfection that all *sekasha* seek." Stormsong had switched to High Elvish, as if nothing else could capture the truth of her words. Tinker wondered what subtle meaning she was totally missing. "Earth Son was a fool to play politics in a war zone with one such as her at his side."

Tinker found the jeans. "Wow, an entire dresser of blue jeans? I never figured you for a clothes horse."

"I was afraid Pittsburgh would go away one day." Stormsong opened the second drawer and pulled out two pair of shorts. "Hmm. I think the low riders."

Tinker tried them on and considered the mirror. "You can see my panties."

"That's the point."

Tinker stuck out her tongue but left the shorts on. They were the most comfortable thing she'd put on since she was dragged to Aum Renau nearly three months earlier.

"We can trust Thorne Scratch completely? What if she became Beholden to Forest Moss or Jewel Tear, and they ordered her to kill me?"

"Even then." Stormsong pulled on a pair of bootcut jeans. "According to the Wyverns, Thorne Scratch refused Forest Moss already."

"What about Jewel Tear?"

"They say that Jewel Tear has not asked." Stormsong seemed slightly puzzled by the fact.

Frankly, as much as Tinker loved her Hand, it drove her slightly nuts to have them constantly underfoot. She could understand why Jewel Tear would skip taking on five more. "Windwolf says she's nearly broke. You guys have to be expensive to keep. I've seen you eat."

"If she had a second Hand, she would be well rewarded by her clan. It is a loop. The more *sekasha* a *domana* holds, the more they can protect, the greater their reputation, the more *sekasha* will offer to them. It behooves the clan to support their *domana* to keep the clan strong."

"Like Prince True Flame and all his zillions of Wyvern?"

"Yes. The Fire Clan supports him so they can send him where he is needed to enforce the queen's rule."

Perhaps she needed to rethink taking a second Hand. How did she *find* more without stealing them off of Windwolf? "Okay, I understand why Jewel Tear should have offered to Thorne Scratch. Maybe she scares Jewel Tear silly. She did lop off Earth Son's head."

"Jewel Tear has many faults, but she is not a coward. I believe that Tiger Eye pressured Jewel Tear into not asking."

"Why?"

"It would be difficult to put into words."

"I'm patient."

Stormsong laughed and pulled on her scale-armor vest. "You are anything but patient. Because I love you, I will try to explain.

"We are considered holy because we are perfect, but perfection has its degrees. While I have my differences with my father, even I have to acknowledge that he is one of the greatest warriors our caste has produced. There are only two or three others that are of his match. Tiger Eye is not of the caliber of Thorne Scratch. He loves his *domi* well, but he treats her like a child. At the tunnel, Jewel Tear should not have felt the need to whisper her order to him. He should not have then so loudly defied her. It is embarrassing that any First would act in that manner."

Tinker had thought the two had been disgustingly cute.

"It would be impossible for Tiger Eye to be First to Thorne Scratch. It would only a matter of time before both Hands would look to her as if she were First, and such a division of power would be a catastrophe."

"The importance of fit," Tinker said.

"Yes."

"So, how do we get *sekasha* to Pittsburgh that we know will fit? I think I should take a second Hand."

Stormsong hugged her tight, laughing. "Tell me again how you're patient!"

11: SPELL LOCK

Her Hand was silently unhappy in the loudest way possible. After what Stormsong had told Tinker about Tiger Eye being a bad First, Tinker was hyperaware of Pony's silence beside her as she carefully examined the chest from the whelping pens. Apparently deemed too dangerous to take deeper into the enclave, it'd been tucked into one of the empty bays of the coach house. Unlike the rough, utilitarian garages of humans, the enclave's coach house was a shrine to transportation. The floor was paved in a herringbone of glazed brick. The walls were rich stained wood. The beveled glass windows gleamed as if freshly cleaned. Still, the chest managed to positively lurk in the shadows.

The chest was two feet high, three feet wide, and four feet long. It had no seams or joints. It looked like one solid hunk of ironwood, as if the chest been carved out of a tree trunk. An eight-phoneme spell-lock was inscribed in a band, three inches down, marking off the lid. Even standing several feet from the chest, she could feel the active spell hidden within. If the trap was explosive in nature, there was enough oomph to it to level the coach house. Her Hand had a good reason to be unhappy.

"The little dragon said you needed to take possession of it, but he did not say you had to open it," Pony murmured quietly for only her to hear.

"If I can't open it safely, I won't try," Tinker promised, because she knew Pony would be in blast range.

Personally Tinker could understand Jewel Tear wanting Tiger Eye out of danger's way. Yet Tinker saw the logic of the male staying beside his *domi*—there could have been any number of other dangers in the tunnel. They were stronger together as a team than apart.

Tinker was clueless, though, as to how to get the chest open safely. She took reference photos and measurements and then retreated across the driveway to the stable's hayloft. With the loft door open, she could see the chest where it lurked in the garage. Pony settled beside her, still silent but no longer unhappy.

Magic basically reduced material to possibilities, and spells realigned the material to the desired end. Spell-locks used magic to flip the locked material between two states. Generally an "open" state was where two halves of the material were separate identities, and "closed" was where they merged into one solid object. When Tinker was learning to create spell-locks, she had reduced several hundred pieces of wood down to instant splinters before she figured out how pre-tune the lock material.

The chest was made of ironwood. The super-dense wood had been bioengineered to have the same structural strength of high-quality steel. Normally boards ran an inch and a half thick and required special spells and tools to cut. She assumed that any attempt cut the chest open would most likely trigger the trap. Without knowing what was inside, even if she managed to shut down the active spell, cutting the chest open might damage the contents.

She could use a magic null spell on the chest. That would wipe out the trap, but it would also render the spell-lock inoperative in the "locked" position, forcing her to cut her way into the chest.

What she needed was a set of picks and something akin to tumblers that she could feel her way through. She needed to experiment.

Several exploded pieces of wood later, she remembered why she hated spell-locks.

12: MORNING AFTER

The fire alarm screamed Oilcan awake. It died moments later, a wooden sword through its heart, but its death only muted the sound slightly as the rest of the fire alarms in the condo were still screaming.

"It's a fire alarm!" he shouted to forestall the death of his other alarms. "Something is burning!"

Sometime during the night, Thorne had pulled on her underwear and arranged her weapons close at hand. She placed her hand against the door and, finding it cool, triggered her shields, jerked open the door, and disappeared down the hall. A moment later, the screams of children joined in that of the fire alarms.

"Shit, shit, shit." Oilcan grabbed clean boxers, tugging them on one leg at a time as he hopped after her.

Smoke was pouring out of his microwave. Thorne looked like she was considering skewering it. The children were ping-ponging around the living room like frightened mice.

"Wait! Wait! Wait!" he shouted over the screaming fire alarms and children to stop Thorne. The microwave was counting down from eighty-seven minutes while a bag of popcorn blazed. He grabbed the fire extinguisher off the wall, flipped open the microwave door, and blasted foam over the burning bag. "There, it's out. We've just got to clear out the smoke to stop the alarms." He wove through the children to open the sliding glass door to the balcony. It was midmorning outside, surprising him by how late he'd slept in. "It's all right! It's all right! The noisc will stop in a little while."

He went to open his front door and discovered the children had built a barricade in front of it out of his recliner and one of his end tables. He picked up the end table and carried it back into the living room. The kitchen counter was covered with his pantry goods. All the boxes and bags, from his baking soda to his polenta—were sitting open. Thankfully they hadn't figured out how to open the cans.

"I'm sorry," Merry said. "We were hungry, so I thought we could make pop pop pop."

"It's called *popcorn*." He gave her the English word. He had made her a bag of it on her first night in Pittsburgh and played her *High School Musical*. "You should have just woken me up."

Merry's glance toward Thorne explained why the children had decided to fend for themselves. This was not the morning he should have slept in.

He muscled the recliner back to where it belonged and then propped open his front door and the building's main entrance down the hall. He came back into his apartment to discover that the children clearly regarded the open door as more alarming than the nearly naked and armed *sekasha*.

"There were people talking." Cattail Reeds pointed out into the hall. "Just beyond the door."

"There are other humans that live in this building. They are . . ." Friendly? Not completely. The other tenants regarded him as their lazy handyman. They resented that he wasn't around every hour of the day, fixing all the little things that went wrong in the building. His lease, though, stipulated that he was only responsible for the heating, the air conditioning, and the elevator. "They're harmless."

Her eyes went wide suddenly, warning him that someone was at the open door.

Margaret was head of the building association. "Do I need to call the fire department, Orville?"

No matter how many times he asked her to use his nickname, she insisted on his real name. "A bag of popcorn just got left in the microwave too long. The alarms will go off as soon as I get the smoke cleared out."

She glanced down over him, making him realize that he was still just in his boxers, and then flicked her gaze over Thorne in her underwear and the children in the hospice gowns that looked like pajamas. "You can't sublet your bedrooms. You can't have these—people move in."

Her voice suggested he had a herd of pigs in his apartment. He was getting so sick and tired of bigotry from every angle. He thought Pittsburgh was better than this. "I'm not subletting. I've adopted these kids. Thorne will not be living here."

She glanced over the elves again. "Five children?" She shook her head. "No."

"I have three bedrooms—"

"The co-op board will never approve six people for your square footage. Four is the most we would consider."

"Fine," he snapped. Thankfully the alarms shut off, so he kicked the prop on his door free. "I'll find another place to live."

He slammed his door shut. Immediately there was a knock on it. He jerked it back open, expecting Margaret.

Blue Sky jumped back from his snarled "What?" and held up a basket. "I brought breakfast!"

"Sorry. Come in." Oilcan stepped back to let the half-elf in. Blue wore tennis shoes, blue jeans, and a black T-shirt that expounded "It's all about racing." Only his eyes and ears gave him away as a half-elf.

"Did you just get kicked out of your building?" Blue Sky pointed over his shoulder to where Margaret had been standing.

"Yes." Oilcan took a deep breath as he realized that Blue would probably tell Tinker, and she would hit the roof. As of late, Tinker had been stomping over everyone in her path Godzilla-style. It was tempting to unleash her but the place was cramped for six and the kids weren't comfortable with strangers living so close. "No. Not really. This place is too small. I needed to move."

Blue Sky took in the chaos of the kitchen, the smoke lingering in the air, and the fact that Oilcan was still in his underwear and smiled brightly. "I thought Tinker was just trying to ditch me when she told me to come help you, but I guess you really do need me."

"Yes, I could use some help." Oilcan really needed to get dressed. He pointed to the Stone Clan children in approximate order of their ages. "This is Fields of Barley, Cattail Reeds, Rustle of Leaves, Merry, and Baby Duck. This is Blue Sky. He was born here in Pittsburgh. Listen to him." And then added in English, "Make sure they don't burn down the place while I'm putting on clothes."

"We're supposed to obey a Wind Clan baby?" Baby Duck whispered to Fields of Barley.

"He is *sekasha* first," Thorne Scratch said. "And you will obey him as you would obey me."

The children flinched back from her, and Baby Duck quietly said, "*Quiee.*"

Oilcan, Tinker, and Blue Sky had all learned how to drive on go-karts that Tinker made out of lawn mowers and leaf blowers. They'd blocked off deserted streets on Neville Island and raced through the abandoned neighborhood at insane speeds. Blue Sky might look ten years old, but he had a driver's license and could probably outdrive anyone in the city—as long as he could reach the pedals and see over the dashboard. Thus it was no surprise that Tinker had sent Blue Sky in one of the viceroy's Rolls Royces. It was raining, after all, and the cab of Oilcan's pickup could only fit three people comfortably.

Figuring out who should ride where was like the logic problem of ferrying a fox, a chicken, and grain across a river in a rowboat. There were eight of them; too many to comfortably fit in the Rolls. He and Blue were the only ones that could drive. All the kids but Merry and Blue were terrified of Thorne. Rustle of Leaves' left arm was splinted, inked with healing spells, and was still healing, so he couldn't be squeezed into a shared seat. In the end, the only logical configuration had Blue driving the Rolls with all the kids, and Oilcan following with Thorne in his pickup.

Luckily for Oilcan's nerves, it was a short trip. No oni leapt out to snatch up the kids and take them away.

Tooloo's was the only store in Pittsburgh that sold used elfin clothes, albeit usually to elf-obsessed humans. Her place was in McKees Rocks, just a few blocks from John Montana's gas station. From the street, her store looked like a tiny little hole in the wall, just one large glass block window and a thick bulletproof glass door. Only the hand-painted English and Elvish running under the window, stating BREAD, BUTTER, EGGS, FISH, FOWL, HONEY, INTERNET ACCESS, MILK, SPELLCASTING, TELEPHONE, TRANSLATIONS, VIDEO RENTALS gave a clue to what lay hidden within.

Tooloo had carved out an entire farm from what had been pure city. Orchards and pastures and terraced gardens climbed a hill that was too steep to build on. Outbuildings that started life as garages had been repurposed into chicken coops, dovecotes and a milking barn. For some unfathomable reason, Oilcan and Tinker had spent endless hours working the farm under the guise of being babysat by the old half-elf. How Tooloo ended up as his grandfather's primary babysitter was one of the unsolved mysteries of his childhood. It was a relationship set in stone by the time Oilcan came to Pittsburgh. He'd asked Tinker about it once when they were little and discovered she was under the delusion it somehow involved spinning straw into gold. (Looking back, he really should have disabused her of that lie, but it was so cute he let it stand.)

"My brother always said that we looked like we poured a can of oil over us and then rolled in dirt all day," Blue was telling the kids as they got out of the car. "At some point we just started to call him 'oil can.' That's what Oilcan means."

The bells on the doorjamb jangled as Thorne opened the door and stalked into the dimly lit store. Oilcan kept close on her heels, not sure how Tooloo would react to the *sekasha*. Hell, there was no telling how Tooloo would react to anything. The old half-elf defied logic and reason; Oilcan suspected she did it to keep people at a distance.

Tooloo was stocking the stand-up refrigerator case with milk and eggs. As always, she was in an elegant dress of elfin silk, faded and threadbare with age, and battered high-top tennis shoes. Her ankle-length silver hair was braided into a thick cord. She glanced up with a look of mild surprise as Thorne entered. Then her eyes went wide when she saw Oilcan and the children.

"No!" Tooloo wailed and leapt up. "No, no, no!"

For one moment he thought she was going to object to the Stone Clan invasion, but she swooped down on Oilcan and caught him by both ears.

"Ow, Tooloo! Thorne!" He caught Thorne by the wrist to keep her from drawing her sword. "Tooloo!"

The old half-elf let go of his ears only to press his face between her hands and peer closely at him. Tooloo smelled of smoke and honey; she must have been working with her beehives prior to opening her store. "Oh, my little wood sprite! It's you, just you."

"Yeah, it's me." Oilcan tried to pull his face out from between her hands, but she had him fast.

"Get your hands off him," Thorne growled.

Tooloo turned her attention to the warrior. "Shame on you. By the sword and the blood." Tooloo spat. "My little wood sprite is not for you."

"This is Thorne Scratch." Who looked like she was about to slice and dice the crazy half-elf into small pieces. "She's a Stone Clan *sekasha*."

"I have eyes. I can see." Tooloo let him go. "Stupid guard dog. Tear the throat out of one master only to give its leash to another. Loves the pat on the head and the toss of the ball too much to leave it for true freedom."

Thankfully Tooloo had switched to English. Thorne Scratch continued to glare hard enough to cut.

"Tooloo, we're just here for stuff for the kids." Oilcan was glad that the kids had already trailed off after Blue Sky, who was explaining the use of the plastic shopping baskets that Tooloo had salvaged from Walgreens.

Tooloo spat again but went back to stocking the refrigerator, muttering darkly. "It be all well and good if they were satisfied at staying on the leash, but they've wound it tight around all the rest, binding everyone in place. Humans understand true revolution. Fight to be free and then stay free—don't just hand the keys over to the next master that rises up."

Oilcan had learned that when the half-elf got on a rant, there was no reasoning with her.

"You be careful of them." Tooloo crashed the milk bottles into the case. "The Stone Clan are the worst of the *domana* bastards. They were so sure that they would be the next masters after the Skin Clan were thrown down. Want is a dangerous thing. It's a seed planted in darkness that grows in secret. It grows and grows until it consumes you. Don't let them get their hands on you, or they'll twist you around and then murder you in your sleep."

"I'll be careful," Oilcan promised.

Tooloo harrumphed and stomped out the back of her store without another word.

Relieved, Oilcan went to check on the kids. He found Fields of Barley down the next aisle, loading bottles of spices into one of the Walgreen baskets.

"There are clothes in the other room," Oilcan said.

Barley nodded. "Cattail Reeds is looking at them. She is a seamstress; she'll find something for me. If I'm going to be doing the cooking, I need more pots, dishes, spices, knives . . ." He closed his eyes tight, his breath suddenly ragged.

"Are you okay?" Oilcan asked gently.

"They took my knives. They used my paring knife to cut my hair, and then they took them."

What could he say in the face of that? "I'm sorry."

Barley nodded rapidly, blinking. "It's—it's just my knives were made for me, the best I could afford."

Oilcan glanced around, but Tooloo had no knives for sale. "There are other places to buy things. I'm sure we can find knives if we look—"

"Yes, I know. In truth, my knives would have not lasted more than one or two hundred years. I feel stupid. I thought I could come and start an enclave. I was in the city no more than an hour before I was captured. What idiocy to think I could protect others when I could not even protect myself."

"One failure does not make a life," Oilcan said. "The important thing is you're alive. You failed because you knew nothing about Pittsburgh. Once you know the city, you can try again."

"The mistake I made was thinking I could do it alone," Barley said. "It's a major undertaking. It takes lots of people."

Oilcan nodded encouragingly.

"We could start one with the six of us. Blue Sky told us that we would be leaving that unsafe place with humans."

"What? Wait. No."

"We're staying there?" Barley's dismay at the condo was clear; the young male's façade started to crumble at the edges. His hands trembled slightly, and he blinked rapidly to keep tears out of his eyes.

"We're not staying," Oilcan quickly reassured him. "I don't know where we will be going. I haven't had time to think about it."

"Good. It's far too small and vulnerable." Barley ticked the points off on his fingers. "Everyone will need their own space to maintain the harmony of our household. The commons needs to be at least five times bigger than where we are now. The bathing room should be separate from the toilets. We need a safe room. We need garden space. We need—"

"Okay." Oilcan held up his hands to stem the flow of information. If opening an enclave was Barley's dream, then the elf had probably spent decades studying their design and function.

Somehow this felt all very familiar. Tinker been this focused when she decided that opening a salvage yard would be the answer to many of their problems. *"No one is going to think we're helpless orphans if we're running a successful business."* She'd been right, as usual. Every cop in Pittsburgh knew they were living on their own but looked the other way since they were obviously doing well enough to be left alone.

"We'll start looking for a new place to live after we leave here," Oilcan promised.

Barley nodded and wiped at his eyes. "Thank you, *Sama*."

Cattail Reeds came up with a bundle of clothes in her arms. She was already dressed in a black-checked miniskirt and a pink-flowered baby-doll shirt. "I will have to take in most of these; everything is too big. Hold this please, *Sama*." She pushed the clothes into Oilcan's arms and then tugged free a pair of black denim jeans. "We'll have to roll up the cuff until I can shorten these, but they should fit Barley in the waist and inseam."

She had to show Barley how to zip up the jeans, but her eye was perfect; the pants were a perfect fit. She sighed at a cotton tunic that was Wind Clan blue. "If we can dye this, it will work well." She flipped it over her shoulder. She pulled out a black Steeler's T-shirt and held it out to Barley. "Will you wear this?"

"What is it?" Barley took the shirt and examined it closely.

"It's human fashion!" Cattail grinned. "Isn't it awesome? They write on their clothes. You should see what they do with patterns. I want to get some of their fabric and make dresses and tops."

"But what does it mean?" Barley held out the shirt so the NFL logo was prominent.

Oilcan spent several minutes trying to explain professional football and the Pittsburgh habit of clinging to the memory of something that didn't exist anymore. All the professional sports teams had left immediately after it became clear that Pittsburgh would routinely be stranded on Elfhome. Hoverbike racing had filled the void.

"*Sama*." Rustle of Leaves came out of the next room, trailing Blue Sky and Merry. He was wearing earbuds linked to an iPod by white cords. He held the MP3 player out to Oilcan. It was old but irreplaceable now that Pittsburgh was stranded permanently on Elfhome.

"I told him it's expensive," Blue Sky said. "Tooloo wants over a hundred dollars for it."

"You can have it," Oilcan said. Rustle of Leaves was the one he was most worried about; the quiet male wouldn't be able to put his captivity behind him if he never regained the use of his arm. Music would be a comfort and a distraction for him.

Rustle of Leaves smiled his thanks.

"Here." Cattail Reeds dug through the clothes to find khaki slacks and a white button-down shirt for Rustle of Leaves. She and Merry helped Rustle strip down and eased him into the new clothes. Oilcan was glad that the kids all seemed to be taking care of each other. It was only after Rustle was dressed that Oilcan realized that Blue seemed to be on the brink of losing it.

"Hey." Oilcan pulled the boy aside. "Are you okay?"

And just like that, Blue Sky wasn't a confident seventeen-year-old but a rattled ten-year-old. He wrapped his arms around Oilcan and buried his face into Oilcan's side. It was always so odd when something like this served as a reminder that Blue Sky wasn't just short for his age, but actually stuck young. Oilcan and Tinker had moved forward, grown up, and somehow Blue Sky had ended up left behind.

"What's wrong?" Oilcan asked quietly in English.

Blue Sky mumbled something into Oilcan's shirt; the only words that Oilcan could pick out were "hurt" and "so bad." The boy had seen Rustle's massive bruises, the fresh ragged wounds, and the ink of all the healing spells needed to save Rustle's life. What could Oilcan say? "It's okay" was so inadequate, especially with the knowledge that the oni were still out there, fully capable of doing it to someone else.

"I know," Oilcan said finally.

To be brutally honest with himself, he'd been grief stricken at first when Tinker had been transformed into an elf and then whisked away to Aum Reanu. What made it bearable was seeing how much she loved her new family and how much they loved her. He constantly searched for ways to be okay with the sudden turn of events. He reminded himself that sooner or later she would have married, that at least she hadn't gone to Earth and been a full universe away, that he didn't have to worry that if something happened to him, she'd be left alone in Pittsburgh. And now he could add that he was glad Tinker would be there for Blue all the years it took for the half-elf to grow up.

"Is that everything?" Tooloo asked at the overflowing checkout counter.

Baby Duck squeezed in between Cattail Reeds and Fields of Barley and held out six baby chicks. "*Quiee.*"

There were exclamations of delight from all the kids, and each picked up a chick to cuddle. He knew, though, that Tooloo never sold live chickens in the store and all her eggs were refrigerated for hours. Baby Duck must have gone out the back and raided Tooloo's chicken coop.

"Oh, Baby Duck." He didn't have a heart to tell her no without even asking Tooloo. "Can we have the chicks, too, please?"

The old half-elf pressed her lips into a tight line, but after a moment, said, "Oh, my poor little wood sprite, you don't stand a chance."

13: KNOCK KNOCK OPEN THE BOX

Windwolf found Tinker deep in mad-scientist mode in Poppymeadow's woodshed. He hadn't come home the night before. She distracted herself from his absence by blowing up wood and telling herself someone would come tell her if something horrible had happened to him. Wraith Arrow—if he were still alive—which would be doubtful. Maynard. True Flame. The Wyverns. Chloe Polanski. *Someone!*

She worked through all of Poppymeadow's spare lumber and had the staff raid the neighboring enclaves for more. She was starting to think she would need to decimate Pittsburgh's entire supply of ironwood, when he appeared.

"Finally!" She launched herself into his arms. He swept her up off her feet. He smelled of blood and smoke and mud. He hugged her so tight she realized that he had had his own fears.

"We really need to work on communication," Tinker said.

"Yes." Windwolf laughed tiredly. He slid up her safety goggles and kissed her. "The marines, once they were able to fight through the oni to my side, told me of your adventure. You impressed them."

She blushed, feeling like a kid again, caught raiding the dynamite locker. "You're not upset with me?"

"You are my *domi*, Beloved. It means we will be together, forever, but it also means that in times like these, you must act for me. I cannot have one without the other, and in truth, I would not want it any other way. I love your courage and your ability to lead."

She supposed that made sense. She hated that he needed to go out and fight, and yet she would not want him to let Pittsburgh fall to the oni, either. Blood and mud were sprayed across the front of his white silk shirt, and there was a bruise on his cheek. Something had gotten through his shield and hurt him. The Stone Clan children had forever, and yet three of them were now dead. She hugged Windwolf tighter, wrapping arms and legs around him. And for a while, all that mattered was that they were together.

After Windwolf examined the chest with her, they ended up in the hayloft, as if they were just two average teenagers sneaking away for some privacy.

They were, of course, being discreetly guarded by their Hands. Tinker wasn't sure which made the *sekasha* more nervous: the chest or her blowing things up.

The problem with going into mad-scientist mode was it didn't shut down for nookie. Even as Windwolf nudged up the blue cheetah-print camisole with his nose, her mind was pointing out inconsistencies in the events she'd just told him.

She sighed and gave up resisting the demand for answers. "Did Sparrow know about Earth Son's offer to sponsor anyone from his clan that came to the Westernlands?"

"I do not believe so." Windwolf used his lips and tongue to quiet the mad scientist . . . for a few minutes.

"The thing I keep going back to with the kids: how did Yutakajodo know? He sent the lesser bloods to the train station because he knew that there would be elves traveling alone. Elves no one would miss. How would Yutakajodo know about the kids when the rest of us were so clueless?"

Windwolf leaned back. Emotions played across Windwolf's face, starting with anger. It gave way to confusion, and he shook his head. "I sent word to the queen after the oni kidnapped you—before they even took Little Horse as your whipping boy. I knew that my cousin would probably request the Stone Clan to send *domana*; they excel at city sieges and guerrilla warfare. If this were a battle all in open fields, Ember would have just sent more Fire Clan. She could only require the Stone Clan to send someone—she could not select the *domana* herself—not without insulting the head of the Stone Clan."

"Gods forbid we insult people," Tinker growled.

He grinned at her and then sobered as he traced circles on her bared stomach. "Ember has a thankless job of keeping four clans that would happily slit each others throats from doing just that."

"Earth Son was at Aum Reanu. Perhaps he told Sparrow while he was there that he planned to sponsor these children. She could have passed that information on to the oni."

Windwolf considered it and then slowly shook his head. "I doubt it. Sparrow was misleading me as to just how strong the oni force was in Pittsburgh. I wasn't willing to give up my holdings for help until the oni took you. Then I was willing to give it all away to get you back."

It made her all fluttery inside to know he meant it. "Wow." She slapped him slightly on the shoulder. "Don't say things like that. It wouldn't have been fair to people like Poppymeadow and Ginger Wine. They depend on you."

He grinned and kissed her. "You are perfect."

She blushed and yet felt giddily happy. "Why?"

"Because you're right."

"Of course I am. I usually am. I don't see how the two relate, though. What does that have to do with Earth Son telling Sparrow about sponsoring people?"

"Because he had no holdings in Westernlands until the Crown awarded him remunerations for coming to Pittsburgh."

She saw the cause and effect then. When Earth Son was at Aum Reanu, he couldn't have known that Windwolf would ask for help. Sparrow was dead by the time Earth Son arrived in Pittsburgh.

"Could someone have sent Sparrow the information before she was killed?"

"No. My cousin came in all haste, leaving behind half of his people just to get here as quickly as possible. No messenger with a letter could have outstripped him. The entire enclave would have known if we received a message via the distant voice. Sparrow couldn't have kept the information secret."

There had been distant voices at Aum Renau.

When Tinker was the all-important pivot who would stop the oni invasion, the elves answered all her questions about the magical devices in great detail but very politely refused her request to experiment with them. With everything else, she'd been given free rein—well, they had made her promise not to disassemble the dreadnaught.

As far as she could determine, the elves had discovered how to entangle elements at the quantum level on a large scale. The distant voices appeared to be two marble slabs. A spell was embedded within the stone. As a special pen was moved over one, a special magic-sensitive paper on the paired slab recorded the pen strokes as they were written. Given earth technology, it wouldn't seem amazing to the casual observer. To know that the distant voices could operate half a world apart without a satellite system or wires connecting them fascinated Tinker. She desperately wanted to take one apart so she could view the spell.

An idea bubbled up. She nudged Windwolf's chest until he rolled them over.

"We have distant voices here?" She sat up. So far she hadn't seen any at Poppymeadow's, but at Aum Renau they were kept in a small locked and guarded room.

"We have four. They work in pairs. We have one to the other three Wind Clan settlements here in Westernlands and one to my father in the Easternlands."

"Show me."

It turned out that the distant voices were as tightly guarded at Poppymeadow's as they had been at Aum Reanu. They were always attended by a member of Windwolf's personal household, who rang a bell as a message was received. The bell summoned someone who could take the message directly to Windwolf without leaving the device unattended. Like Windwolf said, Sparrow couldn't have received information without the entire household knowing.

Tinker would be more worried that other members of Windwolf's household had been in league with Sparrow if she hadn't spent the weeks at Aum Reanu. It been clear that Sparrow had no friends.

"How did you end up with her as your *husepavua*?" Tinker dug through the supplies for the distant voices. Windwolf—being rich and systematic—had stocked the room with several reams of the special paper.

Windwolf laughed. "I inherited her, like so many things in my life. Sparrow was vital to the clan during the clan wars. After my grandfather was killed, my father took certain steps to secure his place as clan head. One was to mark Sparrow with the *dau* to make her *domana* in name, though not in blood. She thought he would make her his *domi*—and perhaps if the war continued he would have. Politically it would have been a good match, although loveless.

"The *sekasha*, however, decided that the war was decimating our people and that it had to end. They united and forced the clans to accept Ashfall as king. He was a wise choice. Ashfall was willing to do whatever it took to create a lasting peace, even sacrificing his children to the cause. He summoned the heads of the clans to court and proposed marriages to tie the clans together with blood. When my parents met for the first time, my father was smitten."

A whopping ten kids later, Windwolf was born. Apparently Ashfall missed out when the Skin Clan was handing out infertility. She wondered what it would mean for her and Windwolf. Babies—gah! She was so not ready for that.

Tinker counted out a dozen pieces of special paper. "Your dad falls for your mom, dumps Sparrow, and she has an axe to grind forever after."

"So it appears." Windwolf followed Tinker back to the woodshed. Pony and Wraith Arrow shadowed them, keeping silent to maintain the illusion of privacy. "My father had no choice. Sparrow would not let go of the war and focus on peace. War would have torn Father's heart and home apart. He all but exiled her to remote holdings. Anyway, I did not want another *domana* taking control of Pittsburgh, and yet I did not want to abandon my holdings on the coast. Using Sparrow seemed the perfect compromise. Since there were no other clans in the Westernlands, I thought she could do no harm. . . ."

Pony had told Tinker once that Sparrow hoped Windwolf would take her as his *domi*. Twice burned. That would piss anyone off—but enough to betray your entire species?

"Other than redecorating Poppymeadow's woodshed, what are you attempting to do?" Windwolf fingered the splinters embedded into the wall, making it look like a cactus.

"I'm trying to safely open the chest from the whelping pens." Tinker laid the distant voice paper on top of one of her newly created spell-locks. "It requires me to pick the lock."

"I did not think that was possible."

She held up a finger to indicate silence. Into the hush, she slowly pronounced, "Three point one four one five nine two."

There was no outward sign from the spell-lock, but the spell glyphs appeared on the paper as she spoke the syllables of the key. Only when she hit "two" did the spell-lock gleam with power and the lumber it was etched on split into two pieces.

"Owned!" she shouted and danced around the wood shop.

Windwolf scooped her up and kissed her.

"I don't understand," Wraith Arrow murmured to Pony. "Yes, it copied the spell, but she made the lock, so she knows the key. How does that help with a lock that she does not know the key to?"

"Ah! Look!" She locked the spell again and put another paper in place. "Two nine five one four one point." She held out the still-blank paper. "Nothing!" She put it in place again. "Three." The first glyph appeared. "It only reacts to the correct phoneme when it's spoken in the correct order. Each glyph as it's unlocked gives off a minuscule amount of magic in order to activate the next section of the spell. The paper transcribes the glyph. Oh, I think I know how they build the distant voices." She frowned at the paper. "But how do they make the paper?"

"That is a Stone Clan secret," Windwolf said.

"Figures." The mad scientist suggested other secrets that the Stone Clan might have. "Do they have distant voices here in Pittsburgh?"

"I assume they do, but at this moment I don't know. I can ask Ginger Wine. She will know."

Tinker considered the possibility that Earth Son had dealt directly with Yutakajodo and frowned as the logic went neatly circular. "Oh, that's ugly."

"What is?" Windwolf asked.

"What if the reason Earth Son offered to sponsor anyone that could get to Pittsburgh was to guarantee a steady stream of elves that no one would miss?"

Windwolf's face went cold. "Earth Son was sacrificing his own people?"

"These kids started arriving weeks ago. Earth Son died last week. Why didn't he make arrangements for his people to get safely to Ginger Wine's? Pittsburgh is a strange and dangerous place. He didn't talk to you about it. He couldn't have told True Flame, because the Wyverns didn't know anything. He didn't even tell his own Hand."

Windwolf started to pace. "It is dangerous to assume it was him."

"Why?"

"Because he's safely dead. There is still Forest Moss to consider. He may or may not be mad, and he was held prisoner by the oni and then conveniently escaped, leading them back to Earth. He was the one that opened the door."

Deeming the woodshed already half ruined, they moved the chest to it for her attempt to unlock it. Elvish had thirty-eight phonemes, so she rigged her datapad to speak each and then check to see there had been a reaction in the paper. After that it was simply reprogramming one of her hacking programs to use Elvish phonemes instead of numbers and the English alphabet. She set up a remote camera and watched from a safe distance. Even using her datapad, it took the entire morning to pick through the lock. Windwolf slept for two hours and left again.

Shortly after lunch, the lock cracked open, but otherwise it was all slightly anticlimactic.

They slid the lid off, and a pair of *laedin* guards took it off someplace. Pony checked the chest for bombs and poisonous snakes and midget ninjas.

Tinker frowned at the contents. There were stacks of used spell papers. "Great, more puzzles to work out."

She lifted them out and carried them to the dining room to spread out on the one sunlit table. The spells scrolled down the left side of tissue-thin papers with such identical precision that they had to have been printed. She lifted two up to the light, aligning the edges of the paper, to check. The spells started and ended in the same exact points. "These were printed on a printer." Smeared across the page were odd blurs of color. "They look like DNA scans."

"D-N-A?" Pony asked.

"It's—it's stuff I don't know much about," she admitted. "Well, my grandfather said when dealing with things outside of your field, go to an expert."

14: MONSTER POPSICLES

"I thought you said that black-willow saplings were non-ambulatory," Tinker grumbled. The one-foot-tall seedlings were zipping around Lain's high-walled nursery bed like mice on crack. They were cute in a very ugly way. Their trunks thickened into a wrinkled old-man "face" and their branches splayed out like a head of mad hair. They looked like little miniature Albert Einsteins racing blindly about the box.

It was a lot easier to focus on the saplings than how badly she missed the ordered serenity of Lain's house. Her earliest memories were filled with the smell of fresh dirt and bruised greens.

Tinker studied Lain out of the corner of her eye. Lain was a head taller than Tinker ever hoped to be, with strong shoulders and arms from decades of relying on her crutches to move around. Her eyes were a pale blue-gray, and her hair had been gray for as long as Tinker could remember. Tinker could see nothing of herself in her aunt. It was like her father's side of the family had won every chromosomal flip of the coin; Tinker was dusky skinned, dark haired and dark eyed, small nosed and chesty. Not that it was all that surprising. The Skin Clan apparently had made sure that the genes that they wanted were extremely dominant.

How much different would her life been if she'd looked more like Lain? Would she have guessed then that Lain was her aunt?

Lain seemed willing to totally ignore their fight and everything that followed. "I said the saplings that I observed were non-ambulatory. After I was able to study the mature black willow, I realized that the level of magic altered the plant's activity level. This bed is on a ley line."

A weak ley line meandered through the back corner of Lain's greenhouse. When Tinker was growing up, it was the corner where her radio-controlled cars would suddenly run amuck. As a *domana*, she could now sense the flow of magic as a slight trickle of power over her toes, like she was standing in a shallow stream of warm water.

While Tinker could understand how magic could influence the saplings' movements, she wasn't sure about accelerated growth. When she last saw Lain, she had been culling seedpods. "Did you grow these from seeds?"

"No, I transplanted them from a very magic-weak area to test my theory."

Tinker leaned down to catch one. She wanted to have a closer look at their feet. "I didn't think plants could move so fast."

"Careful." Lain blocked Tinker's outstretched hand

with the tip of her crutch just as Pony caught Tinker by the shoulder and pulled her backward.

"They bite," Lain said in English as Pony murmured in Elvish, "*Domi*, they can bite."

"Why am I not surprised?" Tinker's shadow seemed to have attracted the saplings' attention; they gathered against the wall in front of her and scrambled wildly at the smooth surface. It was creepy and funny at the same time.

"When the saplings are en masse like this, they act like a school of piranha." Lain seemed inordinately pleased at that. She was probably wallowing in the joy of alien biology. Lain had thought her career as xenobiologist ended with the shuttle explosion that crippled her; Earth's space agencies only tapped the most physically fit for extraterrestrial missions. When Pittsburgh had been accidentally transported to Elfhome, though, Lain had gained a second chance to study life on another planet. "They tore a large groundhog apart in a matter of minutes and swallowed even the bones whole."

The rust-colored splashes on the nursery walls took on ominous meaning. "You fed them a live groundhog?"

"Not intentionally. The stupid thing burrowed into the nursery." Lain pointed out a mound of disturbed dirt near one corner. "So far, when Earth's flora and fauna meet Elfhome's, Elfhome's come out the winner. Magic seems to raise the whole 'survival of the fittest' to a higher level. Just consider the elves themselves. They're taller, stronger, and immortal. If we could use magic to bioengineer—"

"You can study how magic changes plants." Stormsong was the only one of Tinker's *sekasha* fluent in

English, thus the only one following the conversation. "But you must not try to use what you learn. That type of magic is forbidden."

"Forbidden?" Lain looked pointedly toward Tinker, who had been human up to a few months ago and was now undeniably elf.

"There are exceptions, but they are few and strictly controlled," Stormsong said. "Nature did not make us this way. The Skin Clan enslaved us and treated us like animals. They bred us for desired traits and slaughtered any infant that didn't meet their standards."

"Yeah, spell-working—bioengineering using magic—is a major no-no." Tinker waved a warning to Lain to back off the subject. The Skin Clan had set out to create the perfect beings in the *sekasha* to act as their bodyguards. While they wildly succeeded, the perfection worked against them. The *sekasha* were morally horrified by their makers and wiped them out.

"For a long time, spell-working was completely forbidden," Tinker explained. "That's the importance of Tempered Steel, the *sekasha* monk that they make such a big to-do over during the Harvest Faire." While she was growing up, the story competed with the pilgrims and the first Thanksgiving; every Harvest Faire featured a cute little puppet show and an odd fixation on keva beans. Only after becoming an elf did she realize all the little nuances of the story that she'd missed. "Wheat blight was creating a massive famine until Tempered Steel successfully argued for special allowances for spell-working."

What she didn't realize as a child was the fact that despite the *domana*-caste being "the lords" of the elves, it was the *sekasha* that had the final say in all matters. Tempered Steel hadn't gone to the elf king but to the *sekasha* monasteries of all the clans to argue his case. Being *sekasha*, his argument had been backed by serious sword skills. In the puppet show, he would defeat the monastery's champion before uttering his famous line of "Evil lies in the heart of elves, not in magic." In the end, it was the *sekasha* that decided that spell-working would be allowed and created the guidelines.

"Spell-working is really at the heart of why the elves so vehemently oppose the oni. The greater bloods practice wholesale bioengineering on their people. The tengu were humans that an oni greater blood spell-worked as punishment for resisting their takeover. He merged them with the crows who were feasting on their dead fathers and brothers."

Lain sighed. "Yes, I understand that applying bioengineering indiscriminately to sentient beings is morally wrong. But there is so much that the elves and even the oni could teach us. Most biologists coming to Pittsburgh from Earth look down their noses at the 'primitive' elves without realizing that the elves had been manipulating DNA with magic for thousands of years before we even began to imagine what it was."

Tinker didn't want to stand and argue the point in front of Stormsong. She was fairly certain that Stormsong wouldn't hurt Lain, but she didn't want to find out the hard way that she was mistaken. Being wrong once was enough. "Lain. Really?" Tinker motioned to the sapling dashing madly about the nursery bed. "A food we need to chase down and catch?"

Lain scoffed but allowed the subject to be changed back to the saplings. "I'm going to have to do something with them before they get much larger. Based on what I learned from the mature tree, I think they'll freeze nicely. I could thaw them out one at a time to study."

"Monster popsicles," Tinker said. "Black-willow flavored."

Lain smiled at her; a rare and treasured thing. "I've missed you."

Three little words that made Tinker's heart seize up. While she was growing up, Lain was the closest thing to a mother that she had. Betrayed couldn't describe how Tinker felt when she learned that Lain had lied to her every day of her life—she let Tinker believe that they weren't related when in truth Lain was her aunt. She had to cling to the knowledge that Lain had always been there for her. Lain had nursed her through childhood colds, stitched up cuts, cleaned out wounds, taught her how to deal with the mysteries of menstruation, and expanded her knowledge past quantum physics. Without Lain, she wouldn't have been able to save Windwolf's life, escape from the oni, or anything. And wasn't that the truly important thing? "Yeah. I've missed you, too."

Lain took Tinker's right hand and ran light fingers over the spectacular purples and yellows mottling her forearm. "Did you break it?"

Tinker tried not to wince as the feather touch still gave her tinges of pain. "It was just a hairline fracture. I basically slept for a week while the healing spells were running, and it's back to new."

"With all our science, we still can't heal a bone that fast."

"The spell focuses magic onto the elves' regenerative powers, puts it into hyper-drive, which is why I slept for most of the week. Also ate like a pig every time I woke up—which also meant I spent the rest of my awake time in the bathroom. It was a really annoying week."

Lain kissed her on the forehead. "I was worried about you, ladybug. I'm glad to see you're looking like your old self."

"It's the shirt." Tinker didn't want to go out in just a camisole, so she had raided Stormsong's bedroom again. The result was yet another of Roach's limited editions: a hoverbike sliding sideways through a cloud of dust that spelled out "Tinker." (She wouldn't have borrowed it, but Stormsong had pulled it over her head and grinned.)

Lain hugged her and then let her go. "I had a feeling that you would be coming to see me, so I made cookies and lemonade."

A rifle was lying on the island of Lain's sprawling kitchen. It was Lain's Winchester. The twenty-two-caliber rifle was the least powerful of Lain's guns, just a popgun when compared to her Barrett Light Fifty. Any trip into Elfhome's virgin forest required a gun and often a flamethrower. Lain used to collect samples of Elfhome plants, kept them in quarantine for a month, and then shipped them to Earth during Shutdown.

"Are you going out?" Tinker sighed as she realized that Pony and Stormsong had drifted between her and Lain. She wanted to smack them for acting suspicious of Lain. In truth, though, she couldn't entirely blame them. They had been there when Lain finally admitted the truth. They had seen how badly Tinker lost it. They knew how crazy Lain and her sister Esme—Tinker's real biological mother—had made Tinker.

"I've been having a problem with groundhogs." Lain took a pitcher of lemonade out of the refrigerator and set it beside the rifle, making the *sekasha* twitch. "I expanded my outside beds and planted them all with keva beans. The damn rodents act like I set up a feeding trough."

Since Lain didn't need the rifle for anything life threatening, Tinker picked it up and carried it to the gun rack in the center hallway. The Barrett Light Fifty was missing. The big gun was protection against the giant reptilian saurus; it was extreme overkill for groundhogs. What was Lain thinking? "Why aren't you using your live traps?"

"I thought it would be good for my neighbors to know that this little old crippled lady was armed."

The neighborhood of Observatory Hill had been quite wealthy at the end of the eighteenth century and was filled with grand Victorian houses. Lain lived on the edge of the scientific commune huddled around Allegheny Observatory. Her mansion sat apart from the houses that had been converted into dorms for the rotating base of Earth scientists that came to Elfhome to study the parallel universe. The distance of Lain's home from the dorms reflected the fact that normally only Lain lived in Pittsburgh while all the other scientists were transient. That of course changed when Tinker destroyed the hyper-phase gate that shuffled Pittsburgh back and forth between the two worlds.

It was disturbing to realize that all of Lain's neighbors had been on Elfhome for only a couple of months. They were complete strangers who had signed up for a thirty-day visit to an alien planet and found themselves stranded. "They're scientists! Do you really think they'd attack you?"

"I don't know them, ladybug, and they don't know me."

Tinker considered the missing Barrett and how it sounded like a cannon when shot. "At this rate, they might be afraid to get to know you."

"That would be fine with me," Lain said, and Tinker knew that Lain meant it. "Fiercely private" must run in the family. Before Tinker became an elf, she spent days alone at her salvage yard, focusing on her inventions. Looking back, though, she knew that deep down she'd been lonely.

Was Lain lonely? Tinker, at least, had Oilcan while she had been in her mad-scientist phase. He was always quietly but intensely protective of Tinker. Everyone in Pittsburgh knew that the cousins fought as a tag team.

"It's going to be a rough winter," Lain called. "Everyone up here knows that I've been laying in stores of food. Not that I made a point of telling anyone, but an acre of keva beans is hard to miss. These newcomers don't know me. As far as they're concerned, I'm just a harmless crippled geek."

Tinker suddenly hated the idea of Lain being alone. "Is Esme staying with you?"

There was no answer from the kitchen except extremely loud rattling of silverware. Apparently Tinker wasn't the only one annoyed with Lain's little sister.

Tinker put the Winchester in its place and relocked the gun rack. The rifle safely locked away, the *sekasha* drifted off, giving Tinker the illusion of privacy as she went back to the kitchen. "Have you seen Esme?"

Lain laughed. "If you count watching her sleep at Mercy Hospital, yes, I've seen her. She apparently was suffering mostly from exhaustion. When I went back yesterday, she had checked herself out and left."

"You're kidding! She's been gone for—"

"For a few weeks." Lain overrode Tinker. "For Esme, she's was only in space for a few weeks, not eighteen years. According to the nurses, she didn't realize at first that she's basically jumped forward in time nearly twenty years. It apparently sank in yesterday morning."

And Esme promptly checked herself out. "Oh."

"You didn't tell her?" Lain leveled a hard gaze at Tinker.

Tinker could deliberately misunderstand and pretend she thought Lain meant about the time difference, but she knew what Lain really was asking. "No. That didn't come up. We were kind of busy."

Lain snorted and released Tinker from her Medusa gaze. "You two are entirely too much alike. God have pity on me, having to deal with both of you at the same time."

Tinker focused on raiding the cookie jar. It was filled with her favorite—thin, crunchy sugar cookies. Lain had known she was coming. Apparently both sisters could see the future. It explained how Lain had always managed to stay one step ahead of Tinker when her grandfather couldn't.

"So, what's this puzzle that you can't figure out that you've brought me?" Lain proved that she was two steps in front of Tinker.

Stormsong had loaned Tinker a canvas messenger bag to carry the DNA spell sheets. Tinker spread them out on the butcher block–topped island as she explained how the oni had kidnapped the Stone Clan children.

"I'm afraid that the oni might have done something to the kids. It's horrible to say this, but the best thing we can hope for is that the oni simply bred them with an animal. The hospice made sure that's not a worry anymore. Considering what the oni did with the tengu—transforming an entire generation of humans into half-crows—I'm afraid of what the worst could be."

Lain picked up the first sheet and studied it intently. "These look like DNA scans."

"That's what I thought."

Lain picked up another and studied the two side by side. "It's against the treaty to cull any genetic samples from elves."

"I don't think the oni care."

Lain gave her a dark look. "I have nothing to compare these with. Are you even sure these are from the children?"

"Um, no."

Lain sighed. "First you're going to have to get DNA samples from the children and see if these are indeed matches. And it has to be you—I can't do it."

Tinker decided not to point out that the treaty no longer existed. If someone was going to get in trouble for this, she wanted it to be her.

"While you're at it, any other baseline samples you can get me would be good. I would have to build an entire index to see what is normal before I can tell if there's anything abnormal."

Tinker winced. The elves were not going to like that. "I'll see what I can do."

15: SACRED HEART

If Oilcan really hadn't wanted to move, he probably could have sicced Tinker on his condo board, but to be truthful, he had a three-bedroom condo because he liked having space for himself. It would be only a matter of time before having the five kids crowded in with him would drive him nuts.

He needed a much bigger place. He needed someplace like the abandoned hotel that he grew up in. Last time he checked, it was still standing empty. Nothing, however, could get him to brave the spring floods on Neville Island again. He had the barn in the south hills where he often did art, but it was very isolated. He didn't want to drag the kids out where they'd be vulnerable to oni. The remote barn would probably give them nightmares.

If they were going to open an enclave, then it would probably be best to be out by the other enclaves. He knew it was the custom of incoming elves to go from one enclave to the next until they found one with space still available.

Once he started to actually think "enclave," the type of building became clearer in his mind. It would need a large public dining room, a hefty kitchen, multiple bathrooms, sleeping rooms for guests, and separate sleeping quarters for the kids. Too bad he couldn't just move the hotel from Neville Island out to Oakland.

There was a building, though, in Oakland, that had always reminded him of the hotel.

The oni had launched an attack on the enclaves from a house across the street from the faire ground. The elves had evacuated all the buildings and proceeded to level the block. The last building on the street had been a private high school before Pittsburgh first traveled to Elfhome. The lack of high school–age kids had forced the school to close, and it had been turned over to the EIA. It seemed to Oilcan that someone had been squatting in it over the years, but they would have been evicted along with the rest of the street.

"Blue Sky, have they torn down Sacred Heart High School?"

"Not yet."

The elves were tearing down the buildings to keep the oni at arm's length. Surely they wouldn't mind if someone they could trust moved in.

Oilcan was less sure about his decision as he drove up to Sacred Heart. The east side of the street had stayed on Earth; it had been replaced by virgin forest that pressed up against the edge of the ruined side-walks. The ironwood trees had been cut back for over a mile to create a wide-open field that made up the faire grounds and doubled for safe tethering for the living airships. Flocks of *indi,* Elfhome's near cousins to goats, were out grazing, splashes of white against the green. When he thought of this street, the idyllic faire grounds were what came to mind.

Less than a month ago, the west side of the street had been lined with stately brownstone townhomes. The houses had been reduced to rubble, making the street look like a war-zone. He never realized how much this street meant to him until he gazed at the ruin. The juxtaposition between faire grounds and brownstones had been visual perfection of the humans of Pittsburgh living beside the elves of Elfhome—and the war had torn it to shreds.

Baby Duck tumbled out of the Rolls, pointed excitedly at the *indi* and took off running. The others got out, milled about, and then reluctantly followed. The *indi* had *laedin* warriors keeping watch over them to fend off wargs and oni. Blue Sky was along to make sure the Wind Clan adults behaved toward the Stone Clan children.

Oilcan was glad that the kids would be distracted as he checked out Sacred Heart.

The high school was a solid three-story brick building. The first-floor windows were narrow as arrow slits, but higher floors had huge bay windows that promised lots of natural light. Wide stone steps led up to an arched doorway. At one time a stout oak door had protected the opening, but it was lying in pieces in the foyer.

Apparently the previous occupants had been oni. Bullet holes peppered the plaster in the foyer. The stone floor was smeared with blood, showing that the oni had been killed and their bodies pulled from the building. Judging by the amount of blood dried on the carpet in the cavernous room to the right of the foyer, a *sekasha* had beheaded two or more oni and their bodies had gushed out all of their blood. Flies buzzed lazily through the air, and the bloodstain writhed with maggots.

Oilcan steeled himself against the blood and explored deeper into the high school. The building was everything he hoped, although hip deep in garbage. How did the oni live here without attracting notice? Were some humans this disgusting that no one noticed what animals the neighbors were? The volume of work needed to make the place livable was daunting. Still the bones were good. The first floor had three huge rooms that had been a gym, library, and dining room, a small warren of offices, two bathrooms, and an industrial-grade kitchen. The large backyard was already fenced in by a high brick wall, although piled with garbage. The twenty classrooms on the upper floors were large and littered with clothes but had sunshine streaming in through big, dirty windows. While the urine-soaked bathrooms lacked showers, there were enough of them that he could easily turn one into an elfin bathing room. The roof showed no signs of leaking. No one had gutted the cooper pipes. The hot-water tanks were sound. The heating system had been upgraded in the last quarter century. The only glass that needed replacing was in the lower, smaller windows—they'd been smashed outward during the fight.

His grandfather always said that you needed a plan for everything from baking a cake to total global domination. He'd drummed project management into both of his grandchildren. Again and again, Tinker had used her training to change the world: from creating hoverbike racing to defeating the entire oni army single-handedly. Oilcan had always kept his projects smaller and more personal. This was going to be the largest project he had ever taken on. Still, the key to any project was to break it into small, manageable steps.

The first thing he'd need was a path cleared to one of the chalkboards, chalk, and every dumpster he could get his hands on.

The third floor of the school, Oilcan decided, would be the "family" level, while the guest rooms could be on the second. He picked out the room at the head of the stairs for himself. From it, he could keep watch over all the comings and goings. He'd cleared a path to the chalkboard and started sketching out a plan on how to make the kids' lives right.

There was no way he could get the building cleaned all at once, so he needed to prioritize the rooms. He would also have to fix the front door and make sure the back door locked tightly and any other entrances were secure. Utilities were on, but he wasn't sure if all the light fixtures worked—he should check those before it got dark.

The building was silent except for the scratch of his chalk, so he jumped when someone said directly behind him, "I had no idea that project management was genetic."

Last time Oilcan had seen Riki Shoji, the tengu was still pretending to be a human physics grad student who lucked into a job at Tinker's salvage yard. All that remained of the disguise was the tone and cadence of Riki's voice—a wry sense of humor that scraped along the baritone registry. If it weren't for the voice, Oilcan wouldn't have recognized the tengu warrior as Riki. He stood in the door like a dark angel, wingtips brushing the doorframe. From the machine gun on his hip to the steel fighting spurs on his bird-like feet, there was nothing of the witty scholar Oilcan had called friend.

The only other person who ever triggered so many conflicting emotions in Oilcan—most of them negative—was safely dead by Pony's hand. There was a point, just a few days ago, when Oilcan was sure he would kill Riki given a chance. That was before he found out that the oni had been holding Riki's six-year-old cousin, Joey, as hostage.

It was an uncomfortable feeling knowing that Oilcan had the luxury of never having to decide how far he would go to protect Tinker. He'd never had to kill someone. He'd never had to betray someone that trusted him. If faced with the same choice, could he have saved Tinker by allowing the oni to torture someone who trusted him? Especially now that he intimately knew the horrors that the oni could inflict? Oilcan couldn't even imagine choosing either and staying sane.

Rage had been wonderfully simple compared to what Oilcan felt now.

"What are you doing here?" Oilcan growled.

The tengu shifted uneasy. "I heard that you ended up with the kids we rescued yesterday."

Oilcan took a deep breath and let it out. He knew that the tengu had been instrumental in the rescue, but he hadn't known that Riki had been involved. Tinker had told him that as part of the Chosen bloodline, Riki had been considered the leader of the tengu prior to Jin's return. It was why the oni kidnapped Joey Shoji; it gave them a hold on all the tengu through Riki. It would make sense for Riki to lead an assault instead of Jin. "And?"

"I've stayed at your place. It was okay for two, but way too small for six. I figured you needed help moving." Riki nudged the mounds of trash that threatened to block the door. "Looks like you could use a lot of help."

Oilcan snorted and turned back to the chalkboard. What had he been writing? "Wish" was all he had written down. Wish he could go back to comfortably hating Riki? Not that he really was comfortable with all the rage he'd felt. It had felt like putting on his father's skin.

Wish list. He needed to know what the kids had lost to the oni. If Merry was any example, the kids had pared their luggage down to what they must have to start a new life. If the kids were going to put the nightmare of their captivity behind them, they had to have those essentials back. Oilcan wrote "Barley: knives; Rustle: instrument." Assuming, of course, that Rustle could ever use his shattered left arm again.

There was a noise behind him, and he realized that Riki had picked up a handful of the garbage and was carrying it downstairs.

Tinker had clearly forgiven Riki. She talked about how Riki had subtly protected her while she was held captive, and how adorable his cousin Joey was. Riki knew the oni; he knew what they could do to a child and what he was setting Tinker up to endure. How could Oilcan blame Riki for protecting Joey? How could he forgive Riki for hurting Tinker?

✧ ✧ ✧

Oilcan still wasn't sure how to deal with Riki, when an odd tip-tapping in the foyer heralded the return of the children from the faire grounds.

"*Sama*?" Merry's voice echoed through the building.

"Up here." Oilcan went out to the hall and leaned over the banister.

The children hadn't returned empty-handed; they had a pair of baby *indi* on twine leashes.

"Where did you get those?" he asked. Oh, please gods, hopefully Baby Duck hadn't stolen those, too.

"They gave the *indi* to us," Cattail Reeds said.

Blue Sky shrugged his shoulders when Oilcan looked to him for confirmation. "Tinker apparently put the fear of God into everyone. The enclave people were *really* nice."

Merry wrinkled her nose at the smell as she eyed the trash-covered foyer. "What is this place?"

"This is going to be our enclave—once we get it cleaned out."

The kids eyed the mess around them.

"*Quiee.*" Baby Duck said what they all clearly were thinking.

"Yes, I know it looks horrible," he said. "It just needs some work."

There was the rumble of a big truck outside and then the hiss of brakes. The first of the dumpsters had arrived.

Riki was in the kitchen, cleaning. He had slipped on the scholar disguise again; there was no sign of his wings or gun or fighting spurs. His sandals were so nondescript that they camouflaged Riki's bird-like feet with normalcy.

Considering the emotional state of the kids, Oilcan was glad that if Riki was determined to be underfoot, at least he was doing it in the least threatening of modes.

"What are you doing here?" Oilcan whispered, since the kids had followed him into the kitchen.

"First room on your list to clean is the kitchen," Riki said evenly.

Oilcan laughed bitterly and kept picking his way to the back door. "There's been a change in priorities. I'm starting with the backyard."

"Why?"

Oilcan pointed at one of the *indi* as it bleated as if in answer. He already assumed it would be days before the building would be clean enough to actually move into. While he could slip the chicks into his condo, they'd have to leave the *indi* here.

"Yeah, that could be a problem," Riki said.

The backyard lacked any kind of a path to the tall iron back gate. He had to all but wade through the trash. Roach was waiting in the back alley, looking as soulful as the pair of elf hounds sitting beside him. Roach's family handled most of the garbage collection in Pittsburgh. Their place was out by the airport in what was quickly becoming ironwood forest; they had to keep a pack of the massive dogs to safely operate their landfill business.

"Dude, you've got to be kidding," Roach said in greeting. "You're moving into this dump?"

"Probably." He still had to check with Windwolf, since the building was supposed to be torn down. The *indi* made cleaning up the yard a necessity regardless of the end result on the building itself. "Once I get it cleaned up and jump through a few hoops."

The lock was rusted open—something else to put on his list—but the gate would only swing inward a foot or two before grinding to a halt on the trash spilling into the back alley.

"There's a shitload to do." Roach picked up a mangled office chair and tossed it with a deep clang into the dumpster still on the truck bed.

"Yeah." Oilcan had been assuming that the kids would help, but as he moved aside the surface layer of trash, he was uncovering hidden landmines of broken glass and sharp rusted metal. He didn't want the kids near the trash now. "I'm not sure how I'm going to do this."

"I'll call the team." Roach gave him a worried look. "We're still going to race—right?"

"Yeah. It's just going to be little crazy for a while."

Roach laughed. "And this differs from most of this summer how?"

"Little crazy." Oilcan measured with his fingers. "Instead of a lot crazy."

"I can live with that. Tommy Chang called and asked if we were racing this weekend and if you'd be lead, and I told him yes. I'd really rather not have Tommy pissed at me."

"I should have my shit together by the weekend."

Roach worked the hydraulic controls on the truck and dropped the big steel container within a foot of the wall. "You sure you want two more?"

"Yeah, out front so I can build chutes down from the second and third story." The kids could work at cleaning out one room to sleep in if things turned sour fast with his condo association. The stuff in the classrooms seemed fairly harmless compared to the trash in the backyard.

"Okay," Roach said and whistled to his dogs. "Andy's bringing the second one. I'll tell him to drop it in front."

There were ten tengu in the kitchen. Not a feather was showing, but they were unmistakable from the lean muscle builds, beak-like noses, and the flutter of nervousness that went through them as Oilcan walked back into the kitchen. The center island been cleared of clutter, and they were gathered around it like flocking crows.

"Where are the kids?" Oilcan asked.

"Upstairs." Riki pointed above his head. "I told Blue Sky to have them pick out rooms on the third floor, write their names on the chalkboard and make out wish lists."

It was fairly down Oilcan's to-do list, but the tengu weren't on his plan at all.

"And the *indi*?" Oilcan asked.

"My little cousins have them across the street," Riki said. "*Indi* are kind of stupid—they'll eat plastic and other stuff that will make them sick. I figured it would be better to keep them out of the building until it's cleaned."

"Why are you doing this?" Oilcan growled.

"Because you need help."

"Maybe I don't want your help." There was no "maybe" about it, but the logical part of him, the part most like his mother and so different from his father's unreasonable passion, knew that Riki was right. He needed a lot of help to clean out the building and make it livable. He just didn't want to acknowledge that Riki was right.

"I didn't think you would want my help," Riki said.

A reasonable person would stay far away, knowing that they weren't wanted, but then Oilcan wouldn't use words like "reasonable" to describe Riki. "Is this some kind of plan to make me grateful enough to forgive you?"

"No."

"Then what the fuck are you doing here?"

Riki stood silently for a few minutes and then said, "Did you know there were oni children at the whelping pits yesterday?"

Oilcan recoiled as he realized that the elves wouldn't have let a single oni live; the oni children wouldn't have been spared. "What does that have to do with you screwing us over?"

"Tinker went into that warren to save your kids. She didn't go there to kill the oni children. She didn't want that. She hated that."

"Leave Tinker out of this!" Oilcan shouted. "That's—that's totally different. You wormed your way into our lives. You lied to us. You made us trust you. I told you things that I have never told anyone in my life—not even Tinker. And the whole time you were standing there, going 'I watched my mother die, too,' you were planning on killing Tinker."

Riki flinched as if Oilcan had struck him, but didn't deny it. He hunched his shoulders and continued, "Tinker went into the warren because that's what had to be done to rescue those kids."

"That doesn't make what you did right!"

Riki nodded. "What I did was wrong, but I had to do it. The worst of it is: if you ask me what I'd do differently, the honest answer is 'nothing.' I wouldn't dare. I got my baby cousin back safely. I got my uncle out of orbit and on the right planet. I got my whole frigging race protected. I wouldn't change anything, but it still doesn't make it right."

Oilcan's hands clenched into fists against his will. He looked away from Riki and forced his hands to relax. "So this is some insane plan: to make it all right in your head, you're going to force me to take your help?"

"This is trying to do the right thing so I can live with what I had to do."

Apparently doing the right thing involved a small army of tengu. Oilcan saw not a feather and heard no rustle of wings; they simply appeared with ninja stealth. By the time Roach's younger brother, Andy, showed up with the second dumpster, there were tengu in every room and the dumpster in the back alley was full.

"Already?" Andy said when Oilcan told him. The boy glanced at the big steel container he was about to drop under the largest second-story window. "You still want this one in the front, or should I take it around back?"

With the tengu "helping," the dumpsters were going to be filled as fast as Roach and Andy could rotate them. At several hundred dollars a load, hauling away the trash was going to run Oilcan a lot of money, and he still didn't know if Windwolf would allow him to move into the building. It was tempting just to stop all work and wait for permission. Yet if Windwolf said yes, then the work had to be done, and everything was already in motion and running smoothly.

"Here is good," Oilcan told Andy.

"I'll grab the full one after I drop this." Andy worked the hydraulics to lower the container into place. "And bring another empty one back?"

"Yeah." He wished he could be more confident that he was doing the right thing. Tinker sailed forward so sure and true—it was easy to follow in her wake. It made life a joyful ride. This was like being lost at sea.

If they were going to open an enclave, then they would need tables, chairs, dishes, silverware, food—the list went on and on. He had some money saved. Tinker always paid him well, and he lived rent free, but he had expensive hobbies. If things continued at this rate, he'd burn through his savings fast.

He was in a cleared corner of the dining room with the pieces of the front door. He'd found a spell in his family codex that would rejoin them. He carefully copied the spell onto the oak. He'd just triggered the last spell to knit together the splintered wood, when stillness ran through the building. He looked up and found Windwolf standing in the foyer with his *sekasha* arrayed around him.

Oilcan had seen Windwolf helpless, mauled, and bleeding, close to death. Oilcan had also seen Windwolf calling down bolts of lightning like a god. What mattered most to Oilcan was he'd seen the loving way Windwolf treated Tinker. How the elf felt about him, though, was a mystery.

"Wolf Who Rules Wind." Oilcan gave him a bow and used his full name because he needed to talk to Windwolf about official things.

Windwolf raised an eyebrow at the formality. "I

thought I recognized the pattern of chaos," Windwolf said in English. "But I guess I was wrong."

"Oh! Yeah, this is all me." Oilcan slipped back to English since Windwolf obviously wanted to keep the discussion informal. "I'm glad you're here. I need to talk to you."

Windwolf smiled wryly. "Yes, you do. I ordered this building to be torn down."

"I know. I need to discuss with you setting up an enclave."

"Ah." Windwolf considered a moment, apparently thinking about the fact that their conversation would be public. He tilted his head toward the faire grounds. "Let us walk."

Windwolf was nearly a foot taller than Oilcan, but the elf matched his stride as they walked out of the school and across the street to the rolling pasture. Oilcan waited until they were out of earshot before starting up the conversation again.

"I don't know if you've been told, but I've taken in the Stone Clan children."

"Yes, I've been told," Windwolf said. "I know your family will go to extraordinary lengths to protect anyone that lands in your lap. I love you both for your boundless empathy and selfless courage."

It surprised and touched Oilcan how easily Windwolf used the "l" word. He supposed it was a difference in culture. Still, he could hear the "but" lurking in Windwolf's voice.

"So, what's the problem?" Oilcan said.

"I've become aware, too, that you often act without knowledge of the inherent . . ." Windwolf paused, searching for appropriate word.

"Danger?"

"Entanglements." Windwolf smiled. "But, yes, also danger."

"What am I missing?"

"I'm assuming that if you wish to talk to me about starting an enclave, you're seeking Wind Clan sponsorship."

"I think I am," Oilcan said cautiously. "I need to learn more about it before I can be sure."

"Basically I would supply you with money to start an enclave. It is not a gift given freely." Windwolf frowned. "I want to be sure you understand all that sponsorship entails. I do not want to assume that since your Elvish seems flawless you actually understand what I'm saying to you."

Considering Tinker had accepted Windwolf's engagement gift in total ignorance that she was agreeing to marry him, Oilcan couldn't blame Windwolf for being leery.

"I realize it isn't a gift, that I would be somehow indebted to you," Oilcan said. "It's the level of debt that I don't understand."

Windwolf nodded and sighed. "I'll try to explain. I don't know English well enough to feel comfortable that I'm correctly translating the concepts."

Considering Windwolf's English was as good as Oilcan's, the statement was intimidating.

They walked in silence across the grass. The *sekasha* had moved away, giving them the illusion of privacy.

"We have songs and legends that tell of a time, long ago, when we were much like the humans. We were nomadic tribes, bound together mostly by blood ties, waging wars with even friends and family over land and beautiful females. But then the Skin Clan discovered their dark magic and built an army of monstrous beings—wyverns and wargs and *baenae*—that swept over Elfhome, enslaving all before them. The Skin Clan would scatter each newly conquered tribe through their nation. A cousin here. A cousin there. All the children were taken from their parents. No siblings were raised together. They killed our priests and scholars and burned all our books, determined that nothing would bind their slaves together. They could not, though, destroy our hate of them—and in the end, that was what bound us together."

"This is how the clans started?"

Windwolf nodded. "Two slaves with nothing in common but their hate would pledge to protect each other. And two became three. And then three became four. Secretly. Quietly. One by one, we built a society based on vows."

"If I give you my word, I will keep it."

"I trust you, cousin," Windwolf said. "That is not my fear. It's the children."

Oilcan was surprised that Windwolf's statement hurt like a blow. He wanted Windwolf to be better than everyone that he'd dealt with.

"It is not that I don't trust them," Windwolf said gently. "If they give their word, they will keep it. You are, however, about to put them into a terrible quandary."

"I don't understand."

"That was what I was afraid of."

They had come to the great mooring anchors in the center of the field; ironwood timbers were affixed to bedrock by columns of iron. Windwolf sat down on one of the anchors.

"There are layers—hierarchy—to our loyalty," Windwolf said. "The most basic loyalty is to the clan. If a battle is pitched between two clans, you fight with your clan."

Oilcan nodded. It had become blatantly obvious since he took in Merry.

"Our clans, though, are not as united as they seem," Windwolf said. "That's where the layers become important. If two people within your clan are at odds, who do you support? The . . . the . . ." Windwolf frowned, once again searching for the right word. "The strongest is the bind between Beholden. Do you understand what is between Tinker and Little Horse?"

There was a loaded question. It was impossible to miss how Tinker and Pony felt about one another. He knew Tinker was struggling with her feelings. Did Windwolf see how much she loved both Windwolf and Pony? Did Windwolf trust Tinker not to betray him, or did he expect to share her heart? "I know that Pony would die for her. She would do anything to protect him."

Windwolf nodded. "Little Horse was raised as my blade brother. I held him in my arms just minutes after he was born. Whenever I was home, I would spend hours playing with him. We love each other well, but if some strange madness overcame me and I raised my hand to Tinker, I know Little Horse would kill even me to protect her. And if I tried to harm Little Horse, I would expect to have to fight her first. Little Horse is hers and she is his."

It boggled his mind completely how nonchalantly Windwolf explained it. "Even though she is your *domi*?"

"We are like this." Windwolf clenched his fists and

pressed them together, side by side. "My beloved and me. The right hand and the left. *Domi* and *domou*. We are separate and yet we cooperate to create for the benefit of us both. Neither is greater than the other, because it's our cooperation that gives us strength."

Windwolf opened his right hand and held it out, flexing his fingers. "Tinker and Little Horse are like this. They are one. You cannot separate them without harming both. And thus, their loyalty must be first to each other."

Oilcan nodded although he was struggling with how accepting Windwolf could be toward Tinker loving another male. "I'm not sure how this relates to starting an enclave."

Windwolf laughed. "That was what I was worried about. This has everything to do with sponsorship. If I sponsor you, between us would have to be a bond nearly as strong as that between Tinker and Little Horse. I would protect you as you serve me. No other tie that you have can be stronger—not even with your cousin."

Oilcan shook his head. "I couldn't put you above—"

Windwolf waved away his objection. "That problem is simple enough to circumvent. Tinker could sponsor you, and your loyalty need not be tested."

"I'm confused now."

"The problem lies with the children," Windwolf said. "It was agreed that all humans would be considered without a clan unless they entered into an agreement with an elf. You are a human, and it's assumed that you have no clan. If you are sponsored, then you would become Wind Clan. And by extension, your household would be Wind Clan."

The most basic loyalty is to the clan.

"Oh," Oilcan said. He had assumed that since Tinker was the Wind Clan *domi*, he was automatically considered Wind Clan. Perhaps the reason all the Wind Clan elves called him "cousin" was because it was the only way they felt connected to him. How did Thorne Scratch see him? Did she think of him as a free agent? Was that why she asked him to take the children? Did she only trust him because she thought he was completely neutral?

"I think you're starting to understand," Windwolf said quietly. "The moment you agree to sponsorship, the children will have to decide if they want to stay with you and be Wind Clan or to find another household. It would be one thing if you were an elf. They could choose with the knowledge they would have a home forever. You are a human. The household you form will have a lifespan limited by your own. And it would be nearly impossible for the children to be accepted by another household after you died, since they would have abandoned not only the household of their birth, but also their clan."

"Couldn't the household last beyond my life?"

"I cannot give you that reassurance. I do not know these children well enough. My grandfather Howling was head of the Wind Clan for nearly ten thousand years. He would still be head if he hadn't been murdered. His household shattered after his death; many had not found a refuge until I took them in, over a thousand years later."

The worse of it was, even if Oilcan lived to be an old man, the children would barely be considered adults when he died.

The rumble of a big truck announced Roach's return with another dumpster.

"What about the building?" Oilcan asked, standing up. He couldn't afford to pour more money into the school if he couldn't move the children into it.

"I will tell Maynard that it is free to claim, and you can purchase it for a dollar," Windwolf said. "We will help you no matter what path you follow. Sponsorship, however, is more than just money. All that is Wind Clan would be available to you. The children need a clan protecting them, and the Stone Clan does not appear willing to maintain a strong presence in Pittsburgh. My beloved and I will be sure that the children are cared for if they choose the Wind Clan. Our ability to protect them, however, is limited if they remain Stone Clan. Speak with the children."

Team Tinker had assembled while he was gone. They sat on the front steps and hoods of cars parked in the street in front of the school, waiting for his return.

"What did he say?" Roach asked what everyone else wasn't brave enough to ask.

"The building is mine," Oilcan said and waited for the resulting cheer to die down. "We talked about sponsorship, but there's a lot I didn't know about it. Both Windwolf and Tinker are willing to sponsor me—"

"Are they going to arm wrestle for you?" Andy asked and got smacked by Roach.

"If the male is smart, he won't come between Tinker and Oilcan," Roach said, and there was laughing agreement.

"Both are willing," Oilcan repeated. "But I need to think it over."

"I went upstairs to check out the rooms," Abbey Rhode, the team's spotter, said.

"She means she went upstairs to slack off," Roach said.

Abbey stuck out her tongue as everyone laughed. She was often teased because her job was to simply sit, watch, and report. "This place is going to be sweet once it's cleaned up. It's really cool that you got the kids to write out what they need—although it impressed on me how little I can read Elvish. I took photos of their lists and posted them online."

"I'll translate the lists," Gin Blossom offered.

"Thanks," Oilcan said.

"And we managed to get one of the things on the list already," Abbey said.

"We?" Roach said.

"You don't read Elvish, either," Abbey said. "So it was joint effort."

Roach opened the door to his truck and an elfhound puppy tumbled out into his arms. "Pete sired this little one, so we're calling him Repeat."

Another baby animal. Oilcan was going to be able to open a petting zoo by the end of the week.

16: MORGUE BREAKING AND ENTERING

Lain had given Tinker swabs for taking DNA samples from the kids. They drove back into town with the box in her lap as she argued with Stormsong.

"All we're going to do is stick these swabs in their mouth and rub them around a little." Tinker couldn't see why this was so hard to understand.

"Collecting DNA smacks of spell-working," Stormsong repeated, using different words. So far she'd found three ways to say it.

"We're not going to do any spell-working!" Tinker cried. "We need to know what the oni were doing with the kids. The oni could have been designing a plague to wipe out elves, or creating a spell to merge elves into crows like the tengu, or—or—I don't know, and that's what scares me. They could have been planning anything."

"This is a bad idea." Stormsong found a fourth way to say the same thing. "The first step of spell-working is establishing a baseline."

Tinker wanted to scream. "Are you getting hit with a big sledgehammer that says 'duck now or die' or are you just bitching on general principle?"

Stormsong huffed. "Unlike some people, I don't need clairvoyance to see trouble coming."

"The children are Stone Clan." Pony stepped in to mediate. "It is true that their clan is failing them utterly, but Stormsong is concerned that the Stone Clan will attempt to use anything questionable we do against us."

Stormsong finally put her objection into a format Tinker could understand. "If the Stone Clan accuses us of spell-working, then the Wyverns will most likely see it in the worst light. They are the best of us because they were most heavily spell-worked."

"Okay, that's useful to know," Tinker said.

"And since Oilcan is acting as the children's *sama*," Stormsong said, "he could be punished for recklessly endangering them."

"Oh." Tinker considered pitching the swabs out the window.

"*Domi* is right," Pony said. "We need to know why the oni were kidnapping the children and keeping them alive. We will have to use caution in gathering the samples."

Obviously, it was time to prove that she was the smartest person in Pittsburgh.

Which was how they ended up at the morgue.

Tinker avoided the front door on the theory that the fewer people they talked to, the better. She had Pony park where the ambulances and hearses unloaded the bodies. There was a big button marked PRESS

FOR NIGHT ATTENDANT that she ignored. Instead she proceeded to hack the digital lock that required a transmitter key for entrance.

"You have no idea how disturbing it is that you know how to do that," Stormsong murmured.

Tinker blushed. "People lock themselves out of their cars all the time. Since we operated a tow truck, they expected us to be able to help them."

"Cars don't have these types of locks."

"This is just the end of the natural progression of experimentation once you begin playing with locks."

Stormsong laughed, and the lock bleeped as it unlocked.

The body-admittance area was all bare cement, easy to hose down. The place smelled like a hospital, only worse, and their footsteps echoed weirdly.

There seemed to be no one there. It was perfect that the place was deserted, but it was also spooky. The actual morgue was through a series of locked doors that she had to hack the security to get open. She left the doors unlocked behind her so they could leave quickly.

The morgue was one giant walk-in freezer. The door opened to the solid smell of decomposing flesh. There were banks after banks of smaller doors to the drawers that held the actual dead people. The cold made Tinker's skin goose bump over.

What a smart idea: visit the morgue. Who knew it would be so big?

But it made sense. The Pittsburgh area had once had a population in the millions. Considering they were in the middle of a war, the large facility was probably a good thing, too.

She so didn't want to start opening drawers. There were dead naked strangers inside. Only way it could be worse was if they weren't strangers. Gods, surely by now Nathan was safely buried.

Tinker scanned the freezer doors. She was really hoping for labels identifying who was where. The drawers were only numbered. Apparently there was a computerized list somewhere. It would be quicker to open and look than find a computer, hack through its security, and then figure out their filing system.

She just hated how icky it was going to be. It did not help that her Hand looked as freaked out as she felt. From what Windwolf told her in the past, elves had very little experience with the dead. Counting her grandfather, she had known more than a dozen people that died of old age. Morgues, funerals, and graveyards were human territory.

At least when she cracked open the first drawer, she found herself looking down at a bag-shrouded face and not bare feet. She should probably get gloves on and a mask.

After the first dozen or so times, she kind of got used to unzipping the bag and finding someone dead underneath the heavy plastic.

A systematic search was going to take forever. It took longer than she expected to pull out a drawer, unzip the bag, verify that it wasn't an elf inside, zip it back up, and get the drawer back into place with the door closed. It was going to take hours, and every minute they spent at the morgue increased the risk of being caught.

Tinker was reconsidering taking the time to hack their computer system when she realized that Pony and Stormsong were in full Shield mode; close enough to her to cover her with their protective spells, hands riding on their swords, their focus toward the front door. "What is it?"

"Someone is coming," Stormsong said.

"Shit," Tinker whispered.

Tinker heard footsteps nearing, and a moment later the far door opened. "Hello?" a woman bellowed, and only when she yelped, "*Nae, nae, nae*! Scarecrow! Call off your dogs!" did Tinker recognize Esme's voice.

"Hold!" Pony called to the others.

Esme came stomping up the hallway, ignoring the elves now that they had stood down. It was still weird looking at Esme and knowing that she was her mother. Due to a fluke in the hyper-phase gate design, Esme had spent all of Tinker's life stuck in one moment in time and hadn't aged. She was still only a few years older than Tinker. Like Lain, Esme was a head taller than Tinker could ever hope to get, boyishly thin, and, judging by the color of her eyelashes, a pale blonde under the purple hair dye. Despite a week of hospital rest, Esme looked haggard. She still wore her torn, bloody, and soot-smudged jumpsuit.

"I keep running into you at the strangest places," Esme said. "What are you doing here, Scarecrow?"

If Tinker ever heard a stupid question, that was it. *Breaking into the morgue* was so blatant, it had to be obvious. "I've got official business here. What are you doing here?"

"Last I checked," Esme said, "I'm here because a snarky elf princess landed me in Pittsburgh."

Tinker shook her finger at Esme in frustration. "I saved your ass."

"Yes, you did." Esme scrubbed at her face as if she was exhausted. "I'm sorry; it's all just hitting me hard. Everything I've been working for is over and done, and I'm here, and I'm not going to be stuck out in space, trying to piece together a life on whatever was left of a colony on the other side of the galaxy that's been hit by a major disaster. I'm stuck on Elfhome—in a city that's been hit by a major disaster—so there's sixty thousand humans instead of a few hundred—and there's oni and tengu and a talking dragon. And last week was eighteen years ago."

Tinker winced. It hadn't occurred to her that Esme was facing such a wrenching mental readjustment. The tengu had been taking it all in stride, but they knew about the tengu, oni, and talking dragon going in. When all was said and done, Esme had risked her life to save countless others.

"I don't want to talk about what I'm doing here," Tinker admitted reluctantly. "Because it could get me killed."

"Oh." Esme's eyebrows knitted into worry. "Maybe you should just leave. I had a bad dream."

"You dreamed about *domi*?" Pony asked, making Tinker realize that they'd been speaking Elvish with a smattering of English.

Esme shook her head. "No. I—I've been looking for someone. I had a dream about the place where he used to live. I dreamed of him running through the big empty rooms, laughing in hazy sunlight, and when I woke up in the hospital, it suddenly hit me that I could see him. I never thought I'd actually get to see him, and I just about lost it when I realized I would."

"Him?" Tinker was feeling slightly betrayed. Esme realized that eighteen years had past and went looking for an old lover? Did she even remember she had left a kid behind?

Esme gave a laugh that edged along mania. "When I checked out of the hospital, I had some vague plan of calling my sister, but I just kept walking and walking. I hiked the whole way to the island. The place is in ruins—no one has lived there for years. The place looks like it was ransacked. There were pencil marks and dates on the wall—a record of him getting taller and taller—and then five years ago, it just stops!"

Tinker's grandfather must have only told Esme that he was calling his grandchild Alexander Graham Bell. Esme was looking for a son. From the sound of it, Esme had gone to the abandoned hotel on Neville Island where Tinker had grown up. After their grandfather died, Oilcan had talked her into moving to McKees Rocks. He moved their grandfather's books and files to safe storage, leaving behind all their childhood clutter, and boarded shut the hotel.

"There were all the little bits of him scattered around," Esme said wistfully. "Little toy robots and model airplanes and one hallway that had tiny little handprints all up and down it in blue paint—okay, that was kind of *Blair Witch* creepy—but it was his hands. And he had the constellations done in glow-in-the-dark paint on his ceiling—just like I had when I was a kid."

Lain had helped Tinker paint the stars, muttering darkly, "Nature or nurture?"

"He was everywhere and nowhere," Esme whispered. "And that's when I really did lose it."

All of which Tinker could have prevented if she had just told Esme the truth when they were on the *Dahe Hao* together. "I'm sorry."

"I cried myself to sleep on his bed." Esme walked to one of the morgue drawers and pressed her hand to the stainless-steel door. "And then I dreamed where I'd find him."

"What? Oh, no, no, no." Tinker moved to stop her, but Esme opened the door and pulled out the drawer. "You don't need to—"

There was something horribly wrong about the shrouded body inside. The hidden geography was all too short and lacking in landmarks: the peak made by the nose, the valley of the throat, the distant points of the feet. Esme unzipped the bag in one rushed motion, like she was getting it done fast before she chickened out.

It was the male child that the oni had butchered down to eat—a gruesome collection of parts. Laid out like a half-assembled jigsaw puzzle, it was made more horrifying by what was missing.

Esme whimpered and stumbled backward.

Despite coming to the morgue to find the murdered children, Tinker wasn't prepared for the sight. She could only stare dazed at the butchered male and remember the smell of roasting meat that hung in the air of the whelping pen's kitchen.

"*Domi*," Pony murmured. "Can we do what is needed and cover it up?"

Tinker blinked up at him, confused for a minute as to why they were there. Oh, yes, DNA samples.

She fumbled with one of the swabs to unwrap it and then forced herself to rub the clean white tip against the bloody stump of a severed arm.

Only as she closed the cap did she realize Esme was silently weeping.

"Oh, Esme, this isn't your son," Tinker said. "This is a male elf child killed by the oni. I was looking for him."

Esme shook her head. "I dreamed that I'd find him here. I opened the drawer and there he was—newborn like when I left Earth—crying. It's him."

Stormsong snorted. "You've flung wide open a door that's not easy to keep closed in the first place. Your blood tie to *domi* means that her *nuenae* can easily overlap yours. The more you interact with her, the more her *nuenae* will transpose yours."

Esme wasn't listening. "He's here!" She walked halfway down the row of doors and opened another drawer, seemingly at random. "And he's helpless—and flying monkeys are coming for him."

"Oh gods, I thought we were done with that shit," Tinker whimpered. Esme had driven her nearly mad by invading Tinker's dreams, calling for help through the only line of communication available to the astronauts trapped in space. It had been an insane week full of prophetic nightmares. Again and again, Tinker had found herself facing a twisted echo of something she had dreamed. She so didn't want to go through that again.

Esme unzipped the body bag to reveal the young elf female.

Tinker groaned at the sight of the child. None of the dead humans had been battered into broken bones held together with torn flesh. Tinker's hand shook as she swabbed the inside of the female's mouth, trying to ignore that her jaw had been broken so badly that the bones had pierced the skin and half her teeth were missing. Tinker murmured apologies as she plucked a few strands of hair free, just in case.

"What are you doing?" Esme asked.

"I'm trying to figure out why the oni kidnapped these children," Tinker explained. "Only, establishing DNA baselines is the first step of bioengineering magic—which is highly illegal, even for me."

"We should hurry," Pony said. "If someone else is coming."

"There's one more," Tinker told Esme. "A second male. Can you find him, too?"

Esme frowned but nodded. She concentrated for a minute before picking a third drawer on the other side of the room.

Taking samples from the second male was even more emotionally wrenching. His face was relatively undamaged, and he reminded Tinker of Oilcan. Suddenly she couldn't bear to be in the room, wearing the gloves and the mask, breathing in the omnipresent reek of rotting flesh. She fled out of the room, blinking back tears, desperately tearing at the gloves with latex-encased fingers.

Pony wordlessly caught her hands with his and pulled the gloves free and then held her until the need to scream and throw things passed.

"They shouldn't be here," Tinker growled. The children had been innocent and trusting and had forever ahead of them; they shouldn't be locked in these little boxes, surrounded by death.

"No, they should not. They be should be given up to the sky so their souls can be free of their bodies."

"What do you mean? How do we give them up to the sky?"

"They should be cremated as soon as possible. To be trapped in a dead body is torment to the soul."

Tinker remembered then that most elf ghost stories started with someone dying and not being properly cremated. "How—how do I make this happen? Who takes care of these things?"

"Normally their clan." Pony reluctantly added, "But none of the Stone Clan would know how."

"Are you sure about that?" Tinker muttered.

"I did not know that you locked your dead into steel drawers," Pony admitted unhappily. "I would have not known how to find this place even if I had known that was your custom."

Tinker wanted to argue that any of the elves could ask Maynard for directions, but Pony had a point. The Stone Clan might have assumed that the children's bodies had been automatically cremated by the humans once they'd been recovered from the whelping pens.

"Someone is coming." Stormsong moved between Tinker and the door.

"It's the flying monkeys," Esme whispered and wisely moved back, giving the *sekasha* lots of room to move.

Tinker doubted very much it was literally flying monkeys. Riki had been the last person associated with that imagery. He had saved her life two or three times during the week of insane dreams. He had also kidnapped her twice. Tinker hid away the swabs in the messenger bag, freeing up her spell-casting hand.

She listened closely but could hear nothing. The *sekasha*, though, shifted as they tracked someone moving through the otherwise empty building.

Pony signed a question in blade talk.

Stormsong lifted up one finger then indicated that the sole invader was just beyond the last door. They stood tense for a long silence and then the doorknob slowly turned and the door creaked opened.

TV reporter Chloe Polanski stood in the doorway, eyes narrowing as she took in Tinker and the *sekasha*. She was in a flawless black pantsuit belted with a wide swatch of alligator leather. After a moment of calculating study, her predatory smile slid into place. "You're so much easier to catch now, Vicereine. What are you doing here so late at night?"

Oh gods, could it get any worse? By tomorrow, everyone in Pittsburgh could know that Tinker was taking DNA samples.

Pony drew his *ejae*, his face set to a cold warrior death mask. Taking their cue from her First, the others drew their swords.

Yes, it could get worse. Tinker couldn't lie in front of the *sekasha*. If she told Chloe about the DNA scans, her Hand would probably kill the reporter to keep her from spreading the information. Time to dance on the razor-sharp edge of truth.

"Several children of the Stone Clan were killed by oni." Tinker frantically signed *hold* in blade talk. "Their bodies were brought here by mistake. Well, not really a mistake, but elves see storing the dead like this as a torture to the soul. I need to find someone that can cremate the children so their souls are released from their bodies—tonight, if possible."

Yes, as of this moment, that's the new plan, I'm not lying.

Chloe's smile faded several notches. "The coroner and his staff are currently swamped with the oni dead from yesterday. They've set up a mass grave beyond the Rim. I doubt if you can get the bodies officially released tonight."

That would explain why the morgue was so empty.

"I don't need to have them *officially* released." Tinker waved that aside; she was *domi* after all. "I just need someone that can burn the bodies. Tonight."

Get rid of the evidence. Good plan. Who would know about cremation? Lain would.

Lain answered on the first ring with worry in her voice. "Are you okay?"

"I'll have to get back to you on that." It was not a good sign that apparently both Esme and Lain were seeing bad things in store for Tinker. "When you had my grandfather cremated, who did you call?"

"McDermott's in McKees Rocks." Lain didn't ask why; she simply supplied the phone number. Did she already know or did she just stop asking awkward questions when Tinker descended on her with weirdness? "When you see my sister, bring her to me."

Tinker sighed.

"Ladybug." Lain used the "you will obey" tone.

"Okay, I will."

Chloe's smile vanished completely as Tinker dialed McDermott's. "You—you can't just take them."

"Yes, I can. The coroner's office has no jurisdiction over elves—dead or alive." A man picked up the line, identifying himself as Allen McDermott. "Yes, this is Tinker *ze domi*, head of the Wind Clan. Can you come to the morgue? I have three bodies that need to be cremated."

Tinker hung up before the annoying questions on authorizations could start.

Chloe reached into her suit pocket and pulled out her eyepiece. "This is a clear abuse of power. You can't just walk—"

Chloe froze, her eyes going wide as Esme suddenly stepped out of the shadows with a gun leveled at the reporter.

"I don't know who you are, although you look very familiar..." Esme trailed off, cocking her head.

"You've probably seen me on television." Chloe held up her eyepiece as explanation. "Pittsburgh only has three TV stations."

"Put it away," Esme growled. "And stay away from my kid."

"You have a child?" Chloe paled.

"Alexander Graham Bell is my—"

"Daughter," Tinker said to cut off any confusion, since she was fairly sure Chloe—if not all of Pittsburgh—knew her real name by now.

"Daughter?" Esme glanced sharply at Tinker.

"You're Captain Shenske's daughter?" Chloe gave Tinker a horrified look.

"Yes, I'm her daughter." Tinker stayed focused on Chloe, not wanting to see how her mother took the news. Why, though, was it so upsetting to Chloe? It wasn't like she was suddenly getting a daughter dumped in her lap.

"Fine. I'll stay away from her." Chloe backed out the door.

Tinker really wanted to bolt out of the room on Chloe's heels instead of turning around and facing Esme.

She made Lain lie to me. She drove me nearly insane.

With that smoldering anger stoked back to a flame, Tinker turned back to Esme.

Esme was giving her a befuddled look, as if Tinker's words had sunk in but hadn't made any sense. "Wait! What?"

"I'm Alexander Graham Bell." Tinker pointed to herself. "I'm your daughter."

"Scarecrow?" Esme said faintly.

"Daughter," Tinker said. "As in: not a boy."

Esme shook her head. "But—but—you're an elf!"

"Well, that's a little more complicated to explain," Tinker allowed.

Explanation had to wait, though, as city officials descended on them, responding to anonymous phone calls about "someone stealing bodies from the morgue." Chloe must have started calling in strike forces before she even left the building. The police showed up first, followed by the deputy mayor and three city council members for reasons that Tinker couldn't fathom except maybe that they were pigheaded enough to argue with Tinker. Someone made the mistake of contacting Maynard, who was out with Prince True Flame, which led to the Wyverns getting involved.

The sudden incoming wave of red made Tinker's heart hammer in her chest. If the Wyverns found the DNA swipes, things could go ugly quickly. She casually swung her messenger bag with the swipes back behind her so it was hidden from view.

"I will deal with them, *domi*," Pony murmured.

That was what she was afraid of: he would only

tell them the truth. Her fear must have shown on her face as he gave her a slight smile.

"Don't worry," he whispered. "You have taught me that truth is a weapon to wield carefully."

She had? That made her feel weirdly guilty. Pony embodied a hundred years of perfection: corrupted by her in one hectic summer. She nodded, trusting him.

Signing to Cloudwalker to take his place as Shield, Pony intercepted the incoming Wyverns. Their conversation was in machine-gun High Elvish, rattling out faster than Tinker could follow. She focused on keeping the undertaker from McDermott's from leaving empty-handed.

"The coroner would tell you—if he were here—that he doesn't have any jurisdiction over elves—alive or dead." Tinker stood firm on her strongest argument, then pushed on to points she wasn't as sure about. "I'm the Vicereine of the Westernlands." At least that's what people kept telling her. "That means I do have jurisdiction over all elves—not just the Wind Clan." As far as she could tell, that's what it meant. She was going with that until someone told her otherwise. "These children have suffered enough. It's time they are decently put to rest."

"The elves have their laws," the councilwoman said. "And we have our own laws and procedures. We're tired of having your people walk all over our rules. This is still our city."

Her people? Had they forgotten she was a Pittsburgh-born human until Mid-Summer's Eve? And this wasn't about who owned the city but basic decency. "Do you have any kids?"

"Yes, a little boy."

"If your boy died outside the city, on Elfhome, you'll be happy with letting the elves do whatever they want to his dead body? Let it lay out where the animals could eat him? Stuff and mount him?"

The woman gasped with outrage. "They wouldn't dare—"

"That's what you're doing to their children! Locking those kids up in boxes is an abomination on the level of having your boy taxidermied."

"Waiting until tomorrow morning will not make any differ—"

Tinker hadn't noticed that the Wyverns had left the room until they came sweeping back in from the morgue. They projected extremely pissed off, which was good, because they were talking High Elvish full tilt; she suspected none of the humans were following. Unfortunately, they were aiming their conversation at her.

"Forgiveness, I don't understand." Tinker looked to Pony for help.

"They demand that you have the children given to the sky immediately."

Tinker turned to the humans, who thankfully spoke enough Elvish to understand Pony. "Okay, are you going to do what I asked or do *you* want to tell the Wyverns that they need to wait until tomorrow?"

Luckily none of them were totally stupid as well as pigheaded.

Remembering her promise to Lain, Tinker dragged Esme along on the impromptu procession to the funeral home. Her mother hadn't said anything during the entire three-ring circus; she only watched Tinker in unnerving silence. The silent treatment continued even once they were safely isolated in the Rolls-Royce. Tinker figured that Esme was angry that Tinker hadn't explained their connection the first time they met.

"You're the one that popped me in the easy-bake oven and skipped town," Tinker grumbled, slumping down in the front seat between Pony and Stormsong. "If anyone has the right to be pissed off, it's me."

Esme sighed in the backseat. "I knew that the oni would kill every last human in Pittsburgh if Leonardo Dufae didn't have an heir to his genius, a brilliance that could close the door that he opened. So I found your grandfather and talked him into using Leo's sperm to make—to make you. And I knew that I needed to save Jin Wong, so I had to jump through the gate."

Anyone else probably would have just tried talking Lain into leaving Pittsburgh. Lain, though, needed Elf-home like she needed air. Esme couldn't simply move her sister to the safety of Earth; she needed to make Pittsburgh safe. The route she took seemed insane, but it was hard to argue with the proven success of it.

Still, Tinker tried. "So you just handed over an egg and took off? Didn't you even bother to find out your baby's gender?"

In the rearview mirror, Tinker saw Esme flinched as if struck. "No, it wasn't like that. At first, yes, you were just Leo's heir, but then I started to realize that I might not survive the crash, and, if I did, I wasn't ever returning to Earth. You would be all that was left of me after I was gone. You stopped being Leo's child to me. You became mine. You became precious to me."

"No, you thought you had a son. I'm in no way precious to you."

"Yes, you are." Esme leaned forward over the seat to pinch Tinker's cheek. "And you're so much cuter than I ever imagined."

"Oh, gee, don't do that."

Stormsong caught Esme's hand and twisted it hard enough to get a yelp of pain. "I don't care who you are, you will respect *domi*."

"Okay!" Esme sat back, rubbing her hand. "Now, exactly how did you end up an elf princess?"

Tinker started with saving Windwolf's life during Shutdown just before Mid-Summer's Eve and everything that followed. Well—not *everything*—she'd been embarrassingly clueless through many points. Just because Esme was her mother didn't give her rights to a full confession. Tinker got detoured back to the first time she saved Windwolf—the day Blue Sky's father died—when she made an offhand mention about the magical tie she had thought existed between her and Windwolf.

"It happened so fast that my memories are blurred and disjointed. Everyone was running and screaming. There was a big tri-axle Mack dump truck sitting at the edge of the faire ground, and I scooted under it. The saurus pinned Lightning Strikes to the ground beside the truck and was tearing him in half." Tinker shuddered at the memory. "I don't know what I was thinking—I was thirteen and about ninety pounds dripping wet—but I tried to kill it with a tire iron. Not my best plan."

"You saved Wolf," Pony murmured. "He was unconscious next to Lightning Strikes."

"I didn't see him at the time." Tinker laughed. "All

my attention was taken up by a pissed-off saurus trying to dig me out from under the dump truck. When I did finally see Windwolf, I thought he was mad at me. His first words to me were 'Fool, it would have killed you.' It wasn't a very romantic first meeting."

"And this magical tie?" Esme asked.

They were crossing the McKees Rocks Bridge, so Tinker made a long story shorter. "That's just something Tooloo made up. She's an elf that has a small farm at the end of this street." Tinker pointed in the direction of Tooloo's.

"I know Tooloo," Esme said.

Tinker supposed that shouldn't surprise her, but it did. Lain and Tooloo seemed to have a weird unspoken agreement that they would keep to their respective neighborhoods as much as possible. She had assumed that Esme would know only the places that Lain frequented. "Tooloo taught me everything I know about elves, but I'm finding out that she was lying about half of it. The whole 'magical tie' was a way to keep me away from Windwolf."

"She was trying to keep you safe," Esme said. "She knew what kind of danger lay in store for you."

"How the hell would she know?" Tinker snapped. "Did you tell everyone but me who I really was?"

Esme shook her head. "Tooloo is the one that taught me how to control my dreams."

It was totally unfair that at that moment they arrived at McDermott's and Tinker had to go back to being ringmaster. Much as she wanted to grill Esme on Tooloo, she had to focus on the cremation.

McDermott's was a big Victorian mansion full of

dead stillness and memories Tinker thought were long forgotten. Once inside, she remembered the floor plan, the big rooms with stuffed chairs lining the walls and the painful smell of roses and age.

McDermott had endless forms he wanted signed guaranteeing he'd get paid and not arrested by the EIA. He also insisted she tour a room filled with coffins of oak and steel, making it sound like the law required a coffin for cremation. Considering the elves' reaction to the drawers at the morgue—their horror at the idea of "locking the bodies in steel boxes"—the coffins were probably a bad idea. She managed to frighten McDermott into admitting that the coffins were optional and that cardboard boxes were acceptable. She talked him into forgoing even the boxes with assurances that no one would press charges. All the details, though, made her realize how much Lain had quietly taken care of when Tinker's grandfather had died.

Start to finish, the cremations would take a good part of the night. Even though McDerrmott's had four furnaces (a number that slightly boggled her mind,) it would take more than two hours to render the bodies to ash, and then several hours more for the ashes to cool enough to be safely handled. She stayed only long enough to see the bodies safely loaded into the furnaces and talked the Wyverns into standing guard the rest of the night. Tinker wanted to stay in motion so Chloe's strike forces couldn't corner her again. She didn't need witnesses while getting the DNA from the living children—although she wasn't sure how she was going to do that without raising questions.

Back in the Rolls-Royce, Esme proved she had

used the time that Tinker had been distracted to piece together the logical end to Tinker's story. "So, you and Windwolf fell in love and he used magic to change you into an elf?"

"That's the basic gist of it." Tinker was glad she didn't have to go into details.

Esme cocked her head. "What I don't get is why you would be in trouble if you'd been caught at the morgue."

"Collecting DNA smacks of spell-working," Tinker quoted Stormsong.

"So, why is it illegal for you do something that simple when Windwolf is going around doing wholesale transformation?"

Tinker sighed. "Technically, it isn't illegal. The problem is political maneuvering shit. The Stone Clan are being asses."

Esme nodded as if that made perfect sense.

Pony hadn't asked where they were going when they left the funeral home, proof of his nervousness around the Wyverns. He stopped the car at the end of the McKees Rocks Bridge—a good, safe two miles from the Wyverns—to wait for Tinker to choose a direction.

Take the three swabs and Esme to Lain? Track down the other children with Esme still in tow? Surely the less people involved, the better, but the whole deadly trinity of Esme, Lain, and Tooloo could derail Tinker when time was against her. Not Lain's then—and she needed a cover story for tracking down the children and sticking things in their mouths.

"Let's go to Poppymeadow's," Tinker told Pony, and he turned the big gray car toward the gleaming city instead of taking the dark, twisting roads up to the observatory.

"So, you're an elf with all the bells and whistles?" Esme asked.

Tinker nodded.

"And you wanted this?" Esme said it as if worried that Tinker been transformed against her will, or, worse, she had been desperate to be an elf.

Tinker realized her Hand were all listening intently. She had never considered before how they might feel about Windwolf using the nearly forbidden magic to change her. They must have been in full agreement with his decision or they would have stopped him. It was weird knowing that they had gone so against their principles to allow Windwolf to do the spell. They had all been nameless strangers to her then. She couldn't even remember who had been with Windwolf the night he took her to the hunting lodge and changed her. It was a testament of how much they trusted Windwolf.

It seemed dangerous to admit she didn't know what Windwolf had planned. It was her stupidity, not his. And yet she couldn't lie—not to her Hand. They deserved the truth.

"I still don't have a full grasp on what Windwolf was offering me," she said cautiously. "It's too big. I haven't lived long enough to understand the limits of a human life to really wrap my brain around being an elf. I know, though, I have forever now to be with people I love." Pony reached out and took her hand and laced his fingers with hers. "Besides, the bells and whistles are pretty cool."

"Bells and whistles." Esme stared out the window at the night-shrouded city. The streetlights overhead spilled light across her again and again as they drove through the dark streets. "The spell that Windwolf used—could it make anyone perfect as the *sekasha* yet able to use the *domana* spells?"

All the *sekasha* laughed at the question. Pony answered for her Hand. "You cannot see the world as black and white and in color at the same time."

"In theory, though, someone could be godlike?" The light slid through the car and left Esme in shadows.

"We would not allow it," Pony said. The others were so much in agreement that they didn't even nod. "That is what the Skin Clan wanted: to be gods in flesh. We did not hunt them down for thousands of years just for someone else to replace them."

"Sparrow said something about that the night she kept me from escaping the oni," Tinker said. "She said that the Skin Clan had taken elves from one step above apes to one step below gods. She thought the elves were stagnating. She wanted to go back to the old ways."

"What a fool," Pony growled. "The reason we're tall, fair, and immortal is that, in the beginning, the Skin Clan could only improve their bloodline by breeding with us after they had *improved* us." His loathing for how the Skin Clan had genetically screwed over the elves was obvious in his voice. "They couldn't introduce a weakness into our stock without fear of passing it on to their children. After they became immortal, though, they eventually stopped caring about their bloodline; they only wanted to enhance themselves. They created spells that allowed them to safely manipulate their own DNA. They could experiment with us until they found a desirable trait and then duplicate it in themselves. We would have become as twisted as the oni if we had not killed them all."

"Sparrow must have seen the oni as a replacement for the Skin Clan," Tinker said. "I suppose it made sense for her to work with them; she wanted to be made *domana* caste. I don't understand, though, why the Stone Clan *domana* would be working with the oni."

"Wait, what's this?" Esme asked. "They're working *with* the oni?"

Oops. "I told you that they were being asses," Tinker grumbled. "We think—but can't prove—that the Stone Clan lured those children to Pittsburgh and all but handed them over to the oni."

"That's—that's brutal! Why?"

"We don't know," Tinker said. "But I'm going to find out."

17: GIVE ME A BEAT

Oilcan missed the start of the war. He wanted to believe that the tengu had started it, intentionally or not, with a simple show of inhuman speed and strength. More likely, Team Tinker, knowing full well what a scumbag Riki had been, decided that Pittsburghers (meaning humans) weren't going to be outdone by tengu. Certainly showing superiority by going faster fit the mentality of hoverbiker racers. Team Tinker took over cleaning the third floor and trash started to fly out the window, sans chute, as if fired from a confetti cannon. The tengu picked up the challenge and responded with a massive outpouring of trash from all the windows of the second floor. When Team Tinker realized that the tengu were outdoing them simply because the tengu outnumbered the humans, they must have started to call in reinforcements, because soon half of Pittsburgh descended on the school.

The elves at the enclaves would have had to be blind to miss the activity. While they arrived late, the elves made up for it with millennia-practiced teamwork. They plowed through the front door bearing brooms and mops like spears. They took over the foyer and spread outward in all directions, herding the tengu in front of them.

It was only a matter of time before the tengu collided with the humans and things turned violent. Oilcan had lost any pretense of control shortly after Windwolf dragged him off for the talk. In hopes of cutting the tension, he tried to coax Merry into getting out her *olianuni* and playing. Her music, he hoped, would remind everyone that they were working to help the kids, not outstrip the other groups.

"Oh, *sama*, I've never played all by myself." Merry was peering up the foyer staircase where voices were raised in anger. "I—I don't know . . ."

He needed her playing well from the start, not going into a downward spiral from nervousness. He would need to take the lead and let her follow him the best that she could.

Oilcan went out to his pickup and got his Stratocaster and his sixty-watt amp from behind the bench seat. Luckily the gym had been cleared by the tengu and the hardwood floors scrubbed clean by the elves until they gleamed, smelling of lemon polish. If you ignored the bullet holes gouged into the walls, it was a perfect venue. He plugged in his amp, jacked in his guitar, and started into the melody for "America."

"*Sama*!" Merry's eyes went huge and her hands slowly crept up to cover her heart as if she were afraid it would burst out of her chest. "You—you're an artisan?"

Oilcan laughed. "No, no, I can play well enough to get by. Moser is an artisan. But come on, play with me."

At that point she couldn't unpack her instrument fast enough. Looking like a bastard child of a xylophone and steel drum, the *olianuni* wrapped around Merry with twice the range of a piano but played like a percussion instrument. The low notes rumbled like thunder and the high notes chimed, and it jammed like heaven with his Stratocaster.

It was hard to imagine anyone calling Merry's playing just adequate. She glowed as she played, her mallets a blur. As she warmed up, she added mad flourishes with her mallets on the upswing and little yips of excitement. He started with the songs he was fairly sure she knew, those he had glimpsed in her hand-scribed songbook. He had been hoping that she could just keep up with him, but she outstripped him. Encouraged, Oilcan launched into songs that Windchime had been most familiar with and thus most likely taught her.

Almost as if their songs summoned them, the members of *Naekanain* appeared. Snapdragon showed up with his tribal drums, Moser with his bass guitar, and Briar with a bottle of ouzo, and they really let loose, tearing into the human-elf fusion of music that was uniquely Pittsburgh. As always, Moser's deep growl of English and bastardized Low Elvish was electrifying against Briar's angelic High Elvish. As they played, more and more people drifted into the gym to listen.

Oilcan was glad to see that the growing audience was all three races, although they still kept to separate camps. The tengu with their backless tank tops and unruly short black hair perched on the bleachers. Elves, looking ethereal even while leaning on brooms, their glorious long hair braided with ribbons, kept to the back of the room. Humans gathered close to the music, varied as snowflakes: short and tall, thin and wide, ugly and beautiful, white and black and Asian.

"You should have charged a cover for this," Moser shouted at him as Snapdragon and Merry blasted into an instrumental duet that was more like a duel of speed.

"They paid with labor," Oilcan shouted back.

"No food?" Moser pouted.

"There is food." Tinker appeared out of the crowd, carrying a basket fragrant with the scent of meat dumplings. A great deal of food, considering the number of Poppymeadow's people behind her bearing baskets.

"Coz!" Oilcan bumped shoulders with her in greeting. She bumped him back with a grin. She was dressed down in T-shirt and shorts, looking the most like herself in months. She had her five bodyguards with her, although for some odd reason they all had cat whiskers drawn on their faces.

"You always were my favorite." Moser swung his guitar onto his back and snatched the basket out of Tinker's hands.

"What about the next set?" Oilcan cried. While he was glad to see Tinker, her arrival certainly was triggering a shift in the audience. All three groups were moving in, trying to be as close to her as her Hand would allow. He knew that the humans were peeved that the elves had "stolen" their girl. To the elves she was *domi* and had "singlehandedly" defeated the dragon that even Prince True Flame couldn't kill. She held the tengu, and judging by the way they looked at her, that mattered a lot to them.

But none of the groups seemed happy about having

to share her. Stopping the music would be bad. But it wasn't like Moser was being paid to perform beyond the food that Tinker had just handed him.

"Sing your cousin that new song you wrote for her," Moser said.

"You wrote me a song?" Tinker squealed.

"Bastard," Oilcan snarled at Moser. He hadn't told Moser that the song was about Tinker, but the words were obviously inspired by her.

Moser backed away with the basket. "You said I butchered the words anyhow!"

"You wrote me a song?" Tinker said. "You never wrote me a song before."

Oilcan had written lots of songs about Tinker; he'd just never shared them with anyone. The lyrics ranged from angry to loving to overprotective, depending on his mood, and once the moment was passed, the words felt too dangerous. What if Tinker thought he was always that angry with her? How badly would she take (because she would take it badly) the rant against her self-centered obsessive curiosity—especially since the whole thing with Nathan had ended so badly? And gods forbid, someone got the wrong idea about the whole "crawl into my bed, hold me tight, and make me feel all right" that he wrote when he was ten and she was six.

Tinker smacked him. "Don't you dare say no if you sold it to Moser."

"Okay, okay, I'll play it." He had sold it because it felt safe—mostly because it wasn't about his relationship with her. He wasn't sure, though, how she would take it. He led into the melody so Merry had a chance to learn it. "It changes though, watch for it, and—and improvise."

Merry laughed and nodded, eyes gleaming with her joy, her face glistening with sweat.

It was started as a ballad duet in High Elvish between him and Briar. He sang of the attack and defense sword movements of a *sekasha* and moved his guitar into rough approximations of the stances. Briar's counter lines were the *domana* shield and attack spells; she moved her hands elegantly through the movements that a *domi* would use to call magic from the clan's Spell Stones. And then the song changed, dropping into something wilder, untamed, and in Low Elvish, speaking of the shared vow of protection, guarding each other, loving each other. Two people, bound together, each determined to protect the other at all cost.

Tinker was burning red with embarrassment, but she was holding tight to Pony's and Stormsong's hands with tears in her eyes. It didn't seem as if she was going to freak out on him. When they went into the chorus the second time, all the elves joined in on Oilcan's bass line, a thunder of approval.

He thought of himself as Wind Clan not just because Windwolf loved Tinker, although that was part of it. He thought of himself as Wind Clan because all of the clan had opened their hearts to his cousin and taken her in, and she loved them back. Her *sekasha* would die for her, and she would die for them, and for that reason Oilcan was Wind Clan.

And maybe that was the key to breaking the tension between the races. The music was only distracting the audience—and only mildly—from their hostility. The songs weren't trying to unify them. What could he use? What would make them feel as if they were part of the whole? The only thing they had in common was Tinker.

He launched into "Godzilla of Pittsburgh." It was strictly instrumental, and its reference to Tinker was obscure. The crowd, though, seemed to recognize her sweeping nature in the music. He thought about all the other songs he'd ever written for Tinker. Like the Godzilla song, they were obscure by their intimate nature. The people that really knew Tinker would recognize her, but this crowd didn't know the real person—they only knew Tinker via secondhand stories.

What songs would suggest Tinker? Songs about hoverbike racing were obvious, since she had all but invented the sport.

He had just launched into the lyrical "Sky Diving" that he wrote about doing the jumps at Chang's racetrack when he realized that Tinker was doing guerrilla-style face-painting attacks on the audience. He watched with confused amusement as she zigzagged about the gym, grabbing random people, pulling them down to her five-foot level, and, lightning quick, drawing cat whiskers on their faces. She pounced on elves, tengu, and human alike—seemingly at random—but after a dozen or so ambushes, he realized that she was cycling through the races, keeping even the number of painted per race. The oddest thing was that she seemed to be purposely ignoring anyone that was paying attention to her and only ambushing those focused on the music. The result was a growing mass of confused decorated people in her wake, gingerly touching their faces, unsure what Tinker had just done to them.

What was she up to?

The crowd, at least, had stopped snarling at each other and was moving with the music. They were seeing Tinker in the song, taking the massive ramps into the jumps, soaring through the air, and free-falling back to earth. Moser joined him, mouth full but hands free, whiskers drawn on his face, for the instrumental bridge. They were tearing down the last stretch when Merry gave a loud meep of surprise. Oilcan glanced behind him to see that Tinker had whiskered a very startled Merry. A wall of *sekasha* kept the rest of the audience from seeing whatever Tinker had done to the little female.

"Fields of Summer." He shouted the next song in the set to Moser and then sidled up to Tinker. "What's with the whiskers, Tink?"

"Prestidigitation." Tinker waved her left hand in a showy flourish—and sketched whiskers on him quickly with her right. "There, you're one of us now."

Oilcan laughed despite the slight alarm that went through him. What was she distracting people from while she drew whiskers on them? As Wind Clan *domi*, she should have been able to command *this* crowd to do just about anything. It probably wasn't something they should discuss in shouts in front of a crowd.

"Fields of Summer" wasn't holding the whole audience. The humans were getting the reference to the ultimate casual in parties: a big empty field, a campfire, and an acoustic guitar for music. The elves and the tengu were drifting away, unfamiliar with the Pittsburgh tradition. Near the door there was a shove that turned into an angry staring match between the fringe of the tengu flock and some incoming *laedin*-enclave guards.

Oilcan scanned the audience, found Riki at the edge

nearest Tinker, watching her with a slight frown. He caught Riki's attention by playing the jarring notes of the song he had only ever shared with the tengu. *Mother's blood on my toes . . .*

Riki's head whipped around, and he gave Oilcan a look of surprise and—oddly enough—hurt. Had it mattered that much that Oilcan had confided with him? That they shared that kind of pain? Oilcan jerked his head toward the brewing fight, and Riki followed his gaze and then nodded.

"What's that?" Moser asked of the melody. "A new song?"

Oilcan shook his head. There was no way he'd play the sorrowful song publicly, especially with the audience on the edge like it was. He needed a song though, one to tie this whole crowd together. An idea of a song went through his head, and he started to fumble through a melody.

Moser quirked up an eyebrow but followed his lead. His frustration with the crowd fed into the tune. Couldn't they just see that despite everything, they were all one people? At the very core, they had to have the same drive as his kids. Pittsburgh wasn't a sane and simple place to live. You had to have a deep need to live here. The melody was defiant and angry, and the words, when they came, were furious.

"Blood on the pavement, blood on the blade, blood flows through common veins." The words poured from somewhere deep inside of him, like they were being torn from his gut. "Three worlds bridged by a single span, steel that climbs from earth to sky. Freedom to create, freedom to fly—one world, one people, one kind. We are Pittsburgh."

When he hit the chorus the second time, they all sang with him.

He and the rest of the band were all panting and dripping sweat and glowing with joy. It was like they had had a long session of really good sex. The humans in the crowd started to call for an encore, but Oilcan's body felt rubbery with the effort to stay standing.

Tinker appeared out of the crowd, bouncing like a mad thing. She couldn't possibly know how cute she looked, because she would have stopped otherwise. She bound up, claimed the microphone, and shouted, "We are Pittsburgh! We are one people!"

The crowd roared, loving her.

"When you see the whiskers on your face and the faces around you, remember! You're not human, elf, or tengu—you're a Pittsburgher! You're one of us!"

They roared again.

"Thank you for all the help you've given my cousin. Now go home."

The crowd laughed and went.

Despite his obvious exhaustion, Moser was still dancing. "This song is mine!" He had unplugged his electric guitar so there was no music to draw the crowd back but he could still strum through the chords of the new song. "I call dibs on it."

Oilcan laughed. "If you can remember the words."

Moser laughed and pulled out his cell phone. "I saw the gears grinding and knew what was coming. I recorded it."

Oilcan high-fived Moser. "Let me hear."

Tinker made a negative sound and gave Moser a

little push. "You start that and you'll be up all night. Go home, let the boy rest."

"I'll write up the score!" Moser promised as Briar grabbed his arm and hauled him out of the gym.

And suddenly it was all over. He had a massive house, five kids, and no idea if he even had a bed for the night. For all he knew, the upstairs was still filled with trash. He sat down on the floor and then went ahead and sprawled out on the smooth wood.

Tinker went off to make sure everyone actually left. She came back a few minutes later and nudged him with her toe. "I'm pretty surc this is a gym, not a bedroom."

"They're right about you being a genius." Oilcan wished he could just sleep there on the gym floor. He had to find out, though, if the kids had someplace to sleep and if they had gotten some of the food that had circulated. Maybe he should pack up the kids and go back to his condo for the night. Then he remembered the *indi*, the chicks, and the puppy. He climbed back to his feet with a groan.

She poked him in the stomach. "You going to be okay?"

He laughed. He had no idea how to answer that truthfully. All day he had the sense of sinking in over his head until he couldn't even see the surface.

"You know—no matter what—we're always going to be family." Tinker leaned her forehead against his shoulder. "You need something and it's mine to give, it's yours."

He knew it to his core, but it was what he needed to hear. "I'll be fine."

✧ ✧ ✧

Only after Tinker had left did Oilcan realize that he had no idea where his kids were. Even Merry had packed up her instrument and disappeared after the music ended; most likely scared off by the *sekasha*'s presence. The electricity was on in the school, but with the exception of the high fixtures of the gym, most of the light bulbs had been smashed. Trying not to panic, he got a flashlight from his pickup and headed up to the third floor that he had deemed "the family rooms." His footsteps echoed through the dark, empty building.

He checked the classroom at the top of the stairs first. It was disappointingly cluttered. Apparently Team Tinker hadn't finished cleaning the third floor. He started to turn away, when he recognized the smell of burnt popcorn. He turned back and panned the flashlight over the room. His microwave sat on its stand just inside the door. Beyond it was his overstuffed recliner and his nightstand.

It wasn't litter in the classroom—it was the furniture from his condo! Someone had moved him lock, stock, and barrel. There were little towers of cans from his pantry, stacks of his ancient DVDs and CDs and Blueray disks, and heaps of clothes still on hangers from his closet. Everything he owned had been carried up and dropped at the first clear place on the floor. His belongings created island chains in the moonlight. His mattress canted against the far wall beside the windows.

"*Sama*?" Cattail Reeds came down the hall, carrying a spell light in one hand and a basket in the other. "Forgiveness, I didn't have time to fix up your room."

"Cattail! Where are the others?"

"Everyone else is asleep." She yawned, waving the spell light back down the hallway toward the other classrooms.

"Did someone bring your beds?" He hated calling them beds, as they were just mattresses and sheets.

"Tinker *ze domi* had them brought from the small place." Cattail had whiskers drawn on her face. He hadn't seen any of the kids in the gym beyond Merry, but Tinker had obviously found them. "She brought food, too."

It was intimidating how much Tinker could get done while acting silly. She had fed his kids and made sure they had someplace to sleep. "Oh, good. How clean are your rooms?"

"That is why we didn't get your room straightened out." She touched the whiskers on her face. "The Wind Clan was helping us clean our rooms. *Ze domi* made sure they were very kind to us. She said that we should think of ourselves as Pittsburghers first, not Wind Clan or Stone Clan."

Oilcan had forgotten to ask Tinker about the true motive behind the whiskers. By Cattail's tone, the concept of "one people" obviously puzzled her, despite having benefitted from it. Sooner or later, he needed to talk to the kids about being sponsored by the Wind Clan or going on alone as Stone Clan. Not now, though; not in the middle of the night when they were both dead on their feet.

"We saved this for you." Cattail held up the basket that smelled of something warm and savory.

"Thank you." He accepted it with guilt twisting in his stomach. He should have been the one making sure that the kids had food, not the other way around.

"Do you need help righting your room?" Cattail asked.

"No, go to bed. I'm going to eat and then go to sleep. We can do it tomorrow."

He thought about the day as he cleared space for

his mattress. The kids had amazed him with their strength. Just hours after being rescued from horrible torture, they had knitted themselves into a family, taking care of each other and working toward a better future. He knew it was in part, though, because they thought they had found a safe haven.

He could remember after his mother had died. It was months before his grandfather knew what happened and could come get him. He was shuffled between foster homes, not knowing what was going to happen to him. By the time he reached Pittsburgh, he was a fearful mess. Only after Tinker had convinced him that she wouldn't let anyone take him away could he get through the night without crying. Whatever courage he had during the day drained away with the light.

The kids wouldn't be doing so well if they realized how tentative their situation really was. He flipped down his mattress and sprawled onto it. The biggest problem was that he knew how tentative it was. It wasn't even that he was human, but that he was only one person. He was anchor rider for Team Tinker, and both he and Tinker had been lucky not to be hurt in the smashups that occurred at the races. The city was at war, and the oni could attack any place, any time. One stray bullet and where would the kids be?

A hand on his shoulder woke him.

Oilcan opened his eyes to darkness, unsure of where he was. Moonlight streamed through too large a window. The bed felt too low but definitely wasn't one of his friends' couches.

"You left all the doors unlocked." Thorne Scratch's rough voice came out of the dark.

"Um, okay." He sat up in bed, remembering then he'd moved into the school down the street from the enclaves. Worried about the kids, he hadn't thought about locking down for the night. "I'll lock them."

"I already have." She sat on his couch to pull off her boots. He was still sleep clouded enough that he didn't realize what she intended until she stood and slid down her leather pants.

She was staying the night.

That afternoon, when he pulled to a stop in front of the school, she had walked away without saying good-bye or if she would be back. He'd figured last night had been a thing born of alcohol and too much pain to bear alone. A momentary lapse of reason not to be repeated.

Perhaps from her perspective, one afternoon apart wasn't enough time separated to warrant a good-bye. Last night, in his apartment, seemed a lifetime ago for him. Since she was hundreds of years old, though, maybe the day had passed in the blink of an eye.

Which made this—what? A continuation of last night? Or was this more than a one-night stand on an epic scale? Could it ever be more than that since he was just human? Did it matter? Honestly, he wanted her there in his arms, strong and fierce and painfully vulnerable.

The sex had all the slow glide of lovemaking, and afterward she pressed a tear-damp cheek to his shoulder as they lay wrapped together.

"He never understood," she whispered mysteriously. "But you do."

He was afraid that if he asked what she meant, she'd realize that she was mistaken.

18: REPERCUSSIONS

Esme walked into Lain's without ringing the ancient hand-cranked doorbell. Tinker stood on Lain's porch, shocked. She'd been taught to ring and wait for Lain to come to the door. *Only uncivilized heathens simply barged into people's homes.*

"Lain!" Esme's voice drifted back as she went down the hallway.

Then again, Lain usually dead bolted her front door, which required ringing the bell to get in. It was odd that it was open in the middle of the night—although all her astronomer neighbors would be awake.

Tinker glanced to Pony. He nodded, his face mirroring her concern. She cocked her fingers into the summoning, and they followed Esme through the dark house.

Lain was all the way back in her dimly lit lab, a pitcher of lemonade and a platter of sugar cookies waiting beside her microscope. "I don't know why I thought that the two of you together could do anything in a timely fashion. God forbid you hurry because someone is waiting."

"Things got complicated," Tinker said in their defense. She signaled to her Hand to stand down.

"Did you tell her?" Lain asked.

Esme laughed at the confusion on Tinker's face as she tried to connect the question to the last six hours of dealing with illegal DNA collection and the cremation of dead children. "Yes, she told me." Esme caught her older sister in a hug. "God, you sound like Mother. You look like her, too."

Lain laughed bitterly. "Mother wouldn't be caught dead without makeup."

"That's true, but you shouldn't be so old."

"I'm lucky to be old," Lain said. "It means I'm still alive."

Which made Esme hug Lain harder.

"Oh, stop that. I'm still angry with you for going off and nearly getting yourself killed."

"I only wanted you safe and happy, Lain."

"Like I could be happy knowing you'd sacrificed yourself for me." Still, Lain relented and hugged Esme back. Tinker felt an unexpected stab of jealousy. Lain kept everyone but Tinker at arm's length. It was surprisingly hard to know that someone else would be receiving her affection. "You're still on my shit list for any number of things."

Esme laughed. "Now you sound like Nana."

"Stop making me older than I am!" Lain studied the whiskers on her face. "Do I want to know?"

"I had to practice my technique for getting DNA unnoticed before trying it out on the unsuspecting." Tinker unpacked the messenger bag of the swabs.

Lain eyed the growing pile with uneasiness. "How many samples did you get?"

"How many swabs did you give me?"

Lain shook her head. "I should have known you wouldn't do it small. Good thing I only gave you a hundred. You do know who you tagged?"

Tinker nodded. "I kept a list." She found the list of names connected to the swab numbers. Between the elves' long names and the need to quickly scribble down the information, she had used a code instead of writing out the full names. "It's kind of cryptic at the moment."

"Cryptic is good." Lain looked torn between glee and worry. "Are you sure you're not going to get into trouble for this? I studied the treaty. If we destroy these without testing, we're in the clear."

Esme laughed. "Oh, none of them seemed to know what hit them."

Tinker scowled at Esme. "The treaty is the least of my worries, and no, don't destroy them. No one seemed to be the wiser." Riki seemed suspicious; he knew better than anyone how much she could pull off in front of witnesses. She doubted, though, that he would talk to the Wyverns about anything he suspected. The tengu needed her safe and sound and protecting them.

Esme continued to smirk at her.

"What?" Tinker asked.

"You just"—Esme made a slight crashing noise and motioned with one hand to indicate something being plowed over—"go right through people. I think it's very funny."

Tinker scowled at her and turned back to Lain, who was gathering up the swabs. "One through three are the dead children. I'm four—just in case you destroyed what you had from me. Five through nine are my Hand. The other four kids are scattered in among the rest. I didn't want it obvious that I was mainly after them. I hit Merry, too—she's another Stone Clan child, but the oni didn't get a hold of her. She's number ninety-five."

"Good. She can stand as a control." Lain stowed the swabs in a drawer and locked it. "I scanned in the spell. I'll have to print off more copies."

Tinker checked the printouts on top of the printer and found that Lain had already printed a dozen copies. "Do you really need the spell? Can't you use your lab?"

"The spell might not be doing something as straightforward as a simple DNA scan. For all we know, it might be predicting what the children's DNA would be if subjected to gene manipulation. We still don't know if the scans you found were from the children, and a traditional lab scan might not produce the same results as the spell."

Tinker nodded, following Lain's logic. "I'll have to talk to the tengu. They might have some clue what oni spell-working—" Tinker frowned at the spell in her hand. "Damn. This is elf magic, too."

"Are you sure?" Lain asked.

Tinker slowly shook her head. "Not really." She handed it to Pony to study. "I've only done a little with healing spells. You and Grandpa were pretty much against me experimenting with them."

"For a good reason," Lain said. "You could have killed someone if you got the spells wrong."

"Yes, and I understood that, so I left them alone. The first one I ever cast was to save Windwolf's life."

Pony was shaking his head. "You are right that

this is Elvish. The command word is ancient Elvish, common to the type that the Skin Clan would have used. I do not know enough about spell-working to recognize this, *domi*. Wolf would know." He caught her look of surprise. "The *domana* are taught their clan's *esva* and spell-working."

She sighed as it reminded her yet again of what she should know but didn't. She wondered if Windwolf was home yet from the daily wild-goose chase of trying to find the oni encampments. She frowned as she realized that the Stone Clan *domana* always joined Windwolf. And this spell was printed from a computer or . . .

Tinker turned to face both Pony and Stormsong. "Did Sparrow know spell-working?"

"No, *domi*," Pony said.

Tinker continued to frown as facts pointed to a logical answer. "Sparrow could drive. Could she work computers?"

Stormsong laughed. "She could drive badly. She could use the telephone with difficulty. Why she made the effort to learn is now obvious, but she hated technology. Computers were beyond her."

Tinker held up the spell. "Who printed off this spell then? I really doubt the Stone Clan knows computers well enough to set up and print a spell."

"The oni could have done it for them," Stormsong pointed out. "The oni would only need one copy of the spell to scan in."

Tinker considered that. Some of the oni forces, especially the ones raised on Earth like the kitsune Chiyo, knew computers enough for it to work that way, but it still didn't seem right. "The timing keeps being off, over and over again. The Stone Clan just got to

Pittsburgh, and True Flame has had them running in tight circles ever since. There has to be someone else other than Sparrow and the Stone Clan. Could there be other *domana* in Pittsburgh?"

Her Hand shook their heads.

"We would know," Pony said. "*Domana* do not travel without notice."

Was that true? Considering that of the several thousand elves in Pittsburgh, only five were *domana*, the *sekasha* might not have trouble keeping track of the entire caste. How many *domana* were there on Elfhome? A couple thousand? A few hundred? Less than a hundred? She needed more data.

"Who else would know spell-working and computers?" Tinker asked. "The healers at the hospice?"

They shook their heads.

"The magic they do is not the same as spell-working," Pony explained.

"Nor are they any more versed in computers than, say"—Stormsong paused to find the perfect analogy—"Wraith Arrow."

Tinker winced, knowing that Windwolf's First was a technophobe. "Who is taught spell-working? Only *domana*?"

They nodded.

She stared at the spell as the insidious suggested itself. Spell-working had been created by the Skin Clan. The oni's greater bloods took spell-working to levels undreamed of on Elfhome. If this was a sample of the oni's magic, and it was elfin, then perhaps the oni greater bloods weren't oni at all. "Is it possible that the Skin Clan escaped to Onihida?"

✧ ✧ ✧

All the dangerous links to spell-working locked away, they drove toward McDermott's in dark, brooding silence. By now the dead children had been reduced to small piles of cold ash. Their betrayal, though, might have been the tip of a massive iceberg.

"We have no proof," Stormsong finally murmured.

Pony was behind the steering wheel. The dash lights gleamed on his profile as he gave Stormsong a hard look.

"The others will want proof," Stormsong said. "We can't take them wild guesses. We will look like babies afraid of the lightning."

Tinker gave her one shaky proof. "How did Sparrow expect to control the oni once the *domana* were overthrown? If the Skin Clan are the greater bloods, then the oni are already under their control."

Pony looked pained as he focused on the dark roads. "*Domi*, if you believe this, then I am sure you are right. Stormsong is also correct in saying that the others will need proof."

Tinker slunk down in her seat, wishing she felt as sure as Pony did. His trust in her was intimidating. "No, I could be wrong. It's just a hunch."

"Your mother is a very strong *intanyai seyosa*." Stormsong used the Elvish name for one who could see the future. "It passes through the female line. You have it to some degree."

Tinker snorted in disbelief.

"I've seen you race, Beloved," Stormsong said. "You were aggressive beyond reason because you let your ability guide you."

It went against Tinker's grain to go without solid proof. Science was about facts, not hunches. This hunch, though, was eating away at her gut.

Stormsong suddenly shouted "Out!" as she threw open the door, caught Tinker by the waist, and flung them both out into the night. They hit the highway hard, Stormsong taking the brunt of the fall, and tumbled on the rough asphalt before Stormsong's shields wrapped around them in brilliant blue. A second later, the Rolls erupted into flame. Tinker screamed in pain and horror as searing heat and deafening noise blasted over them. *Pony!*

Stormsong held her close, muffling Tinker's scream against her shoulder. "Shhh." Stormsong tucked them behind a concrete Jersey barrier. The gas tank burst in a secondary explosion even as random car pieces rained down onto the roadway around them. Thick black smoke rolled up into the night, awash with the blaze of the roaring fire.

Tinker locked her jaw tight against the pain and anguish. Someone had hit the Rolls with a rocket. Had the others reacted in time to Stormsong's warning? Were they safe? There was something wrong with her right arm; it felt like it was on fire. She couldn't make her fingers move. She couldn't summon her shields. The ammo in the trunk started to go off in random cracks of gunfire.

There was movement and Pony was beside them, shields up and face set to cold hardness. Tinker wanted to hug him tight and reassure herself that he was safe. She contented herself with leaning lightly against him. He kissed her on the temple.

Stormsong signed "*no shields*" in blade talk. Pony glanced at Tinker's arm and nodded. In the flickering light from the burning Rolls, he made a motion and Cloudwalker appeared beside him.

"*Attack?*" Cloudwalker asked in blade talk.

Pony shook his head, and signed back, "*Retreat.*"

Cloudwalker frowned and signed a question that Tinker couldn't follow.

Pony shook his head again and repeated firmly, "*Retreat.*"

Obviously if she weren't there, helpless, they would have engaged the oni, but Pony was putting her safety first. She put out her left hand to Pony to get his attention, held up all her fingers, and folded over all but the last two and ended with a question. She wasn't going to leave if the other two were hurt.

He nodded first right and then left, indicating that Rainlily and Little Egret were flanking them.

She nodded her understanding. If her Hand was safe, then she was all for retreating. Cloudwalker sheathed his sword and scooped her up.

She was trying to remember the sign that meant she could walk when they took off running. Stormsong was in the lead, picking the path.

The ambush had hit them in the middle span of Mckees Rocks Bridge. A hundred feet over the Ohio River and no way down except toward one of the banks, over a half-mile away. The smoke masked their escape the first few minutes, and then they were out in the open, only the night to hide them. Gunfire cracked and bullets ricocheted off the pavement at their feet.

"Under!" Stormsong yelled and leaped off the bridge.

Pony followed without a pause, and a second later Cloudwalker leapt, still carrying Tinker. She gasped, trying not to scream as they fell down toward the river, hundreds of feet below, and then Stormsong and Pony yanked Cloudwalker into the underbracing of the bridge. Something hit hard overhead, exploding in a great thunder of noise, and the steel under them jumped and rattled.

"This way," Stormsong whispered in the darkness.

And they were running again, weaving through the huge girders of the understructure. The others raced forward again and took turns acting as Cloudwalker's hands so he didn't have to shift his hold on Tinker. Years of working as a team let them move silently through the steelwork as if they were a circus act.

She tried to get her bearings in the darkness. They had left an entire Hand of Wyverns at the funeral home. She realized that they were on the wrong side of the bridge in more ways than one. To connect with any of the elf forces, they had to cross a river. They hit the far bank and scrambled up to the road, ironically just feet from where Nathan had died.

False dawn was graying the sky. The streets were empty and still as the *sekasha* ran fast and silent downhill toward the North Shore. Downtown Pittsburgh appeared around the hillside, pale towers in the mist, seeming impossibly far. She wasn't the one running, but she couldn't get her breath.

"She's going into shock," Cloudwalker said.

They stopped in the shelter of an overpass, and Pony pressed his hand to her forehead. It felt like a warm blanket against her skin.

"We need to get her to the hospice quickly," Pony said.

Rainlily swore softly. "That's nearly five miles and on the other side of the river."

"Take me to Lain's," Tinker said. "It's closer."

Stormsong glanced back the way they had come. "No. We have to move, and we have to head into the city."

✧ ✧ ✧

Dawn was a blur light and motion, inexplicable starts and stops, and the sound of gunfire growing loud and more frequent.

There was a sudden crack of rifles, and silence fell.

"Tinker!" Riki's voice came from up high. A moment later he came winging down. "*Domi*! Tinker!"

Pony blocked the tengu male short of Tinker.

"She's hurt?" Riki cried.

"How did you know to come?" Pony growled.

"We have lookouts all over the city. The one in McKees Rocks saw the Rolls go up. How badly is she hurt?"

Pony didn't move out of the way. "We need to get her to the hospice."

"I have a van close by." Riki pointed in the direction of the car.

Pony glared at Riki without answering.

"Pony, trust him," Tinker said.

"Yes, *domi*."

Despite being Wind Clan healers, the hospice staff had always fallen into the "outsiders" range of the *sekasha* trust. The night had just shoved everyone down a couple of notches. Unfortunately, the healers didn't realize the change until they tried to use a pair of scissors on Tinker.

The poor scissor-wielder suddenly found himself facedown on the floor. The following discussion was conducted in loud, fast and ultra-polite High Elvish that Tinker had no hope of following.

"Oh gods, not High Elvish!" Tinker cried. Everything was confusing enough without adding a language she wasn't fluent in. "What happened? Did someone hit him? Why?"

"They want to remove your shirt." Riki seemed to be the only person paying attention to her, even though he was giving the *sekasha* plenty of space. He looked horribly out of place among the elves. He had dismissed his wings, but he was a head shorter than everyone else and the only scruffy-looking one.

It took her a minute to process, but when she realized that they intended to cut her Team Tinker T-shirt off, she objected. Loudly.

"It is just a shirt," Stormsong said.

"It's a very cool, limited-edition shirt."

"No belonging lasts forever." Stormsong took the scissors from the healers. "And technically it's my shirt, so it goes."

It was gone before Tinker could form an alternate plan of dealing with getting it off.

Tinker had gotten to know all the healers at the hospice through one painful misadventure after another. Soothing Breeze of Wind was head of their household. She always seemed amused by how often Tinker managed to hurt herself. As Tinker gained *sekasha*, however, the healer kept her amusement more and more to herself.

At least, Tinker hoped that was why there wasn't even laughter in the female's eyes as she examined Tinker's arm.

"I am so sorry, but it is broken much worse than before." Soothing Breeze used High Elvish but spoke slowly, so Tinker could follow it. "I'm afraid that it will be very painful to treat, *ze domi*." And obviously afraid of the *sekasha*'s reaction to her pain. "It would be best if you let us give you *saijin*."

"No," Tinker growled. "Don't you have something else for pain?"

Soothing Breeze glanced at Pony. Tinker couldn't tell the healer was afraid that Pony would start lopping off heads or hoping that he'd just pin Tinker down and dose her himself. "*Saijin* is by far the safest we can give you. We need to set the bones, brace them straight, and then ink the healing spell into place. It will be long and painful. If you take the *saijin*, you'll sleep through all of it."

Tinker shook her head.

Soothing Breeze took hold of Tinker's broken arm, and pain jolted through Tinker so hard that it seemed like thunder. Tinker whimpered, and all her *sekasha* shifted closer, as if yanked by a string. Cloudwalker put a hand on the healer's shoulder.

"Forgiveness." Soothing Breeze's eyes went wide with sudden fear.

"I'm fine," Tinker hissed. "Let her finish."

"You should just take the *saijin* and sleep through this," Stormsong said in English.

"No," Tinker snapped. "Every time I've turned around this summer, someone has been drugging me with *saijin*. No way I'm going to take it by choice." She made the mistake of glancing at Riki, who had been one of the people that had forcibly dosed her. Once to kidnap her, and another time to keep her from realizing how easily she could escape. Judging by his sorrowful look, he was regretting the experience as much as she did.

The glance also reminded Pony of everything Riki had done to Tinker. He shifted next to the tengu.

"I'm fine," Tinker growled, mostly for Pony's sake.

"Besides, *saijin* gives me nightmares that have the nasty habit of coming true."

Soothing Breeze gave an apologetic look to Cloudwalker. "The pain will get worse."

Oh joy.

"Just do it." Tinker tried to brace herself against the promised pain.

She didn't succeed.

It was like getting hit by lightning. Everything flashed white, and she was only vaguely aware that she had screamed.

When her vision cleared, Cloudwalker had tightened his hold on Soothing Breeze, and Pony had Riki pinned to the far wall with a palm to Riki's chest. At least none of her Hand had drawn their swords yet.

"Leave them alone!" Tinker growled between clenched teeth. Her arm had been a low pulse of pain since she broke it; now it was a hard, agonizing throb keeping time with her heart. A whimper slipped out, and a strongly felt "Shit-shit-shit-shit-shit." If she made the healers continue without drugs, she'd probably just get Riki killed. "Get me the freaking flower."

Pony snapped an order, and one of the other healers fetched the glass jar holding a single large golden bloom of the *saijin* flower.

"Go home," Tinker told Riki, and then, because it seemed abruptly rude after all his help, "Thank you. Oh, and I need to talk to you about greater bloods when I wake up."

Riki nodded, but his eyes were on Pony, who still had him pinned.

"Pony, let him go."

As Riki slipped out the door, Tinker held out her hand for the flower. If she had to take the drug, she was going to administer it herself. The sweet, powerful scent only held bad memories for her. She steeled herself, praying that she wouldn't have nightmares, and breathed deep. Sweet whiteness claimed her.

19: FOR THE WIN

Tommy and his cousins stormed the garage of Team Providence first. The building was completely empty of everything, even dust.

"We just not let them race!" Syn said as Bingo sniffed around the room, trying to find a scent.

Bingo shook his head. "They waited until the *Post Gazette* listed the teams. We provided the list after the teams all paid the entrance fee. The elves would see that as a contractual promise—"

"Fuck the elves." Tommy snarled. "Okay, so to hit all of us at once, there had to be at least twenty of them. Were any of them part of Team Providence?"

His cousins shook their heads.

"Thirty tengu. We only need one. One little bird to sing."

The tengu had at one time been humans who lost their way onto Onihida through natural gateways. Gathered into one mountain tribe, they were conquered by an oni greater blood, who merged the survivors with the crows feeding on the dead. Typical oni stupidity—use what was at hand and not worry about the consequences. Thus the tengu were clever with languages, were attracted to bright and shiny things, and tended to flock together against their enemies. Like Tommy, the tengu had thrown in with the elves during the last battle and won their limited freedom.

The Four and Twenty was the tengu bar in town. On a Friday night, it was crowded with tengu. Wading into it would have been an invitation for a full-out war, with a good possibility that the tengu they wanted was not even in the crowd.

Tommy didn't have his father's talent. Lord Tomtom's ability to pass an army invisibly through a crowd was the reason his father had been chosen to oversee the invasion of Elfhome. Tommy couldn't completely mask a moving object from multiple watchers. With stage props, dark lighting, and concentration, though, he could pass as someone else in a crowded space.

He tore up one of his T-shirts to match the backless style favored by the tengu. With matte black paint, they painted a close approximation to the spell that was tattooed onto the back of every tengu. His black hair needed no work, but he wore a hat pulled low, to cover the fact his nose wasn't a large hooked beak.

He startled Bingo at the door on his way out.

"Tommy?" Bingo sniffed a few times to verify his scent. "Why Riki?"

"He has some influence, so I'm going to use it. Besides, I can nail him cold." They had worked with Riki during the summer, serving as a go-between as Riki spied for the oni. In the confusion following

Lord Tomtom's death, Riki managed to free his baby cousin and break free of the oni. Ironically, it had given Tommy the courage to rebel.

"How are you going to know he's not in the Four and Twenty already?"

"You're going to sniff around the outside first. Still remember his scent?"

"Yeah, I can do that."

Four and Twenty was in the Strip District, giving Tommy reason to suspect that the tengu village was north of Pittsburgh. Tengu would fly in out of the dark on wings of glossy black feathers. With a word, they would cancel the spell that created their wings and walk into the bar. While Tommy masked them from the tengu coming and going, Bingo sniffed around both the front door and the back.

"Riki doesn't seem to be here, Tommy." Bingo drifted back into the shadows across the street. "Be careful. If you need me, just yell."

The bar was crowded but dim. Tommy avoided the bar. The people sitting there looked in too many random directions, and the mirror behind the bartender doubled his danger. Tommy slipped back to the corner of the room, trying to keep focused on his appearance while listening in to the conversations that he passed. He found an empty table without hearing one mention of racing. He wished he could take the hat off; it was muffling his hearing. Still, he could make out conversations that the various parties thought were under the general level of noise. He focused on each discussion around him in turn.

In the corner booth, four males were discussing the weather report for the next day. They made travel arrangements without indicating where they would be heading, but Tommy listened with interest. There were few places in Pittsburgh where tengu would find driving easier than flying. The racetrack was one. He didn't recognize any of them, but as three got up to leave they called the fourth by name. Kenji. Babe's cap bet was placed by a Kenji Toshihiko. Was it the same person?

Tommy caught Kenji as he counted out money for the tab. He slid into the booth and put out his leg, trapping the tengu into his side. Tommy said nothing, only glared, waiting to see if this male knew Riki.

Kenji's eyes went wide. "Shoji, what are you doing here?"

"I've been worried about how things are going." There, nice and vague.

The tengu male got a slightly guilty look on his face that he banished away. *Oh, what is this? Something that Shoji—and ultimately, the spiritual leader—wouldn't like?*

"The city is a powder keg." Tommy poked at the tengu's conscience. "One little thing, and it's going to blow to pieces. If it does, I'm afraid a lot of our people will be hurt."

"Most of our people don't go into the city," Kenji said.

"The race tomorrow is sure to pull some of them," Tommy said.

Again, another guilty look.

"I heard what you've done, and I don't like it," Tommy said.

"Does your uncle know?"

"Not yet."

"It's only the one time. The only ones hurt by the phones going down were the oni brats. It was the only way to sucker them into a big payoff. They wouldn't have taken a big bet at the long odds, and with each small bet, they would have adjusted the odds down."

Damn right he would have. Unlike the people making the bets, Tommy didn't gamble. Only outright fraud like the tengu could have forced him into losing money. He controlled the urge to rip Kenji's throat out. He still had to find out how they planned to win the race.

The waitress came to collect Kenji's bill.

"Let's talk about this where we will not be overheard." Tommy let Kenji lead him out the door, concentrating on keeping his appearance through the crowds. Once outside, he caught hold of Kenji's arm and urged him toward where Bingo was hidden. His cousin gave a wolfish grin but stood silent as Tommy kept him invisible from the tengu. Once they were past him, Bingo quietly followed.

"You're putting our people's safety on the line to cheat on a race?" Tommy talked to distract Kenji as he led the tengu even farther from the bar, where cries of pain wouldn't be heard.

"We checked carefully. The rules allow you to switch out bikes up to the last minute."

They'd found a loophole. Tinker had invented the hoverbikes and up till now was the only one that understood the blend of magic and technology enough to improve on the basic design. It was such common knowledge when Tinker sold one of her custom Deltas, Tommy could easily adjust the odds.

"I don't see how you're going to get your hoverbike past the oni brats." Tommy hated using the words to describe himself. He spat them out in anger.

Kenji mistook his tone. "The dogs won't be able to

do anything. It took careful manipulations, but the Wyverns will be there—seeing what the newly found baby *sekasha* does in his spare time. We're going to show up just before the first race, wipe everyone off the track with our bike, collect our winnings and leave."

With the Wyverns unintentionally protecting them every step of the way. If Tommy didn't get to the bike before they got to the track, there would be no stopping them without getting the elves involved.

Kenji finally noticed that they'd walked for several blocks into a warehouse district. He laughed nervously. "Are we walking back to the Nest?"

"Here's far enough." Tommy pinned the tengu to the wall. "Where's the bike?"

Kenji looked at the hand pinning him, seemingly still unaware he was in danger. "I don't know where they moved it to."

Was he telling the truth? "Who would know where it is?"

"Look, you shouldn't even get involved in all this. It could get messy. We didn't want to get you or Jin pulled in."

Behind Tommy, he heard Bingo shift with a scrape of boot on pavement. Kenji glanced toward the noise and went stiff with alarm.

"It's an oni brat!" Kenji cried and tried to push Tommy aside.

"Yes." Tommy lifted his head and dropped his illusion. "It is. Now, tell me, where's the bike, or this *will* get messy."

Unfortunately, they had to get very messy, but without learning anything useful. If Kenji knew where the bike was stored, he took the information to his death. After what they'd done to him, however, Tommy doubted that the tengu had ever known. At first light, they dumped his body into the river.

Tommy knew that his father would have raided the tengu village, taken hostages, and executed them for the surrender of the bike. He couldn't. Even if he could bear to be that much like his father, the elves were watching him too closely. He'd be putting every half-oni in Pittsburgh at risk.

He didn't know what to do. The race would start in a few hours, and he didn't know where the bike was being stored. The tengu had outwitted him so far at every step, so staking everything on a chance to intercept it and destroy it would be stupid. He needed to act, not react. He had no proof that the tengu had defrauded him, while, for all he knew, this was a clever trap, forcing him to betray himself by cheating.

No, he needed a plan, one that the elves couldn't object to. Kenji had admitted that the tengu's bike could outstrip the Delta in speed. Speed wasn't everything.

Tommy's luck was good for once. John and Blue Sky were at the Team Big Sky's pit at the racetrack, keeping to their habit of showing up early. The only sign of change was a basket of food from the enclave instead of their normal brunch of hot dogs and sauerkraut from the concession stands. John eyed him with faint suspicion as Tommy crossed the racetrack.

"I need help," Tommy said.

"You?" John said.

"Yes. I put up all the money to rebuild my family's restaurant to back my bets." Tommy went on to explain how Team Providence had disrupted the phones in order to defraud him. "They have a new bike. It's faster than yours. They plan on blowing you out of the water and bankrupting me."

"It's not my problem," John said.

"They'll take everything I own, including this racetrack. These bigoted frauds will be running the races, screwing people over whenever they feel like it. You think you don't trust me—but if you really didn't, you wouldn't be letting your little brother race here. I run a clean track. For the last five years, I've kept this kind of bullshit out. You might be scared to let me anywhere near Blue Sky, but you've always felt this place was safe for him."

John studied him, the line of his jaw tight.

Blue came to lean against his brother. "There's nothing wrong with Tommy. He's just trying to protect his family."

"He does it by hurting people," John said.

Blue shrugged. "He likes to fight. And so do I. John, what's the point of me racing today if I'm not trying to win?"

John looked down at his little brother and then sighed. "Give me a minute to think." He paced the pit for a minute. "Most of the racing bikes are stripped down so that they're lighter. The Delta has a beefed up power plant, and Blue is one of the lightest riders, so we've never stripped down the Delta."

"We should tell Oilcan about this," Blue Sky said.

"What?" Tommy was surprised that Blue would be willing to share an advantage.

"It is only fair," Blue said. "Oilcan could have stripped down his Delta to get an edge on me, but he's been keeping the playing field even."

Ah, yes, the *honorable* thing. "We need to keep it quiet, or the tengu will strip their model, too."

"Oilcan can be trusted," Blue said.

It went against Tommy's grain to trust anyone. Part of him, though, envied Blue's easy faith in someone. Having another team on a more equal footing, though, would be to Tommy's advantage.

"Fine, tell Oilcan," Tommy said. "Let him know that we have to keep it secret."

Blue nodded and dashed off.

John took out his drill and started to dismantle his Delta.

Blue Sky came back a few minutes later with a spell stencil. "Oilcan gave this to me. Tinker designed it. It goes on the handle bar. It gives a bike a more aero-dy-namic profile . . . whatever that means. He was going to use it this race to try and gain speed on me, since I'm lighter than him."

A few minutes before race time, the tengu team arrived, bike intact. Tommy wasn't sure how they slipped it past the various traps his cousins had laid outside the racetrack, but it didn't matter. It was here, and he was out of time. Everything rode now on Team Big Sky and Team Tinker.

Blue pulled on his racing leathers and mounted the Delta.

John caught his brother's chin and made the boy look at him. "You do not take unnecessary risks. This is just a race. It is only money. Your life is more important than either one of those. Do you understand?"

Blue glanced to Tommy.

"It's only money," Tommy forced himself to say.

Blue pulled on his helmet, started up the Delta, and swung it out onto the racecourse.

Oilcan came out of Team Tinker's pit, his Delta as bare as John's. While he was bigger than Blue Sky, Oilcan was a compact man. Both teams were in Wind Clan Blue, near twins as they slid up into their starting gates. Oilcan looked in Tommy's direction, giving him a long, unreadable study. As Windwolf's in-law, Tommy realized, Oilcan probably knew that Tommy was half-oni.

Team Providence brought their bike out last, trailing the pack. It was a standard street frame and enlarged power housing. The rider was a tall, lean male with a tengu nose in the team's bright red color. He frowned at the stripped Deltas as he took his gate at the end.

There was a moment of near quiet with only the deep rumble of the engines as the clock counted down the last second. Then the horn blared, the gates dropped open, and the hoverbikes leaped forward. The crowd roared. Blue Sky darted into the lead position with Oilcan on his flank, and a second later the tengu surged forward out of the pack to close the distance. The lead three flashed around the corner into the first series of jumps. The last bike cleared the gates. As the gate crew moved to swing the gates out of the way, Tommy crossed the track and swung over the retaining wall. He wanted to watch from the stands in order to see the full racecourse.

It was clear that his bike gave the tengu the advantage. In the straights he pulled ahead, only to lose the lead again and again to the more experienced Blue Sky and Oilcan on the smaller bikes. He was shifting too much power into his lift drive to make each jump, stealing too much from his spell chain that provided the speed. Blue Sky had the lead, shaving the clearance of his jumps down to fractions of an inch. Oilcan kissed down each time, seconds behind him, but with nearly a foot in on his landings.

"Yes!" Tommy hissed. His nails bit deep into his palm as he clenched his fist tight. If the two could hold out the entire race, they might win.

There was another straight after the jumps, and the tengu pulled ahead but slowed for the hairpin second turn. Blue Sky flashed past him, riding high up the wall to slip around the tengu. Oilcan took back second and then pushed into first as they went through the moguls, perfectly timing his liftoff to grab the most airspace.

Tommy pulled his eyes off the racers to check on the tengu pit. Their spotter was down off his perch, huddled with the rest of the crew. They knew they were in trouble. What would they do? Tommy watched them carefully. While the elves had accepted the tengu's claims of being humans crossed with crows, it didn't make them any less oni in Tommy's eyes. And oni were capable of anything.

The crew captain broke away from the huddle, talking on his headset, shielding the earpiece from the unending roar of the crowd. Tommy tried to read his lips but couldn't tell which of the many languages in Pittsburgh the tengu was using. The captain was repeating the word. What was he telling his rider to do?

The captain turned and looked not out at the riders, but up at the grandstand. He was talking to someone in the stands. No, he was looking too high. On the grandstand roof!

The leaders flashed in front of the pits, and the captain gestured at them and repeated the word. Tommy guessed the word—*shoot.*

Fury filled him, like a cold dark storm. He shoved his way through the crowd to the stairs down to the concession level. The dim cement hallway was empty of people and echoed with the wild cheering.

"I've got a shooter on the roof!" Tommy shouted at Trixie as he ran past her in the concession stand. "Get someone to back me up!"

He had to jump to grab the bottom of the access ladder. Then he scrambled up it. A tengu male was crouched at the far lip of the roof, a rifle at his shoulder, aiming at the leaders. Tommy clenched his ability tight around the tengu's mind and willed him blind. The tengu lowered the gun, shaking his head as if trying to clear his vision. Tommy stalked forward, all need to hurry over, letting his fury carry him. The tengu got to his feet and cautiously backed away from the edge of the roof. Tommy grabbed the rifle and jerked it from the tengu's hands. Changing his grip on the rifle, Tommy swung it like a club.

"This!" The stock hit with satisfying solidness. *"Is!"* His hit smashed the tengu to the ground. *"My!"* The tengu's nose disintegrated in a spray of blood. *"Track!"*

The tengu writhed on the ground, trying to escape him. Tommy pinned him in place with his foot, reversed the rifle, and placed the tip of the barrel at the center of the tengu's forehead. He released his hold on the tengu's mind, letting him see the rifle. "And no one fucks with what is mine."

The roaring of the crowd grew, indicating that the race was nearly done. The tengu team would be free to look for their missing shooter, and the grandstand would be swarming with idle racegoers hanging out between races. If he killed the tengu, there could be hell to pay. He kicked the tengu in the temple, knocking him unconscious. Bingo scrambled up the ladder to join Tommy on the roof.

"Don't kill him, but get him down off here." Tommy turned to watch the end of the race.

The leaders were coming around the last turn. Blue was tight and low, leaned so close to the inside wall it seemed like it had to be peeling off his jacket. Oilcan was tucked close behind, his spell chain nearly touching Blue's lift engine. The human flicked out as they hit the straight, moving to try and pass the half-elf. The tengu whipped around the curve and poured all his power into speed and surged forward. Oilcan continued to slide right, blocking him. The tengu tried to shift left, and Blue darted into his path. They roared toward the finish line, the lead two weaving a dance to keep the tengu blocked.

Team Big Sky won. Team Tinker took second. Team Providence took third.

Oilcan stopped Tommy before he reached the tengu team. "Don't hurt them, Tommy. This has been bad enough for the racing. Don't take it any further."

"This is their gun. They were going to use it on you and Blue."

Oilcan's eyes widened at the blood-splattered rifle, but still he shook his head. "You beat them. If you take it further, it's only going to look bad on you." He indicated the *sekasha* in the stands.

Tommy flung the rifle into the tengu's pit. "Clear out

and don't come back. All tengu teams, from here on out, are banned from the race. All tengu are banned from the racetrack. They are banned from every place that I have influence over. I offered a fair race and fair odds, and you tried to grind that into the mud, and I will not deal with you again."

"Do you think we care?" .the captain asked.

"Take your dishonor back to your flock. Tell your shame to Jin. Then tell me if you care."

It took a minute, but then it dawned on the male that in Pittsburgh, with the elves holding a sword's edge to the throat of all that was non-elf, he and his cohorts had just fucked themselves over royally.

Windwolf arrived while Tommy was working in the money room, totaling up the day's take. His *sekasha* walked in like they owned the place, and he swept in behind them. The large, normally very secure room suddenly felt like a broom closet.

"What are you doing here?" Tommy saved his work and closed the windows on his datapad.

"I heard there was trouble here today," Windwolf said.

"Nothing I couldn't handle."

The tengu team had slunk away, taking their unconscious shooter with them. The races continued without incident and no surprises in the betting. Between the attendance fees and concession receipts, they covered all their expenses and made a good profit. All in all, a good day.

Windwolf tilted his head, as if utterly confounded by Tommy. "Why do you fight the idea of forming a household beholden to me so much?"

"Why do you expect me to put my life into your

hands? Because you were humane enough to recognize the truth—that we're more human than we are oni? That we hate the oni as much as you do? Why should that be enough to make you our master?"

"As part of the new treaty, all of Pittsburgh must become part of the elfin culture. The half-oni must form a household."

"We are a household."

"And be part of a clan."

"Because you refuse to trust us unless we're your slaves? We're good and honorable people." He had realized today that he had always had, at his core, that human nobility that he recognized in John. For years he had run a fair race for no other reason than it seemed the right thing to do.

"It is the elfin way. Those who serve are protected, those who protect are served."

"The elfin way is wrong. You have no right to be my master. You're no better a being than I am, and you don't have my trust, and I don't owe you anything. I will not enslave myself and my entire people just because you say I have to."

"Yes, you owe me nothing," Windwolf said patiently, as if he were speaking to a child. "But I owe you my life. I do not seek to enslave you but to protect you from my people and the others that would harm you."

"I will protect my people. I always have. And I always will."

20: BLACKBIRD SING

"Tommy, Keiko Shoji is at the gate. She says that Jin Wong wants to meet with you."

The great and holy Jin Wong. The Buddha of the tengu. He was a secret legend of Pittsburgh the entire time Tommy was growing up. Somehow it was fitting that Tinker had produced Jin out of thin air. And the mighty Jin wanted to meet with the half-oni?

Tommy leaned forward to see the front gate. At a distance, Riki's young female cousin looked like a little fierce bird. What was Jin thinking, sending her? Did he think Tommy would be less likely to hurt a female? If he did, then he was an idiot.

But Tommy was curious. This was the mountain coming to Mohammed. If he was going to make the ban on tengu stick, he couldn't meet with Jin at the racetrack. He needed a neutral ground. Someplace where the tengu were at a disadvantage, which meant indoors. "Tell him that we'll meet him at the aviary in an hour."

"The what?"

"He'll know what it is."

The National Aviary was on the North Side. His mother used to bring Tommy down to see the birds. When he was very small, it was an ancient facility with a few hundred Earth birds and curious elves. Over the years, new buildings had been added and filled with birds from Elfhome and researchers from Earth.

It wasn't until he was inside and watching the brightly colored songbirds flit through the mock woodland that he remembered why he'd loved the aviary as a child. In the American cartoons, the small and defenseless birds always outwitted the bigger cats and dogs. He could come and see the tiny yellow finches and the small roadrunners and have hope that one day he would be able to defeat his father.

Tommy avoided the new buildings, keeping to the birds of Earth in the old sections. He settled among the owls and waited for the common enemy. The tengu swept into the aviary, a flock of crow black. Jin wore nothing to single him out as the leader of the tengu except the lack of weapons.

Jin was a surprisingly slight man. Tall. Lean. Quiet. He had a weird sense of presence, though, that made him impossible to miss. It was like every cell in his body was silently shouting, *"I am."*

He came with a platoon of bodyguards that Tommy knew by sight as the most kickass of the tengu. Males and females that even the best of his father's warriors would be leery of tangling with. It was clear that they would all die to keep Jin safe. Warriors of the cause.

That Jin was bound to the whim of a little girl like

Tinker would be nearly laughable if she didn't have the habit of redefining the world.

"I'm here," Tommy growled. "What do you want?"

Jin spoke quietly, without any anger in his voice. "I wish to apologize." Jin bowed deeply to Tommy. "Those who have wronged you have been punished. I have made it clear to my people that I will not tolerate this type of activity."

Tommy bit down on the disdaining laugh that wanted out. A man like Jin Wong didn't come in person and apologize, not to the likes of him. There was more to this. "And?"

"I ask that you reopen the racetrack to my people."

Yeah, that's what he thought. "No. Saying you're sorry and slapping your people on the wrists will not make this better between us."

"I put to death those that wronged you."

Tommy went still in surprise. "You killed them?"

"What they did was inexcusable." Jin's eyes were hard and cold. The male was deadly serious.

"You killed all ten of Team Providence?" Tommy asked just to be clear.

"There were thirty tengu involved. The ten on the team and the twenty that laid the bets. I questioned them all closely to discover what they had done and why. They all knew what was planned and cooperated in it, so they were all treated equally. I executed all but one for their crimes. We're still looking for the last one."

They weren't going to find him. Tommy had made sure of that. Was this an elaborate scam to get Tommy to confess? Jin could wait for the end of time if that was the case. Oh, wait, Jin had been to the end of time and had come back.

"You killed twenty-nine of your own people for trying to cheat me?"

"We were enslaved by the oni for thousands of years." Jin tapped the cage holding a great horned owl. The large bird clicked its beak at the crow. "For the first time ever, we have the hope for lasting peace. At this moment, though, that is all it is: a hope. The elves must win this war with the oni, and we must fight alongside the elves, the humans, and the half-oni."

"No, no, don't put us into that mix. We're flying solo. Hell, half my people are under the age of ten, and a quarter of the other half are pregnant. We don't want to fight anyone."

Jin gave Tommy a sad smile. "You have broken your ties with the oni—that is all that is important to me. The tengu has one enemy, and only one enemy. I do not want my people to ever lose sight of that."

Twenty-nine tengu. Dead. Tommy couldn't quite wrap his head around it. That was more than his three aunts and all his younger cousins combined. Lined up and killed in cold blood by the person they would die to protect. The one person that should have been protecting them.

"I don't get it," Tommy said. "They lost. They didn't win the race or get the money."

"This is not about the race or the money," Jin said. "This is about truth, trust, and vigilance. Team Providence knew that I would have stopped them, so they kept their plans secret from me. They lied by omission."

Kenji had admitted that much before Tommy killed him.

Jin continued to list Team Providence's crimes. "They

knew that Team Big Sky and Team Tinker were favorites, so they took the rifle with them to assure a win. They knew too that Oilcan is our *domi*'s cousin and that she has adopted Blue Sky. Yet still they loaded the gun and sent their shooter to the grandstand roof."

Tommy hadn't considered the connections of the two targets. Talk about shooting yourself in the foot. Team Providence might have won the race if they had shot Blue or Oilcan, but their people would have been washed in blood immediately afterward.

And how soon after the tengu's apparent betrayal would the half-oni massacre follow?

Jin read the flow of realizations on Tommy's face. "Yes, our fate is tied. Windwolf was willing to trust the tengu because the half-oni saved him from Malice. Because I could stand as *sama* for all of the tengu, the elves were willing to believe that you would become Beholden to a *domana*."

Tommy didn't like that cause and effect.

"In this war, we are allies," Jin said softly. "And we have only one enemy—the oni. Team Providence shut their eyes and closed their ears and let our enemy take them by the hand."

"The oni set this up?"

"There was a human in a bar, buying drinks and talking loudly. They don't remember his name or what he looked like, but they let him fill their hearts with poison. He scattered all the little bits of the plan on the ground like bright jewels and walked away, leaving them to gather them up, piece them together, and then congratulate each other for being so clever to have figured it all out by themselves."

"Kajo." Tommy spat the name. The greater blood

was famous for using spies to infiltrate groups and splintering them apart. Kenji mentioned something about getting the idea from a drunk human spouting off about how much money he'd won betting on long shots. Tommy had been too focused on finding the hoverbike to delve deeper.

"Yes, it was Kajo. The drunk gave them information that could have only come from Tinker's datapad that the oni had hacked. No one else in Pittsburgh could have developed the new hoverbike. The snake in the grass poisoned these few and tried to destroy both our people. For that treason, I executed Team Providence."

Put all together, yes, it was damning. Tommy nodded his understanding of why Jin had killed the tengu involved. Bigotry, greed, and stupidity had combined to nearly destroy them all.

Jin gazed at Tommy levelly. "To continue your ban of my people from your racetracks and other businesses is to allow Kajo to keep the handhold he's created. He will use it to drive one wedge after another between our people. Do not give the oni control over you. Take back your ban."

Tommy made a show of lighting a cigarette to give himself time to think. There was no doubt in his mind that Kajo had been behind Team Providence's scam. The greater blood had always been three steps ahead of Lord Tomtom. Tommy had been torn between joy and embarrassment as Kajo had made his father run in circles. It was all painfully clear that this time, Tommy was the one jerked around. Team Providence were typical tools of the greater blood. People nudged hard in a direction they would already go, given information that they couldn't otherwise obtain, twisted and lied to and then released to wreak havoc. And all the roadblocks that Tommy had faced had been Kajo maneuvering. The exploited loophole in the rules. The entire bullshit of Tommy not being able to stop a race at his own racetrack. The Wyverns in the stands to watch the baby *sekasha* race. Tommy flicked the barely smoked cigarette onto the floor and angrily ground it out.

What a sack of shit.

And Jin—the frigging spiritual leader—quietly explaining why he had to blow the brains out of his own people. You don't kill your people. You protect your people against *them*—them being everyone else in the world. But then, Tommy never had any of his family spit in his face and try to knife him in the back. A few thousand half-oni might have been born to human mothers since the first Startup, but only a couple hundred had survived to see freedom. Like Tommy had told Jin, half his people were under ten years old.

Was it only a matter of time before Tommy needed to kill cousins to keep the others in line?

Jin was waiting patiently for an answer. Lift the ban? Tommy was still angry with Team Providence, but they were all dead. Keeping the ban in place would be like pissing on a dead man. Easy but pointless.

All this came looping back to Windwolf wanting Tommy to be Beholden. Jin saw them as allies because he thought their fates were linked. They'd be bookends to Tinker and Windwolf. A glorious future of lasting peace, choke-chained by the elves.

"You're wrong," Tommy growled. "There's no happily ever after to chase after. All you did was swap masters, oni for elves. Beholden is just another word for slave."

Jin gave a bird-like tilt of his head to peer quizzically at Tommy. "Is that how you see it? I don't. I see myself as a knight at the Round Table."

"What?"

"Once upon a time, far, far away." Jin jumped up lightly to the railing in front of the cage. He startled the owl inside, making it rustle its wings nervously. "On Earth, to be exact, in land called England, there was a king by the name of Arthur Pendragon."

"I know all about that sword in the stone bullshit," Tommy roared. "I was raised in Pittsburgh, not on Onihida."

Jin crouched while still balanced on the railing. "The basis for the legend was that Arthur had many powerful warriors who were tearing the land apart with their petty bickering. He brought them together and made them allies by creating a code of conduct. His code contains virtues such as protection of the weak, courage, mercy, and generosity. It was a code that would not allow them to engage in pointless fighting with each other."

Tommy laughed. "What a fairy tale."

"No, no, see, it's actually pure genius. You can't change other people. You can only change yourself. King Arthur set this high bar, this perfection of justice and good, and said 'This is what a knight of the Round Table is' and then left it up to his warriors to prove to themselves that they could measure up to it."

"You really believe King Arthur existed? Merlin the magician, living backward in time?"

"Odder things have happened—to me." Jin stood

and started to walk down the railing as he talked. "But consider a second example: the bushido code that the samurai followed. They believed that the perfect warrior strove to achieve seven virtues." He ticked them off with his fingers. "Courage. Respect. Honesty. Honor. Loyalty. Benevolence. Righteousness."

"Get to the damn point."

"The elves are not asking you to be a slave. They're offering you a place at the Round Table. All that they ask is that you strive to be a good man. To be truthful. To be just. To be honorable and loyal."

"Loyal lapdog. I've heard how Tinker calls and you come running like chickens, ready to die in her crazy plan of the day."

"She is good and kind." There was steel behind the words. Jin didn't like people knocking his *domi*. He stepped down off the railing. "And you know she is. You've spent too much time around her not to know."

"She has you doing things like highjacking dreadnaughts in midair and clearing oni nests."

"We want to live in peace, and for that, we must create peace to live in."

Jin locked gazes with him. "Let there be peace between our people. Those that wronged you have been punished. Lift your ban."

"I'll think about it."

21: SHADOW BOXING

Oni moved through Tinker's nightmares. They were all through the enclave, slipping unseen into position for attack. No one seemed to notice them, even when the oni were standing right in front of the elves. She whimpered as the oni crept into the room where Pony slept. Her First lay sprawled facedown in his bed, confident in the safety of the enclave, his naked back to the invaders. An oni warrior eased a long dagger from his belt and moved silently toward Pony's bed.

She tried to call out, tried to shout, but the words caught in her throat.

The oni struck downwards and Pony jerked once and then went still. Blood sprayed from the wound, a fountain pulsing to Pony's still beating heart.

There was a noise behind her and Tinker turned, caught sight of an oni appearing out of nowhere as if suddenly teleported there, reaching for her. She started to run, bringing up her left hand, fingers crooked in position to summon her shields. The oni caught her by her long braid and jerked her back, slamming her onto the ground.

Stormsong burst into the room, her shields wrapped around her like black mist.

A third oni warrior with a machine gun opened fire on Stormsong as the female *sekasha* charged toward where Tinker was still pinned on the ground. Stormsong's shields flared at the striking bullets, again and again, and then vanished. A bullet caught her in the face, dropping her instantly.

"No!" Tinker sat up with a scream.

"*Domi*, hush, it's all right, I'm here." Pony crooned into her ear, his arms around her. The nightmare vanished and she was in her own bed, warm sheets cocooning her and Pony. There was no wound on his bare back—no blood pouring from his neck—yet.

"Oh God! Oh God! There's oni in the enclave!" She tried to bring up her right hand and cried out as she realized that her arm was bound tight and useless. "No! I need my shields. They'll kill everyone!"

"Arm yourself!" Pony shouted and activated his shields without taking his arms from around her.

Stormsong burst into the room, shields up brilliant blue and *ejae* out. "What is it?"

Tinker cried out in relief and held out her left hand to Stormsong, desperate to feel the life in her. Stormsong crossed the room to Tinker's bed, but her eyes flicked about the room, looking for something to kill.

"*Domi* dreamed that oni attacked," Pony said.

Stormsong's shield blocked Tinker's hand from reaching her. Tinker pressed her hand flat against the solid air, frustrated even as she was reassured by its presence. "We couldn't see them. It was like Lord Tomtom—they were there, but we couldn't see them."

Pony swept Tinker up off her bed. "We'll move to the practice hall. It's more secure."

Stormsong nodded and took the lead out of the bedroom. They collected the rest of her Hand as they moved through the enclave. Except for Pony, they were all fully dressed, apparently on alert as long as Windwolf was out of the enclave and Tinker was in a drugged sleep.

"Put me down," Tinker said. "Let me call my shields. They have machine guns. It just eats right through your shield. They'll kill you."

"Your arm is broken," Pony said in a tone he rarely used with her. He'd shifted into the one in charge. There would be no arguing with him. "You'll cripple yourself for life if you unbind it while the healing spell is active."

"So I'll cancel the damn spell." She slapped uselessly at his bare shoulder.

He wouldn't put her down. "The pain will keep you from maintaining a shield for any useful length of time."

The *laedin*-caste guards of the enclave were added to the *sekasha*, herding Poppymeadow's staff and members of Wolf's personal household out of the way for Tinker's Hand to move through first, and then swept into their wake.

She had never noticed that the practice hall had reinforced doors and narrow arrow slits for windows. The *laedin* slammed the doors shut, threw heavy bars into place, and activated defense shields built into the framework.

The elves relaxed slightly.

If the dream hadn't been so vivid and horrific, if her dreams didn't have a habit of coming true, then Tinker would be embarrassed at disrupting the entire enclave based on a nightmare. She couldn't get the images out of her mind. Pony's blood pumping out. Stormsong's face shattering under the force of the bullet.

She gasped slightly as she realized something odd had been playing through her dream.

"What is it, *domi*?"

"Stormsong's shields! Your spell tattoos!" Tinker pressed her hand to Pony's blue-inked tattoos that ran down his arms. "In my dream—they were black."

"Black?" Stormsong murmured and looked to the right intently as if she had suddenly developed X-ray vision and was scanning beyond the wall.

"Yes. And the oni—they caught me by my hair." Tinker caught a fistful of her short, scruffy hair. "I had a long braid."

"Jewel Tear," Stormsong said. "The oni aren't in this enclave. They're at Ginger Wine's. They're going to attack the Stone Clan. We'll have to warn them."

The *sekasha* glanced at each other and came to a silent agreement. They nodded.

Tinker guessed that they had decided to go together. "I'm coming with you."

"*Domi*—" Pony started.

She cut him short by cocking the undamaged fingers of her left hand and activating a protection shield. She wasn't sure it would work; she'd never tried it before and was relieved when the shields wrapped solidly around her. Even better, there was no pain. She should have tried this for the fight in the whelping pens.

"What the hell?" Stormsong cried in English.

"*Domi*?" Pony frowned at the black misting shield she'd summoned. "How—how are you doing that?"

"I can tap the Stone Clan Spell Stones," she admitted.

"How—how?" Pony sputtered.

"And how did you learn their *esva*?" Stormsong asked.

She canceled the spell and answered the simpler question. "Blue Sky recorded Jewel Tear activating her shields. I ran it through a video editor to analyze the spell she used."

They looked so scandalized that she didn't add in that she had done the same with True Flame calling a flame strike. Nor that she'd practiced the parts of the flame strike, keeping the activation command and hand gestures separate so there was no chance she might actually cast it.

"It's a *domana* shield. It's a thousand times stronger than your personal shields. That's what I'm here for: to protect you as you protect me. I am not letting you go over to that enclave alone."

"Stone Clan defense spells are actually stronger than Wind Clan," Stormsong pointed out, always the realist.

"She's wounded," Pony said.

"It feels—best—to take her." Stormsong meant that her own precog ability suggested that disaster lay in leaving Tinker behind.

"I am going," Tinker growled.

Pony didn't look happy, but he nodded compliance.

They were too late.

They came through the front gate, let in by Ginger

Wine's door guard, just as the first round of machine-gun fire announced the death of Jewel Tear's Second.

"Get everyone out," Tinker ordered and cast the Stone *esva* shield. The rest of Jewel Tear's Hand would die as surely as her Second trying to rescue Jewel Tear. The shield encompassed an annoyingly small area, enveloping half of what she would cover with her Wind *esva* shield. "Stay close."

They went through the sprawling compound, pushing through Ginger Wine's staff as they fled away from the gunfire. They got as far as the inner courtyard when Pony paused her.

"*Domi*, they've barricaded themselves into the training hall." He pointed to the low building across the yard full of apple trees. The doors were closed, and rifle barrels bristled from the arrow slits.

"Watch out!" Tinker cried as one of the rifles jerked back and made room for a rocket launcher. A missile blasted toward them and slammed into the *domana* shield. The force of the explosion plowed back through the trees, snapping off limbs and making it rain down half-ripe fruit.

"That missile launcher is really starting to piss me off," Tinker growled.

"We need to cover Ginger Wine's people." Pony studied the building with narrowed eyes. "It would be unwise to force our way into the training hall—even if we could breach the doors. There are at least a dozen warriors inside; we would be overwhelmed if there's more than three for each of us to fight."

"Do you think they have Jewel Tear in there?" Tinker winced as a second missile slammed into her *domana* shield.

Stormsong shook her head. "No, this force is just to slow us down as they take Jewel out another way."

"We'll need Wolf to get them out of the training hall," Pony said.

"Fuck that." Tinker glanced around. There was a stone wall beside them. "Take cover."

She dropped the shield and aimed a flame strike at the training hall.

It had a lot more power behind it than she expected. The night erupted into brilliance as flame blasted up through the roof of the training hall. Burning timbers and ceramic roofing tiles came raining back down.

Tinker ducked back beside her Hand. They were staring at her in stunned shock. "Shit! I thought the training hall was shielded!"

"The oni wouldn't know the activation command." Pony broke the silence. "Only Ginger Wine and a handful of her people would know."

Stormsong found her voice. "Are you nuts? Do you have any idea how dangerous that spell is?"

"It's a calculated risk." Tinker recast the shield. "We need to find Jewel and what's left of her Hand."

22: HELPLESS

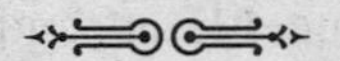

Gunfire woke Oilcan. He tumbled out of bed, once again disoriented by the pattern of light and shadows in his bedroom. *Where was he? Oh, yes, Sacred Heart. Was it gunfire he actually heard?*

The thunder of a machine gun answered his question. It sounded far too close for comfort. Thorne Scratch was dressing hurriedly in the darkness.

"Where's that coming from?" He didn't bother fumbling for his discarded clothes. He pulled fresh out of his dresser.

"Ginger Wine's," Thorne Scratch growled.

There was a sudden draconic roar and the flare of crimson-tainted brilliance. Thorne had her vest armor on; the light gleamed off the slick black of the scales.

"Thank gods," Thorne Scratch breathed out.

"What was that?"

"Fire Clan *esva*." She tugged on her pants. "I need to go. Take the children to the safe room and lock yourself in."

He stepped into his tennis shoes without bothering with socks.

Thorne Scratch was pulling on boots as he went out his door. The kids were spilling into the hallway, all in nightgowns, whimpering in distress. There was another roar. Through the hallway window, he saw a crest of flame rise up out of buildings down the street, temporarily lighting the night to day. The kids cried out and ran to him. He was suddenly trapped by a dozen arms clinging tightly to him.

"It's okay! It's okay! Prince True Flame and the Wyverns are fighting the oni. We'll be fine."

"Get to the safe room!" Thorne snapped from his bedroom. "Go!"

He started them moving, shuffling forward like a giant amoeba of fear. It wasn't until Thorne swept past them like a dark shadow that the kids let go of him enough to cling to each other in more manageable groups.

Thorne Scratch unlocked the front door and then stood waiting for him to catch up to her.

"Go to the safe room." He pushed the kids toward the hallway.

Thorne caught him by the front of his T-shirt and kissed him hard. "I hate leaving you here with nothing to protect you," she whispered.

"You're the one running toward the fight," he said. "I'll be tucked behind several feet of stone."

Thorne Scratch gave him one last long stare as if it was going to be the last time she'd see him alive. "Lock this behind me. I'll be back as soon as I can."

And then she was gone.

Locking the door was the hardest thing he ever had to do.

He hurried back to the small windowless safe room. He did a head count—five kids looking scared to hell—before shutting the heavy door and sliding the bars into place. Even through the thick walls, he could hear the muffled gunfire. And then there was a loud explosion of such force that he could feel the earth underneath him shift. An explosion like that would kill a *sekasha* regardless of their protective shield—and Thorne Scratch didn't have a *domana* protecting her.

Oh, Thorne, he thought. *Be safe.*

Hours passed. The night had gone silent.

Windwolf and Prince True Flame had most likely won, but he didn't know how to find out short of leaving the kids alone or waiting for Thorne.

And Thorne still hadn't returned.

He hadn't felt so helpless since hiding in the pantry, watching his father keen over his mother's body.

23: SCISSOR PAPER STONE

Two spells were woefully inadequate.

Or at least, two spells that Tinker didn't know all the parameters for. The lack of control was driving her nuts. There was no time to even guess how to increase the size of the Stone *esva* shield since the gunfire required her to keep it up nearly constantly. The flame strike dealt out a satisfyingly massive blow of damage, but she was in the process of burning down Ginger Wine's entire enclave. She felt like she should be shouting "Sorry!" every time she blasted another tight knot of oni.

The enclave was a pure chaos of bodies. The oni were taking advantage of the enclave's defenses, fortifying themselves behind stout doors and stone walls. The Stone Clan forces—alarmingly only *laedin*-caste—seemed unsure if they should be escorting their unarmed clansmen to safety or be attacking the oni. They careened around the enclave, randomly chasing or fleeing the oni.

"Where the hell are the Stone Clan *sekasha*?"

Tinker carefully picked her way over smoldering rubble. There should be sliced and diced oni someplace as the *sekasha* kicked collective butt.

"The oni must have taken them by surprise," Pony said. "It is the only reason the oni would still be alive."

"They're all dead?"

"Those you saw die, those were probably not the first to die, but the last."

She shifted sideways hurriedly to protect a knot of Ginger Wine's staff from machine-gun fire. "Go! Get to Poppymeadow's." She was too late to save the *sekasha*, but she could make sure everyone else got out safely.

She and her Hand pushed forward, driving the oni back and freeing the elves that had been trapped behind them. Since she was dropping her shield to cast the flame strike, her Hand scattered evenly around her so their shields would protect her from stray gunfire. It made her nervous, so she blasted away without mercy or regard to the property damage she was causing.

They reached the far corner of the enclave and discovered that the handful of oni they'd been chasing had backed into a dead end. The *sekasha* leapt forward, a whirlwind of blades, and moments later she was surrounded by dismembered bodies.

"They weren't the main force," Pony growled. "They were just a distraction. They took Jewel Tear out another way."

Tinker felt like she was nine years old when Prince True Flame and Windwolf appeared. There she was, surrounded by the burning rubble of Ginger Wine's enclave, with no rescued Jewel Tear to show for all the destruction.

"Beloved," Windwolf ignored the ruin to focus on her. "Are you hurt?"

And that's one of the reasons she loved him so much. He understood the important part of this mess. "No." She dropped her shield, suddenly feeling bone weary, and let him wrap his arms around her. It felt wonderful to lean on his strength, knowing he would make everything right.

Obviously the prince wasn't going to ignore the fact that she had just leveled an enclave. He was staring down at her with an odd expression. "She was maintaining a Stone Clan shield."

As Stormsong had pointed out with her limited edition T-shirt, things wear out. Usually not so spectacularly. . . .

"My right hand is broken," Tinker offered as an excuse.

Windwolf tightened his hold on her. "The Wind *esva* doesn't have shields cast by the left hand."

"It was Stone Clan *esva*." True Flame's tone demanded an answer.

Oh gods, all this burning rubble and dead bodies, and they were going to argue about that? "One of my ancestors was an elf. Apparently he was a Stone Clan *domana*."

The prince glared at Windwolf. "You changed the *domana* of another clan?"

If Tinker hadn't been pressed against him, she would have missed Windwolf's anger. He stood quietly, only the tension of his body betraying him. Finally he calmly said, "Her grandfather died of old age before he was out of his doubles. If I hadn't changed her, she would have had the lifespan of a human."

"She was a child of another clan." True Flame stressed the word "child."

"She was an adult by human counting," Wolf snapped. "Her family made no attempt to contact the Stone Clan. The ties were severed."

"She called their Spell Stones," True Flame said.

"You told me to protect my Hand!" Tinker cried. "Protect the ones that serve! They would have all died if I'd let them come here alone. I did what I had to do to protect them."

Judging by the annoyance on True Flame's face and his silence, she'd found the argument that he couldn't reply to. It was the fundamental basis of the entire elf culture: that obedience demanded protection. Tinker would have felt triumphant over the win if she hadn't just snapped out the first thing that came to her. How could she feel so tired after sleeping all day? Almost in answer, pain flared through her right arm. Oh, yes, the damn healing spells.

Someone started to scream nearby. The fact that the screamer was male made the sound more horrific.

"That's Forest Moss," True Flame said.

They found the one-eyed *domana* crouched in the blood of one of Jewel Tear's *sekasha*. Forest Moss was holding out his bloody hands and screaming. The female *sekasha* had been shot in the face at close range. In Tinker's dream, she had been Stormsong. Tiger Eye was in his bed just beyond the female's body, his spine cut. Judging by the blood splatter, he'd been paralyzed by the blow, helpless as his lifeblood pumped out.

Tinker completely understood the need to scream. She turned to hug Pony close. "In my dream, it was you and Stormsong."

"You are hurt and tired," Pony murmured only loud enough for her to hear. "Let me take you back home."

It didn't seem right to leave the mess for Windwolf to clean up, but she could feel the healing spell taking its toll. In a matter of minutes, she'd be asleep, regardless of her standing upright or lying down. Besides, what was the point of her staying? She'd already leveled the place and failed to stop the oni.

24: SCAPEGOAT

The Wyvern washed into the warren like a flood of blood.

Tommy shouted, "Don't fight! Don't fight!" A moment later, he was on the floor, in too much pain to focus his mind and heart hammering with fear for his family. Had the elves decided to fuck it all and kill them anyhow?

His family was all so used to having the snot beat of them that even the smallest just lay silent where they were pinned to the floor. The only reason he knew they weren't dead was their fearful breathing and that there was no smell of blood in the air—yet.

The scrape of boots announced that the true powers had entered the warren.

Prince True Flame was a schoolgirl's wet dream of an elf, from golden hair to skin that looked carved from white marble. He was dressed in spotless white.

Prince True Flame came to tower over Tommy. "Where is she?"

"Where is who?" Had Tinker disappeared again?

God forbid, since the world turned upside down every time she did.

"The Stone Clan *domi* Jewel Tear on Stone. Where is she?"

"I don't know!" Tommy shouted.

"True Flame." Windwolf blocked the prince's kick to Tommy's head. "We have no proof that they had anything to do with it."

"He has his father's powers." True Flame glared down at Tommy.

"I told you, his powers are limited." Windwolf stayed between Tommy and the prince. "Look around you. This is a household, not a camp of warriors fresh from battle."

"They are oni spawn with no one trustworthy standing responsible for their actions. They refuse your protection, so they are not part of us."

"They do not trust us, and if this is how we treat them with no proof to support an attack, then they have full right to mistrust us."

They searched for proof. They were thorough but strangely neat about it. The oni would have broken everything as they searched, but when the elves were done, nothing seemed disturbed.

"What's going on?" Tommy growled into the battered floor.

"Ginger Wine's enclave was attacked. Jewel Tear was taken," Windwolf said.

"And you suspect us?"

"The oni clouded the minds of the *sekasha* and took them unawares."

And Tommy was one of the few people in Pittsburgh that had the ability, but he wasn't the only one. "The oni had a kitsune. She's better at the mind tricks than I am."

"Yes, so my *domi* tells me."

Windwolf trusted Tommy, but obviously he wasn't top dog in Pittsburgh anymore. Prince True Flame was now the one that said who lived and died. The half-oni had fallen into an "all or nothing" category. If the elves decided Tommy was guilty of helping the oni, then all his cousins would be ruled guilty, too. It would be a quick slaughter.

He needed to get the elves away from his warren so his family could disappear. "Let me help find her."

Windwolf's eyebrows rose in surprise. "You want to help?"

"No one knows Pittsburgh better than me. I need to go to Ginger Wine's, though, where it all started."

"It's a Wind Clan enclave. I can grant you access to it." Windwolf motioned to the soldiers pinning Tommy down.

Tommy carefully freed his eight-year-old cousin, Spot, and tucked the small boy under his arm. "Spot has a better nose than me. He might be able to smell something out."

From across the room, Bingo gave him puzzled look and murmured, "What are you doing?"

They'd found out long ago that if they whispered without moving their mouths, their extra-sharp ears would pick it up without them being overheard.

"Move the warren," Tommy whispered back.

"What about you?" Bingo asked.

"I'll get them away from here so you can disappear."

"Tommy..."

"Do it." Tommy hissed.

Bingo hung his head and looked away.

✧ ✧ ✧

All three TV channels had their news trucks outside of Ginger Wine's smoldering enclave. Under bright mobile spotlights, the reporters were recording the human take on the night's activities. They were making a big fuss over the fact that the dead oni were being stacked like cordwood on the curb. Didn't they know that the oni fed their dead to their dogs?

Tommy used the brilliance and shadows to stay hidden from the reporters as he slipped through Ginger Wine's front gate. A full battle had been pitched inside the enclave. Half the buildings were leveled, the ruins still smoldering. Empty bullet casings brightly littered the ground, and blood was sprayed across the walls. It was going to be hard to find anything useful in the rubble.

The elves frightened Spot. When Tommy put him down, the boy clung to Tommy's hand. Spot was silent as usual, but his solid amber eyes drank in every detail. The elves shied away from them, trying not to look at the boy's short black fur, doglike muzzle and long, floppy ears. Spot had his mother's sweetness; he didn't deserve the frightened glances.

"We need to track the oni." Tommy kept the anger out of his voice—it wasn't the boy he was angry with. "You understand?"

Spot nodded wordlessly and crouched down to sniff at the gleaming wooden floors. Hands flat on the ground, he half ran in circles around Tommy, trying to make sense out of the confusion of scents. Windwolf, Ginger Wine, and the viceroy's bodyguards stood back, silently watching the boy track.

Spot picked his way through the maze of the enclaves. The oni had avoided the great inner courtyard, instead working their way through almost all of the back passages that the staff used to access the guest rooms. All but one of the dead elves had been killed unaware, not that it lessened the carnage done to their bodies. Oni were like sharks when it came to blood; once they smelled it, they went a little mad. Unarmed members of Ginger Wine's staff and several of her *laedin*-caste guards had been hacked apart in hallways and public rooms. Eight of the *sekasha* been killed in their bedrooms. Obviously the oni had moved unseen and unheard through the enclave. No wonder the elves suspected him.

The boy suddenly veered off to a little back room stacked with baskets, rakes, and snow shovels. Tucked in the very back, hidden from a casual search of the room, was a bed complete with goose-down pillows, silk sheets, and rich wool blankets. Apples, keva beans, and smoked river shark had been squirreled in easy reach of the luxurious bed. Even Tommy's weak nose could identify the musky scent of a kitsune.

"Chiyo was living here." Tommy nudged two baskets that were lined with towels. "Looks like she planned to have her litter here. She's got another week or two before she's due."

Ginger Wine gasped and dropped to her knees. "I didn't know, *domou*. Please. I didn't know."

"You came to me with your concerns weeks ago," Windwolf said. "I should have investigated. This is not your fault."

Tommy locked down on a bitter laugh. The elves got completely forgiven for housing an oni—not even yelled at—but his entire family was blamed for something they had nothing to do with.

✧ ✧ ✧

The moon was rising as Spot followed the track to the side gate that gave cars and horses access to a barnlike outbuilding. The boy lost the scent there.

"They probably had a truck waiting." Tommy patted the boy on the head and gave him an apple stolen from the courtyard. "At sixty miles per hour, they could be anywhere in Pittsburgh by now."

Prince True Flame huffed. "I think they will take her west. There are no Spell Stones there. She will be helpless, as will we."

"I'm not leaving the city," Windwolf said quietly. "They almost killed my beloved yesterday. Her arm is broken, and she is—nearly—helpless. The healing spells will keep her weak for days."

"Your *domi* will be safe in the enclave."

Windwolf stood firm. "I have given up three hundred thousand *sen* of virgin forest to the Stone Clan, and what have they managed to do? Earth Son forced his Hand against him. Forest Moss has gone mad." As if summoned by his name, the *domana* started to scream. "And now this idiocy. A single ground scry would have picked up the kitsune. Three Stone Clan *domana*, and not one checked the buildings they slept in? This is a war zone!"

"That is not how the Stone Clan will see this. They will see it as a failure on the Wind Clan's part. You should have made sure that the enclave was safe."

"You know that the wind scry couldn't have found the kitsune. That was the whole point of requesting Stone Clan to send help."

Prince True Flame glanced toward Tommy. "I will send word to my sister. She will have to deal with the Stone Clan somehow. We need more *domana* or we will fall here. The Stone Clan will want a scapegoat for this if we cannot recover Jewel Tear. They will want you, cousin, but I will offer them the oni spawn."

They let him go. At first he was surprised, but then he realized that they wanted the Stone Clan to waste time trying to find him. So far the elves couldn't find their ass with both hands. An elfin carpenter, however, was more thorough than a human one, because the elf had forever to hammer down nails. The Stone Clan would find Tommy eventually.

Prince True Flame had suggested that if they recovered Jewel Tear before the Stone Clan sent more *domana*, everything would be fine. Tommy wasn't going to leave it to the elves to find the female.

He circled Ginger Wine's, considering all he knew about Chiyo, the oni, and what he had seen in the smoldering enclave. Chiyo had disappeared the night Lord Tomtom had died. Tommy had heard that Kajo wanted the pregnant female for the whelping pens. The kitsune abilities allowed the fox-tainted oni to wield a great deal of political power despite their status of lesser bloods. Normally Kajo wouldn't have been able to cage Chiyo, but with Pittsburgh stranded on Elfhome she was fair game. Much to his father's annoyance, Kajo had ordered Chiyo turned over to the whelping pens and its experienced midwives. The rumor was that if the kitsune survived the birth of her oversized puppies, Kajo planned to endlessly bred Chiyo to his kennel of wargs.

Something messed with his timing, making him rush the attack. One thing the oni were good at was waiting for the perfect moment—immortality gave them infinite patience when it came to hunting. What triggered the attack? The timing seemed randomly chosen—like something a human running on clocks would pick instead of the timeless oni.

And why had Kajo taken Jewel Tear? To use her as bait so the elves ran in circles, screaming at each other? If that was his plan, it was working.

The biggest freaking problem with this so-called war was that Kajo was keeping one step in front of the elves. What Tommy needed was the elves find the oni so that both sides would forget about his family.

Where the hell was Kajo hiding his army?

Tommy had known of a handful of small camps within the city, but they'd all been abandoned after Tomtom's attempt to kill Windwolf exposed the oni's presence. It was one thing to hide in the city when oni were myths, but now the humans were in the middle of a war they couldn't ignore. Pittsburgh was a sprawling, half-abandoned city, but filled with eyes. Sixty thousand humans meant someone would notice masses of oni eating and sleeping and shitting. Even the humans should be able to smell a nest in this heat.

The oni had been gearing up for war since the first Startup. Thirty years was a long time to stay completely hidden, even in Pittsburgh. There had to be a main camp outside of the city. Certainly there were hundreds of miles of virgin forest in all directions. Prince True Flame might be right that the oni were taking Jewel Tear west, out of range of Spell Stones. Anything northeast of the city would be visible from incoming gossamers. Straight east was the train. . . .

Kajo had lesser bloods working the trains since the elves laid the last track. It would have been simple to load up a train in Pittsburgh, stop somewhere between the city and the east coast, and drop supplies to an oni camp. The oni could build as large a camp they wanted as long as they stayed out of sight of the train and incoming gossamers. Hell, if they stopped the train on one of the bridges, they could have used a crane and pallet system to load onto barges. That way they could ship heavy equipment without leaving a road for the elves to notice.

The odd timing made sense, too. Since Tinker had rattled cages at the train station, Kajo might be losing access to it shortly. Tonight might have been the last chance to move something risky—like a female elf.

If Tommy could find this camp, he could collide the elves and the oni together, and maybe get Jewel Tear back. Between the two, maybe his family would be left alone.

25: UNBOUNDED BRILLIANCE

Banging woke Oilcan. It sounded like someone was trying to break down the front door with their knocking. Oni wouldn't knock, so Oilcan felt safe answering it. He slipped out of the safe room without waking the children.

The peephole showed a wall of *sekasha* on his porch. He recognized Windwolf's First, Wraith Arrow, and Prince True Flame's First, Red Knife, among the Hand of Wyverns. Red Knife stepped forward, eclipsing Oilcan's view as the male raised his fist to knock again.

"Shit," Oilcan breathed. Why were the Firsts of two clans pounding on his door? What could possibly unite them on his doorstep? The door jumped under the assault of Red Knife's knocking.

"I'm here!" he shouted and worked the locks. "One moment!"

He jerked open the door. The *sekasha* had shifted slightly, and the three abreast were Red Knife, Wraith Arrow, and Thorne Scratch.

"Thorne!" he cried with relief and then realized she

had her face set to the cold *sekasha* warrior's mask. He'd seen it enough times on Pony to know that she was in full working mode. "What's wrong?"

"This is him," Wraith Arrow said quietly to the Wyvern First.

Red Knife gazed down at Oilcan, eyes going wide with surprise. "I know she's tiny, but I did not expect him to be as well. Is this as tall as he's going to get?"

The question scored a hit on Thorne's face that was quickly smoothed back to warrior's mask. "He is fully grown." Thorne's High Elvish was carefully polite. It was intimidating that even the *sekasha* were cautious around each other.

"He is older than Beloved Tinker *ze domi*," Wraith Arrow added.

"Have you lost all influence on your *domana* that this is what you're reduced to?" Red Knife asked Thorne Scratch. "Your clan was requested support, not offered babysitting."

The muscles in Thorne Scratch's jaw went rigid in anger, but she answered levelly. "I have sent word to my clan's First that this is unacceptable. It will be rectified."

Red Knife put a hand on Oilcan's chest and gently but firmly backed him into the foyer. *Sekasha* flowed into the building.

"Forgiveness," Oilcan said cautiously. If the *sekasha* were sparring with words, how long until they drew their swords? He didn't want to be in the middle when the blades were drawn. "I don't understand why you are here. Has something happened to my cousin?"

Wraith Arrow shook his head. "*Domi* has not been harmed, *nagarou*."

Thorne Scratch all but ignored Oilcan in favor

of keeping her focus on Red Knife. "This might be totally unnecessary."

"Let us be done with it then." The Wyvern waved a hand at Oilcan.

Oilcan's heart jumped in his chest. Done with what?

Thorne Scratch caught hold of Oilcan's left hand. With thunderstorms raging in her eyes, she molded his fingers into an odd position and lifted his hand to her lips. For a moment he thought she meant to kiss his fingers. Instead Thorne Scratch sounded out a long, drawn-out vowel. He felt an odd thrumming down in his bones, like he gripped hard to a big engine.

Thorne reshaped his fingers into another position and spoke another vowel.

The air pressure changed, making Oilcan's ears pop like he just taken an express elevator in a skyscraper, and all around him the air distorted oddly.

Red Knife grunted while both Thorne Scratch and Wraith Arrow looked horrified.

"What—what just happened?" Oilcan asked. "What did you do?"

"What do you see?" Thorne Scratch kept him from moving his hand.

"There's something—a shield, I think—around us," Oilcan said. "What did you do?"

Thorne Scratch dropped Oilcan's hand, and the distortion in the air rippled and vanished. She put on her warrior mask again, but the thunderstorm continued to rage in her eyes. "He doesn't have the magic sense, but he retains enough of the genome to tap the Stones. He'd have to be trained, though, to use the *esva*."

Red Knife laughed. "If he's as clever as his cousin, he'll pick it up quickly enough."

Wraith Arrow still looked as if Oilcan had just dropped over dead. The Wind Clan *sekasha* wasn't even trying to mask his grief.

"What is going on?" Oilcan struggled to keep his voice level. He could tap the Stone Clan Spell Stones? Judging by Thorne's anger and Wraith Arrow's grief, in the eyes of the elves, it changed everything.

"We're trying to determine what is to be done with you," Red Knife said, confirming his fear.

"What was the name of the one that started your blood line?" Thorne Scratch growled.

He could understand Wraith Arrow's reaction, but why was Thorne angry? "He went by the human name of Guillaume Dufae. He died a long time ago."

"How long ago?" Thorne asked.

"Nearly three hundred years ago," Oilcan said.

Red Knife laughed bitterly. "I was already a quad when he died then."

Which meant Red Knife was well over a thousand years old and needed four numbers to count his age. Considering that perspective, three hundred wasn't that long ago. Was that why Thorne was mad? That he hadn't told her about his Stone Clan ancestor?

Oilcan tried to put it in human perspective for them. "We've considered ourselves fully human since his great-grandson, several generations back."

"His true name," Thorne Scratch said firmly.

"Um . . ." Oilcan pinched the bridge of his nose, trying to dredge up the name. Guillaume was a corruption of the Elvish name that meant "Unbounded." What had been Guillaume's middle name again? "I think it was Unbounded Bright—no, Brilliance. Unbounded Brilliance."

A noise came from the direction of the safe room as the children gasped in discovery that that the foyer was filled with warriors. The *sekasha* glanced toward the noise, hands going to their *ejae*.

"It's just the children." Oilcan shifted between the warriors and the hallway.

Red Knife gave a dry laugh. "Your family's courage is disproportionate to your size."

"Courage comes from the spirit, not the body," Oilcan said.

Red Knife nodded at the truth. The Wyvern First came to tower over Oilcan again. "How old are you?"

Oilcan learned a long time ago not to tell elves his age. A human never lived long enough to seem to be anything more than a child. "I'm an adult."

"That isn't what I asked." There was no mistaking the edge in the Wyvern's voice despite the politeness of the High Elvish.

Thorne Scratch gave her head a nearly imperceptible shake, telling him not to annoy the Wyvern.

Oilcan gritted his teeth and confessed. "I'm twenty-two years old." It made him basically about five years old in elf terms.

Red Knife laughed, murmuring, "Just a baby." He glanced down the hall again at the children cowering there. "Babies taking care of babies."

"I am an adult now," Oilcan stated. "My family is no longer immortal. I will not live beyond my doubles."

"And yet you can tap the Spell Stones." Red Knife shook his head and then turned to Thorne. "Stay with him until someone sane from your clan can decide what is to be done."

✧ ✧ ✧

"What's happened?" he asked after the other *seka-sha* had left.

"They're dead. The oni killed them all," Thorne said bleakly. "They took Jewel Tear. Forest Moss is not currently lucid."

The gunfire had been part of a massacre. Elves that Thorne had known for hundreds of years had been cut down in the battle.

"I'm so sorry," Oilcan said. "But I don't understand how this relates to me."

"If you can tap the Stone Clan Spell Stones, then you are Stone Clan *domana*."

"No, I'm not."

"You are the only functioning Stone Clan *domana* in Pittsburgh at this moment," Thorne Scratch continued as if he hadn't spoken. "You are head of the clan."

"No!" Oilcan caught her by the shoulders and turned her to face him. "Look at me! See me! I'm human!"

She studied him hard with her warrior mask on, but then she let the mask drop. She stepped forward and pressed her forehead to his. "I see you."

26: PROVIDENCE

"*Domi.*" Pony woke Tinker in full dark. "The tengu have come to speak with you."

She flailed in bed, momentarily confounded by darkness and the fact that her right arm was bound tight to her side. "Which ones?"

"It is Jin Wong." Pony helped her sit up. "And I believe he has brought his entire household."

Surely Pony wasn't right; Jin's entire household was all twenty thousand tengu.

"In the middle of the night?"

"You wanted to talk to them."

She did? It took her a minute to remember that when they were splinting her arm, she had told Riki that that she wanted to ask him about greater bloods. Apparently Riki decided that Jin would have more information.

"Yes, I did." Only, she wanted to talk to them in small, manageable numbers. *All* did not sound small to her. Now that she was awake, she could hear the rustle of wings, and distant drumming. "Get me some light."

As Pony activated a spell light, Tinker stumbled into her closet to grab something to wear. She had on the blue cheetah-print cami and boy shorts, but she'd rather meet the entire tengu flock in something other than her Victoria Secrets. She grabbed a dress of deep green silk. She really needed to do something about her wardrobe.

Lemonseed was waiting as Tinker came out of the closet. "*Domi*, they are asking if we can cancel the defensive spells."

Pony had on his warrior's mask and gave Tinker a shake of his head, meaning he didn't think it was safe to let down their guard. Lemonseed, though, was waiting for Tinker's word.

When she had called Jin, he had come to her alone and unarmed, trusting that he'd be safe with her. He was asking her to trust him this time.

"Cancel them," Tinker said. "And bring Jin into the courtyard. That way the overflow of tengu can perch on the roof."

Lemonseed's eyes widened at the thought of tengu on the roof, but she bowed and hurried away.

Tinker went out into the courtyard to find that all the spell lights had been removed, pitching the acre of peach trees into darkness. Black wings churned unseen in the sky overhead, masked by branches. Shrill flutes and thin tin gongs had joined the drumming, growing louder as the musicians came through the main hall.

Her Hand pressed in tightly around her, hands gripped tight to their *ejae*, ready to draw.

Small figures came spilling out the hall, carrying paper lanterns. Tinker lost count after the first dozen that swarmed through the courtyard, slowly lighting up the area as more and more moved among the trees. One came hurrying up to her. It was little Joey Shoji, dressed in a white tunic trimmed in red and carrying a lantern nearly as big as he was.

"Joey, what's going on?" Tinker asked.

He pressed a finger to his lips. "Shhh, Providence is coming."

Jin had told her once that Providence was the guardian spirit of the tengu. As the Chosen, he was considered Providence's child. From what she could gather, though, the guardian spirit was actually a dragon.

Did that mean there was yet another dragon in Pittsburgh?

Behind the lantern bearers came musicians. The flutes were shrill. The gongs looked like and sounded like battered cooking pots. The drums ranged in tones from high and thin to sharp and woody. They made a sharp-edged music with no discernible melody. Just as she thought musicians were playing completely solo to each other, they all sped up slightly at the same moment.

Finally Jin appeared, dressed in robes of white. He was dancing, slowly, mechanically, almost like a series of poses. Before each new pose, he would take a quick step forward, so that he was stuttering his way through the dark trees, like a series of still photographs.

Riki followed behind Jin, dressed in black, winged, armed with swords, and his face painted for war. A dozen armed tengu followed, all with swords but no pistols and rifles. Riki's younger cousin, Kieko, was among the armed honor guard.

The possession included a small shrine being carried by a dozen males and a drum nearly eight feet across carried by another dozen. The big drum was settled into a stand; six drummers circled it and stood waiting. There was no sign of Providence. It seemed like an elaborate party to have without the guest of honor in attendance. Then again, if Providence was in Pittsburgh, Riki probably wouldn't have kidnapped and strip-searched Tinker two weeks earlier, looking for signs that she was Impatience's Chosen. He seemed desperate for a new guardian for the tengu. Or was it that without Jin, Providence wouldn't protect the tengu?

The thrilling near-discordant flute music suddenly stopped, and for a moment the only noise was the wind through the leaves.

All six drummers struck once, a single deep heartbeat of sound.

A second simultaneous downbeat. Then a third.

Then in a sudden, wild of assault of drumming, all the drummers, perfectly in time with each other, beat out one massive rhythm.

Jin moved to the shrine, bowed low to it, and opened the front.

Tinker gasped as she saw what lay inside the little shrine: a dragon hide.

Jin lifted out the hide and turned, holding the head above him. The hide settled over his shoulders, cloaking him from view. The flutes broke out in their shrill discord and the gongs clattered fast and furious.

Jin started to dance forward again, faster, but still in the odd stuttering poses. This time the poses made more sense. Each could have been a photograph of Impatience as the little dragon moved without the fluidity of life.

Tinker realized she had covered her mouth in horror and her hand was still pressed tight to her mouth. For one horrific moment, she thought that the skin might belong to Impatience, but the color was wrong: a deep gold instead of blood red. This was Providence? Or at least the skin of the tengu's guardian spirit? What had happened to him? What kind of monster skinned a massively intelligent being? And why in hell had the tengu brought his skin to her? The elves' insistence on burning their dead seemed suddenly sane and pure.

Jin the dragon danced in a wide circle around Tinker and her Hand. The big drum throbbed like a massive heartbeat against her skin as the flutes shrieked. The dragon head dipped and rose and turned in a parody of Impatience's curious investigation of his surroundings. Empty eyes took in the night sky, the rooftops crowded with silent tengu, the honor guard kneeling on the ground, the little lantern bearers. Louder and faster the music rushed toward a climax.

A wind suddenly blasted through the trees, and Tinker felt magic surge up as Jin suddenly froze and the music instantly stopped.

The dragon head had been turned away from her.

The hairs on the back of her neck rose as it slowly turned to look at her with gleaming eyes. The mane that had laid down Jin's back rose, crackling with power.

"Tinker *haenanan*." The voice was too deep, too gravelly, too loud to be Jin's. "*Manamana daaaaa sobadadada*."

"Princess Tinker," Riki murmured in Elvish from his bowed position. "Our great guardian Providence greets you."

This was entirely too creepy.

"You never told me that he was dead," Tinker whispered in English.

Riki winced and gave a slight warning shake of his head. Providence, apparently, could understand English fine; the dragon laughed. Its breath blasted warm over her, smelling like wind after a rainstorm. His words rolled over her, seemingly unending. Jin had told her once that dragons were long-winded and indirect and trying to hurry them was considered impolite.

"It is the folly of youth," Riki translated even as Providence spoke. "Ignorant of great pain and death, the young believe that they are above harm. We moved through the worlds, following our whims, believing nothing could hurt us. But we were wrong. Like all things, it was only a matter of time.

"I was not the first to fall. The earliest ones were caught fast by their bodies, their minds free to seek out help. They bore stories of a growing evil, covetous of our powers, which sought to take them for themselves. This evil rendered down our helpless brothers, tearing them asunder and gifting their slaves with tattered pieces of our souls.

"Still, we did not understand our danger. We simply put this world under edict and left it to its own fate. We felt it was not our place to act, as it was not the world we were born to. But then the evil branched out to Earth, like a growing cancer, and this time we attempted to check its spread. We searched out bridges to Onihida, the next world in harmony with this one, and eliminated them. To our horror, we soon realized that we were too late. All we had done was seal the evil on Onihida."

It sounded like her theory was right. "So the greater bloods are elves?"

"This evil has had many names across many worlds.

We did not witness the start of their rise. We do not know from whence they came nor what they were at the birth. They still seek what they have always sought—to become gods. They want what we have by natural right. They grow more and more powerful, piece by stolen piece."

Sparrow had claimed that the Skin Clan had been one step below gods. She had claimed that the elves were stagnating. She had wanted to go back to the old ways, so the elves could once again "advance."

"Long I have watched over my tengu," Riki/Providence said. "It is my shame that I am the cause of their misery—for the evil came searching for me and caught my body and laid siege to my mind. I asked of the tengu to commit the ultimate of blasphemy, to slay their own god to free me from my captors. As punishment for that deed, they were merged with crows and yet left bound to earth."

"But the greater bloods were here first, on Elfhome, as elves?"

Providence nodded his great head. "They gave your father's people our intelligence. They gave your mother's people our sight. They gave the warriors at your back our morality."

"Eons have come to a balance point on this moment, like great rocks pressing on fractures of the Earth. The time is at hand for pressure to cause a shift and all the worlds to be rewritten—not only this world, but all the worlds in harmony with it."

That didn't sound good. "What's going to happen?"

Providence gazed down at her with gleaming eyes. "All is at hand for the evil to achieve their goal."

27: ON TRACK

Tommy was starting to think he was wrong. With Spot tucked behind him on his hoverbike, he'd followed the railroad tracks out for mind-numbing hours. Beyond the Rim, the tracks were the only sign of civilization. They cut through a virgin forest of towering ironwood trees. On either side of the iron rails were spell lights to keep down the ambient level of magic that would otherwise snare and tangle on the metal. Beyond the graveled embankments, he could pick out wards on stone posts, to keep everything from black willows to rabbits from wandering onto the tracks. Still, every few miles there was a massive skeleton of a saurus that had managed to blunder into the path of the train anyhow. For the first time, the massive axe-like nose on the Elfhome engines made sense to Tommy.

There wasn't, however, a single sign of the oni.

Hoverbikes had amazing gas mileage since half their power came from magic. He'd filled his tank and strapped on a extra can behind Spot, but he was nearing the point where he would have to turn around or not be able to get his hoverbike all the way back to Pittsburgh.

Spot beat on his shoulder and pointed behind them.

Tommy skidded to a stop and looked back, the hoverbike rumbling loudly in the forest silence. They were running alongside a shallow river, the train tracks cut into the shoulder of a hill above the flood plain.

"Here?"

Spot didn't answer, but his nose was working, trying to catch whatever elusive scent had made him stop Tommy.

Tommy turned the hoverbike around and slowly made his way back toward Pittsburgh, eyeing the landscape closely. The oni had been careful, but years of use had left small, indelible marks on the landscape. He hadn't noticed them at fifty miles per hour, but at a crawl he could pick them out. The rocky embankment was bare of vegetation all the way down to the river's edge. On the far side of the shallow water, there was a break in the brush, too wide to be a deer trail.

Tommy pulled up against the cliff, just in case a train came through, and shut down his hoverbike to conserve gas. The forest quiet pressed in on them.

Spot swung down off the hoverbike and pressed nose to soil.

"Is it the same group?" Tommy checked his pistol to make sure it was loaded, not that a dozen shots would help much if they were jumped by an entire platoon.

On hands and knees, Spot crisscrossed the embankment sniffing and then nodded.

"Do they still have the elf female?"

Spot nodded again.

"Is the kitsune with them?"

Spot shook his head, making his long ears flap.

Good. Tommy wasn't immune to her powers. "How recent?"

Spot held up both hands to measure out a long time. The oni must have driven straight to the station and boarded a train just as it left. The oni were hours in front of them.

Tommy didn't bother to ask how many oni—Spot was still having trouble counting past five.

So he was right that the oni were using the train to travel far out of Pittsburgh in large numbers. Yay, him; out in the frigging nowhere with a pistol and an eight-year-old. Somehow this didn't seem like a smart plan.

Tommy considered the river and the far bank. The brush screened the area beyond now, but the leaves were already turning color with the approaching autumn. It was only a matter of time before all the leaves came down, leaving the far bank exposed. The oni camp was probably miles south from the track so there was no chance of it being discovered by train work crews. Hopefully it was far enough out that no one had heard his engine. This was as far as he could go on his hoverbike, though, without bringing the oni down on his head.

He turned in a full circle, looking for a place to hide the big bike. Someplace where the oni wouldn't see it or stumble over it or even find it easily if they were looking. There were niches in the cliff running alongside the tracks. He could pop up and land on one of the larger ledges.

Spot tried to scramble back up onto the hoverbike when Tommy restarted the bike.

"No, stay here. I'll be back."

Spot gave him big hurt puppy-dog eyes but backed off. Tommy took the bike around the bend of the hill until he found a likely ledge. He raced the engine and then, dropping all power to the lift chain, popped up onto the wide shelf. Shutting down the motor, he unflattened the brush that he crashed through until the bike was screened from a casual glance.

Spot wriggled with joy when he saw Tommy trotting back down the track toward him. His cheeks were wet with silent tears.

"I told you I'd be back." Tommy patted the boy on the head as Spot hugged him tight. "I need you to be a big boy. No crying."

Spot nodded, rubbing his face dry against Tommy's shirt.

They had to go quietly and carefully. The band of oni had fanned out, taking various trails so that none would be too heavily traveled. After the second ridge, two miles south from the river, they rejoined on one well-worn path. Five miles farther south, another wide trail crossed it.

Half-oni or not, Spot was still just eight. He couldn't hike all day. Tommy detoured to the nearest hilltop where he could keep an eye on the path. Spot curled up beside Tommy and tossed and turned exactly enough to get his head into Tommy's lap before falling asleep.

Tommy sighed, shaking his head, but didn't bother to push Spot off. The only affection that the boy was ever going to get was from his own family. As he got older, even that would be less and less often.

While Spot slept, Tommy considered the crossroads.

Where did the east-west path lead? It seemed to be running parallel to the distant train track. Was it simply that the oni had multiple stops where they could get on and off the train? It would be comforting to think so, because it meant he wouldn't be caught between two oni forces if they continued south. There was only one train in and one train out every day, and both had passed through this area hours ago. If the east-west path led to other camps, though, there could be oni coming and going all day and even into the night. He considered heading back to Pittsburgh, but what would he say? He'd found a path?

After twenty minutes of resting, he shook Spot awake and they continued south. Another ten miles and two longer breaks, and they came to a second crossroad. Dusk was falling and Spot was starting to stagger. He lifted his head, nose working.

Tommy crouched down beside Spot and sniffed. Wood smoke lightly scented the air. They were getting close. "Follow me."

Spot nodded, eyes wide. He might not be able to count, but he understood the danger of tracking the oni.

Tommy veered off the well-beaten path on the valley floor to push through the thick laurel that covered the steep hillside. At points they had to scramble up rock walls. When they reached the hilltop, he motioned to Spot to keep belly down on the ground. Tommy moved forward in a crouch along the ridgeline until he came to a drop-off.

In the valley below was a massive ironwood fort and beyond it hundreds of tents. Thousands of oni moved through the dusk. He could make out hundreds of cages holding muzzled wargs. In the far south of the camp, there was a huge pen. Whatever was caged there roared, the noise echoing up the valley like distant thunder.

"Shit," Tommy whispered.

Spot tapped his shoulder and pointed off to the west. There was a faint smoke haze between them and the setting sun. Another camp lay beyond the hill. The path heading west from the crossroad seemed to lead toward it. Judging by the smoke, the western camp was probably as big as the camp just to the south. Tommy turned and studied the eastern horizon. Darkness was already spreading over the land, and light from campfires in a third site gleamed off a haze of smoke.

There weren't thousands of oni hidden in the forest—there were tens of thousands. And somewhere, down in the spreading darkness, was one female elf.

28: TEA AND CRUMPETS

How do you fight your shadow?

Tinker sat in the courtyard, staring down at her shadow. Around her, the *sekasha* prowled, restless but silent as caged tigers. The wind moved through the peach trees, stirring the branches. She watched the play of light move over her shadow, thinking of Providence.

The dragons had somehow evolved two different levels of existence. There was the body that lived and breathed. Their minds—no, not mind—awareness? Soul? Whatever made up moral conscious thought—that existed beyond their bodies. Jin had warned her that dragon bodies could operate on autopilot without their minds guiding their actions. "Lights are on, but no one's home." It was disturbing to know that their minds could continue too, without the body still alive. And yet wasn't that the whole thing with the elf cremation? To free the spirit of the dead body so it could move on to heaven?

She had tried to get details from Providence about what the Skin Clan planned, but he merely told her that she'd be fighting her shadow.

She held out her hand and studied the dark fingers on the ground. What did the dragon mean by that?

Shadow knows what you're doing because you block the light, telegraphing intention. Actions cause reaction.

Tinker squinted up at the morning sun. Light created the shadow. The absence of light meant there was no shadow. Could that actually be counted as fighting it? Considering the dragon's dual existence, what if the shadow continued to exist in total darkness? What if you could only see it because of the light? Without light, you would no longer be aware of the shadow's reaction. But then again, the shadow wouldn't be connected to you anymore, and it wouldn't be aware of your actions. In darkness, a fight would become a two-way blindman's bluff.

Tinker sighed. She was wasting time with the metaphysical. She would be better off dealing with science. Good hard numbers. So far, Oilcan's kids were the only clue to what the Skin Clan planned. By now Lain should have the preliminary findings on the children's DNA.

Of course, there was the small problem of how to get the information. Her cell phone had been toasted in the Rolls-Royce explosion.

Fate was determined to reduce her down to the Stone Age.

Tinker stood up. "I want to go see Lain."

"Are you sure?" Pony continued to pace restlessly. "Prince True Flame has taken many of the Wyverns with him, and all the other Hands have gone with Wolf."

And you are hurt, he did not say.

"Since there is no phone here, the only way I'll be able to talk to her—"

"Was if she came and saw you," Lain said from behind Lemonseed.

Under the guise of having innocent conversation with her estranged (and strange) mother and aunt, a picnic tea was set up in the courtyard under the peach trees. Lemonseed apparently sensed the real importance of the occasion—she only provided teacups and assorted finger sandwiches for three.

Pony and Stormsong stood guard as Shields at the edge of the picnic blanket. Cloudwalker, Rainlily, and Little Egret roamed the courtyard as Blades, keeping the rest of the elves at bay.

"I focused on the children first," Lain whispered as she spread out the DNA scans on the picnic blanket. "All the children—the living and the dead—were related. They're all distant cousins."

"Are you sure?" Tinker frowned at the smudges. That was all they had to work with? "The Skin Clan spell-worked everyone. Could this just be DNA they bred into the Stone Clan? Look at Oilcan and me. We both look like Stone Clan even though we're only like one-sixteenth or less elf."

Lain sighed. "You have the intelligence to know all this, if you just applied yourself."

"I don't like biology," Tinker said. "Blood and guts and all that. Bleah."

Esme snickered, earning a hard look from both Tinker and Lain. "That's what I said when I was eighteen and Lain tried to talk me into a biology major. Almost those exact words."

Lain decided to ignore both of them. "Yes, I'm sure. All the children share the same great-great-grandmother." Lain pulled out sets of the computer-printed spell papers paper-clipped together. "To verify that the scans you found in the chest were those of the children, I used the spell on the DNA swipes." She divided the paper-clipped papers into two stacks. "These three are the dead children. These are Barley, Cattail, Rustle, and Baby Duck." She laid a lone sheet between the two stacks. "And this is the control, Merry. Notice these markers at the top. This spell is testing for a certain set of DNA markers and showing positive and negative. The three children that were killed tested negative. The four that survived tested positive. Merry also tested positive."

Pony growled out an impressive string of foul words. "We thought ourselves free of the Skin Clan and yet they're still breeding us."

The Skin Clan was working within the Stone Clan, carrying on their breeding programs? It boggled Tinker's mind, but she supposed in the confusion of war, a member of the Skin Clan could disappear in one corner of the world and surface in another, claiming to be part of a different caste and clan. In the time she had lived with Windwolf, she hadn't seen any drawings or paintings of individual elves. Without DNA testing, there was no way to be sure if someone was who they really claimed to be.

"But why bring the kids all the way over here?" Tinker said. "No one has even suspected there's anything wrong in Easternlands."

Pony started to pace. "If Skin Clan is working from within the Stone Clan, they could influence mating:

encourage a marriage, introduce partners, discourage couplings that they didn't want. The Skin Clan couldn't do any spell-working. Every *domana* within a *mei* would feel any massive spell use. Even if they had brought one or two *domana* into their fold, there would be others in range."

"But if we felt something here, we'd assume it was the oni doing stuff," Tinker said. "Did they spell-work the kids?"

Lain sighed. "I only have you as a basis of comparison, and what Windwolf did to you was massive. There's no way to miss it. Merry's sample seems to indicate that nothing has been done to the other children—their abnormality was there when they were born."

"They seem so normal," Tinker complained, thinking of Providence's warning. The Skin Clan tipped their hand in luring the kids to Pittsburgh. What had been worth that risk?

Tinker glanced to Esme, who was plundering the sandwiches that Lemonseed had left behind with the tea. "What about your dreams? Did you see anything—useful?"

Esme looked unhappy. "You and your cousin, the musician, have been playing hide-and-seek with your shadow at that beat-up old hotel where you two used to live. You're just little kids, with your hands covered with blue paint, laughing and singing. Your shadow is this horrible thing—when your back is turned, it's a massive beast with sharp teeth—but when you look at your shadow, it's just a little girl, all pigtails and laughter."

"I never had pigtails," Tinker growled.

Esme frowned, eyes unfocused, as she munched on a cucumber sandwich. "Come to think of it, you have always looked like a little boy in my dreams: short hair, ragged clothes, and covered with mud. Your shadow, though, has pigtails and is wearing a dress."

"So it's not really me," Tinker said.

"It's a monster and it wants you dead and it's very good at the game."

29: SPOT ON

Tommy had raided the fridge for food that could travel and stuffed it into an insulated delivery bag. They sat on the hilltop as the sun set, eating egg rolls, cold pork buns, and fried rice. Afterward Spot curled up against Tommy and slept.

Tommy studied the camp through binoculars, grinding his teeth together. He couldn't stop thinking of what Jin had said about the elves needing to win the war.

After watching the royal troops flood the city and Windwolf fight, Tommy had been assuming that the elves winning was a given. Now he wasn't so sure. Yeah, for a while there the elves were pulling rats out of their holes and hacking them to pieces. The most recent score, however, had oni kicking elf butt. Earth Son was dead. Forest Moss had gone over the edge. Jewel Tear had been taken and all her people killed. Tinker was hurt. Windwolf was in protective overdrive. It left Prince True Flame to take on the entire oni army—if Tommy went back and drew a detailed map and the elves believed him.

Windwolf might listen, but he wasn't calling the shots.

True Flame would believe Jewel Tear.

Of course there was the small matter of finding her and then freeing her—if she was still alive—and then running nearly twenty miles back to his hoverbike with the entire oni army chasing them. He'd have to be insane even to consider it.

Jin had said that you had to create peace to live in it.

Tommy should have grabbed a tengu to drag along. The elves were treating the tengu as trusted allies. If Riki took back reports of the camps, they'd believe him. The bastard had helped kidnap Tinker, but they still called him in on raids of oni whelping pens. Tommy took out his cell phone and checked to see if he had a signal. No surprise: he didn't.

He sighed and scanned the torchlit camp once more. Most of the warriors were obviously right out of whelping pens, and the camp was pure chaos for it. He probably could walk right into camp, passing as one of them, except for the fact he was too well known. He spotted dozens of officers that had reported to his father. They knew his scent, knew his face, knew that he'd slipped free of the oni hold and joined the elves.

Spot turned in his sleep, and Tommy glanced down at the boy. Spot scrubbed his hand over the fur on his face, rubbed at his dog-like muzzle, and then stilled, his floppy ears covering his eyes.

Spot could move through camp unnoticed. He looked bred in a whelping pen. None of the officers knew the boy; Tommy had kept him well hidden.

Spot could track Jewel Tear through the camp, find out where the oni were holding her and—

Tommy laughed. And what? Take on the entire oni army?

But then again, this wasn't one of his aunts. This was elf *domi*. If Tommy could free her, then she could take on the oni army herself.

Still, it was dependent on Spot finding Jewel Tear without getting caught. Tommy hated the idea of sending him down into the camp. The oni wouldn't just kill him if they caught him; the oni were too cruel for anything so merciful.

Tommy's nose wasn't keen enough to pick up Jewel Tear's scent. If he didn't send Spot, then Tommy would have to search all of the camp.

He shook Spot awake.

Spot thought Tommy was insane—it was clear in his gaze. His eyes would slowly slide off Tommy's to the oni-choked camp, and one eyebrow would climb in confusion. And then he'd look back at Tommy, the other eyebrow cocked.

Tommy didn't sugarcoat it, but he didn't want to scare Spot either. "You can do this. You know how when I bring you home a chew toy? You know how you have to act so the big kids won't steal it off you? I've seen you do it. You hide it in your pocket and just pretend you're doing chores and walk around the warren, looking for someplace you can chew on it without anyone seeing?"

Spot thought and then nodded slowly.

"You're going to go down and walk through the camp like you have a chore to do. No one will stop you." Tommy hoped and prayed that they wouldn't. "You just need to find out where they have her and come back to me. I know you can do this. You just have to be brave. Okay?"

"Okay," Spot whispered.

The hardest thing Tommy had ever done was to sit and watch Spot slip out of the shadows and walk toward the oni camp. Fear was roaring through him—a small, cold certainty that the boy was heading for a painful death. Tommy blanked Spot from the guard's vision so his cousin could walk in unchallenged.

Spot paused only slightly just inside the gate, nose working, and then set off in a determined walk.

Tommy lost sight of him among the taller, shifting bodies.

He frantically scanned the oni, looking for the small boy. There were other small oni moving through the camp, their size making Tommy think he'd found Spot only to realize he was wrong.

"Shit, shit, shit. Where is he?"

Time crawled. Half an hour. Then an hour. The small, cold certainty grew until it filled him. What was he thinking? Oni ate their own children if they found one that seemed too weak.

Then the mass shifted, and there was Spot, walking determinedly toward Tommy again.

"Yes!" Tommy blinded the guard, and when Spot reached him, hugged him hard. "Good boy. Good boy."

Spot grinned up at him, nearly vibrating with nerves.

"Did you find her?" Tommy asked. "Is she still alive?"

Spot shook his head but continued to grin.

Tommy's stomach roiled. "She's dead?"

Spot shook his head, his grin slipping.

"You didn't find her?"

Spot cringed from Tommy's scowl. "They took elf to whelping pens."

Tommy swore but rubbed behind Spot's ears in apology. "Good boy."

30: CODEX MOMENT

Tinker was still in healing mode, which meant she slept whether she wanted to or not, usually without warning. One minute she was talking with Esme in the courtyard, and the next she was asleep, dreaming about playing as a child on Neville Island as evil danced underfoot, pretending innocence.

She bolted out of her nightmare to find herself back in her own bed.

"You are safe." Pony wrapped arms around her. "We are all safe."

"This was almost as bad as the oni in the enclave." Tinker clung to him tightly, using his warm, strong presence to force away the skittering fear. "We couldn't see the danger. It was right there in front of us."

"Stormsong will see through the shadows." Pony's voice was full of trust at her Second's ability.

"I've got to stop this. I have to find a way to stop this." Tinker disentangled herself from the sheets and stumbled out of bed. "I think what Providence really meant was that the Skin Clan are going to do something big to take over Elfhome again. Once they do, they could use it to attack Earth from two sides. Obviously the oni are another army of monsters they're going to use. Oilcan's kids work into this somehow—"

Pony winced at the mention of Oilcan.

"What? Is he okay?" Tinker cried, suddenly afraid.

"He is . . . unhurt."

"What then?"

"Prince True Flame has ruled that *nagarou* is to be considered Stone Clan since he can tap their Spell Stones."

"He can?" It amazed her that they'd gone this long without knowing that. She realized that if Oilcan didn't know the connection spell, the one that opened him up to the stored power of the Spell Stones, the rest of the spells would be inert.

That was all? But judging by Pony's look, it was not as harmless as it sounded.

"This is bad how?"

"He is no longer automatically under Windwolf's protection. It is unclear what will happen once the Stone Clan sends new *domana* to help fight the oni."

"They wouldn't try to hurt him, would they?"

Pony looked unhappy. "There are many ways to bring harm without drawing blood."

She didn't like the sound of that. "How soon before they arrive?"

"The Wyverns do not like our situation here. We are spread dangerously thin. They have demanded that the *sekasha* of the Stone Clan act. There will be more *domana* here shortly, whether they want to come or not."

"But any one of them could be the ones working with the Skin Clan."

"We have no choice. We must accept them as trustworthy until they prove otherwise."

Another raid on Stormsong's wardrobe later and she headed down the street to find out what was so special about Oilcan's kids. They seemed completely normal to her, but she was starting to think maybe she was clueless about constituted as "average." It wasn't as if she and Oilcan had ever lived a "normal" life before saving Windwolf's life. Since then, both of their lives had gone off track into completely strange. All manner of inexplicable things had happened to them both. She had become an elf, accidentally stranded Pittsburgh on Elfhome, and fallen into space to save a spaceship that had been trapped in time for her entire life. Oilcan had befriended a dragon, derailed the Skin Clan's collection of the children by adopting Merry, and now was considered head of Stone Clan in Westernlands.

All of that was made even odder because, by rights, neither of them should even be in Pittsburgh. Her father died childless long before the first Startup; her entire existence was an anomaly. Her grandfather once said that he'd brought Oilcan to Elfhome only because he couldn't move Tinker to Earth. If Tinker hadn't existed, then Oilcan wouldn't have been in Pittsburgh. Given those two points, everything that followed was even more improbable. Someone of religious bent—say Riki—might even say everything was miraculous.

Tinker paused on wide stone front steps of Sacred Heart.

Why couldn't her grandfather take her to Earth?

At the time, she had thought it was because she would have fought like a hellion to stay on Elfhome. She realized now that the temper tantrums of a six-year-old wouldn't have swayed her grandfather from doing what was best for his grandchildren. They were his sun and his moon—he would have killed to protect them.

Had Leo warned her grandfather that Jin was tengu and there were oni on Earth? Then again, how did Leo know about the oni? The war had broken out after her ancestor left Elfhome.

"Hey." Oilcan came down the steps to hug her, being overly careful and awkward because of her broken arm. "Been worried about you."

"To quote Blue Sky, 'I have the Great Wall of Kick Butt.'" Tinker was glad to see that Thorne Scratch had survived the oni attack on Ginger Wine's. The female stood within shield range of Oilcan, her "on duty" light on. The story of Tinker's life lately was how a few days of insanity altered how she saw someone without them changing. She had to remind herself that while she now saw Thorne Scratch as a solid ally, there was no way of knowing how the warrior felt about Tinker. She kept to English. "We've got lots and lots of trouble."

Oilcan's sudden grin warned her that he was going to say something stupid. "Right here in River City. Trouble with a capital 'T' that stands for Tinker."

She smacked him with her good hand. "I'm serious. This is majorly bad."

Oilcan listened to her explain the tengu visit, what Providence had told her, and Lain's findings. "Coz, your life is strange."

"Yeah, I was just thinking that. It makes me a bad judge on what is normal. What do you think—how normal are your kids?"

The laughter drained out of his face. "They're good kids. I know it's part of the way elves think—that your household is your family—but they really bonded to each other. I wouldn't blame them for being hysterical messes after all they've been through, but it seems sometimes like they've pulled themselves together just so they can be strong for the others."

She explained what Lain had discovered. "So, you haven't noticed anything strange?"

"Rustle would lose his head if it wasn't screwed on, but no, nothing else."

"There's some reason the Skin Clan wants these kids bad."

Oilcan half turned to stare back at the school building. "Tink, how am I going to keep them safe?"

She understood the feeling completely. "Here." She reached out and caught his hand. "I'll show you how to set up a shield. Just hold it until help comes."

She explained setting up the resonance and calling the shield into existence. He had no problem getting his fingers into position, but then he played several musical instruments, so he was used to twisting his fingers into pretzels. It reminded her of the song he'd written for her. "I really like the song. The one with the *domi* and her First. That was cool."

"Thanks."

"Where did you get those words and hand gestures for Briar's part?" Tinker asked. "Did Briar teach them to you? I've been going nuts trying to learn more of the Wind Clan *esva*."

"My mom taught them to me." He danced out of reach of her angry swing, laughing. "I thought they were just a kid's game. I'd forgotten most of them. That's why I never taught you. I didn't even know what they were until I helped Windwolf with Malice."

"Looks like you remember a lot to me," Tinker grumbled.

"I just copied what was in the codex."

The Dufae codex was her personal bible while she was growing up; she had nearly every page memorized. "They're not in the codex."

"Yes, they are." He let her smack him this time; he knew it only made her madder if he stayed out of reach indefinitely. "Some of the pages have little pictograms above a Elvish phoneme. Those are finger positions."

She suddenly realized what "pictograms" he meant. Sprinkled through the codex was a set of diagrams that she had analyzed to death between the ages of eight and ten. They were two sets of five symbols. She felt stupid that she never realized they represented the right or left hands. "Damn! I asked both Grandpa and Tooloo about those and they lied. Grandpa said he didn't know what they were—"

"He might not have," Oilcan allowed.

"—And Tooloo said that they were footprints of fairies."

Oilcan snickered. "And you believed that?"

"No. I asked her again, and she said—" Tinker stopped, mouth open, startled.

"What?"

"She said they were notations for a song."

Oilcan laughed. "They are now."

"Yes, they are." Tinker frowned, shaking her head. "This was years ago. Could she have really known you were going to write that song?"

"Who can tell with Tooloo?" Oilcan said.

Esme had said that Tooloo had taught her how to control her dreams. The damn half-elf had woven all sorts of lies trying to discourage Tinker from interacting with Windwolf. Somehow Tooloo knew that one day Windwolf would use a Skin Clan spell to change Tinker.

And Tooloo had known Tinker dating Nathan would end with him dead.

All this time, Tooloo was an *intanyai seyosa*?

Tinker blew out her breath and tugged at her hair in frustration. "Sometimes, I just want to beat that female," she said low and quiet so only he could hear. Tooloo might not be on the Wind Clan side of this war, but she wasn't on the Skin Clan's side, either, or the oni would have known exactly where to find Tinker.

Most annoying was the knowledge that trying to get any kind of answer out of Tooloo was probably hopeless. It might even prove deadly for the old half-elf—as the *sekasha* might not take well to her evasion.

31: JEWEL TEAR ON STONE

Successful bookies did not gamble. They always set odds that benefited them and let other people take the risks. Tommy was no exception. Thus, he didn't want to bet his life on the odds spread out before him. In the clearing below him were twelve oni warriors entrusted with dragging Jewel Tear through the wilderness to wherever Kajo's new whelping pen lay. The warriors were the smart kind that needed face paint to make an impression on their more animalistic subordinates. They were so heavily armed it was a wonder that they could move; he had spotted everything from rocket launchers down to grenades hanging like unripe apples of pure evil. The sprawling encampment was miles behind them, but there could be patrols within earshot. Tommy had one pistol with a silencer, eight clips of ammo, his limited ability to cloud minds, and his eight-year-old cousin.

No, he didn't like the odds.

He was starting to wish he'd brought Bingo instead of Spot.

As Tommy mulled over his problem, the oni started to fuss with their prisoner. He couldn't tell what they were doing to her, but the female, who had silently taken their rough treatment, started to scream in terror. Spot cowered, pressing close to Tommy, and looked pleadingly up at him. Obviously the boy expected him to do something. Oh, hell. He really wished he'd brought Bingo.

"Stay." Tommy checked his pistol. "If something happens to me, go home."

He worked his way down to the clearing, trying to remain calm. The silencer made his pistol wildly inaccurate, but he had no hope of keeping his true position secret without it. He would need ice coolness to pull this off. His oni father could have clouded the mind of all the warriors, walked through the clearing unseen, and killed them at leisure. But he didn't have his father's ability to mask a moving object from multiple beings. And his father wouldn't be moved by the whimpers of a child.

"This is so stupid," Tommy whispered to himself. He reached out with his ability and grabbed hold of the oni's minds. It was like trying to hold a dozen large marbles in his hands, shifting around, nearly spilling out of control. *Just trees.* He fed the image into their thoughts, erasing himself from the landscape. *Nothing else.*

Jewel Tear's hands were bundled up with leather to keep her from casting spells. While Tommy had shifted positions, the oni stripped off the covering and now were tying Jewel Tear's arms straight out, hands splayed, so they could amputate her fingers. A *domana* without fingers could do no magic, and she would be forever harmless. Apparently Kajo hadn't trusted the lesser bloods that infiltrated Ginger Wine's enclave to carefully maim the elf without killing her. Considering the carnage that the oni left behind, it'd been wise of Kajo. This new set of guards, though, could do the job right.

Fighting to stay focused, Tommy stood still and aimed at the oni holding the elf. He missed the first shot, making the oni flinch aside as the bullet whined past his ear. The second bullet caught the warrior behind the ear, and he went down. The other oni holding Jewel Tear had been focused on the elf and had missed any sign of the first shot. He looked over at his fallen leader with surprise and took the third bullet in the throat.

The oni started to react to Tommy's attack, but they couldn't tell where he was. Jewel Tear scrambled to her feet and bolted into the woods. Tommy locked down on a curse, which would have given away his position. He didn't need her finding more trouble. He had enough here in the clearing. At least she served as a distraction. The oni were reacting as if they thought she must be running to their attacker. Three charged after her. He managed to kill two, but the third vanished into the trees.

"There's just one." The leader identified himself. He'd taken cover on the wrong side of a tree, shielding himself against attackers in the direction that Jewel Tear had run.

Tommy crouched down as they scanned the wrong direction, and took careful aim.

"I don't see any—" The second-in-command glanced to the leader as Tommy's bullet sprayed blood and brains against the tree trunk. "Behind us!"

Tommy froze in place, trying to not even breathe, as the warriors whipped around, leveling guns in his direction. None were pointed directly at him.

Empty clearing. He held on as tight as he could to their minds. Six was easier than twelve, but they were still slick and unwieldy in his hold. *Nothing to see.*

"Where is he?" the nearest growled to the second-in-command.

They were clumped too close together. There were six tight around him, and he only had four bullets left. They'd cut him to ribbons before he could change his clip.

Carefully, he fed them the image of someone darting through the trees, running from them.

"There!" one bayed and leapt after the phantom image. A second and third were quick on his heels.

"Idiots!" the second-in-command shouted. "There's no—"

Tommy shot him. The first bullet hit the male in the left shoulder. The oni roared with pain, lifting up his machine gun and firing blindly. The others aimed in Tommy's general direction and fired.

Dust, lots of billowing dust, something staggering to the right as bullets slammed into it.

Tommy gritted his teeth, staying still as the bullets tore up the ground beside him, spraying him with dirt and bits of stones. He emptied his clip into the second-in-command, dropping him. After that, he could only wait until the other two warriors reached the end of their clips, hoping they didn't hit him.

As he hoped, they both emptied their guns at the same time. For one moment, they lost their focus as they changed their clips. He ejected the clip from his pistol, slammed a fresh clip home, and gave them a new image.

Dust billows, revealing and hiding a body laying on the ground. Elf long hair, wyvern armor, sekasha *tattoos.*

After the thunder of guns, the silence rang loud in his ears.

Slowly the warriors moved closer to look at the phantom body.

"Can they do that?" the one asked. "Be invisible?"

The other was shaking his head like a wet dog. "Isn't right. Isn't right," the male growled.

"Can they or can't they?" the first asked.

The second worked his nose, sniffing. "Not the right scent," the male growled. "I smell that damn cat."

Shit. How good was the warrior's nose? Would he be able to track Tommy?

The three that had charged into the woods, though, were returning. He reached for their minds and made them see two elves standing over the fallen oni. Their response was satisfyingly violent. In a matter of minutes, only one warrior was left alive.

And one warrior he could completely blindside easily.

From the woods came Spot's cry of anger. Tommy's heart leapt in his chest, followed hard by rage. He had told the boy to stay put! He dashed toward the sound, rejecting the spent clip and inserting a new one.

The lone oni warrior had caught the elf female by her long dark hair, but as he had struggled to subdue her, Spot had jumped the oni from behind. Tommy couldn't shoot in fear of hitting his cousin. The oni reached over his shoulder and grabbed the boy. Spot bit down hard on the oni's hand. Roaring with pain and anger, the oni flung the boy down onto the ground, stomped down on Spot, and pulled his gutting knife. Pinned, the boy was at least out of the line of fire. Tommy took aim and shot.

The oni went down, and both Spot and Jewel went for the knife. The elf was closer and snatched it up awkwardly with her tied hands.

"Don't hurt him!" Tommy roared in Elvish, leveling the gun at her. "Hurt him and I'll gut you myself!"

Jewel backed away from the boy, bound arms bent at the elbow to hold the knife ready to strike. Luckily her hands were still tied too tightly to let her cast magic.

Spot scrambled up and dashed to Tommy, wrapping his arms around him and burying his head into Tommy's side. The boy was shaking hard.

"Are you okay?" Tommy asked him in Mandarin. The boy only whimpered. "Damn it, are you hurt or not?"

Spot shook his head. Tommy sighed out relief and patted the boy on the back. Reassured, he focused back on Jewel Tear. The greater blood oni bred for brute force, not caring that the lesser bloods looked like monsters. In the case of the oni warriors, it might even be a benefit. The elves went for looks; there was no such thing as an ugly elf. Jewel Tear was radiant even when muddy, bruised, and battered. Her rich sable-colored hair fell to her knees. Her eyes were a stunning amber brown with thick long lashes and dark elegant eyebrows. Her skin was a warm caramel color. The oni had torn rends into her green silk gown, and, through the tears, Tommy could see tantalizing glimpses of her body.

That she was bound and yet armed and ready to fight only made her more erotic to him. They eyed each other over the oni gutting blade.

"I don't want to hurt you." He indicated with his pistol that she should drop the knife. "But I will if I have to."

"You will have to kill me. I will not submit."

He reach out with his ability and projected an image of him standing before her, gun leveled, thinking out the problem. Keeping that firm in her mind, he holstered his gun, stepped forward, jerked the knife out of her hand, and shoved her to the ground. She landed with a cry of dismay. He stepped back out of her range and let go of her mind.

"What—what did you do?" she cried as she struggled to free her fingers.

"I told you, I don't want to hurt you." Tommy handed the gutting knife to Spot. It had been a mistake not arming the boy so he could defend himself. "If you haven't noticed, I'm trying to rescue you."

Her eyes narrowed in study of them. She in took in Tommy's catlike ears and Spot's doglike features. "You're Wolf Who Rule's half-oni?"

"We don't belong to the viceroy."

"But you're saving me? For him?"

"True Flame thinks I had something to do with your kidnapping."

She grasped it instantly. "Because the oni used the kitsune's illusions? And you have that mind trick of yours."

"Yes." Tommy hauled her to her feet. "Come on. I'm taking you back to Pittsburgh."

She gave a laugh that ended with a sob. "Back? Back to what? The ruined shambles of my life?"

Tommy laughed and put a hand to her slender neck. "I could kill you and end all your suffering."

She gasped in surprise and gazed at him with doe-eyed amazement.

"Well?" He ran his thumb down her windpipe, feeling her pulse flutter like a moth under his palm. God, he found holding the life of a little, naïve female in the palm of his hand such a turn-on. It made him want to tear off what remained of her clothes and take her, but he controlled the urge. That was his father's way—to force himself on unwilling females.

Her eyes flicked to Spot, reminding Tommy that the boy watched. "Your son?"

"My mother's sister's son, but he's my responsibility. I'm head of our household."

She looked back to Tommy and studied him.

"What do you want?" He knew what he wanted.

"I want to live." Amazingly, the pupils of her eyes dilated in anticipation, and she leaned toward him, seeking his mouth with hers.

It was all the invitation he needed.

It was a crazy-making fuck. She was on him like a sack of mud: clinging, demanding, and impossible to scrape off. His body responded too fast, leaving his brain struggling to catch up.

After Tommy collapsed on her, panting, Spot nudged him. His cousin looked north, his ears twitching. Tommy had forgotten about the possibility of other oni. The rest of the oni force couldn't be close, or Spot would be more anxious. Still, it would be best to get moving.

Tommy leaned back onto his knees. Jewel Tear lay in the green moss, her sable hair a dark halo around her. Her silk dress was in tatters, showing alluring flashes of her tawny skin through the shredded fabric.

She gazed up at him with a lazy, satiated look. She lifted her leg and ran her foot up his bare thigh and hooked it around his hip and tugged slightly on him. "Untie me."

He took out his knife and cut her free, careful not to cut her fingers as he sliced away the bindings. She sat up, feline graceful.

"What's your name?" she said.

"Tommy."

She echoed it, running her hand up to play with the hair at the back of his neck. "What does it mean?"

"It's a human name. It doesn't mean anything." He fought the urge to nuzzle the full breasts that nearly spilled out of her tattered dress. Forget not having time for it. Now that he'd taken the edge off his desire, his basic mistrust of people was kicking in. Why was this highborn elf acting like a cat in heat?

Danger had a way of doing that to some people. Was she one? Or was it more than that?

"We need to get going." He forced himself to stand up, breaking her hold on him, and pulled on his clothes. "I killed twelve warriors. Were there more?"

That rattled her, as if she, too, had forgotten the oni in the heat of the moment. She scrambled to her feet and brought her freed left hand to her mouth. Tommy flinched as she cast a spell. The last *domana* he'd seen casting spells had been Windwolf as the male set oni on fire like giant candles.

Nothing seemed to happen, but Jewel's eyes went wide.

"What is it?" Tommy was fairly sure he wasn't going to like the answer.

"We need to move." She stripped a food pack off

one of the dead oni and then headed straight east in a fast walk.

He grabbed a second pack and followed even though he could hear nothing. "Do you know where you're going?"

"Away from the oni." Jewel Tear dug through the bag and found an apple that she ate hungrily. "Big camp back there." She waved the apple toward the camp that Spot had searched for her. "And another there, there, and there." The apple traveled in a circle. "And the whelping pens that they were taking me to."

She shuddered and flung the apple away with a curse.

He was surprised that she knew where the oni were taking her. "You speak oni?"

"Forest Moss has insisted on teaching it to me. Hours of tramping all over that damn city with him using it as an excuse to say vile, disgusting things to me."

"Oni doesn't have nice words."

"I'm of that opinion now." She walked faster. "Since, in the last two days, there were only a smattering of words that I didn't understand."

Her guards must have realized that she understood them and used that to terrorize her. They probably delighted in explaining what would happen to her at the whelping pens.

Tommy realized that Spot was trotting to keep up with them. The boy wouldn't be able to keep that pace. He caught Jewel Tear's arm. She screamed, dropped the food bag and whipped her hand toward her mouth. He caught her wrist before she could cast a spell.

"We'll wear ourselves out at this speed," he growled.

"There's a platoon behind us! They'll find their dead, and they'll come after us at a run."

Tommy swore but kept hold of her, keeping her helpless. "Can you fight like Wolf Who Rules? Prince True Flame? Set things on fire?"

"I can fight." She tugged carefully, testing his hold, trying to free herself. He was careful not to hurt her. They both knew a broken arm would make her helpless. Her wriggling ended with her pressed against him, head tilted so she could glare up at him, lips nearly brushing his. "I can't set things on fire. That's Fire Clan *esva*."

He breathed in her rich scent and resisted the urge to kiss her. "They'll scout and see that there's only the three of us. They probably won't send for reinforcements. Let's lure them farther away from the rest and deal with them. Most of the oni haven't fought a *domana*—and lived. They don't know how dangerous you are."

She gave a wicked laugh that promised hurt in the oni's future.

He cautiously released her and backed away.

She rubbed her wrist where he had held her helpless. "Don't ever grab my arms again."

The earlier sex had only whetted Tommy's taste for Jewel Tear. When he was sixteen, he and his cousins had stolen a canister of nitric oxide and spent a blur of days falling into sweet oblivion. Afterward, he felt he could easily kill to gain another canister, and the feeling had made him both scared and angry. Frightened because he already had one master: the oni. He didn't need one that he willingly served. Angry because he had given himself the weakness.

Now he was feeling the same lingering want, tainted again with fear and anger. He'd never wanted a female like this before—but then he'd never had a female this fine. He avoided humans. Even if the woman was drunk and he had her pinned facedown in the bed—the fear of discovery always ruined his pleasure. That cold niggling feeling reached down in him and awoke long-buried memories of his own rape. It kept him from the very lush University of Pittsburgh students with their painted-on leggings and tight shirts. The half-oni girls were safe but never as fine. Not that it really was their fault: they didn't get enough to eat and sometimes had literal dogs for fathers.

No, his experiences weren't with females this beautiful, rounded, soft, and wonderfully scented. Even her mouth tasted of some sweetness he couldn't name. In the quick hard fuck, there hadn't been time to wallow in it all. The oni army was breathing down his neck, and yet he was wondering what it be like to bare her chest and suckle to his heart's content.

It scared him that he couldn't keep his mind off her. On Elfhome, more than a dozen nasty plants liked to lure in prey and then pin them helpless to be eaten alive. The plants were all sweet-smelling, beautiful things. Did this elf female have him already pinned? Had she used some kind of magic to ensnare him so tightly? Having time to think about it, he couldn't come up with any sane reason she would spread her legs so willingly for him otherwise.

But if she didn't use magic, then his weakness was all his fault.

Spot couldn't keep up. They were moving too fast. They needed to keep ahead of the platoon until they could find a place to trap the oni. They needed a gorge or cliff to take out the entire platoon at once. If even one escaped, they would have the entire oni force chasing them.

It was becoming apparent that Tommy had to either carry his cousin or leave him behind. Tommy couldn't afford to wear himself out; not with the rest of the family depending on him getting the damn elf bitch back to Pittsburgh. They were a hundred miles deep in a forest filled with oni, wargs, and man-eating plants. It would be kinder to kill the boy than to leave him—but Tommy couldn't bring himself to do it. He put it off even as the boy fell farther and farther behind. As Tommy hit the top of a tall ridge, he realized Spot was totally out of sight. Sighing, he stopped on the pretense of studying the lay of the land.

As if their situation wasn't bad enough, the valley beyond was broad and glittered with standing water half hidden behind dying trees. He growled at the sight, shaking his head.

"What is it?" Jewel's breasts glistened with sweat and strained her dress with every deep panting breath.

Tommy turned away from the distraction her chest presented. "We're boxed in. Black willows prefer marshes." He spotted one of the massive trees stalking through the wetland and pointed it out to her. "My illusions don't work on creatures like them."

He glanced back the way they had come. From their perch on the ridge, he could now see the oni following them. A full platoon of thirty warriors was cresting the last hill and pouring down it at a fast trot.

Spot scrambled up the final bit to the top of the ridge, gasping for breath between whimpers of distress.

"It's okay," Tommy said despite the sick feeling

roiling in his stomach. He couldn't delay his decision any longer. He couldn't keep both Jewel Tear and Spot safe, and for the sake of the rest of the family, the female had to be the one he saved. He scratched Spot behind each floppy ear. One quick twist and he could break the boy's neck cleanly.

Spot looked up at him, trusting him completely.

Jewel put a hand on Tommy's shoulder. "I can use the marsh to kill the oni."

Could he trust her? For Spot's sake, did he really have a choice?

"Let's go then." He hefted Spot onto his back.

It went against everything Tommy had ever felt or believed to trust Jewel Tear, but still he followed her into the swamp. She cast spell after spell as they pushed through the underbrush. He could hear the calls of the oni as they hit the top of the ridge and spotted them.

"They've seen us," he warned.

She gestured, and he felt the change of air pressure as her shield encircled them. "Good! Let them chase us!"

He laughed at the savage tone of her voice. The ground underfoot was firm despite looking water-soaked. Somehow she was building them a path and, most likely, destroying it behind them. A bullet hit a tree in front of them and ricocheted with a whine. Jewel ignored it, shouldering her way through the underbrush to keep her hands free to cast spells.

He felt the ground shake and heard the crashing of something huge moving in front of them. "It's a black willow."

"I know." Jewel turned toward the tree.

"What are you doing?" He paused only to be shoved

from behind by her shield. He suspected if he didn't keep moving she might be able to drag him along behind her with it.

"I'm going to use the tree against them." Jewel Tear crashed through a stand of tall cattails, and suddenly they were face-to-face with a black willow. It was a huge, ancient thing, nearly two hundred feet tall, with a massive trunk completely blocking their way. One of the root-feet tore itself up out of the soil, stretched out and slammed its way back into the soft earth. The ground shook and the tree lurched closer. The whip-like branches snaked out and snared a rabbit darting through the cattails a dozen yards to their right. With a rustle like wind through leaves, more branches reached down and wrapped around the animal, cocooning it in green wicker even as it lifted the squirming, helpless animal upward. A muffled scream came from inside the wriggling ball. Blood was dripping from between the tightly woven branches even as it stuffed the rabbit into a huge maw where the trunk forked.

Spot yipped in fear and Tommy bit down on a curse.

"Come on." Jewel stepped calmly over one of the splayed feet of the willow.

"Crazy elf bitch," Tommy growled lowly. He had no choice but to follow.

"They hunt by vibration of the ground," Jewel said. "I'm masking our footsteps. It's blind to us."

She led them several hundred feet deeper into the marsh. "Hold very still." She cast another spell, a second, and then a third. "This way."

From behind them there was suddenly screaming and rapid gunfire. They plunged through chokeberries, pussy willows, and nettles. There was an unnatural bridge of land through a pond filled with fairy lilies gleaming in the gathering dusk, and they stopped within sight of another towering black willow.

"Shh, don't move," Jewel whispered.

Tommy hadn't planned on it, not even if someone set fire to his feet.

There was the deep cough of a flamethrower, and dusk lit up with the sudden flare. He glanced back to see the distant tree lift up the oni with the flamethrower. It cocooned the warrior even as its massive crown caught fire. The crushing branches ruptured the weapon's fuel tank, and the entire bundle became a bright sun. The black willow seemed unable to unwrap its branches from the oni and waved the flaming ball even as it tried to back quickly away from its own limbs.

"That tree is toast," Tommy whispered.

"I'm sending in this one," Jewel whispered and cast a spell.

The black willow in front of them shifted as if she had prodded it hard. The world shook as it stomped toward them, and then, with branches trailing over Jewel's shield, it walked past them. Spot whimpered, burying his face into Tommy's hair.

"Hush," Tommy breathed. "You're not hurt. Be brave."

Jewel stood still, casting spell after spell, watching the black willow as it forged its way toward the burning tree.

"How did you do that?" Tommy asked.

"They like soft earth, but they instinctively move away from land that's too unstable. They can't right themselves if they topple over."

"You can't let any of the oni out of this swamp alive."

"Don't worry. They're all mine now."

✧ ✧ ✧

An hour later, they reached the far side of the marsh. Jewel Tear had set a total of four black willows onto the oni. By the second one, the oni were no longer giving chase but trying only to escape the marsh alive. Jewel Tear continually cast spells to keep the platoon trapped in the thick mud while herding the black willows into their midst. The gunshots and screaming decreased slowly until the swamp went silent. All that marked the oni was the burning tree and three well-fed black willows.

"You got them all?" Tommy wanted to be sure.

"Trust me." Jewel Tear had no idea how impossible that was. "I got them all."

The food bags held very little in terms of fruit and bread. Tommy didn't want to trust the smoked meat that the oni had been carrying; it could be anything from pork to human. He built a small fire and then went out to set snares for rabbits.

By the time he returned to their hidden camp, Jewel Tear had worked her female magic on Spot. The boy was asleep, sprawled halfway across Jewel Tear's lap as she picked nettles out of Spot's dark fur.

"His fur is so soft," Jewel murmured as she ran her hand over the boy's head. She found another little black seed caught in his fur and plucked it out.

"It's soft because he's young." Tommy lit his last cigarette, dragged the smoke deep into his lungs, and wished he had a whiskey to chase it. It had been a shit day. "It will shed out to coarser fur when he gets older."

"I've never seen a child before."

Tommy thought she meant "oni child" and started to bristle. Why did the elves insist that they were always "oni" and not "human?" They were equally half of each.

Jewel Tear, though, took no notice of his soft growl. "He's so small. I don't remember being so little, but I suppose I was."

It was then he realized she meant "child" in general, but that didn't seem possible. Elves weren't adult until they were over a hundred years old. "You've *never* seen a child before?"

"They're like mythical things. Oh, I've met a few older doubles at Summer Court, but you can't really count them. They're all but adults by that time. They're not tiny like this."

The elves' terror of the oni's proliferation suddenly made a great deal more sense. Tommy couldn't put a number to the infants he'd fed, diapered, held as they died from beatings their own fathers gave them, and quietly disposed of. He was only twenty-four. To live to be more than a hundred and never have seen a child?

"Can he talk?" Jewel petted the sleeping boy like he was a puppy. "Or isn't he old enough yet? When do children start to talk? My mother was horrified that all I did for months after I was born was laugh and cry—she thought there was something wrong with me."

"Yes, he can talk. He's just shy. He's never met anyone outside our family."

"Because of how he looks."

"Yes."

Jewel took Spot's very small and human hand in hers and studied it closely. "His mother was human? Your mother's sister?"

"Yes."

Carefully she shifted the boy off her lap and gave his furry head one last pet. "What of his father?"

He took another drag on his cigarette and breathed out the truth. "I killed him."

He'd never told anyone. He might have been Lord Tomtom's bastard son, but the warriors his father had brought from Onihida were all considered royalty compared to the half-bloods born in Pittsburgh. His father would have executed Tommy if he'd found out. It had always been too dangerous to tell anyone. Tommy wasn't even sure why he told her.

She nodded, neither shocked nor dismayed.

Tommy found himself explaining. "The oni used my mother and aunts as whores. It was safest just to suffer. But Spot's father was more animal than most oni. He hurt my aunt badly. I had to do something."

She watched Spot sleeping for a minute before murmuring, "It was good of you to hate the father but love the child."

He laughed at the use of the word "love." He cared for his family and valued them, but only the weak used words like "love" and "cherish."

Any intelligent reply he had in his head vanished when she plucked at her dress bodice to cool herself. It left him with just hard want. For a moment or two, she didn't notice his focus. Then she realized where his gaze was riveted. She stilled. And then, hooking her fingers into her bodice, she slid it down, freeing her right breast.

His hand cupped it before he even realized he had moved. It was perfection of a breast, filling his palm without overflowing, softer than silk, the nipple red and beautiful as a flower. He caressed it lightly with the pad of his thumb, and her gasp made it feel like a cord had been threaded down through his body, wrapped tight around the base of his dick, and yanked tight.

He managed to stop himself inches from kissing her. She had her head tilted up, lips parted, ready for him. "Why? Why are you doing this?"

She blushed and tried to look away.

"Answer me!"

Anger flared in her eyes. "I'm fertile. I know what they did to the kitsune. They promised me the same when they got me to the whelping pens."

"So you're using me to get yourself pregnant?"

"It's not as if you haven't enjoyed the process," she snarled. "And yes, if I can fill my womb with your child, there won't be room for them to get some monster on me, no matter what they mate me with."

Her eyes blazed at him, full of fury and determination. He had the sudden image of her knocking him down and straddling him to get what she wanted. The thought took him to his knees. She tangled her fingers tightly in his hair and pulled him to her breast. It tasted as perfect as it looked. It was even better as he watched her anger melt to pure wanton pleasure.

He had heard once that the original lords of the elves had bred the *domana* to be the perfect whores. He could readily believe it as he stripped her bare. Everything from the unbelievable softness of her skin to how she contracted around him as he nibbled on her ears—it was as if she'd been created to bring pleasure. He would never again have a female so perfect in every way. He wallowed in her perfection.

Yes, he was going to enjoy filling her womb. He'd worry about the consequences later.

32: SCRY

"This shouldn't hurt," Tinker assured everyone as she used a handcrafted wax and iron-filing crayon to mark out a spell on the white stone.

Merry meeped nervously at the center of the spell.

Tinker was slightly mystified by the lack of trust she'd been encountering all day. She had heard rumors that the University of Pittsburgh had set up a magic-research lab near the enclaves, complete with a large-scale spell-casting area. It took her several hours to track down the small building, tucked just across the Rim, downhill and out of sight of the faire ground. All the university people she talked to acted like she was going to blow it up or something. They'd been reluctant to admit that the building existed at first, and then to give her permission to use it.

Really—the only thing she'd personally blown up was parts of Ginger Wine's enclave—and she didn't think that should be held against her.

"It took three years and ten million dollars to

build!" the university officials kept repeating, although when she finally reached the building, she had no idea why. While well built with cunning use of glass, stone, ironwood, and poly-resin, it was basically just one massive slab of polished white marble resting on bedrock with a glass roof overhead to keep off the rain and snow.

Yet even Oilcan was voicing concern. "Tink, I don't really think this is a good idea."

"I've done this spell before." Tinker paused to dredge up memories of the last time she experimented with it. If she remembered correctly, the results had been disappointingly unimpressive. "On you even."

"Yes, I know." Oilcan flipped his datapad so she could read his notes. They read: *The little mad scientist cast this on all of us today, she's not pleased, is all I can say. Shakalakaboomboom.* "I've let you talk me into lots of crazy things."

"Did it hurt?"

"No. That's not the point. You've never known what this spell does."

"Not entirely." She had to bow to the truth of that statement. "But I think I understand it now. It's been a very informative summer. It didn't hurt you, and it won't hurt her." At least she was fairly sure it wouldn't. "I've cast it on Blue Sky, and it didn't hurt him."

"It made me dizzy for the rest of the day," Blue Sky said unhelpfully. "John told me never to let you cast spells on me again."

"It was the two hours in the Tilt-A-Whirl that made you dizzy," Tinker said. "And I warned you about that."

No one looked confident about her except for Pony and Stormsong, which was why she loved them best.

"Look, it's a divination spell." She paused in transcribing the spell onto the floor to show Oilcan her datapad.

Her grandfather had given her the non-indexed digital copy of the Dufae codex after teaching her the key to the ancient book's spell-lock. Most likely it was his way of sharing the family secrets with her while slowing her down with the non-searchable copy. She spent most of her childhood building indexes and cross-linking the pages, testing various spells and adding her own notes to those of Dufae. She had this spell memorized, but for everyone's peace of mind, including her own, she was triple-checking her work.

"The spell doesn't act on the focus at all, but detects power connected to the focus. That's why it didn't seem to do anything when we were kids. Blue Sky has no connections, and our link to the Stone Clan Spell Stones is active only when we cast the resonance spell."

"Why do you think they're linked to an active power source?" He meant the kids in general. Merry was acting as guinea pig since the others had been so traumatized by the oni.

"I'm just gathering data. It's what a scientist does when presented with the unknown. If it would make you feel better, I can do the spell on you first, just to prove it does what I think it does."

"Yes, it would."

Tinker finished drawing the spell as Oilcan and Merry changed places. There were several divination spells in the codex and it delighted her to no end to see that all the others had fingering diagrams beside them. Once she had Oilcan and the kids comfortable with her casting spells on the children, she planned to cut loose.

She quadruple-checked her transcription and spoke the command word. The outer shell of the spell powered up, creating a soft glowing dome over the entire spell, enclosing Oilcan inside the spell's influence. The first inner ring powered up, a looping function that would keep the spell active until she canceled it. The symbols flickered one after another as the spell cycled around and around. The third ring created a second dome, fractions of an inch smaller than the first, marking out the true divination section of the spell. Showy but static at the moment.

"Okay, set up resonance," Tinker told Oilcan.

Oilcan smoothly called the Stones, and a bright spike appeared in the spell's half-dome, pointing roughly south by southwest.

"Is that the direction of the Stone Clan Spell Stones?" Tinker asked.

Pony nodded and Stormsong added, "It's roughly in the same place as Huntsville, Alabama, is on Earth."

Tinker knew where Huntsville was—birthplace of Saturn rockets—so it gave her a good idea of the location. "Wow, why so far from the coast?"

"The Stones must be built on very powerful springs of magic. There are very few points in the world where they can be placed."

Oilcan dropped his resonance with the Spell Stones and waited for her to cancel the spell. "Okay, so you do know what the spell does."

"I'm so hurt by your lack of faith."

"I let you cast the spell on me."

Tinker supposed that did forgive a host of things.

She canceled the divination spell and shooed him out of the center.

Merry took courage from the lack of any harm to Oilcan and returned to the center without any prodding.

Tinker made sure that none of the lines had blurred or shorted out. Once she was sure that the spell hadn't been altered by the previous casting, she spoke the command word.

The entire building lit up brilliantly with streams of energy pouring through the focus.

Merry danced at the center of the spell, whimpering. "*Sama*?"

"It's okay!" Oilcan called. "Cancel the spell."

Tinker canceled the spell, and Merry darted out of the center and into Oilcan's arms.

"What was that?" Oilcan whispered urgently in English.

Tinker shook her head mutely. She didn't know, but it couldn't have been good.

What the hell were Oilcan's kids?

Tinker couldn't even be sure all of the kids were like Merry. She wanted to test them all, but the spell's spectacular reaction to Merry had rattled the kids badly. She couldn't look into their fear-filled eyes—remember the excrement-filled pits she found them in—and force them to cooperate. They were still too fragile. She let Oilcan take them off to do something soothing: play music or pet baby animals or something.

It left Tinker with two meager data points: the children were all genetically similar, and Merry, the control, was connected to something big.

Tinker had theories. The Skin Clan obviously had

bred the kids to harness some kind of exotic power. Just like her and Oilcan, the ability had been passed down, generation after generation, locked away only by ignorance. Obviously the Skin Clan knew the key to unlock the kids' abilities and desperately wanted control of that power.

Tinker flicked through the digital pages of the codex, tapping on the links to her notes relating to the various finger diagrams. She had applied every encryption method she could think of to the diagrams. The closest she had gotten was assigning five-digit numbers to each set of drawings. Zero for *laedin* position, where the finger curled tight. One for *sekasha* position, where the finger curled from the first knuckle. Two for *domana* position with the difficult only first knuckle crooked. Three for the full royal position with the finger fully extended, bowing to no one.

She had noticed the "numbers" corresponded to a periodic table–like hierarchy, since the numbers never repeated. She had theorized that the codex was missing spells since there were numbers skipped—like 32103—which set up resonance to the Spell Stones.

If she had ever grasped the meaning of the drawings, it would have been only a matter of time before she unlocked it all. She giggled at the thought of a six-year-old human wielding the power of the Spell Stones. Oh, the elves would have been horrified.

She sobered as she considered everything that could have happened. Sooner or later, the Stone Clan *domana* in Huntsville would have noticed that she was tapping their Spell Stones. The *sekasha* would have been alerted that there were unaccountable *domana* in Pittsburgh. The Wind Clan elves would have searched for the interlopers. If they had been found, she and Oilcan would have been exiled to Stone Clan holdings.

Tinker frowned down at her datapad. Had her grandfather withheld the one spell, rendering the rest inert? Had he kept it secret to protect her and Oilcan?

She blew out her breath. She should be focusing on the kids.

The children themselves might be ignorant of what they were—but it was possible that one of the Stone Clan adults would know. Unfortunately, Forest Moss was the only adult in Pittsburgh.

33: HIT BY AN ARROW

Tommy was so screwed. Strange he didn't see it coming.

He should have known when they fell asleep locked together and he noticed that she fit perfectly to him. He should have realized it when she woke him up by sliding down onto him and he had to smile at her look of fierce determination. All day he had little warning signs as they scrambled up and down hills, across streams and marshes, dodging lone oni scouts here and killing them there. He missed the subtle evidence.

So he'd been completely clueless when she stopped on a ridge, cast a spell and then murmured, "We're safe here, for now." She made a slight noise of protest as he pulled her into his arms that ended with a laugh smothered by his lips.

"Insatiable," she groaned as he kissed his way down her neck. Judging by the way she clung tight to him, it wasn't a complaint.

Whoever invented dresses had ready access in mind.

After the quick hard fuck, she nuzzled into his

neck and murmured, "You say you don't belong to the viceroy. Were his terms so bad that you rejected his offer?"

He growled and pushed her away. "I'm done with having masters."

She gave him a puzzled look and then understanding flooded her face, followed by exasperation. "Oh! I see. He has done it again."

"Done what?"

"Wolf Who Rules has a way of expecting you to trust blindly. To leap at his command, with no reassurance there is a safe landing beyond. For those who love him dearly, I suppose that is enough. Those of us, though, who don't love him enough . . ."

Apparently the viceroy had a thing for small, dusky females with a temper. "You didn't."

"No. I didn't." She tugged and shimmied her breasts back into her bodice.

"Forming a household in a clan is not enslavement any more than starting a business. It is, in fact, one and the same."

"Not the way Windwolf explains it."

"He may be beautiful, intelligent, rich, blessed with two *esva*—"

Tommy kissed her to stop her from going on about the male elf.

"But he does not kiss nearly as well as you," she murmured. "And he fails at speaking his heart plainly."

"He had no tender words for you?"

She laughed. "It is the plain words I want, not the tender ones. The humans call him a prince, and they are not far from the truth. His mother was sister to the king, and his father is the head of the Wind

Clan. I, on the other hand . . ." She pulled the hem of her skirt down over her hips and tried to smooth it with her hands. "My parents oversaw three small holdings that made glue and shoes from animals unfit for eating. I spent my childhood with blood-soaked slaughter yards, the omnipresent stench of the curing pits, death, rotting flesh, and the constant struggle to make enough money to eat. I loathed it. I didn't want to live forever in that hell."

"You didn't trust him to keep you safe?"

"No." Jewel laughed, held out her hands, and turned in a full circle. "And look how well I've done on my own."

"They could have gone after Tinker just as easy as you."

"Grab any bitch and breed her? No, this wasn't a simpleminded act of war. This was betrayal at the deepest level. Earth Son's First has been guarding over children that the Wind Clan believes were lured here by someone in the Stone Clan. I decided to go through his things and see if they're right. Two days ago, I discovered he used a camouflage spell to hide a spell-locked chest within a closet. I spent hours trying to get the damned thing open and failed. I was going to ask the Wind Clan *domi* for help."

Tommy remembered the massive destruction at the enclave and guessed the fate of the locked chest. "The oni warriors blew it up when they took you?"

"I'm just a distraction from the truth."

She looked so distraught that he put out his hand, but she had already turned away.

He reached and caught her braid and gave it a playful tug. "Hey—"

She cried out and flinched away from him.

"You said not to grab your arms," he snapped and then realized it wasn't him that she was reacting to. She jerked the braid out of his hand and stared at it with loathing and horror.

"They caught me by my hair. If I'd stayed free of them a minute more, I could have summoned my magic. But they caught me by my hair. They pulled me back and pinned my arms and made me helpless. There was nothing I could do but watch as they killed my people!"

She pulled out her oni gutting knife and started to hack ruthlessly at her hair.

Seductive elves, Tommy had no experience in. Females battered to pieces by the oni, he knew too well. She needed to vent the anger. He mourned the loss of her beautiful hair, but it would grow back. He watched only for a more permanent cut. Her hair fell around her in long, silky locks. When her hair was cropped close to her skull, she tried to cut it shorter and he caught her hand, taking the knife from her. He'd learned that there was nothing he could say to make things right. Wordlessly, he took her in his arms and did the best he could to comfort her while keeping her safe from herself.

And it was then that he realized he was screwed.

He'd broken the cardinal rule. He forgot to disengage the heart when engaging the dick. He *cared* for her. Shit! What a stupid twelve-year-old mistake. The last thing he needed was to go all gooey over an elf.

"I should have never come to Pittsburgh." She cried into his shoulder as he railed silently at himself. "I cast my lot *nae hae* ago, when Wolf brought me to the Westernlands and his household was living in tents and there was nothing but trees. I didn't trust him then. I didn't believe he could carve prosperous holdings out of the wilderness."

And of course, because Tommy was thinking with the wrong head, he was happy that she hadn't trusted the male, that it was his shoulder that she was crying on.

"All I could see was ruin," she wailed. "So I put distance between us and left him to fail alone."

That was what Tommy needed to do. He couldn't afford to be softhearted over any female, especially an elf. Of course, there was the annoying problem that he needed to deliver her alive and well to Prince True Flame.

"I should have lived with my failure." Jewel Tear sobbed and clung tighter to him. "But everything was unraveling and word came that his child bride had been taken and might be dead. I thought if I was here when they found her body—"

He kissed her to silence her. He didn't want to hear how she planned to win Windwolf back. He didn't want to think of her in bed with the male—true stupidity to feel jealous—to feel *anything*. Still, he couldn't help holding her and soothing her and feeling like an idiot for wanting to protect her.

She calmed down enough to realize that they really didn't have time to screw around anymore. When she pulled out of his arms, it felt like something tore inside of him because he knew he would have to keep her at arm's length from then on. It made him angry that it hurt—angry at himself and at her and at the elves and the stupid oni.

Spot tugged at Tommy's shirt and pointed upward.

A gossamer swam on the horizon, the bulk of its

giant body just a shimmer of light. Its passage was marked by the massive gondola gliding underneath it like a black needle threading through the blue.

Jewel Tear gasped. "It's one of ours."

Ours. Like he was an elf, too. But she didn't sound any more happy about it than he did.

"And that's bad?"

"I don't know how many of my clan are working with the oni."

34: AMARANTH AND FORGE

Since finding Merry outside the train station, Oilcan's life had veered off onto a strange road. Despite the fact that the way was full of twists and turns, winding through a dark country, he had felt in control. He'd decided to be responsible for the kids. He'd chosen to move to Sacred Heart. He had been holding off on sponsorship, trying to see if they could open an enclave without the commitment to any one clan.

He had an uneasy feeling, though, that the brakes on his life were going. Any moment, he would go hurtling down a steep hill, stomp down to stop it all, and the pedal would sink to the floor and nothing would grab the wheels.

He went to his project board in an attempt to find things that would make him feel like he was staying in control. Of the countless projects yet to be done, the one that spoke to him was painting. The bullet holes had been filled and the plaster sanded and primed, but none of the walls had been given a final coat of paint. The whole building looked infected with the countless white spots bright against the grimy walls. Fresh paint would erase the last traces of the oni on the enclave and make it wholly theirs. Buying paint would also take him to one of his favorite places: the hardware store.

Wollerton's had ruled over the South Side, like so many of the successful surviving businesses in Pittsburgh, for generations out of mind. Its narrow, dim aisles had everything conceivable for keeping a home livable on Elfhome, from paint and ladders to flamethrowers and wolf traps. Becky Wollerton leaned toward crockpot dishes while tending the store, which wreathed the place with the smell of stewing meat. Occasionally there was the thunder of little feet overhead as the next generation of storekeepers played soccer or tag in their sprawling apartment. It was a comforting safe place for Oilcan.

He guided his kids to the painting section while Thorne slipped through the aisles like a grim shadow. He couldn't imagine the pain she was going through, losing all her brother warriors in one night. At night, in bed, she allowed herself the freedom to cry, but he'd learned that daylight meant she was working, and she preferred her space.

The kids stood silent and still in front of the massive array of colors, apparently stunned at the number of choices.

"They're so pretty." Merry fingered the paint chips. "We can only choose one?"

"You can choose two or three if you want." He pulled out cream and paired it with a dark green in the same family. "The trick is to pick colors that look good together. See, we could paint three of the walls this cream and one wall this green."

He put the chips back into the trays. "The rooms are big. We can paint them any way you want, but the easiest is just to pick one color you like a lot."

"What does this say?" Cattail Reeds held out a warm gold to him.

"Each color has a name. That one is"—he paused a moment to translate into Elvish—"Happily Ever After."

"Happily Ever After," Baby Duck echoed and took the chip from Cattail.

"But what kind of name is that?" Cattail protested. "It doesn't tell you anything."

Oilcan waved a hand at the large section of yellows. "We ran out of names and started to make up new ones."

"I like this." Merry held out a chip of pale buttery yellow. "What's it called?"

He translated the name. "Pure Joy."

Merry did a little dance. "I love it."

Cattail laughed dryly at Merry and drifted toward the reds.

Rustle of Leaves picked out a deep green called Paradise Valley and Barley chose a warm tan called Honey Oak. Oilcan found a rich brown called Weathered Oak for his bedroom and paired it with a cream.

"This one." Cattail held out a strong purplish red called Raspberry Truffle. "And this one." A warm dark gray called Stardust. "And this one." An off-white called Mannequin Cream. "And this." A lighter gray called Sandlot Gray.

Oilcan laughed. He had no idea how she was going to use all four, but he trusted that she would figure it out. The four chips harmonized in his hand. "Okay."

Cattail and Barley started into a debate on colors for the foyer. Oilcan deposited the chips with the paint mixer, ordering three five-gallon buckets of every color that the kids picked out. After the "family" bedrooms, they would need to paint the guest bedrooms, too. It would cost over a thousand dollars in paint, but it would be another step closer to opening the enclave.

Paint ordered, he went in search of drop cloths, paint brushes, rollers, paint pans, and ladders. The tile section reached out and took hold of him as he passed through it, reminding him that he needed to start on the bathing room on the third floor. They were doing bathing out of the sinks. There was a marvelous iridescent glass tile of blues and purples that whispered to his soul. Of course it was hideously expensive, but it would be beautiful.

"He shapes stone with coarse hands,
 rough as rock, unyielding.
Builds a palace to capture light, a stolen gem,
 an artist's restless eye.
She illuminates his silent walls and empty rooms,
 fills the lonely
Corners with impossible color,
 paints a secret language
Only he can read; every word fractures
 the jewel of his heart."

He realized he was singing and laughed at the tune. It was the song about the quirky romance between Forge and Amaranth. The male had loved the painter Amaranth at first sight but for some reason didn't think his love was returned. He hired her to paint the palace he'd built, and then to be sure the task would take as long as needed to win her heart, he'd added rooms and wings and outbuildings to it. The chorus was an urge to build faster, as Amaranth had nearly finished painting.

Oilcan tore himself away from the tile and moved on to the painting equipment. The bathing room would have to come later.

"*Sama.*" Baby Duck was suddenly beside him with two kittens in her hands. All three stared at him intently.

"Where did you find those?"

"Upstairs."

Oilcan sighed. He was going to have to have a long talk about privacy with her. "I'll see if they're for sale."

Aaron Wollerton laughed as he explained the situation. "We're about drowning in cats, so she can have them."

They started with his room; his theory was that he liked to repaint often anyhow. It wasn't so much he grew tired of the old color, but that he enjoyed trying new colors. If the children messed up painting his room, he would only have to live with it for a short time.

He taught them how to prep the room, taking covers off the light switches and electrical boxes. He showed them how to tape off the areas that were going to be painted later. He trained them on cutting in with brushes and rolling with rollers.

"Please, no painting each other," he said as he stepped back to let them work.

"Why would we paint one another?" Merry asked as they all stared at him in confusion.

"I'm not sure." He and Tinker had done it when they painted for the first time; he could no longer remember why. He was sure it made sense at the time. "Just don't."

They were neat and careful painters, if painfully slow. He'd never realized that living forever meant there was no rush to get work done quickly; apparently their whole lives they'd been taught to do things right, however long it took. They kept stepping back and frowning at the coverage. For having paintbrushes in their hands for the first time, they were doing a wonderful job. If they expected perfection, though, painting the entire building could take forever.

"Sometimes it takes two or three coats for complete coverage," he cautioned them. "Just be as neat as you can and keep working. Trust that the end product will reflect the care you put into it."

"*Sama.*" Barley was cutting along the chalkboard at the front of the room. "How are you paying for everything?"

"I'm using my own savings for now," Oilcan said. "I don't have enough to buy everything to open an enclave, but it's more than enough to make this place livable."

"What are we doing for sponsorship?" Barley asked.

The others paused in mid-work to look at Oilcan. He didn't really want to talk about this now; it felt too soon. Still, they had a right to meet it head on. "Wind Clan is willing to give me sponsorship, but if I took it, all of you would have to become Wind Clan."

Their looks told him everything. Their clan was their last anchor. They'd been utterly lost once—the idea of being adrift again terrified them.

"I'm waiting to see how far my money will take us." Oilcan tried to temporize.

"If you're *domana*," Cattail Reeds said, "can't you get funding from Stone Clan?"

He laughed, shaking his head. There were so many things wrong with that question, starting with the idea that he was *domana*. What he was, though, wasn't the heart of the issue. "Even if the Stone Clan offered me sponsorship, I probably wouldn't accept."

"Why not?" Barley had given up everything for the dream of sponsorship. Obviously he couldn't conceive of refusing. It felt so selfish to deny the kids. If there were only one or two of them, it would be a simple balancing act, but with five of them and Thorne to consider . . .

He knew, though, he couldn't sacrifice his heart and not become bitter at them. "I was raised in Pittsburgh, surrounded by Wind Clan," he said gently as he could. "I saw myself as part of the Wind Clan before my cousin became Wolf Who Rules' *domi*. I'm sorry, but I don't want to change clans any more than you want to."

"But we're still a household." Merry reached out a hand to him, imploring him to say "yes" with her eyes.

"Yes." He gripped her hand tight. "We're a household. We have money to make this place livable. And we will be able to scrape enough money together, eventually, to furnish it as an enclave. Let's just focus on today."

Merry had picked the bedroom beside his, so he decided that they would do hers next. They painted the walls the cheery yellow called Pure Joy, the ceiling a very pale yellow called Lemon Ice, and the trim a crisp white. Cattail insisted on painting Merry's bed the crisp white and draped one of the fresh painter's cloths above it. The voluminous canopy made the room seem a little less empty.

"Window dresses. Paintings here." Cattail Reeds motioned to the long blank wall opposite the windows, then pointed at the hardwood floors. "And put down some sort of rug, it will look even better."

Oilcan nodded, making note to add the items to his growing list of things they needed. The other kids only had mattresses donated by the hospice. None had lamps or bulbs for the overhead light fixtures and had been relying on elf shines. Still, the room was a hundred times better with its bright and cheery color than it had been with its pockmarked grimy white.

After their six bedrooms, they painted the four spare classrooms on the "family" level, the hallway, and the restrooms. It surprised him that Cattail Reeds and Barley settled on Merry's color scheme for the "family" level. With the clean windows, it made the entire third floor a happy place.

In just a day, the children had become seasoned painters. They set up the ladders, opened up buckets, stirred the paint, and laid out drop cloths without him having to give direction. Cattail taped, deciding what would be painted which color. Barley cut in high, carefully balancing on the ladders. Rustle cut in low, using his one good hand. He had only lost one paintbrush and his left shoe. Merry and Baby Duck rolled. And they talked and talked.

Cattail Reeds' household made clothes for all the *domana* that attended Winter Court. "Oh, the clothes are so beautiful that they bring tears to your eyes." Cattail sighed as she ran blue painter's tape along the wainscoting. "But the dresses are all basically the same. Show the charms." She cupped her breasts. "Nip the waist. Train, train, train." She motioned as if to an invisible train of fabric behind her. "But then the *slickies* started to come from Pittsburgh." She used the English word for the high-end digital magazines. "*Vogue. Elle.* Such colors! Such beautiful fabric! So wearable!" With the magazines came rumors that the Wind Clan artists that had made their way to Pittsburgh were selling their crafts to humans. "Earth Son's offer of sponsorship seemed like the perfect opportunity. I could open a boutique that catered to humans that wanted a hybrid of fashion. Elf high couture meets human common sense."

"We can still do it," Merry said.

Cattail Reeds nodded. "I intend to once we're settled and have more people."

Barley looked slightly worried until Oilcan said, "Most human enclaves—we call them hotels—have boutiques."

Barley talked about the remote enclave where he grew up. "It's perched on this mountain alongside the silk road. We're high up where no trees grow, so the land is all wind-swept bare. On clear days you can see far, far away far in the distance, to the next enclave. There's a female there that is seven hundred and twelve years old; she's the only person under a thousand years old for a hundred miles, and she's already in love."

"There was no one our age in my village, either," Rustle said. "It was nice going to Summer Court to study, and meeting Merry."

Merry blushed.

Fields of Barley continued from his high perch. "I liked working at the enclave, but no one would ever listen to me. My mother was the youngest before I was born; my father was a weaver that passed through once a year until he'd been killed in a landslide. My household taught me how to cook, but I could never choose what we would make. We would order a new set of dishes every fifty years, retiring the old dishes which were now chipped and worn. It showed how well-to-do we were to our returning clients to have an obviously new pattern. The salesman would bring books with the china patterns and everyone would sit and marvel over them. There was this one pattern that I loved. It was elegant in its simplicity; nothing about the dish called attention away from the food being served. Our *sama*, though, believed that the dish itself should be stunning, so when it sat empty after the meal and the bill came, the customer felt that the tab was justified. I realized as I sat looking at the patterns that we would never, never pick one that I wanted, not that day or in all the years to come. I would never be able to decide what to cook or choose how we would serve it. The only way I'd have a say in anything would be if I started a new enclave."

After years of trying to find a means to follow his dream, Barley had heard of Earth Son's offer and immediately set out for the coast. "And that went so well."

Baby Duck quacked nervously. She had little to offer as to why she'd traveled to Pittsburgh; her life prior to the whelping pen was still a complete mystery to her. "I remember we had big barns with kittens and chicks. I remember the smell of hay, like the barn was one big nest, and how safe it made me feel."

Oilcan mentally added hay to the list of things to track down. There were farms in the south hills, source of most of the locally grown produce. They were going to need a shelter for the *indi* and would have to find enough food to get the animals through the winter.

They were finishing the last classroom when Baby Duck suddenly pointed out the large window to the faire grounds and cried, "Gossamer!"

They paused to watch the great living airship glide in from the east. The sunlight gleamed thru the massive translucent body, rendering it into a moving cloud of cut diamonds.

"It's one of the Stone Clan's," Thorne Scratch murmured as they watched ropes being thrown down to the ground crew to be tied off at the anchors.

The gossamer itself looked no different than those that Windwolf owned, but the teak gondola slung under the creature was painted black with accents of gold.

"You'll need to go out and meet it," Thorne said.

"Me?"

"You're the senior Stone Clan *domana* in Westernlands."

"How do I outrank Forest Moss when I'm human?"

"He does not have a household. Also, currently he's not lucid."

"Fine." He put down the paintbrush he'd been using and started out of the room.

"Do you really want to meet them dressed that way?" Thorne asked.

Oilcan glanced down at his painting clothes. His old blue jeans and black T-shirt were splattered with years of paint. "I look more human this way."

Thorne made a little noise of agreement with that and followed him down the stairs.

Who had the Stone Clan sent and how would they change things in Pittsburgh? They couldn't take the children from him, but they certainly could offer them a more secure household. They couldn't take Thorne Scratch from him, but they could offer her a true beholding.

It hurt to think of losing them. He knew he could fall back to how his life had been before he met Merry, but that life seemed achingly empty. He had grown to love this new pattern of his life.

He reached out and took Thorne's left hand. She looked down in surprise at their fingers intertwined.

"It's something humans do," he said.

She smiled slightly and tightened her hold on his hand. Together they strolled across the wide meadows toward the incoming Stone Clan *domana* who could steal all his newfound happiness away.

The first of the newcomers was landing from the gondola via a steel-caged elevator as Oilcan and Thorne strolled up to the anchors. *Laedin* warriors in black were securing the area. They gave Oilcan and Thorne surprised looks but moved off to establish a perimeter.

The elevator climbed back to the gondola and then glided downwards again, this time loaded with *sekasha*. Thorne slipped her hand free. Oilcan expected Thorne to start a conversation with the newly arrived *sekasha*, but apparently that wasn't how it was handled. After one surprised glance to Oilcan, one of the males shifted forward and squared off against Thorne Scratch, locking into a silent stare-down. Thorne Scratch had her warrior's mask on and looked wildly beautiful, stone cold and deadly.

A minute later, the elevator returned again, this time bearing a male *domana.* For an elf, he was plainly dressed. He wore slouch boots, doeskin pants, and a white silk shirt that showed off the fact he was strongly built through the shoulders and chest. All the hair in his braid was dark brown, and the only lines on his face were laugh lines at the edges of his dark eyes, but there was something vaguely grandfatherly about him.

Oilcan knew enough about elf customs that he should introduce himself first. "Welcome to Pittsburgh. I'm Oilcan Wright. Lacking any other candidates, Prince True Flame has deemed me head of the Stone Clan, because I'm a descendent of Unbounded Brilliance of Stone."

The male stared at him with hurt and dismay on his face. His gaze dropped, taking in Oilcan's clothes and paint-speckled hands.

"Forgiveness, I was painting." Oilcan held out his hands as evidence.

The male breathed out a laugh like it been kicked out of him. "You could always tell what room she was working in by what colors were on her hands." He reached out and rubbed at Oilcan's face, scrubbing at a splotch of paint. "You have her eyes and her smile."

"Forgiveness—I—I don't understand."

"You have your grandmother's eyes." And the male wrapped him tight in a hug. "My child, I have prayed for this day."

And then the whole grandfatherly feel became clear. The male was a weirdly younger, elfin ghost of his grandfather, Tim Bell. "You're Forge of Stone?"

Forge smiled. "I've come to take you home."

35: FOREST MOSS

Tinker had heard that Forest Moss was not lucid, so she expected finding him would be fairly simple. A quick check with the hospice—where she expected to find him drugged—and Ginger Wine's—where she was hoping to find him locked up—both turned up empty.

The elves were letting a mad howitzer roam Pittsburgh unchecked? A quick scry showed that Forest Moss wasn't even in Oakland.

In the end, she called Riki. "Do you have any idea where I can find Forest Moss?"

"He's at Kaufmann's."

Kaufmann's been built in the heart of Pittsburgh back in the 1800s. Clad in limestone, decorated with carved stone arches, cherubs, and lion heads, it stood like a fortress, resisting time and space. The elevators boasted bronze doors with art deco designs. The ancient escalators on the upper floors were clad in wood. The only department store that survived relocation to

Elfhome, it was normally overstocked with all that humans might want to stay well-heeled while isolated on another planet. Two months being stranded without restocking from Earth, and even Kaufmann's was starting to look picked over.

There was something slightly incongruent about riding up the wooden escalators with her Hand in armor and carrying swords and bows. . . .

It all became very surreal when they found Forest Moss.

The crazed elf was in the children's department. There were no humans on the floor—both customers and salesclerks had abandoned it to the elf. The air was oddly hazed, as if a sudden dust storm had erupted in the department. Forest Moss sat in the back corner at a tiny tea table, not exactly alone. All of the pint-sized mannequins were gathered tightly around the table, clothed and naked, brightly smiling and headless, hands and amputated arms all outstretched to the elf in silent welcome. Someone had supplied Forest Moss with a china toy tea set, a plate of the bakery's fancy cookies, and real tea for the teapot. He had shared out the cookies and tea and was now imploring the children to eat. All the while, a fine dust snowed down on the mannequins, the table, and the white-haired, one-eyed elf.

"Try the yellow ones," he murmured to the mannequin standing beside him.. It was a little brunette eight-year-old-girl in a white tank top and blue flowered pants. He put his arm about it and pulled the doll close, rubbing his empty eye socket along the mannequin's pale cheek. "They are sweet perfection like you."

Somehow, Tinker doubted that questioning the

insane elf was going to useful, but she had to try. "Forest Moss?"

The male's good eye flicked to Tinker even as he continued rubbing his wound over the curves of the mannequin's face. "Hmm, Wolf's child bride, so young and waif-like. What could she want with one such as me?"

"I want to talk to you about the children," Tinker said.

"My beautiful, lovely children are all so happy and carefree." His hands slipped under the tank top to caress the flawless plastic skin underneath.

Tinker controlled the urge to rip the mannequin out of the elf's hold. He was better off playing with the dolls than pinning down real children. She tried to ignore the way that the fabric of the tank top stretched tight, molding to Forest Moss' large hand as it traveled over the small, anatomically correct body.

"Do you know that Earth Son told people that he would sponsor them if they came to Pittsburgh?"

"Earth Son? Now, there was a disappointing child." Forest Moss frowned and glanced at one of the boy mannequins standing to his right. "Whine. Whine. Whine. I told you to shut up, you spoiled little coward!"

Forest Moss flicked his free hand up to his mouth, set up a resonance, and gave a quick closed-fist gesture. Pony snatched Tinker up and whirled her about, putting himself between her and Forest Moss. She didn't see the boy mannequin explode, but fingers and toes and part of an ear tumbled by as white dust woofed out around Pony's shields. Only then did she notice that the floor was already littered with plastic body parts and tattered clothes. The explanation for the haze became evident.

If Forest Moss had been just pretending to be crazy before, he wasn't acting any longer.

Pony cautiously put Tinker down but stayed between her and Forest Moss.

Forest Moss pulled the girl mannequin close and nuzzled into its neck, keening slightly. "All this is his fault."

"Earth Son's?"

Forest Moss keened more, his caressing hand making its way into the tight flowered pants. Judging by the gender ratio of his plastic audience, Forest Moss had a beef with little boys. "What a spoiled child he was! He could swallow the moon and still be hungry for the sun. He could not be happy with the prosperity of peace; he clung to the grudges of the past. It did not matter that his lovelies, the ones that loved to fight the best, begged him to give up such pettiness. Endless war would take us to extinction. It was time to put away old hates."

Tinker wasn't sure if Forest Moss' rant had anything to do with Earth Son and the children. She'd been under the impression that Earth Son wasn't that much older than Windwolf.

"Shut up!" Forest Moss suddenly bellowed at one of the few remaining boy mannequins. "Shut up! Yes, they chose the Fire Clan over us! Whining spoiled . . ."

And he snapped out the closed-fist spell, reducing the silent mannequin to dust, and started to keen again. Tinker found herself teleported back a dozen feet more, both Stormsong and Pony between her and the crazed elf.

Was Forest Moss destroying himself again and again, the one that made the mistake that led to the slaughter of his household?

"Did you know—did he know that the pathway led to Onihida?"

"He should have been more cautious!" Forest Moss howled. "They trusted him to be careful! Some near stranger comes to him and whispers of a chance to beat all the other clans to wealth, and he leaps at the chance without wondering why him."

"Someone else told you about the path to Onihida?"

"Oh, how hard he searched for their deaths. In and out of caves, over mountains, round and round, searching for the way to oblivion."

"Who told him about the path?" Tinker pressed.

"You cannot find what you cannot see," Forest Moss whispered. "That's all *domana* are good for on Earth—to see the way home."

Tinker nudged Stormsong aside and caught Forest Moss' face between her hands and made him look at her with his one good eye. "Tell me who wanted the pathway found!"

Forest Moss whimpered softly and let drop the mannequin. As it clattered on the ground, he lunged forward, wrapping his arms around her.

"Wait," Tinker growled as Pony and Stormsong grabbed hold of the male, trying to pry him away from her. "Let me deal with him."

While Pony watched with concern, Stormsong had murderous hate in her eyes.

Forest Moss sobbed as he ran his hands over her, rubbing his face against her stomach. "So long! So long since I've held true flesh—soft and warm and yielding."

"Tell me," Tinker said. "Tell me about him or I'll go away."

"Oh, child, you can't imagine what it is like to live

so long. Memories do not stay bright and sharp. Years wear away the polish and then all details. Even with those you love, everything slowly washes away, the shape of their face, the sound of their voice, the scent of their hair. Names of friends and even enemies slip away, lost in the dark waters of time."

"You don't remember?" Tinker cried.

"No!" Forest Moss tightened his hold as if afraid she would tear away from him. "It was at one of countless parties at Summer Court. I remember I was on a bridge, somewhere in the gardens, and he found me there. We talked, but I don't remember the words. All there is left is a dark wind smelling of cherry blossom, and the murmur of voices just over that of running water."

"How could you forget the male that destroyed everything?"

"We searched for years!" Forest Moss wailed. "I deemed him unimportant. A *nivasa*, beautiful and talented but nothing more than a sweet, nearly forbidden treat."

Any questions about what that all might have entailed were driven from Tinker's mind as Forest Moss pushed his trembling hands up under her shirt. A moment later, he had his face pressed against her bared stomach, his scars rough against her skin.

"*Domi*," Pony growled softly.

Tinker caught Forest Moss' braid and yanked his head back.

"Please, oh, please, let me taste you!" Forest Moss begged.

Tinker flinched at the thought but growled, "Tell me something worthwhile!"

Forest Moss whimpered and groaned, running his hands over her stomach. "Something worthwhile? Something worthwhile? Something worthwhile? Gods above, nothing in my life has been worthwhile since the oni took my eye. Time has taken all that I had. There is only darkness where my lovelies once lived."

"Did this *nivasa* talk with Earth Son? Convince him to lure the children here?"

Forest Moss went still, and his eye slowly widened. "Oh." He finally breathed. "I did not recognize him. Yes, I saw him with Earth Son." He pushed his face into her stomach again and moaned softly as he rubbed against her. "I thought nothing of him whispering in Earth Son's ear, twisting him around and around until he was just as warped inside as I was. Ah, but Earth Son's lovelies were much more wise than mine—they killed the spoiled brat before he could be the death of all."

"What about the children? What are the children?"

"They are beautiful—until they're unmade—then they're like everything else—just so much dust."

There was a ding, and the elevator door opened. Blue Sky leaned out. When he caught sight of them, he leapt out of the elevator.

"Tinker! Tinker!"

"What is it?"

"It's your grandfather!"

"What?"

"Your grandfather! He's here!"

"What? My grandfather is dead. You know that. You were at his funeral."

"No, no, the other one! Your great-great-great-something-grandfather. The elf one! He's here and he's taking Oilcan away!"

36: BETWEEN A STONE AND AN IRON MACE

Somehow Oilcan managed to escape without being immediately loaded onto the gossamer and hauled back to Easternlands, kicking and screaming. He quickly explained that he had a household and frantically pointed back toward Sacred Heart.

All the while the back of his brain screamed reminders that this man had built a massive palace to trap his heart's desire in—endlessly painting—until she agreed to become his lover. The male was relentless. Suddenly the story seemed creepy instead of sweetly romantic.

Forge nodded without glancing toward the enclave, his focus wholly on Oilcan. "We were told nothing except that my son's orphan had been found in the middle of the war zone and there were no clansmen here to protect him. We came as quickly as we could."

"We?" Oilcan had the sinking feeling he was about to be outnumbered.

"Your grandmother's brother came with me." Forge waved a hand upward toward the gossamer. "Iron Mace against Stone."

"Against" implied violent force. It seemed an ill-omened name to Oilcan, especially if the force was applied to him. As if summoned by name, the elevator started to descend again.

"I am just an architect," Forge said. "While being methodical and exacting makes me excellent in my craft, I react too slowly for battle. Mace would not hear of me going into a war zone alone."

The elevator reached the ground. The door rattled open and a lone male stepped off. He was all that Oilcan expected in a high-caste elf: tall, elegantly beautiful, and ornately dressed. He wore gold-hued wyvern armor, rich green breeches tucked into tall gleaming boots, and a duster of green fairy silk painted with dragons. Beside him, Forge was short, rough, and earthy. Was that why Forge had felt like he had to court Amaranth so cautiously?

"Mace." Forge put an arm about Oilcan's shoulders. "This is my grandson, Oilcan Wright."

"He's human." Mace frowned down at Oilcan.

"Yes, I am." Oilcan felt the need to underscore that. *Not an elf. Not a child. Not to be taken from Pittsburgh*. "Unbounded Brilliance was my great-great-great-grandfather."

The look on Mace's face made Thorne Scratch shift forward. "He can call the Spell Stones. He is still *domana*-caste."

Forge squeezed Oilcan's shoulders. "He has Amaranth's eyes and smile, and that's all that matters. Besides, what is one generation or five to our cruel overlord's work? We breed true whether we like it or not. Look at him. Is he not all wood sprite?"

"Wh-what?" Oilcan asked.

"The clever little spirits of the woods." Forge gave Oilcan another half hug. "My mother was part of a new caste that the Skin Clan were creating. Small and clever."

"Dangerously clever," Mace said.

Forge grinned at his brother-in-law. "Yes. We are. We remind people of mythical forest guardians, especially after we escaped en masse and set up the first Spell Stones."

The elevator spilled out Mace's Hand, and there was a subtle shift of *sekasha*.

"Come." Forge gently tugged Oilcan toward the enclaves. "Tell me about my son."

Forge did not ask *"How did my son die?"* but clearly that was what he wanted to know.

Mace's First, though, was asking Thorne Scratch what had happened to the *domana* and *sekasha* that came to Pittsburgh. His questions were in High Elvish, and polite, but implied *"Why are you still alive when you should be dead?"*

Oilcan resisted Forge's pull to look back at Thorne Scratch. She was squared off against Iron Mace's First. He didn't want to leave her having to face all the assembled alone, but he wouldn't know what was safe to say. His defense might damn her in their eyes.

As Oilcan wavered, Forge's First noticed him, and his look softened. He minutely shook his head and gave one pushing motion with his hand.

Forge tugged again, and this time Oilcan didn't resist. Still, it felt like he was betraying Thorne Scratch as he let Forge lead him away.

✧ ✧ ✧

At first Oilcan was too distracted to panic.

It was one thing to tell someone that their son was dead and quite another to tell him that his son was beheaded in front of a jeering crowd. To be kind, Oilcan focused on what little he knew of Unbounded Brilliance's life at the French court. His elfin beauty and knowledge of advanced biology had made him a favorite of the queen. Unfortunately, it also made him a target when the nobles fell. While other commoners were overlooked, the elf had been hunted down and put to death. Oilcan merely said, "A civil war broke out, and he was killed in the fighting." Unbounded's son, Etienne, had been as slow to mature as Blue Sky and was still very young. "His wife brought their child to this continent to keep him safe. He became a jeweler and watchmaker."

By then they had reached Sacred Heart, and Oilcan was beginning to realize that compressed down, his family history was one long tragedy. Unbounded Brilliance had died in the Reign of Terror. Etienne had been killed by jewel thieves. Etienne's son drowned in the Johnstown Flood. Of all Unbounded Brilliance's descendants, only Oilcan's grandfather had died peacefully in bed.

A full Hand of *sekasha* swept into the school building ahead of them, and all thoughts of past tragedies vanished.

"Wait!" Oilcan cried, dashing after them. "Forgiveness, but please wait."

The children had gone back to painting. Still clutching dripping paintbrushes, they fled toward the safe room.

Oilcan managed to get between them and the *sekasha*. "Forgiveness. The children have been through much. They frighten easily."

With smiles that seemed almost shy, the warriors backed off.

"*Sama*?" Merry tucked close to Oilcan, ignoring the fact that she was pressing a wet paintbrush into his side.

"This is Forge of Stone." Oilcan pried the paintbrush out of her hands. "He is my ancestor."

"Call me Grandfather." Forge shook his head as he studied the five doubles. "I've never seen so many children together in one place before. What are they doing in this war zone?"

Oilcan hoped that Forge wasn't counting him as one of the children. "Earth Son offered sponsorship to anyone that came to Pittsburgh, but he's—he's dead." Oilcan skirted around explaining how Earth Son had ended up dead. "The children broke ties with their households—they can't go back."

Forge continued to shake his head. "I had not heard—but I'm not privy to most clan business. I work too closely with the Fire Clan to be trusted by most of our clan. Still—what was he thinking? *Laedin* I could understand in a war zone, but *naelinsanota*?"

"*Naelinsanota*?" Oilcan had never heard the term before. If he was translating the word correctly, it meant "unclean blood."

"Forgiveness, the habits of your youth are the deepest ingrained. It's been *nae hou*, and yet the old words are the ones that come easiest. Our cruel overlords each had their own breeding projects. Just as my mother's people were clever, the *naelinsanota* were just as gifted, although more artistically inclined. After the liberation, the *naelinsanota* were absorbed into the *taunlae*."

"My parents were *naelinsanota*," Merry whispered, blushing brightly. "But they let people believe they're *taunlae*."

Rustle took her hand and squeezed it tight. "So were mine."

"Mine, too," Cattail said.

"I'm not sure," Barley said. "I think my father may have been. He wasn't *nivasa* caste, and that was all my mother's household talked about—like she'd lowered herself."

"*Quiee*." It clearly distressed Baby Duck that she didn't know what she was.

Oilcan frowned. It was one thing if Earth Son had put out a general summons. If he had selectively tapped only the children of a certain caste, then the *domana* had definitely been working with the oni greater bloods. But to what end?

"Where will Grandfather be staying?" Barley reminded Oilcan that there was a more important problem at hand. "Grandfather" was here on a mission. The young male added with a mix of hope and dread, "With us?"

That seemed too close. "In the house" seemed like it would lead directly to "in control."

Oilcan shook his head. "We don't have extra beds."

"We don't have any beds," Cattail Reeds pointed out.

"We won't be here long." By "we" Forge probably meant himself, Oilcan, and the children.

This was Oilcan's life without brakes. "Wait here a minute." Oilcan backpedaled into the kitchen. He was running by the time he hit the back door. He ran out the back gate and down the back alley, praying that Windwolf was at Poppymeadow's.

He nearly careened into the male halfway down the road. "Windwolf!" He caught hold of the tall male.

"What is wrong, cousin?"

"Forge of Stone is here. He is the father of Unbounded Brilliance—my ancestor. He is claiming me as his child and wants to take me to Easternlands."

"I will not allow it," Windwolf snapped.

Oilcan breathed out in relief. "So, you can stop him?"

Windwolf looked angry. "I am not sure, but I intend to try."

Apparently it was the arrival of the gossamer that triggered the gathering of *domana.* Prince True Flame was on the edge of the faire grounds, already exchanging introductions with Iron Mace. Forge's First and Thorne Scratch weren't with the knot of elves: apparently they'd gone on to Sacred Heart.

Oilcan was glad to note that Iron Mace introduced himself to Windwolf, meaning that he was lower ranked. Prince True Flame, though, in the end would be the one that decided Oilcan's fate.

"Wolf Who Rules Wind." Windwolf growled out his name and then turned to his cousin. "True, I will not have my territory plundered while I'm dealing with a common enemy. If they are not here to help, they are not welcomed."

"They just arrived." True Flame shifted the conversation to High Elvish and made a motion for Windwolf to stay calm.

For reasons that eluded Oilcan, the more polite the conversation, the faster the elves talked.

Windwolf's response was machine-gun fast but courteous. "I will not stand by and let them take what is mine. It was agreed that humans would be considered neutral but under Wind Clan rule."

"What is this?" Iron Mace noticed Oilcan and frowned. "You would deny us our own blood?"

Windwolf nodded. "If he does not want to leave Pittsburgh, then yes, I would deny you. He is not yours to take."

Iron Mace waved a hand toward Oilcan. "He is—what? Thirty? Forty years old? He is not old enough to choose his clan. He is the clan of his birth."

"I was not born into a clan," Oilcan pointed out as calmly as he could in High Elvish. "Nor was my mother or my grandfather or his father."

True Flame looked at him with surprise clear on his face. He glanced to Windwolf. "How is it that the one that is human speaks High Tongue better than the one that is an elf?"

Iron Mace plowed through any answer from Windwolf beyond a spreading of hands. "My sister's son was lost to us. His children were born to the Stone Clan regardless if they knew it or not."

Windwolf shook his head. "One's clan is a personal choice. Loyalty must be freely given."

"As I said." Iron Mace raised his voice and talked faster. "He is not old enough to choose."

None of the elves seem to be considering Oilcan as part of the conversation. They were like dogs fighting over a bone.

"Forgiveness." Oilcan fought to stay civil. "I am a human, not an elf."

Iron Mace didn't even glance in Oilcan's direction. "If he is *domana* enough to tap the Stones, then he must be considered an elf."

Oilcan shifted closer to Prince True Flame. He wasn't sure what it said that none of the prince's *sekasha* considered him threat enough to block his move. It did not help his cause that he only came up to mid-chest on them.

"Honorable one, the question is not how much an elf I am, but if I'm an adult and can determine my own fate. By human reckoning, I reached my adulthood years ago. My mother gave birth to me when she was only a few years older than I am now." Actually, she had been over a decade older, but it was close enough in elf years. "My grandfather died before he reached his triples. If you don't consider me adult now, then I will never live long enough for you to see me as an adult."

"Your grandfather died a double?" Forge joined the fray without bothering to introduce himself.

"He was ninety-eight," Oilcan said. "His heart gave out."

At least, that was what the coroner ruled. His grandfather had been fighting pneumonia for a week before he died. It was possible that if he had let them take him to the hospice and use magic to battle the illness, he would have survived.

"He was no taller than I am now. I am full grown." Oilcan hammered home on the fact that he had a human lifespan. "I will not live to see my triples. The average lifespan of a human male is only mid-seventies."

Only then did he see Thorne Scratch behind Forge. Her warrior's mask slipped, and her eyes filled with sorrow. He wished she was close enough to reach out and take her hand, but he would have had to go through Forge's Hand to get to her.

"How old are you now?" Forge dragged Oilcan's attention back to the debate.

Oilcan sighed, hating to answer. "Humans reach maturity in less than two decades."

"I realize that. How old are you?" Forge pressed for an answer.

"Twenty-two." Judging by the dismayed looks all around, he had just reduced himself back to a five-year-old in their eyes. "Pittsburgh is my home and if I had to choose a clan, I would choose the Wind Clan. Because of the children, though, it would be best if I could merely stay neutral."

"Wind Clan?" Iron Mace cried. "What idiocy is that? You are Stone Clan!"

"He is not!" Tinker pushed her way through Windwolf's Hand to stand between Oilcan and the Stone Clan *domana*. She was wearing shorts, a Team Tinker T-shirt, and tennis shoes. She had her right arm in a sling and was snarling in Low Elvish. "He's old enough to decide his clan, and he decided to be neutral, so back off!"

"Who is this?" Iron Mace demanded.

"This is Beloved Tinker of Wind." Prince True Flame gave Windwolf a look that clearly demanded his cousin to take control of his child bride. "She is the Wind Clan *domi*."

The Stone Clan continued to look confused.

"She is my cousin." Oilcan added the High Elvish term that clearly mapped out how they were related. He shifted back to Low Elvish as Tinker wouldn't be able to follow the conversation otherwise. "But we were raised as brother and sister."

Forge instantly grasped Windwolf's reasons. "You returned her immortality!"

Iron Mace, though, focused on the negative. "You spell-worked one of our clan's children?"

"I am not a child," Tinker snapped. "And I've never been Stone Clan. I have always considered myself Wind Clan."

"It is all we've ever known," Oilcan added.

Iron Mace shook his head. "Clearly Unbounded Brilliance's children lost all memory of who they really were along with their immortality."

Tinker shook her head. "Our grandfather knew that we were once Stone Clan, and he chose not to have any communication with them."

Their grandfather had viewed almost everything connected to elves with faint distrust. Oilcan had always attributed their grandfather's wariness to the fact that Tooloo seemed incapable of telling the truth. Perhaps he knew that contacting the Stone Clan meant they would be scooped up and forced to be children the rest of their lives.

"Why didn't he send word?" Forge asked. "I've been searching for *nae hae* for my son."

"It does not matter." Iron Mace snapped. "The Wind Clan has no right—"

"Wolf Who Rules offered, I accepted—there doesn't need to be anything more than that!" Tinker shouted.

"Enough!" Prince True Flame roared. "We are at war. We do not have time for this petty bickering. Humans are considered adult at eighteen, so he can choose to be Stone Clan or not, if he wishes."

"Forgiveness," Oilcan said to Forge and to Thorne Scratch. "But I choose not to be Stone Clan."

Oilcan fled back to Sacred Heart while Prince True Flame dragooned Iron Mace into the war effort and dragged him off for a war council. Forge begged off, pointing out that he could lay defenses but was generally a noncombatant. Prince True Flame allowed it; maybe seeing it as payment for losing his grandchildren, or maybe so he could babysit the two baby *domana* cousins.

Oilcan wished he didn't feel so guilty for protecting himself. But if his mother's death had taught him anything, it was that you couldn't live your life ignoring your own heart for the sake of someone else's happiness. He'd watched his mother die a little bit at a time for years before his father landed the killing blow. She should have fled to Elfhome, following her love of elf culture, instead of worrying about making his father unhappy. Her leaving his father wouldn't have been as bad as his father rotting in a prison cell, knowing he'd killed the only good thing in his life.

Tinker walked beside Oilcan, occasionally bumping shoulders with him and giving him worried looks.

"Oh, oh, what's the look for? You're the one with the broken arm."

Tinker bumped him a little harder and stuck out her tongue. He laughed; it made him happy that despite all the madness of her change and the war, they were fundamentally the same. He could understand Forge's immediate obsession. In Tinker, Oilcan heard echoes of his mother's voice and grandfather's sharp humor. If he lost Tinker, it would be like he lost his mother and grandfather all over again. He couldn't bear the loss.

It didn't surprise him that Forge followed them up the steps to Sacred Heart. Oilcan wasn't sure how to deal with the elf that reminded him of his grandfather. Would the elf obey Prince True Flame or would he steamroll over everything to drag Oilcan back to the Easternlands?

Tinker turned to glare with suspicion at their great-grandfather. "What do you want—besides the obvious? You can't have Oilcan."

Unstoppable force met unmovable object. If Oilcan wasn't sandwiched between the two, it would be entertaining.

Forge stared back at Tinker, seemingly fascinated by her. "You were as human as your cousin? Before Wolf Who Rules spell-worked you?"

"Yes," Tinker growled. "Most people thought we were brother and sister, not cousins. I won't let you take him away. This is his home—not some huge sprawling palace with a bunch of strangers."

Forge nodded slowly. "Forgiveness. Of course. I—I didn't think..." He faltered to a halt, and then sudden hope dawned on his face. "Are there more of you? They say humans are more prolific—"

"No," Oilcan said, and then to soften it added, "Grandfather. Most of Unbounded's descendants had only one child to carry on the bloodline. Tinker and I are the only ones left."

"I see. Oh, well." He smiled sadly. "It is two more than I had ever hoped for. My son disappeared so suddenly, without a word to anyone, taking no one with him and seemingly without any of his things. He left behind his brushes and paints and lute. What was missing were things a thief would take. We were afraid he'd been killed and his body buried in some shallow grave. The not knowing what had happened to him: that was the worst."

Oilcan understood all too well. When the oni kidnapped Tinker a few weeks earlier, they made it seem as if she had crashed into the river. For weeks, he hadn't known if she was dead or alive. He had the prophecy, though, that Tinker would be the one to stop the oni from invading. Oilcan had clung to that hope despite all the evidence. He could not imagine three hundred years of nothing. He could imagine how overwhelming the grief would be. Just the glimmer of hope would keep fresh the wounds, and every day would be a cycle of sorrow.

"Amaranth had every foot of soil within a day's walk overturned. We dragged all the nearby lakes. She endlessly questioned everyone that might have seen him those last days. In the end, she couldn't take not knowing what had happened to our son. She killed herself."

To lose first your child and then your wife. Gods have pity on the male.

"I'm sorry for your loss," Oilcan said.

"We came at all haste once we heard the news about his orphan being in the war zone. We only have our *sekasha* with us; we left behind the rest of our households. We'll have to send my gossamer back to fetch them."

"You're staying?" Tinker's voice was full of suspicion.

"Of course we're staying. We can't leave you two here defenseless. We have cots and blankets on the gossamer, and while we're here, we can build your defenses for this enclave."

Oilcan realized that when Forge said "staying," he meant at Sacred Heart.

The children were ecstatic at the news. They saw it as a dry run toward opening an enclave. As Forge went off to collect gear from the gossamer and send it back for his household, the kids argued over what to do to prepare.

"We should paint the dining hall!" Cattail doggedly rolled as fast as she could.

"That's pointless. We only have one table and six chairs." Rustle waved his paintbrush at Oilcan's small dinette table and mismatched collection of chairs.

"They can eat in shifts." Barley had stopped edging and was cleaning his paintbrush. "But I need to start dinner now. We need food for what—nineteen people? How many Hands did they bring? A couple days of this and we'll end up with nothing but keva beans."

Baby Duck was trotting in tight circles, clutching her roller. "Where will they sleep? None of the guest rooms have been painted. Shouldn't we be working on those instead?"

That brought them all to a complete halt, and they turned to Oilcan with pleading eyes.

"For now, we'll put them in the finished rooms on the third floor." Oilcan hated the whole plan. He wasn't sure if he could trust Forge, but they needed funds if they were to stay neutral, and the *domana* did have *sekasha* to keep the children safe. "Only for a day or two until we can paint the rooms on the second floor."

"And put up window dresses and artwork," Cattail added quietly.

"And make them nice," Oilcan promised. He wasn't sure where they'd get fabric for the curtains, but artwork he could handle. "Beans will be fine. They know this is a war zone. I can see if they can have supplies from Easternlands brought across. I'll chase down another table and some more chairs." He caught Baby Duck by the shoulders and pointed her at the nearest unfinished wall. "Go ahead and finish this coat. You're almost done, and then you'll have to wait for it to dry anyhow. Merry, why don't you take over edging for Barley?"

Tinker was watching him marshal his troops with amusement. "Grandpa would be proud."

"He'd be happier if they weren't elves," Oilcan murmured in English to spare the kids' feelings. He pulled out a tablet and started a new to-do list. If he wanted Forge's gossamer to bring back food supplies, he'd better talk to Forge immediately. "Grandpa never really trusted elves."

"Lately, I've been empathizing with him," Tinker grumbled low but back in Elvish. She kept pace with Oilcan as he headed toward the distant gossamer. Apparently she intended to keep an eye on Oilcan while the gossamer was still close enough to whisk him away. "If you read between the lines in his codex, Dufae was hiding on Earth. He never comes out and says it, but I think he found out that someone in the Stone Clan was cooperating with the Skin Clan. It might seem like a long time ago for us, but most likely, all the parties except Dufae are still alive."

Dufae and his mother, who'd been desperately trying to figure out what had happened to her son—searching to find what had made him disappear. He wondered how Amaranth had died. Had Amaranth actually killed herself?

If she hadn't, then two households' worth of possible killers were about to arrive.

Would the kids be safe? Someone in the Stone Clan had already betrayed them once. "I found something out," Oilcan said. "All the kids are *naelinsanota*—a caste that the Skin Clan was developing. The weird thing was that it's a bit of a stigma—families weren't advertising the fact that they were *naelinsanota*."

Tinker cursed loudly, looking like she wanted to hit someone hard. Frustrated, she settled for kicking at a clump of grass. "I bet the dead children were hiding the fact that they were *naelinsanota*, too. Lain says all the kids, the ones that lived and the ones that were killed, were related. It means they're all the same caste—even Baby Duck, even though she can't remember. All seven! This wasn't a random call for sponsorship. Earth Son, or whoever was using his name, had to have all but hand-delivered his offer to specific families."

"To specific children," Oilcan said. "It can't be a coincidence that all of them are still doubles."

"Only doubles are free to change households without shame." Pony's voice echoed Tinker's anger. "The only caste that waits until their hundredth year to choose their beholding are *sekasha*. But to find seven doubles of any one caste—that is not coincidence."

"Do you think Forge has anything to do with this?" Tinker eyed Oilcan. He could almost see the little cogs and wheels in her brain spinning quickly, planning ways to kidnap him herself.

"No," Oilcan said firmly. "Thorne asked me for our lineage. The news traveled to Forge, and he came to find us. Me." Forge's emotions felt too genuine to be faked. "He loved Amaranth beyond reason. There's no way he could have killed her and stayed sane."

"So maybe he's crazy," Tinker said.

"I—I doubt it." Pony shook himself like a wet dog at the idea. "His Hand would know if he's unstable enough for that, and if they suspected he was monster enough to kill his *domi*, then—no—he can't be insane."

It was comforting to know—assuming that the *sekasha* were as all-knowing as Pony thought. Certainly Pony had been the first to realize Tinker was slipping over the edge when Esme was invading her dreams. But what if Tinker had been twisted before Pony met her? Would Pony see past a mask of sanity? Thorne Scratch hadn't.

There was chaos on the faire ground by the massive anchors. Apparently Earth Son's and Jewel Tear's orphaned households had heard of the arrival of a Stone Clan airship. They were gathered around Forge, carrying travel bags. Some stoically quiet. Some in tears. Some pleading and weeping loudly.

"Anyone that wants to go back to Easternlands can." Forge must have cast an amplification spell, because his voice carried as if he were using a bullhorn. "Anyone seeking to join my household will need to stay here in Pittsburgh and wait until I can decide to accept anyone."

Oilcan glanced to Thorne Scratch. He hadn't even considered that she might leave completely. Certainly there was nothing he could offer to make her stay. He took comfort that she made no move to leave his side, collect her gear, and go back to the Easternlands on the great living airship. Did she plan to offer to Forge or Iron Mace? Surrounded by Tinker's and Forge's Hands, Thorne had her face set to warrior neutral, so he could glean nothing of her intentions.

Forge pushed through the throng to where Oilcan and Tinker stood. "Is something wrong?"

Oilcan realized then that they hadn't actually talked about how much he'd charge Forge. Maybe the elf thought he was staying in exchange for the defensive spells he planned—but Tinker could probably do just as good a job. It was food that Oilcan couldn't get easily elsewhere. "The city is under siege and running low on food. We'll be happy to have you stay with us—but there's no place we can buy enough food to feed everyone. I was hoping that part of your—"

He wasn't sure what elves called it.

"*Mau*," Pony murmured.

"*Mau* would be in supplies from Easternland. Flour, salt, sugar, keva beans."

Forge nodded. "Of course, of course. If you need something, and if it is mine to give, you may have it."

It was nearly the same thing that Tinker had said just days before. It touched Oilcan deeply that this male he had just met was so willing to commit completely. It reminded him of his own instant affinity to Merry because she had reminded him of his lost mother.

"Thank you, Grandfather." He put his hand on the male's shoulder, ignoring the slight snort from Tinker.

Forge swallowed him into a full hug. "Oh, my child, I don't know if I'll be able to bear losing you so soon after finding you."

"You can stay as long as you want," Oilcan said. Really, they needed all the *domana* they could get.

Forge hugged him tighter. "I will stay to the end."

For a moment, Oilcan thought he meant until the end of the war. Only when he caught sight of Thorne giving him a look full of understanding sorrow did Oilcan realize that Forge meant until Oilcan died of old age.

37: DAYS OF PAST NOT FORGOTTEN

Oilcan spent the next few days finding tables and chairs, buying paint, tracking down yards and yards of fabric and a sewing machine, raiding his various stashes of paintings for artwork emotionally safe enough to hang, and making countless trips to Wollerton's for the massive bathing-room renovation. He also tracked down yet another cell phone for Tinker and programed it for her. All of this meant he spent a lot of time away from Sacred Heart. Since Thorne always came with him (and usually a rotating foursome of Forge's *sekasha* in the name of learning the city), it left the children alone. With the oni doing raids all over the city, he was glad that Forge was at the enclave, overseeing construction of outer walls and defensive spells.

When Oilcan found time to spare, he would check in on Forge. The male was more than willing to patiently explain how he was building the spells into the wall's foundations to create the enclave's powerful barrier protection. Again and again, Oilcan found echoes of his grandfather in the elf. From the way Forge handled his project management to the way he pulled at his hair in frustration, it was obvious that more than just genetics had been handed down through the family.

It delighted Forge to see the habits in Oilcan. "Amaranth always had paint on her hands and in her hair and on her face, usually right on the end of her nose. I think it was because she would do this." Forge pressed the back of his hand to his nose to demonstrate.

Oilcan laughed and checked. He had a swipe of soldering paste across his nose from welding the bathing room's water pipes. "Yeah, that's how it got there. Tinker is worse than me. Five minutes into anything and she's got a smudged nose."

Forge was showing Oilcan how to vary the shield spell when a slight tension went through Forge's Hand.

Iron Mace drifted onto the worksite. "Ah, I wondered who was tapping the stones."

"I'm just teaching him how to protect himself," Forge said.

"You weren't taught our *esva* as a child?" Iron Mace motioned with his hand as if conceding a point. "Well, more of a child."

Oilcan sighed. Insisting he was an adult made him feel like a four-year-old shouting "I'm a big boy now!" Forge had studied architecture during the days of the pharaohs and Iron Mace had been using four numbers to record his age when Amaranth had been born. It was no wonder that the two couldn't see him as anything but hopelessly young. "My mother knew Elvish, both Low and High, and a handful of songs, but not much more."

Mace pressed, apparently not believing that Oilcan was untrained. "Unbounded Brilliance made no permanent record to school his children in their inheritance? He left them ignorant of his clan and his family and all the vast store of knowledge we had when humans were still squatting in caves?"

If his ancestor had left anything, it was in the codex with a warning built into the spell-lock: *trust no one.* Still, Oilcan had to keep to the truth. "We didn't know that Unbounded Brilliance was Stone Clan *domana* until a few days ago. If he'd told his son anything about the Spell Stones or the *esva*, it was lost long ago." Certainly they hadn't been aware that the spells of the codex were inscribed on stones and could be cast remotely. His mother had taught him the *domana* finger exercises between rounds of patty-cake and cat's cradle.

"How does your cousin know the *esva* then?" Mace asked.

Oilcan wasn't sure, but he could guess. "She probably saw Jewel Tear and Forest Moss cast spells and copied them."

Forge laughed. "What did I say, Mace? We breed true—too clever for our own good."

Iron Mace snorted.

Forge glanced beyond Iron Mace and shook his head. "This is a war zone, Mace. You should keep your people closer."

Iron Mace laughed. "I'm safe here." He waved to the nearly completed wall. "You have the passive protections in place, and you are here with two of your Hands. I see no point to wearing my people to the bone. They have to rest sometime."

"You would not have this problem if you took another Hand."

"And have five more mouths to feed."

"The clan would more than double your support."

"Things are not that simple. This is why you fail so badly at politics." Mace gave a slight wave and strolled away.

Forge frowned after him.

"He cannot take what hasn't been offered," Forge's First, Dark Scythe, said.

"If you change your mind," the note read in messy English, followed by a phone number and then lots of *x*'s and *o*'s. Oilcan frowned at the scrap of paper tucked into his glove box. Who was this from? The phone number had an area code, so it wasn't a Pittsburgh number.

He rooted a little more until he came up with a fresh pad of paper and a pen and headed back into Sacred Heart, trying not to think about the note. Undoubtedly it was from a female post-doc that he'd met at one of Lain's Startup Cookouts. It really didn't matter which one—they all ended messy.

Ryan MacDonald was the last woman he had dated. She had been delightfully laid-back. Toward the end of her thirty-day stay on Elfhome, though, they slipped into the familiar pattern of all his relationships. The conversations that danced around the depth of his feelings. The tentative testing of his commitment to Elfhome. Ryan at least didn't push for him to move to Earth; instead she hinted that she could return to Elfhome for a permanent position.

It ended like all the others. Her in tears and the familiar refrain "If you would only say that you loved me."

Any other Shutdown, he would have locked himself away at his barn and drunk himself into a stupor. On the off chance that Tinker would return from Aum Renau, though, he got permission to ride out Shutdown at the enclaves and thus was there to welcome her home.

He flipped open the pad and tried to distract himself by scribbling down the start of a new to-do list. (Tinker teased him about using paper, but sometimes writing something down and then burning the paper was the only way to deal with things.) Roach had hauled away the last dumpster filled with rubble from the restroom demolition. He needed to take down the three-story chute, carefully, in case he needed it for a second story remodel of the bathrooms. The cement board was up and the seams sealed. All that was left was the tiling.

His footsteps echoed in the front foyer, reminding him that he was alone for the first time since he found Merry. Not completely alone. Blue Sky was treating the kids to DVDs. Oilcan could hear the faint strains of music from somewhere upstairs, and buttered popcorn perfumed the air. Iron Mace was working in his rooms. His Hand was using the gym as a training hall. Forge was consulting with Prince True Flame on defenses out by the faire grounds.

But Thorne Scratch wasn't quietly shadowing Oilcan for the first time in days. Iron Mace had called her aside while Roach was loading up the dumpster. She had left Sacred Heart to do Iron Mace's bidding—making Oilcan wonder if they had quietly come to an arrangement already.

The mystery note reminded him that this time he

was the one that was leaving "in just a few decades." He was the one wondering how Thorne Scratch felt. He was the one that desperately wanted to ask the measure of her feelings. And it was probably going to be the same messy end.

He crumpled up the note and shoved it into his pocket to burn later.

Blue Sky and Baby Duck came charging down the stairs, Repeat the elfhound puppy half tumbling on their heels. "Out of popcorn!" Blue yelled as they ran past. "And Rustle lost his belt buckle!"

Oilcan sighed. "How?"

"I don't know!" Blue shouted back as all three vanished into the dining room.

Oilcan shook his head. Rustle was a black hole for personal items. He had lost everything from the irreplaceable iPod to three left shoes. Oilcan added "Rustle: belt buckle" to his to-do list and continued up the stairs.

He had used up the last of his money to buy tile for the bathing room. Wollerton's didn't have enough of the gorgeous blue glass tile to cover the entire room. He had to buy other tiles to have enough square footage. Before he could start laying the tile, he needed to decide on a design. The project should relax him, as art was always soothing. It let him take a big hunk of chaos and reduce it down to something neat and orderly.

It was a brainless choice for the swimming pool-like tub. The elves liked to add salt and minerals to the heated water. Since the cloudy water would obscure most of the inner walls, the tub itself could be of plain white tiles.

He switched to his datapad to do calculations on

how much square footage the glass tile would cover. He sang to himself as he sketched out a 3-D model of the room and overlaid a grid to show coverage. Once he got the room tiled, the acoustics were going to be amazing.

His brain went back to Rustle. The musician's arm was still not healing readily. True, Tinker's arm wasn't as badly broken, but she had regained limited use of hers in two days of the same aggressive healing spells. Nor was Rustle sleeping as much as Tinker did while healing. Maybe he should take Rustle back to the hospice. Perhaps something about the kids' weird genetic makeup meant that the healing spells didn't work the same on them. What Pandora's box did Tinker open when she picked the chest's lock?

"Knock, knock, pick the lock," he sang. "Open the box, take the spell from uncle's room, run away, save the day..."

Oilcan trailed off as he realized the song wasn't some innocent children's song, but a literal history of his family.

Strong arms caught hold of him, and he was jerked off the ground.

"So he did leave a record, after all," Iron Mace growled into Oilcan's ear. "I was afraid he would. It was obvious he must have, the way all his children turned against their clan. No, no, no." Mace pressed something soft against Oilcan's face to muffle his shouts. "We don't want to get the doubles involved in this. Too many innocents have suffered already."

Oilcan stopped shouting as he realized only the kids were on the third floor. Mace's Hand was down on the first floor, and Forge was across the street. Even

Thorne was out—carefully sent away. He focused on trying to get free, but Mace had him tight.

"Just relax, let the *saijin* do its work." Mace carried him toward the bank of windows standing open to let out the construction dust.

Oilcan buckled in Mace's hold even as the edges of his vision went shimmering white with the drug.

"Go to sleep," Iron Mace growled. "That way you won't feel anything."

Oilcan struggled to keep his eyes open. He couldn't move. He felt like he was sinking into warm, bright quicksand. Even Oilcan's fear was slow, seeping through him. Was this how Amaranth really died? Drugged to helplessness and then murdered in a way to look like she had killed herself? Had Mace dropped her from a window, too?

Forge's voice came thundering from a great distance. "What are you doing? Put him down! Get away from him!"

The world was washed in brightness as Mace laid him on the floor, the flower kissing his face. Oilcan struggled to roll his head, but Mace was holding him still. Mace hovered above, a darkness in the shimmering light. "You didn't do anything to save my sister. I told you that she was driving herself insane with all that digging through the moors for his body. I told you that you had to take her away from that place, take her somewhere not haunted by his ghost. You didn't listen. You did nothing, and she slipped through your fingers."

Forge's voice lost its thunder. "I didn't think she would—I didn't think—"

Oilcan tried to shout his fear, and it came out a moan. *No, no, don't listen to him!*

"If you do nothing, we're going to lose all we have left of her!" Iron Mace raged, sounding like a grief-stricken older brother—but then, he'd had centuries to perfect the act. "The Wind Clan already took one of our little ones. She's gone to us. Are you going to let him slip through your fingers, too?"

"I've done what I can." Forge finally eclipsed Oilcan's view of the ceiling. He gazed down at Oilcan with eyes dark and luminous with tears. "You can't—"

"Save him!" Mace shouted. "Or are you going to let him die, too?"

"You can't just drug him and change him." Forge reached for the flower.

Iron Mace caught Forge's hand. "He's twenty-two years old, Forge. Twenty-two! What does he know about life and death? He's still a baby. The law says a parent can act for the good of their child."

Oilcan's eyes closed against his will, and he sank down into the light.

"He—he's not a baby." Forge's voice was full of despair. "He's good and kind and patient. . . ."

The light was dimming, fading to black. Tooloo had warned Oilcan to be careful, that the Stone Clan would twist him around and then murder him in his sleep.

"And he'll be gone soon if we don't save him," Mace thundered in the darkness. "Don't fail him like you failed Amaranth."

The last thing Oilcan heard was Forge groan and whisper softly, "Oh, child, forgive me, but he's right."

And then Oilcan was lost in the darkness.

38: UNCLEAN BLOOD

Lemonseed was Windwolf's major domo. She was patient and unmovable as a mountain. She looked no older than Lain, her face only lightly touched by time. Small wrinkles gathered at the corners of her Lady Madonna smile. She had two locks of pure white hair that she wove like silk ribbons through her Wind Clan glossy black hair. She was, however, the oldest member of Windwolf's household and well over nine thousand years old. She had been born when humans were just wrapping their brains around the idea of keeping animals as pets and planting seeds into the ground to create farms. She had lived through thousands of years of Skin Clan rule before the clans won their freedom.

Most importantly, she was Windwolf's Beholden. She could be trusted not to talk to the Wyverns about anything damning Tinker let slip.

They cornered her in the kitchen garden among the laundered sheets hung out to dry on strands of steel-spinner silk. The walls of damp white cotton gave them privacy without making it obvious that they were trying to hide.

"What do you know about the *naelinsanota*?" Tinker asked.

"Oh, that is not a term I've heard for *nae hou*," Lemonseed said. "It is not something I would tell you lightly. Do you really need to know?"

Tinker nodded. "Please. Everything that you can tell me."

Lemonseed laughed and smiled and cupped Tinker's face in her hands. "Oh, sweetness, it would take years to tell you all that I know." A measure of her Hand's trust of the old female, neither Pony or Stormsong moved as Lemonseed touched her. "Judging on the last few months, we do not have years for you to hear it all."

"Unfortunately, no. I'm not sure if I even have days or hours."

"Ah, the unclean ones?" Lemonseed tilted her head to consider the clouds passing over their narrow cloth hallway. "I was born slave to King Boar Bristle of the Eastern Steppes. He had been born the second son of King War Axe, but he had murdered his father and older brother for his title and was quite determined not to spawn any children that could wrestle away his power. We lived in a great jewellike palace built over a lake that was stocked with the most heavenly smelling water lilies, and glow fish so beautiful it would take your breath away. And yet there wasn't a moment of the day where you were totally safe. To the king, we were cattle, there to be used and slaughtered. To his favorites, he gave free rein to take their pleasures however they wished. Half of the people that lived in the palace were loyal to the Skin Clan, but the rest of us were secretly Wind Clan. It was my mother who was wet nurse to Quick Blade, Windwolf's great-grandfather, the king's bastard who he had ordered drowned in the lake at birth. My older half-brother was drowned in his stead."

Tinker wondered when Lemonseed would get to her point; and the tengu thought that dragons were long-winded. "So, the unclean ones?"

"That was how it was," Lemonseed said. "The Skin Clan had great palaces scattered across the known world where we lived like frightened mice as they moved like gods among us, taking pleasure and killing where they desired. But every century, we were growing stronger and bolder. The Soulless One lived on the Inner Sea, half a world away, where Winter Court lies now."

Obviously there was a huge hole in Tinker's knowledge, as Lemonseed had said the name as if Tinker should recognize the person. "Who?"

"The emperor of the Skin Clan, Heaven's Blessing. We called him the Soulless One because he was an albino."

"Albinos are born without a soul." Pony sounded like he believed it totally.

"Fortunately, albinos are almost unheard of among elves," Stormsong added. "Mostly because it was ruthlessly eliminated from the main breed stock shortly after Heaven's Blessing was born."

"He was brilliant and ruthless. He sensed the coming years of resistance where we would fight open battles against our masters. The greatest at spell-working, he chose to create his ultimate weapons. Of that, we of the Wind Clan only know the rumors."

In other words—much fewer words: *I wasn't there, I'm not sure how much of this is true.* The reason for the disclaimer became obvious with Lemonseed's next sentence.

"It is said," Lemonseed whispered, "that the emperor captured a god. He distilled down its essence and used it to create new castes. The first that he made were the *naelinsanota.* They were flawed because of his impatience. The second he made were the *intanyai seyosa.* They looked upon their maker and saw his wickedness. They saw too that he was about to create his own downfall, so they kept their silence. It was with the god's holy perfection that he made the *sekasha.*"

Providence had claimed that the Skin Clan had used a dragon to create the *sekasha.* The children were descended from "brothers" of the *sekasha*? If the caste was considered flawed, why did the Skin Clan want the children? What abilities had the Emperor been trying to breed into the *naelinsanota*?

"Why were they considered unclean while the *sekasha* are holy?" Tinker asked.

"Because of their mothers." Lemonseed blushed and looked down at the ground. "The Soulless One had developed a spell in which a child would be produced within a female's womb without her having sex. It has never been clear if the resulting child was the mother's flesh and blood, or if she was merely a vessel for another's child. He tested it first using wargs—he was trying to make a creature strictly for war." Lemonseed waved her hands as she floundered. "The offspring looked like elves. Many did not survive their births. They were eaten by their beast mothers."

"Gods," Tinker breathed.

"When he saw he could make elves with the god's essence, he used *filintau*-caste to bear the children."

The *filintau* were "the clean folk." The caste had been created to be a pure breeding stock, free of defects. Apparently the mother's "purity" was enough to affect how the other elves saw the offspring.

Still, how did you even take something like Impatience, render it down, and produce an elf born to a beast? Tinker couldn't imagine the level of knowledge on gene manipulation that the Skin Clan had to possess. Even the horrific twisting of the oni didn't compare.

Her new cell phone started to play "Sky Diving"—Blue Sky's ringtone.

"What is it, Blue?" Tinker answered her phone.

"Everyone is gone, and someone's here." Blue's voice was thin with fear. "I think it's oni."

"What? Where are you?"

"Sacred Heart. Someone just broke down the door."

"Get to the safe room!"

"We can't! They're downstairs and we're upstairs."

She was running toward the door, aware that warriors were sweeping up behind her. Her mind was racing through the school's layout. The bedroom doors had frosted glass inset into wooden frames. Only the restrooms had solid doors. "Go to one of the restrooms and barricade yourself in."

"The toilets or the bathing room?"

It doesn't matter, she almost wailed and then realized it did. "The bathing room!"

Judging by the shouts and screams and sudden gunfire, Blue Sky had the other kids with him and a gun. Where was Oilcan? Where were Forge and his

Hands? There should be a horde of *sekasha* between the kids and the oni!

There was an awful possibility that the oni didn't need or want the children alive. Maybe body parts were sufficient, or maybe they would rather that the kids were dead than have Tinker able to discover what was different about them.

"Tinker!" Blue cried over the phone. "They're breaking down the door!"

"The chute! Come down the chute!"

She waved Pony to head into the school as she detoured to the construction chute. The boxed-in slide slanted down the side of the building, leading from the third-story bathroom to where the dumpster had been parked. What were the numbers of "soft?" She dropped her phone and cast the spell, praying she remembered the fingering chart correctly.

A moment later Baby Duck came shrieking down the slide and landed in soft, yielding nothingness.

"No, no!" Tinker used her foot to block the screaming little female's attempt to climb her. "I've got to catch the others. Someone get her!"

One of the *laedin* caught hold of Baby Duck and was, in turn, frantically scaled until the little female was latched tight around the warrior's neck.

Tinker tried to ignore the sudden outbreak of gunfire as Pony led the elves into the school house.

Rustle slid down the chute next, quiet and white. He stumbled to his feet and turned to catch hold of Merry as she slid down to safety. They clung to each other.

Tinker wanted Oilcan's kids safe and sound, but it was Blue Sky she desperately wanted on the ground beside her. The little idiot would probably wait until last—his father's genes wouldn't let him go any earlier. The sound of open warfare came from the school. Cattail appeared, then Barley, but no baby *sekasha*. "Blue!" There was an explosion above. "Blue!"

And then he was there, safe. She canceled the spell so she could hug him tight. "Idiot!"

She was aware of royal troops arriving, summoned too late by the gunfire and explosion. The kids would have been taken if not for Blue Sky. Half of the troops rushed into Sacred Heart while the rest spread out, flooding the area with red. "Where is Oilcan?"

"I don't know. We were watching *Rocky Horror Picture Show* and the dog suddenly started growling."

The elfhound puppy, Repeat, wasn't accounted for, either. She could guess its fate—elfhounds were prized because of their courage and selfless loyalty. They were just as bad as *sekasha* in regard to dying for the ones they loved. She tightened her hold on Blue Sky, reassuring herself that he was fine.

The gunfire stopped. All the oni were most likely dead.

It still left the mystery of what the oni wanted with the kids and where all the adults had gone. Had the oni intended to take the kids or just kill them? Did the oni manufacture some emergency that pulled the adults away? Or had Forge stolen Oilcan, whisking him off to Easternlands? But why would he leave the kids helpless? Tinker swore as she realized she couldn't question the oni.

She turned to study the faire grounds, and her heart leapt up her throat. Three gossamers drifted above the field, waiting to be tied off at the anchors. All the gondolas were Stone Clan black but edged with red and green. None of them were Forge's gossamer, but she'd been asleep for hours before she cornered Lemonseed. "Did Forge's ship come and go while I was sleeping?"

Stormsong shook her head. "No, it didn't. Forge could have taken Oilcan on the train. Do not worry, *domi*. The train goes only to Wind Clan holdings. We could use the distant voice to have them detained."

Pony returned, thankfully unharmed. His anger showed clearly on his face. "They did not leave Pittsburgh. Iron Mace's Hand has only their primary weapons. Forge's Hands took all their field weapons, but their shipping crates are here."

Obviously then, Forge hadn't gone far, but he didn't plan to return soon.

Thorne Scratch came pushing her way through the Wyverns and Wind Clan forces, a lone black mote in the wash of blue and red.

"Where is my cousin?" Tinker cried. "Where are Forge and Iron Mace? Why wasn't there anyone here with the children?"

Thorne Scratch blinked at her, confused, and then looked up at the school and then back to the children. "They were here when I left. I was just down the street. Why would they leave?"

Tinker wasn't going to get anything useful out of Thorne Scratch. She snatched up her phone.

She tried Oilcan's number first. "Godzilla of Pittsburgh" started to play in the grass nearby. She let out a cry of hurt as she spotted Oilcan's phone lying in the weeds. She hung up and called Riki.

Riki answered his phone on the first ring. "How can I serve you, *domi*?"

"Tell me that you have eyes on Oilcan."

"I did," he said cautiously.

"Where is he?"

"I'll find out," Riki promised and hung up.

Thorne Scratch had snapped out of her dismay and had gone into fury. "That pig came to me as clan head. He pointed out that with three *domana* and three Hands of *sekasha* and the perimeter defenses nearly complete, Oilcan's enclave was by far the safest place in Pittsburgh. He asked me to go to the other enclaves and find out how many of our people are still in the city. He said that I should go because I would know all of Earth Son's household who stayed and some of Jewel Tear's. He made it sound so reasonable. He even suggested that Oilcan would be receiving the funds that the Wind Clan enclaves were receiving for housing our clansmen. Gods, he wove such a web that I never once considered he had some other reason to see me gone."

Iron Mace was the current Stone Clan head in Pittsburgh. Tinker had assumed Forge had taken Oilcan as a poor substitute for his lost son, but Iron Mace? There was only one reason why a *domana* would send a *sekasha* away—and that was because he was about to commit acts that would turn them against him.

Tinker clenched her fist against the fear racing through her. "They wouldn't hurt Oilcan—would they?"

"This is a war zone," Pony said. "Protocol would be for Forge's people to take their field weapons for any extended stay. A transformation spell, such as the one that Windwolf cast on you, would take hours to prepare and then days for Oilcan to recover from."

Forge had been in the city for days; he could have set the spell up already. Windwolf had cast the spell on her minutes after they arrived at his remote hunting lodge. Forge could transform Oilcan as soon as they reached the casting room. They had to find Oilcan quickly.

"Would Forge's Hand even allow this—if Oilcan refused?"

Pony and Stormsong exchanged bleak looks and then turned to Thorne Scratch.

The Stone Clan *sekasha* shook her head slowly. "They see him as a child. They believe he has a child's grasp of time and ignorance of death. That he can call the Spell Stones is proof that he was born Stone Clan, despite all his protests. To transform him back to full elf would be returning to him what should have been rightfully his—if they had not failed Amaranth."

There was a flurry of wings, and Riki winged down beside her. He sketched a bow, panting heavily. He was bare chested and without war paint. One look at his face and she knew that he didn't have good news.

"Someone took out all three spotters that we had watching this block." Riki waved toward distant rooftops that had tight knots of tengu on them. "The shooters used high-powered rifles. One of our people is dead. The other two are still alive but badly hurt."

She should have heard the shots. The shooters must have used silencers. "Did they see Oilcan leave with the Stone Clan?"

"He and Iron Mace were at Sacred Heart. Forge was with Prince True Flame."

It couldn't have been just a coincidence that the spotters were shot just before Oilcan was whisked away. It terrified her that it was Iron Mace that spearheaded taking Oilcan and not Forge. Her only comfort was that Forge's Hands had taken their backup weapons. But what if Forge had gone someplace on Prince True Flame's bidding?

She grabbed a royal marine by the front of his uniform. He went wide-eyed, as her act made him the collected focus of her entire Hand plus one. "Where's Prince True Flame?"

"He and the viceroy are providing cover for the ground crews and the incoming gossamers in case the fighting spills over to the airfield."

Yes, she could feel the twin pull on the Spell Stones. Was it a good thing that she couldn't feel anything from the Stone Clan Stones?

"Is Forge with them?" She was afraid of the answer. "Yes" would be worse than "no," because it would mean that Iron Mace had acted alone. Oilcan trusted Forge. Normally Oilcan was a much better judge of people than she was. She sucked at it.

"N-n-no," the marine stammered. "He returned to his enclave prior to the fighting."

Tinker let the marine go, and he nearly tripped backing quickly away.

Tinker moved through the crowd, grabbing Wind Clan *laedin* as she spotted them. The area was being flooded by royal troops, and her people were increasingly harder to single out. "Fan out," she ordered each of them. "Find out if anyone saw the Stone Clan leaving my cousin's enclave before the shooting started." The last she told, "Have someone at Poppymeadow's take you to the train station and see if the Stone Clan left on the train."

As she turned to question Thorne Scratch in more detail, she realized that there was a sweep of movement that always preceded Prince True Flame. She didn't want to talk to him; she wasn't sure if she could do "polite" at this point. She wanted Windwolf there, making everything right, but today was determined to piss her off.

She remembered to bow in greeting. "The Stone Clan *domana* are working in collusion with the oni. The oni killed the tengu lookouts so the Stone Clan would take my cousin—most likely to spell-work him in secret—and in return, the Stone Clan left his children unprotected."

Prince True Flame glanced back at the incoming gossamers. "You do not know if that is what happened."

"What other possible answer could there be?" Tinker cried. "Elves would have used arrows to take out the lookouts. Even my people do not know how to use—use—" She ran into the lack of an Elvish word for the simple gun attachment. "Things that make rifles silent."

"That is not proof that the Stone Clan colluded with the oni. The oni spawn and the tengu have been at war with each other."

"That was resolved." Riki's High Elvish sounded perfect to Tinker, not that she was much of a judge, only spoken slowly enough that she could follow the conversation. "The tengu that acted against the half-oni were punished, and Jin apologized to the half-oni."

Prince True Flame waved that aside. "Your *sama* has taken the proper action, but there's no telling what the oni spawn might do. They have no *sama* to take responsibility for their actions, so they can run amok at will."

The prince didn't know Tommy Chang if he thought that they had no *sama*, but she wasn't going to be distracted by fighting that battle. "My Beholden are dead and wounded, and my cousin is missing."

"I understand." True sighed and then, surprisingly, went down on bended knee in front of her. It made her painfully aware of how very tall the prince truly was. They were now eye to eye. Around them was the subtle shift of Wyverns and her Hand to give them the illusion of privacy. "Beloved Tinker, I beg of you to consider Wolf's position in this."

It felt like a trick question. "He—he wants to protect my cousin as much as I do."

"Yes, he does. He will fling himself off cliffs for you. That is why I ask that you consider his safety first."

It still felt like a trick question. "Are you saying that I have to choose between Wolf and my cousin?"

"You are so blatantly human that I do not blame Wolf for never considering that you may be Stone Clan. No sane being would, but war does not foster sanity. I love my cousin well. He came to court barely fifty, wise for his age and yet modest for all his abilities." True Flame measured off a size that was just a hair over Tinker's head. It was intimidating to know that it had been hundreds of years since Windwolf was young enough to look her in the eyes. "Much as I love him, there is little I can do to protect him without endangering our hard-won peace.

"The clan wars are fresh wounds for most of our people. We have lost mothers and fathers, sisters and brothers, lovers and children. There are those who will never let the war end, and they are the ones who watch for any slight to excuse a new attack."

A week ago she would have brushed it off, but she had seen how much the Wind Clan hated Oilcan's kids just because they were Stone Clan. "You want me to just let them take my cousin?"

"Because Wolf took you as his *domi* and you have taken him as your *domou*, there is nothing that the Stone Clan can say. Your cousin is another matter. Forge lost so much, and his grief was made so public, that none would deny him the comfort of an orphaned grandchild. If you block Forge, all will be against you, and by default, Wolf."

"How can I just let them do whatever they want to my cousin?"

"To suggest Forge means harm to his grandson is slander, and the Stone Clan will call foul. You are under the queen's protection, but Wolf is not. If you continue to insist that Forge is acting in collusion with the oni when there is no proof that this is true—then Wolf will have to deal with the consequences."

"This is not right." Tinker controlled the urge to kick something. She didn't have her steel-toe boots on, and it would probably be bad form to kick the prince while he was kneeling before her. She glared at Red Knife behind the prince. "My cousin would not leave his household unprotected. Iron Mace deliberately sent Thorne Scratch away so she could not object to my cousin being taken against his will. If not for Blue Sky, the children would have vanished into the city for the second time. Three are dead by the oni's hand already. My Beholden who stood guard on my cousin is dead. It is not right that the Stone Clan has clemency because I cannot hold up a bloody knife."

"Politics is a battle of wits, not swords," Red Knife said. "You are well armed. Apply the rules."

✧ ✧ ✧

"Are you really going to take that as an answer?" Riki asked.

She kept tightly focused on the ground because she didn't want to kick him, either. He wasn't the one that she was angry with. "Yes. For now. I'm not starting a war with the Stone Clan."

When they first returned from Aum Renau she hadn't been sure that she loved Windwolf. How horrible was it that she knew with all certainty that she loved him beyond reason, because otherwise she would have sacrificed him for Oilcan in a heartbeat.

"I'll deal with them after I've taken care of the greater bloods," she growled. "But if they hurt Oilcan . . ."

Power suddenly burned across her magic sense. Somewhere to the south a spell flared into existence, blazing brilliant.

She whimpered.

"*Domi*?" Pony asked.

"It's too late. They changed him." She turned to Riki. "Find Oilcan. Make sure he's safe, but don't pick a fight with the Stone Clan *domana*. I just need to know he's okay."

"Yes, *domi*." He bowed and took wing. A moment later there was a thunder of black wings, and the skies filled with tengu.

A battle of wits.

Tinker paced the empty halls of Sacred Heart looking for clues.

A battle of wits.

Tinker's grandfather had taught her chess when she stopped trying to eat the pieces, sometime around her second birthday. She beat him regularly by the time she was five, but she never liked the game. It was fine and good to puzzle around the limits of the pieces, but it ignored the humanity of the game piece's names. One knight should be able to best the rest in combat. One bishop should be able to perform miracles and raise the dead. One of the rooks should be a genius inventor of impenetrable defenses. One of the pawns should be a coward and another a spy for the other side. While she couldn't remember the source of this opinion, she suspected Tooloo, since chess with the half-elf often ended with the white queen seduced by the black knight, or the black bishop killing his own king as a heretic.

The thing about chess—it was only hard if you couldn't guess what your opponent's next move would be. Once you recognized the pattern of attack, you could run circles around the other player.

Like the oni had been doing to them.

Over and over again, the oni had been one step ahead of the elves.

"Shit," Tinker breathed as chess, Tooloo, and the events of the last few days collided in her brain.

Fight your shadow, Providence had told her.

A shadow was right there, under her feet, watching every move.

"Shit!" Tinker slapped her hand over her mouth. If she was right, then anything she said could be heard.

"Are you okay?" Stormsong asked.

Hand still over her mouth, Tinker nodded, eyes wide.

How was she going to beat someone that knew what she was about to do?

39: MAKING PEACE

If Jewel Tear was a drug, then Tommy was addicted. He tried quitting cold turkey, pushing on ahead, carrying Spot to fill his hands. Like any good drug, though, the hooks were sunk deep into him already, urging him to do stupid things. He clung tight to his anger to armor himself against the urges. He might care about Jewel Tear against his will and all common sense, but she wasn't in love with him. The oni made sure she understood all the horrors of the whelping pens. Tommy was a convenient tool, a way to delay the inevitable if she was recaptured by the oni.

The thing that pissed him off the most was the fact that Jin was right. Jewel Tear kept going on and on about Windwolf offering sponsorship to Tommy. Behind that "bitch about my ex" was the assumption that the half-oni would follow the tengu's lead and tie themselves to a *domana*. Despite the cat ears and the little cousin that was more dog than boy, Tommy was an acceptable boy toy because one day he was going to be Beholden.

Someone's. Anyone's. Not hers—at least she wasn't asking.

Part of him—linked strongly to his dick—desperately wanted her to ask.

The intelligent part of him was terrified that she might, because his dick would agree in an instant. And the intelligent part knew that it would be a bad, bad thing. The half-oni wanted a seat at the in-crowd's Round Table. Pittsburgh was a Wind Clan town, and the way things were going, it was going to stay that way. Windwolf had hinted that the Stone Clan *domana* were chosen by their clan to be sacrificial lambs. Someone had picked Jewel Tear for shits and giggles because she was Windwolf's ex. Now that she had lost all her *sekasha*, she was in danger of becoming as much a social leper as Forest Moss. Yeah, part of him wanted to be her knight in shining armor and save her from that whole mess, but that was the little head talking. Teaming up with Jewel Tear would be throwing his people in a tar pit.

Of course it might be just his little head talking to assume she would even ask. She might be planning on digging a big hole and burying him in it as soon as they got close to Pittsburgh. She might not want the other elves to find out she was screwing the oni spawn. Once she was safe in town, she would have no more need of him as a boy toy. If she still "needed" him, it would be as muscle, and Tommy didn't want to set his family up to be anyone's goons. All he wanted for his family was to live in peace.

But that took Tommy back to how Jin was right, which only made him even more annoyed. Jin claimed that you had to create peace first before you could live in it. Tommy had already proven Jin right once by saving Windwolf from Malice. He was proving it again by taking Jewel Tear back to Pittsburgh with detailed information about where the oni forces were located. He thought he could make his stand once and retreat to the back line and let the elves duke it out. Obviously he was going to have sit at the damn Round Table, be an ally, and be part of the war effort if he was going to protect his family.

The question was, whose knight in shining armor was he going to be?

He still didn't know the answer to that question when they reached train tracks and his hidden hoverbike.

Nor did he know when they rumbled through Pittsburgh. There were gossamers hanging over the faire grounds, unloading hordes of elves in Stone Clan black. Fire Clan red surrounded the field. There was no sign of Wind Clan blue.

What the hell had happened while he was gone?

They threaded their way through the royal forces, drawing stares. Jewel Tear was tucked behind him, pressed tight and arms around him. Spot was balanced in front of him, legs and feet dangling over the handlebar. They found Prince True Flame at a tent, leaning over a table covered with maps.

"Where's Wolf Who Rules?" Tommy asked. He wanted Windwolf there when Jewel Tear gave the oni position. He wanted the elves to unite and kick oni butt—not each other's.

Prince True Flame ignored him, staring at Jewel Tear's shorn hair. "Are you hurt, child?"

"Where is Wolf?" Jewel Tear flipped through the maps on the table. "He should hear what I have to say. And who is arriving?"

"Darkness, Sunder, and Cana Lily."

The names meant nothing to Tommy, but Jewel Tear's eyes went wide.

"They sent two Harbingers!" Jewel Tear gasped.

He did know what Harbingers were. They were the seasoned warlords that the elves had used to fight the oni on Earth. There had been a dozen that kicked oni butt back to Onihida while the elves pulled down the pathways between Earth and Elfhome. Tommy could guess which two of the three were the Harbingers. *One of these things is not like the others.*

"The *sekasha* demanded that the Stone Clan send veterans," Prince True Flame said.

"We'll need them." Jewel Tear found the map she wanted and traced the train track as it slashed through wilderness. "The oni have strongholds built deep in the wilderness that they access by train." She marked a point on the train tracks and ran her fingers southward. "The camps are south enough that we wouldn't see them via gossamer as we come in from Aum Renau. I counted four in all, but there could be more. There were thousands of warriors at each camp—wargs and horrors. They also have another whelping pen."

Jewel Tear shivered only slightly, but Prince True Flame caught it.

The prince flicked a hand to signal a female Wyvern forward. "My people will see you to the hospice to be cared for."

Such a polite way of saying that she would be given an abortion.

"There is no need." Jewel Tear tried to wave off the Wyvern. "I was not raped. They did not have time."

Only a lifetime serving his brutal father allowed Tommy to keep surprise off his face. If Jewel Tear were truly fertile, they'd done it more than enough times to almost guarantee that she was pregnant. She could have stayed quiet and let their assumptions stand and be rid of any child he'd gotten on her.

"You have been battered and sorely used." The female warrior chided Jewel Tear like a mother dealing with a cranky child.

Jewel Tear's gaze turned cold and hard. "Yes, I am sore and tired and dirty and hungry, but there is much I need to explain about the oni force. This one freed me." She indicated Tommy with a wave of her hand. "While I was being moved from one camp to the whelping pens. We were able to kill all the oni transporting me, but sooner or later they will realize I've slipped through their fingers, and they will move. We must act quickly before they can shift again."

This one? He didn't even rate a name?

"We cannot attack until the Harbingers have offloaded all their people and given them a chance to organize themselves. Go, see to your health."

Jewel Tear warned the female Wyvern off with a look. "I should find what is left of my own household, and they will attend me."

Prince True Flame gave her a pitying look. "Many of those who survived the attack have left Pittsburgh."

Jewel Tear flinched as if struck but still managed, "Please, let me go to what little I have left."

Tommy watched her walk away, flanked by two Hands of Wyverns. He hated that he wanted to hold and comfort her even as she walked away without a glance toward him or a thank-you.

The hurt of it was such that he drove the whole way back to the warren before he remembered that he'd had Bingo move his family. He pulled to stop in front of the warehouse, feeling as hollow and empty as the building. He had known she didn't love him, that she was just using him, so really it had all gone the way he'd expected. Somehow, he thought it wouldn't hurt because he knew how it was going to end.

And the very worst of it—he missed the feel of her pressed against his back.

"Stupid elf bitch," Tommy growled.

Spot gave him a sad look, reached up, and petted Tommy on the head.

Tommy sighed and took out his phone. They both needed a bath, something to eat, and sleep. Depending on where Bingo moved their family, they might as well stay here for the night. Bingo had probably texted him. There were a dozen messages on his phone, all from Bingo. The most recent just a desperate "call me."

His cousin answered his phone with "Shit is flying all over the place. You better have the bitch."

"I delivered her to True Flame already," Tommy growled. "What's happening?"

"Two Stone Clan *domana* showed up after you left. Forge and Iron Mace. The dumb fucks grabbed Oilcan and disappeared. Tinker's crazy pissed off—she's got the tengu tearing the city apart trying to find her cousin. Then, to top it off, she's taken off without telling anyone where she was going, and Windwolf is out trying to find her."

He felt completely blindsided. Prince True Flame hadn't even mentioned the two *domana*. "Why did they take Oilcan?"

Bingo explained what had happened in Pittsburgh since Tommy left, from the discovery that the cousins were descended from Stone Clan *domana* to Oilcan being named head of the clan to the arrival of their great-grandfather, who apparently was bent on transforming Oilcan "back" into an elf. "It's all over the news. Chloe Polanski is having a field day. The humans are pissed to hell at the elves, and the elves look like they're about to start carving each other up."

No wonder there weren't any Wind Clan elves in Oakland as the Stone Clan Harbingers off-loaded. That Prince True Flame had ignored the question of Windwolf's whereabouts. Was it really the *sekasha*'s demands that brought the Harbingers to Pittsburgh, or, after egging the Wind Clan into a fight, had the Stone Clan just loaded the deck?

"Stupid-ass shits!" This was not the time that the elves should be jerking each other off. He was aware that Bingo was telling him where he'd moved the warren. It was a good safe place as long as the oni weren't overrunning the city. If the elves went to war with each other, the oni might just do that.

Tommy cursed. He had just jumped through hoops, risked his life and Spot's to get Jewel Tear back to Pittsburgh, and the elves were about to render it all useless. Of all the shit-stupid luck . . .

No, this wasn't bad luck—this was careful planning. If Earth Son was working with the oni, it wasn't with Lord Tomtom, it was with Kajo. The damn greater blood was a master of twisting everyone and everything. This had all the hallmarks of a Kajo plot.

"Tommy?" Bingo realized that Tommy had gone silent.

"The tengu haven't found Oilcan yet?"

"Still looking, last I heard. Tinker told them just to find him, not to take him back. Apparently this grandfather of theirs has a lot of clout in the Stone Clan. She doesn't want to start a war."

Tinker might not, but Kajo did. If Forge made Oilcan an elf, Tinker would be pissed, but she wouldn't start a war. Not the girl Tommy knew from the racetrack; she was too smart for that. But he was fairly sure that she would deal out a world of pain on anyone that hurt Oilcan. Kajo only needed to make sure that Oilcan died in his grandfather's care.

Unless the tengu realized that Kajo was pulling the strings, they wouldn't find Oilcan in time. Tommy hurried through the warren to his room, hoping that Bingo had been in too much of a rush to think of everything. He'd learned very young that information was the key to staying alive—gathering it up and then keeping it to yourself. He opened his closet and triggered the latch to his secret storage cubbyhole. Everything was still in place. He pulled out his maps.

Forge was newly arrived in Pittsburgh. The tengu would assume that the *domana* didn't know his way around or have access to cars or trucks. They'd be searching Oakland and downtown and maybe beyond the Rim, in the virgin forest. Kajo, though, would make sure that Forge could get to any place easily. A random human that had a truck. An elf that knew how to drive would be bumped into Forge's path. A tengu? No, not a tengu, not after what Jin did to the last ones that endangered Oilcan. But maybe a half-oni that didn't know how pissed off Tommy would be if he found out.

So someplace impossible to find, controlled by the Stone Clan, and that had enough magic to power a transformation spell.

He found his map of magic springs within a hundred miles. The oni built camps on top of a handful of the strongest and used cloaking spells to hide them. The Stone Clan had been given a huge chunk of land to the south of Pittsburgh, just beyond the Rim. Last week the *Pittsburgh Post-Gazette* had published a map showing how the land was divided up. Forest Moss didn't have the resources to develop his land, nor had Jewel Tear. Earth Son—Kajo's little puppet—could have started clearing land. And yes, not far from the Rim, in Earth Son's parcel, was a very strong magical spring.

"I'm going here." He showed Spot the map. "Right here where I marked this. Take this to Bingo. Tell him to have these other springs checked out. I think I'm right, but I'm not sure. We need to find Oilcan and protect him. Kajo is after him."

40: CHILDHOOD'S END

The Rim had grown up and over Neville Island. The ironwood saplings of her childhood were now tall enough to choke out the Earth brush trees. *Esfatiki*, touch-me-nots, skunkweed, and jagger bushes had replaced the lawn down to the riverbank. There was no sign of the groundhogs that had plagued her grandfather's attempts at a garden; Elfhome's flora and fauna had done what her grandfather couldn't. All thc nearby houses—abandoned since the first Startup—had collapsed under the weight of thick wild grape vines.

It'd been three years since Tinker last visited the hotel where she grew up. She expected after the sprawling luxury of Poppymeadow's that it would seem smaller and seedier, but it seemed just as large and imposing and rundown as ever. She had heard through Team Tinker that paparazzi had pried the plywood off the first-floor doors and windows to photograph the princess' birthplace. Judging by the footprints in the dust, though, Esme was the only person who'd recently visited the grand old hotel.

Just to be sure, she let the small army she'd brought with her sweep into the building. There was no telling if she'd managed to jump ahead of her shadow or not with this move.

A loud splash made her jerk around and count heads. One, two, three, four . . . and Blue Sky pulling Baby Duck away from the river's edge.

"Stay away from the banks!" Tinker called. This was why she really shouldn't be in charge of the kids—she sucked at taking care of helpless things. She didn't have much choice in the matter. "The jump fish are really bad in this area."

"Your grandfather raised two children here?" Thorne Scratch sounded like all the people who didn't know her grandfather well. He had an unfounded reputation for being insane. There was method to his madness: they'd been far from any prying eyes on Neville Island.

"The jump-fish population was a lot lower when we were little. Every Shutdown thinned them down until Earth constructed a fish dam to keep them in Pittsburgh waters." Since Thorne was looking unconvinced, Tinker added, "He'd throw out sticks of dynamite once a week, just to be sure."

Maybe part of her problem with being a parent was she'd had such bad examples as role models. The dead father. The mother trapped in time. The mad-scientist grandfather.

She was halfway through the lobby when she realized she'd lost her Shields. She glanced back to the wide front doors. Stormsong and Pony were still outside, standing under the portico, gazing raptly at the lintel.

"What is it?" She called back.

"Hay Bell Ringing in Wind?" Pony read the glyphs printed there.

"My grandfather went by the name of Timothy Bell. Timothy is a type of grass commonly used for hay."

"He claimed to be Wind Clan?" Stormsong asked.

"Oh, no, I did that, not him." Tinker went back to the faded blue door to gaze up at the Elvish painted above it. She'd done a good job for only being six and balanced on a ladder. "He was angry with me for doing it and was going to paint it out until I told him it was because our family was too small. It was just before Oilcan came to live with us. We'd gotten the news that his mother had been killed. I started to have nightmares about something happening to my grandfather and being left alone. I wanted to be part of something bigger."

Pony hugged her as Stormsong kissed her temple. "You are now."

What was scary was that some little part of her always suspected she would retreat to the island for some desperate battle. She had left so much behind; telling everyone and herself that the grief was too fresh. On the third floor, behind a spell-locked door disguised as a bookcase, was her old server room. Oilcan had carefully mothballed it for her. Everything hummed to life as she flicked on her various computers and coaxed them to once again to talk to one another.

Her poor abandoned AI, Pixel, greeted her once she typed in all her passwords. "Hi, Tinker Bell."

Was there a time she actually thought that was cute? "Do a systems check on all perimeter monitors."

"Okay, Tinker Bell."

She rooted through a box of headsets until she found one that she'd insulated for magic-work. It took her a while longer to get it to ride comfortably on her elf-pointed ears. She settled the headset in place just as Pixel reported back on various motion detectors and cameras she had scattered across the island. Despite years of neglect, over half were working. Since she had gone nuts on monitors, the overlap was enough to cover the island.

"Show me all moving objects."

Pixel displayed the *sekasha*, the *laedin*, the children, a feral cat, and the ragged remains of a checkered flag waving in the wind.

"Mark all current moving objects as nonthreatening and ignore."

"Okay, Tinker Bell."

She sighed out. She didn't want to spend time changing her user name.

"Go to code red."

"Code Red initiated, Tinker Bell. No unidentified targets found."

Good. That meant Neville Island was as deserted as she'd hoped. If she blew the island off the face of the planet, only the guilty would get caught in the crossfire.

Tinker took it as a good sign that Stormsong had to ask, "What exactly are we doing?"

Tinker finished pouring the treacle into the 55-gallon plastic barrel filled with ammonium nitrate. She waited until Stormsong duct-taped the lid shut before asking, "Can't you tell?"

"No," Stormsong growled. "That's why I asked."

"Good." Tinker adhered a spell printed out onto circuit paper onto the top of the sealed barrel. She was working with one broken arm, her clueless Hand, and a small army of *laedin*-caste warriors who were mostly technologically inept. Even with Blue Sky helping (and warned not to explain anything), things were going hellishly slow. She had no idea how much time she had. A few minutes or forever? It depended on if her plan worked or not. So far: maybe.

Her only barometer was annoyed but mystified. "So, what are we doing?" Stormsong asked again.

"I'll explain later."

Tinker worked at ignoring the guilt at keeping her Hand clueless. Red Knife had told her that she was well armed and to apply the rules. Well, she was, perhaps more than he'd intended. If Prince True Flame said that she couldn't track down the Stone Clan, then she would have to force them to come to her. Once she started to consider how to make them find her, she realized that was the answer to everything.

Providence had said she would have to fight her own shadow. The key, she hoped, was to keep her shadow in the dark.

41: SOUTHERN RIM

Tommy filled his hoverbike's tank again and roared through the city flat out, as the crow flew. Down paved streets. Through backyards and parking lots. Up and down Pittsburgh's countless steep hills. Across scores of creek beds. The sun was setting, throwing long shadows over the city.

His mind kept going back to Jewel Tear walking away. If he had played it different, would have it ended better? There was a niggling little voice that said he should have talked to her about beholding, but no, once he went over all reasons again, he'd been right not to. He would never completely trust anyone outside of family, but if he understood how they thought, he could at least work with them. Windwolf and Jewel Tear were about as understandable as space aliens. Tinker had always been impossible to guess—her brilliance took her careening all over the map.

Oilcan, though . . .

Tommy had watched Oilcan grow up on the racetrack.

Even at sixteen, he'd been quiet, serious, and responsible. Tinker was the brains and the media darling, but Oilcan had been the one that kept everything going smoothly on the team. Listening to the songs that Oilcan had written, it was obvious that the man understood the weird collision of humans and elf culture that made Pittsburgh. The city was going to need people like him and Tinker to keep things from exploding, as the elves got more and more insistent that the humans conform. They didn't get that most of the humans in Pittsburgh were in the city because they didn't want to conform. It was people that liked living on the edge that stayed, everyone that wanted safe and familiar had fled to Earth the first chance they got.

The elves had been treating Oilcan as one of them, even while he was still fully human. Chances were that by now, Oilcan was as much an elf as Tinker. But if she was any indication, no matter how pointy the ears got, a human still thought like a human.

He'd guessed right. There was a fresh path cut through the dark forest where Route 88 hit the Rim. The trees were hacked down in one clean cut, as if felled by a giant axe, and their massive stumps blasted away. He had to give one thing to the elves: at least the people in charge were scary powerful. This close to the Rim, all the houses stood empty. He glided his hoverbike through the missing sliding door of a nearby ranch house into a cave-dark living room. Plaster from the ceiling crunched underfoot as he spun the bike, parking it ready for a quick getaway later.

The night echoed with life. Someplace far off, children were playing baseball, the crack of ball against bat triggering excited joyous shouting. The bass from a distant stereo thumped to an inaudible melody. A dog barked for attention. It was the sound of peaceful life. The kind of life he wanted for his family, where dark was nothing more than time to relax and play.

He checked his clip and headed into the forest.

Less than two miles from the Rim, the path hacked through the towering ironwoods ended in a wide clearing. The perimeter guards were few and far apart, with eyes only watching outward. Once Tommy blinded them to his presence and slipped past them, he had no trouble moving unnoticed through the camp. It was a matter of walking with purpose, as if he had full right to be there, while keeping to the shadows.

Bingo had said that the Stone Clan *domana* had come to Pittsburgh with only their *sekasha* and *laedin*-caste guards. As a result, the camp wasn't as refined as was normal for elves. There were only a few elfshines drifting among a dozen tents done in dark fairy silk, which made it easy to move unnoticed.

Tommy found Oilcan asleep in a small, unguarded tent. Tommy breathed out in relief. He'd gotten to the man before Kajo managed to have him killed. Tommy only needed to get Oilcan safely to Tinker.

Unless Kajo set Tommy in motion without him realizing he was being played.

Tommy paused at the tent's flap with the sudden doubt. What if Kajo planned all along for Tommy to find Oilcan and whisk him out from under the elf's watch to someplace that Kajo could easily kill him? Kajo had him running circles with the tengu scam. Only Oilcan and Blue Sky had kept him from that trap. What if this was another snare?

No, the tengu scam had been Tommy acting like normal. Watching out for himself and his family. Flying solo. Caring only about what was his. The only thing that saved him was that he'd swallowed his pride and asked for help. Kajo apparently hadn't counted on Oilcan and Blue Sky working together to save the half-oni.

So it was probably safe to assume that Kajo wouldn't know how much meeting Jin had changed Tommy. Hell, even Tommy hadn't realized it until he was deep in the wilderness, staring down at the massive oni army and realizing how fragile the peace of Pittsburgh was. How he would have to join the fight to protect it. How the only way he could protect his family was doing stupid-ass things like sneaking into elf camps.

No, Kajo wasn't pulling his strings.

Tommy stepped into the tent and let the flap close behind him. He needed to get Oilcan to Tinker—wherever she was—before Kajo could land his killing blow. He moved quietly to the cot and reached out to shake Oilcan awake.

They had changed Oilcan into an elf.

The sight kicked Tommy to a full stop. He'd expected it, but still . . .

The elves had completely remade Oilcan in their image. His closed eyes were now almond-shaped. His ears were pointed. His fingernails were perfect half-moons on fingers innocent of hard-earned calluses. The newly flawless skin and lack of facial hair made Oilcan look more like a boy than a man, child-vulnerable to what they had done to him. Anger for Oilcan's sake flashed through Tommy, igniting a hotter fire of annoyance for letting himself care. They were basically strangers to each other—certainly not family—and Tommy didn't make friends with anyone.

He reminded himself that it was better for him and his family that Oilcan was an elf with all the bells and whistles. An elf with a human soul.

Still, he couldn't stop thinking of the last time he had seen Oilcan. The human had been in his racing leathers, five o'clock shadow dusting his face, smelling of sweat, oil, gas, and some lucky female. He had fought hard to save Tommy's family and dared to face Tommy's rage to keep the half-oni from bringing harm to himself. The elves had taken that good and decent man and tried to make it as if he had never breathed life as a human.

Fighting down his anger, Tommy put a hand to Oilcan's shoulder and tried to shake him awake. Oilcan's eyes fluttered, opened a moment to gaze guilelessly up at him, and then slowly closed. A second shake failed to rouse him at all. No wonder the man hadn't tried to escape; he was drugged and helpless.

Breathing out a curse, Tommy hauled Oilcan up and hiked him over his shoulder.

Getting out of the camp was going to be harder than getting in.

Boot steps warned Tommy that someone was coming. He jerked back away from the empty cot and focused on the elf beyond the tent flap. He locked down on the elf's mind as the male slipped into the tent.

Oilcan asleep on the cot, drugged beyond waking.

Going by Bingo's description of the Stone Clan *domana*, the newcomer was Iron Mace. The male stood a moment, intent not on the cot but on the movement of the camp beyond the silk walls. Had

Iron Mace heard Tommy? The night was still and quiet as Tommy erased himself from the male's awareness.

Apparently satisfied that there was nothing to hear, the male turned toward the cot. He pulled the pillow out from under Tommy's illusion and then pressed it firmly down onto the illusion's face.

Tommy clamped down on a curse. The bastard would have killed Oilcan while he was completely helpless. This was Kajo's puppet. If Tommy were caught by the elves after witnessing this attack on Oilcan, Iron Mace would have to kill him. Oilcan's "murder" needed to be convincing.

Tommy had suffocated Spot's father while the oni warrior was drunk. He'd been sixteen and scared shitless, but he could still feel the male struggling under him like it was yesterday. He fed the *domana* the memory: the drunken body weakly flailing under the pillow, the muffled cries, and slow but inevitable stillness.

Iron Mace leaned his whole body weight down on the illusion of the much smaller male and held the pillow tight even after the body went limp. He panted hoarsely in the stillness. Finally Iron Mace slowly lifted the pillow. Tommy planted the image of a dead Oilcan, unseeing eyes open and mouth slack. The elf gave a quiet, shaky laugh and carefully replaced the pillow under the illusion's head. His crime hidden, Iron Mace strolled out of the tent as if he had merely checked on the sleeping Oilcan.

Tommy rested a hand on Oilcan's back and felt the reassuring rhythm of his breathing. He needed to get both of them out of here safely.

42: AWAKING

"Wake up." The command was growl low and menacing. "Damn it, wake up."

Oilcan opened his eyes, feeling strangely hollow and light.

"About fucking time," Tommy growled. A noise made the man glance off into the gray of oncoming dawn, giving Oilcan his tense profile. Tommy's black-furred cat ears twitched as he listened to the distant noises.

Oilcan felt like a house open to the spring wind, blown clean and cold. He could remember Iron Mace drugging him and convincing Forge to change him, and then nothing. He put his hands to his ears and found elfin tips. "God damn him," he growled as anger flowed into the emptiness and filled him with hot murderous rage. "Damn lying bastard. I-I-I . . ."

He wanted to kill Iron Mace. Never in his life had he wanted so desperately to destroy someone. Beat them with his hands so he felt the blows land hard and vicious. Hear their bones break. Reduce them to a smear of blood and then wash that away. He clenched his fist against the rage.

Tommy coldly watched him fight the anger as he took a pistol out of a kidney holster and screwed a silencer into place. "That anger isn't a bad thing. If I were you, I'd hold tight and ride it, because you need it to be hard enough to do what needs to be done."

"Iron Mace drugged me and was going to throw me out a third-story window. When my grandfather stopped him, the damn fucking lying bastard used Forge's grief to keep me helpless."

In a cold, hard voice, Tommy explained how Iron Mace had tried to smother Oilcan in his sleep. "What did you do to piss him off so bad?"

"Not me—Forge's son. He stole something from Iron Mace, a spell of some sort, something I think was deadly incriminating. He ran away from home, all the way to Earth, and handed down bits and pieces of a puzzle. I'm not sure what he took from Iron Mace, but the bastard came to Pittsburgh just to make sure nothing incriminating was floating around after nearly three hundred years."

"Kajo pulled Iron Mace's strings. The damn greater blood probably made sure Iron Mace had good reason to believe you and Tinker know more than you really do. Iron Mace will probably go after her next."

"He wouldn't dare," Oilcan whispered and realized Iron Mace had killed his own sister to keep his secret. He would try to eliminate Tinker, too.

"Don't let the fear in," Tommy said. "That doesn't do you any good. Keep hold of the anger—that's what you're going to need. Let your rage make you strong."

Oilcan struggled to come up with calm, rational things to say as his mind screamed in rage and fear. "How long have I been out of it?"

"I'm not sure. I was out of the city when the shit started flying. I got back yesterday afternoon, so it's been at least a day, maybe two. I've been trying to get you to wake up for six hours now."

Oilcan swore quietly as he studied their surroundings. They were someplace in Pittsburgh, tucked up into the superstructure of an overpass. A roadway crossed over their heads on spans of steel. The ground was half a dozen feet down; a steep graveled slope led down to yet another road and then a stream that glittered in pale dawn. "Where are we?"

"Close to the Southern Rim, somewhere near 88. I'm not completely sure—I cut through the woods instead of following the path out. I figured that the Stone Clan would start chasing us the minute they found you gone. Jewel Tear said that metal interferes with the Stone Clan's scrying spells."

Hence the nest of steel. They needed to move quickly once they left the safety of the overpass. They weren't far from his barn retreat, where he had his spare hoverbikes. And clothes. All he had on were loose cotton pajamas three sizes too big. He was missing all his normal pocket clutter, including his cell phone. "You have a phone?"

Tommy handed him a cell phone. Tinker's phone went straight to voice mail. He tried his own number. No messages. Tinker hadn't left him word where she was going. With Tinker, the possibilities of where she might run off to were mindboggling. Who might know where she was?

Lain didn't know. "Try the tengu," she said. "They're looking for you, so they might know how to find her."

He hated that he still had Riki's number memorized and that as he punched it in, Tommy's phone recognized it. Obviously the oni ex-slaves had worked together when they were both enslaved.

Riki answered on the first ring with "What is it, Chang?"

"It's Oilcan. Tommy pulled me out of danger—"

Riki gave a heartfelt, "Oh, thank God."

Oilcan tried to ignore Riki's relief. "I need to find Tinker. Iron Mace tried to kill me twice. He's going after Tinker."

"She disappeared on us," Riki said. "I've got all eyes that I can trust completely looking for the both of you."

If the tengu didn't know where she was, then it was unlikely that the elves knew. "Where's Windwolf?"

"The inbound train was captured by oni. They tried to ram it into the outbound train with all the elves onboard. The elves managed to derail the inbound engine on the South Side. The *domana* are blowing hell out of everything, and there's oni everywhere."

"Jesus," Oilcan breathed, thinking about the Wollertons and everyone else he knew that lived on the South Side.

Tommy's sharp ears had followed the conversation. "It's a diversion. Kajo is keeping the *domana* occupied so a smaller force can attack someplace else."

"Shit, you're probably right!" Riki said.

"Kajo will keep the elves shadowboxing until he gets whatever he's really after," Tommy said.

Providence had told Tinker to fight her shadow.

Both Esme and Tinker had dreamed of playing hide-and-seek on Neville Island. To play, you first shut your eyes. If Tinker dropped contact with the tengu—her eyes—then she might be playing hide-and-seek already. If Kajo had a force of oni heading for Tinker, there was no way she could take on Iron Mace, too.

The question was: Did he tell Riki where she might be? Forgive and trust wasn't the same thing. Riki's people needed Tinker alive and well and had proven that they were willing to fight and die for her. Tinker might have started the game of hide-and-seek, but this Kajo had her outclassed.

"Riki, get everyone you can trust to Neville Island. I think that Tinker's at the hotel where we grew up. Both Kajo's oni strike force and his puppet, Iron Mace, are headed for her. She's going to need backup or they'll roll right over her."

43: LOST

The elves eyed the casting room with confusion and suspicion. With all her outer-perimeter defenses activated, Tinker had her Hand, Thorne Scratch, Blue Sky, Oilcan's kids, and all the *laedin* warriors gathered in the big room with her. At one time it had been an outdoor pool, but her grandfather had enclosed it with ironwood and glass. The morning sun dawned through the windowed ceiling, starting the cycle of turning the chilly room into a stifling oven. The unused buckets of chlorine already scented the air with ghosts of summers past.

"*Quiee.*" Baby Duck broke the silence.

"And you and *sama* lived here alone with your grandfather?" Cattail asked for the zillionth time.

"What a waste of a wonderful bathing room," Barley said.

"It is . . . it was a—" What was the Elvish word for swimming? She settled for the English. "Swimming pool, not a bathing tub."

Everyone but Blue Sky gazed at her blankly. Maybe elves didn't swim. Considering what lived in most large bodies of water on Elfhome, she didn't blame them.

The casting room had been one of the epic wars between Lain and her grandfather. Lain maintained that if her grandfather was going to raise Tinker in the middle of a river that routinely flooded, Tinker should know how to swim. Her grandfather believed that if Tinker could swim, she would be more likely to play in the river. (Ironically, they were both right on the subject.) They both ordered supplies, and the race was on. Her grandfather's cement truck beat Lain's water truck by a few hours, sealing the swimming pool's fate. The pool-maintenance supplies—from algaecide to winter pills—shipped from Earth and nonreturnable—were still piled in one corner of the room, unused.

As a measure of her childhood, her greatest despair had been watching the gray cement slosh across the pool's pale blue floor. She had been planning on building an entire fleet of toy submarines. She could only wish that her problems had stayed that trivial. It had been over a day since Iron Mace and Forge disappeared with Oilcan. So far, the tengu hadn't found where they'd gone.

Tinker tried to stay focused on the spell she was transcribing on the white marble slab that been laid on the cement insulating layer. It was the same spell she had tried on Merry earlier, only slightly modified. She needed to know what the oni wanted from the kids if she was going to protect them. She was afraid that the condition she found them in reflected how little the oni needed the children alive. Was it mere chance that the three that died lacked whatever the other five had? Statistically, it was unlikely, but she didn't want to stake their lives on what could have been random luck. Perhaps in time, the oni would have killed all the children.

Tinker finished the spell and stepped back. "Merry, could you come down here?"

Merry meeped quietly and backed up slightly, wide-eyed.

"No," Rustle said. "Not Merry. Let me do this. I've felt so useless."

"Your arm will be better soon," Merry cried. "You shouldn't feel useless."

"You should have gone down the chute before me. You're younger than me. You're smaller. I should have been the one holding back to protect you."

Merry rested her head against Rustle's chest. Unfortunately, it only made it more obvious that she was so much smaller than him. "You're hurt now, so I'm the one that should be brave."

"I'll hate myself if I let you take all the risks for all of us." Rustle wrapped his one good arm about her shoulders. "We should share the risk of being hurt."

"It's just a spell." Blue Sky didn't have an ounce of romance in him yet. He was giving the two an impatient scowl. "It won't hurt." He turned to Tinker, full of blind trust. "Right?"

This was where Oilcan normally smacked her until she admitted that she only vaguely knew what she was doing. She ached deep inside. It felt so wrong not to be charging around, looking for him. She hated this feeling that she was doing the wrong thing. Especially since it made her aware of how much of her life she sailed through, assuming she was doing the right thing, just because *she* had thought it up. It was thinking like that which had gotten Nathan killed.

Blue Sky's trusting look started to fade as he saw the doubt on her face. "It isn't going to hurt him?"

"The spell I did earlier on Merry indicated that she was connected to an infinite number of points—evenly." It was simpler to ramble, trying to be reassuring while not lying. The kids were scared enough without telling them that she really wasn't sure what she was doing. "Normally magic is affected by a number of things: gravity being one of them. Springs and ley lines are side effects of gravity's influence on magic. That the points were evenly distributed indicates that the connections weren't affected by gravity."

Blue Sky knew her too well. He knew that she was overwhelming them with technobabble until they were too numb to form an intelligent resistance. "Is this going to hurt him?"

"If it hurts him, I can cancel the spell." She didn't want to say more, not with her shadow possibly hearing every word, seeing every move.

There was a group hug, as if Rustle were going in front of a firing squad, and then the male came down the wide swimming pool's steps to stand beside her. She tried not to notice that he was only a head taller than her and slender as a reed.

She canceled the healing spell that was inked onto his arm. "Go stand in the middle. Be careful not to step on any of the glyphs."

She paced around the outside of the spell, checking her work. Her insides churned with the fear that she might really mess things up. She'd run simulations, but she couldn't account for all the variables because she didn't really know which of the draconic powers the Skin Clan might have bred into the children. Nor, to be truthful, did she understand most of their powers.

Science was about discovering the unknown through experimentation and careful observation.

The dragons owed most of their powers to their dual nature, which seemed dependent on the presence of magic. Jin had asked that the enclaves' defenses be lowered not to allow the tengu to enter but so there would be the abundance of magic necessary for Providence to manifest. When she first encountered Impatience, he'd been entirely animal, but after tapping the Spell Stones' power through her, he gained "consciousness" enough to realize that he was hurting her and stopped.

It stood to reason, if the kids had powers, much like her and Oilcan, they needed some type of trigger to be able to access them. If you analyzed the initialization spell, it became obvious that it used the least common phoneme in the Elvish language and one of the more difficult hand positions. Considering how much time one spent talking and waving hands around, it was good that it was nearly impossible to accidently tap the Spell Stones.

On the other hand, it was possible that the kids—like the dragons—simply needed a vast amount of magic focused on them before their abilities became apparent. There was the fact that while she and Rustle both had a broken arm, hers was nearly healed while Rustle's was still barely healed. The spell used on both of them simply funneled magic into their natural regenerative powers. On her, the spell was doing what was expected, but not on Rustle.

She made another lap around the completed spell,

making sure Rustle hadn't smudged anything by walking through it and that everything was correct. It shouldn't hurt Rustle, she told herself. All it would do was focus magic on him.

She bent low and activated the spell with the command word. The first ring shimmered to life as the resonance of the phonemes triggered the spell. She stood and stepped back as the second ring flared to power.

The detection ring rose, instantly gleaming with the countless connections. So Rustle was just like Merry in that regard. The innermost ring kicked in—like the healing spell—its function was to focus latent magic to Rustle.

The entire spell flared to unbearable brilliance.

Oh, that did not seem good.

"Is it supposed to do that?" Blue Sky asked. "Is he all right?"

Good question.

Tinker shielded her eyes with her hand as she tried to make Rustle out inside the spell. There seemed to be things raining down inside, like exploding corn kernels in a popcorn maker. Oh gods, she hoped it wasn't pieces of Rustle. She edged as close as she dared and squinted at the odd-shaped pieces on the edges of the glare. It *was* popcorn.

Somehow she doubted that Rustle had his pockets stuffed with popcorn. Where was it coming from? An iPod landed next to the fluffy kernels, trailing earbuds that floated down and settled up against the brilliant shell. The color of the spell changed infinitesimally, as pinpoints of blues and greens flared beside the earbuds.

Oilcan had said that Rustle had been losing things right and left, including the expensive MP3 player.

The male had been inconsolable over the loss and had torn the enclave apart looking for it. What if things had been shifting out of phase all this time—little things—like popcorn?

And with more magic, did Rustle just shift out of phase?

"Tink!" Blue Sky cried. "Is he all right? What's happening to him?"

"I'm canceling the spell." She could recast it once she was sure he was fine.

"Inner breach," Pixel announced. "South corridor, lone armed intruder."

How did anyone get into the hotel without being detected? Oh gods, she should have known her shadow would be able to walk through all her defenses.

Tinker backpedaled from the active spell, waving a hand toward the main doors into the casting room. "We've got incoming! Pixel, system status?"

"Twenty-five percent monitor failure detected."

Her shadow had blasted a hole in her defenses. Was there a wave of oni following close behind?

Tinker tapped the Spell Stones and cast a quick scry.

Oni were pouring down Grand Avenue toward the hotel.

Part One of her plan was working. She just really expected more of a warning.

"Pixel, sticks and stones, words will always hurt."

"Broadcasting."

Tinker shouted the command word for the spells scattered across the island. Her voice, amplified by dozens of hidden speakers, echoed up the river valley. There was a deep cough as the blast spell fired, and then a deep roar as flame engulfed everything.

"Incoming: rocket," Pixel announced. "Impact in ten seconds. Nine. Eight..."

She snapped up a shield wall between her people and the hallway just as a rocket blasted away the door. Flames blossomed in a deafening roar. The kids all shrieked counterpoint.

The children were not part of the battle plan—beyond a vague idea that they would serve as bait. She needed to get them out of the war zone somehow—all of them—and that included Rustle.

Tinker shouted out the cancelation command of the spell on Rustle. Her voice echoed up all around, still broadcasted over the hidden speakers. The spell continued to blaze with impossible brightness. "Oh fuck!"

"What's wrong, little princess?" An electronically scrambled voice mocked her from down the now-darkened hallway. "Bite off a little more than you can chew?"

So they both needed time. Her shadow hadn't expected her to be able to block that attack—and she wouldn't have if she hadn't realized her old numbering system allowed her to shortcut to spells she had memorized as a child.

It was a race now, but a race to what? What did her shadow need time for?

"Not as much as you have, Chloe!" Tinker shouted back, thinking frantically. She needed to get Rustle out of the spell and block whatever Chloe was about to throw at her. "I know it's you. A pigtailed little girl, wearing pretty dresses, pretending not to be the monster that you really are! Nice cover, while it lasted. Too bad it's over."

"You were born on this island, and you're going to die on it." Chloe used her own voice this time.

"Actually, I was born at Mercy Hospital!" Tinker shouted back. "And if you were sure I was going to die here, we wouldn't be having this conversation! You only talk when things don't go as planned, when I've done something just so off-the-wall that even you couldn't see it coming. I've figured something out about you: if you don't *understand* what I'm doing, you can't stop me."

"What's so hard to figure out? You just lost the child, and you have no idea how to get him back."

Tinker hated it when the bad guy was right.

"No, I haven't lost him." Just temporarily misplaced him. Hopefully. The spell was out of phase but was reacting to music from the iPod. The dragons cast their spells via their mane. It was possible that the vibrating filaments set up harmonics that controlled their ability to phase in and out. Change the frequency and you could key into another universe.

When she applied magic to Rustle, she triggered his ability to step into another world. Oilcan was just going to kill Tinker. All she'd had to do was keep the kids safe . . .

And with that, Tinker realized why Chloe was here. What the whole mess was about. The Skin Clan had bred the kids, but they didn't know how to "use" the kids. It was nearly as complicated as Oilcan and her trying to figure out the Spell Stones without knowing of their existence. The Skin Clan might have several hundred children tucked in the wings back in Easternlands, but no way to experiment on them safely.

But Tinker was a clever, clever little tool. You just had to be careful when applying her to any puzzle that she didn't figure out what you were doing. . . .

Close by, a Stone Clan shield flared across Tinker's senses. One of the *domana* was about to join the battle. Since Tinker hadn't passed out invitations, they were here on Chloe's invite list, most likely under "secondary distraction." If Tinker had to guess, it was Iron Mace closing fast.

"Get her!" Tinker dropped her shield and cast a force strike at the hallway to nuke it closed behind Chloe. "She's going to try and run! Stop her!"

The collection of warriors let loose a thunderous volley of rifles down the darkened hallway. *Note for future reference: elves will translate "stop her" to "try and kill the bitch."*

Try was the key word as Chloe came bounding down the hallway, twin daggers in hand and dodging like a hyperactive ninja. All pretense of being human was gone; she snaked past Cloudwalker and Rainlily like they were standing still and mowed her way into the *laedin*.

Tinker backpedaled. This was going to be one of those times where it was a pain to be only five feet tall. She couldn't unleash her attack spells without hitting her own people, which was probably why Chloe had closed on the warriors. If she tried to protect her people, they couldn't attack Chloe. Iron Mace was incoming at a fast walk, destruction flaring on her magic sense, followed by the rumble of nearing explosions. Chloe only had to survive until Iron Mace smashed his way into the casting room, and then she could flee in the chaos.

"Get the children out!" Tinker yelled at the still-standing *laedin* to get them out of the way.

She snapped up her shield and shifted to protect

the *laedin*'s retreat with the children. Pony nodded to her as she stopped in the doorway, blocking the only way out of the casting room. He and Stormsong closed on Chloe, *ejae* drawn, their *sekasha* shields glimmering Wind Clan blue.

It was like they had spent weeks choreographing the fight. Her Hand attacked, swinging furiously, only avoiding each other because of their years of practice together. Chloe ducked and whirled and spun, dodging every blow.

Think, Tinker, think. All you have to do is outsmart this bitch, and you know you can.

There was a closer roar of destruction that boomed through the timbers of the old building.

"Lobby door, breached," Pixel reported.

She was running out of time to be brilliant. She'd have to settle for just devious.

"Blue!" she called.

"Tink?" The brave little idiot was right behind her.

"Get this thing off me." She tugged at the bandage that strapped her arm.

There was a lifesaving ring on the wall beside her. Tinker shifted forward slightly and jerked it off the wall. Kneeling in place, she sketched a spell quickly on stiff foam. She dropped her shield and flung the ring. Pain flared up her arm as the motion tortured the fragile knits in her bones.

Chloe laughed as she ducked. "Wake up, princess. Even your half-breed can't hit me!"

The life preserver skidded across the room and careened into the pool supplies.

Tinker snapped up her shield around her Hand and shouted the command word.

The life preserver exploded right on top of the algaecide. A moment later the chemical exploded with a massive fireball.

Thank God, Chloe had apparently failed chemistry.

44: IRON MACE

Oilcan watched as Neville Island erupted. Flame and smoke billowed upward. In that one thunderous moment, the oni army descending on his childhood home vanished.

Tinker!

Beside him, Tommy breathed a curse. "You know, for someone so small, your cousin is freaking destructive."

Oilcan forced himself to nod. The smoke parted, and the hotel was still standing. "Yeah, she is." Godzilla-like. Only a scattered handful of oni seemed unharmed.

The sound of gunfire continued from inside the hotel. There was a flare of magic on Grand Avenue, and Oilcan realized that a Stone Clan *domana* was wading into the fight. He scanned down the street until he spotted Iron Mace heading for the hotel, left hand holding a shield while flicking oni out of his way with his right. In the distance was a black cloud of tengu winging their way to Neville Island, but they couldn't take on the *domana*.

"Damn him." Oilcan turned his hoverbike toward the steep cliff. "No time to follow the roads."

Tommy eyed the steep drop-off and muttered a curse.

They dropped down the cliff, nearly in free-fall, skipping off projections to slow their descent, and then raced flat-out across the steel catwalk above the sluicegates of Emsworth Dam. Jump fish leapt in their wake, reacting too late to their darting shadows.

"You sure your cousin doesn't have more bombs planted?" Tommy shouted as they gunned down Grand Avenue in Iron Mace's wake.

"She doesn't have the patience for planning more than one level of backup defenses. She's all or nothing."

"Yeah, that sounds like her."

Which meant she probably hadn't held back anything to deal with Iron Mace. With a broken arm, there was no way she could take the male. As they raced toward the hotel, he could feel Tinker and the bright motes of her *sekasha* desperately fighting something at close quarters in the casting room. His kids and a handful of adults spilled out the casting room's back door. Iron Mace blasted open the lobby doors, now less than a hundred feet from Tinker.

"Circle around," Oilcan shouted to Tommy. "Save my kids. I'll take Iron Mace."

Oilcan gunned his hoverbike, darted alongside of the hotel to smash through the window into the ballroom. Momentum slid him across muddy marble floor to the doorless opening. Leaping from his bike, he stepped out into the dim hallway and snapped up a shield between him and Iron Mace.

"You!" Iron Mace rocked back in surprise. "I killed you."

"Like you killed Amaranth?"

Iron Mace sneered, all pretense of being a grieving brother abandoned. "My baby sister had the decency to stay dead. I understand your mother knew the trick. If I'm lucky, it's a female trait."

Oilcan squared off behind his shield. "I'm not going to let you hurt my cousin."

Iron Mace laughed. "Go ahead and bark, little mutt puppy. What Forge taught you doesn't mean you can bite."

"I already could bite!" Oilcan took out the floor supports in the hotel's nice deep basement and dropped four stories of hotel on top of Iron Mace. Half a lifetime of good memories—and one surprised *domana*—thundered down into the sudden hole. Oilcan knew it wouldn't hurt Iron Mace, but he figured it might piss him off enough to forget about Tinker. He took off running, keeping his shield up as he ran.

Maybe if Oilcan hadn't spent his childhood playing lab assistant to a mad scientist determined to bend the hell out of reality, he might be clueless as to how to hurt Iron Mace behind his shield. It was just a matter of hitting the male fast and hard with the right series of spells.

Out in the parking lot, Oilcan snapped through a set of spells. Alone they were utilitarian and innocuous; combined by a mad scientist, they reduced asphalt to a frictionless surface. It had taken all three of them days to copy over the glyphs and spell rings to convert a driveway to a hockey rink. The massive power of the Spell Stones transformed the hotel's expansive parking lot to a glassy sheen in a matter of seconds.

The broken rubble of the hotel rumbled, heaved,

shuddered, and then exploded upward, disgorging Iron Mace in a roil of dust.

"Lying brat!" Iron Mace shouted. "You said you didn't know your *esva*."

"I just need to know physics!" Tinker had explained about the strength of *domana* shields, how they redirected kinetic energy around the caster and were nearly impenetrable. Oilcan had been paying attention when his grandfather taught him physics. He just rarely had any need to apply the principles. "This is all science."

And science was all about experimentation. Taking out the floor supports told him that he could control the ground under Iron Mace's feet. He *pulled*—yanking the elf onto the frictionless parking lot. Still pulling, he added his momentum to Iron Mace by running forward, hitting the edge of the shining surface, and sliding.

In a frictionless environment, things in motion stayed in motion—including elves.

They slid fast toward each other. Oilcan tried a blast against Iron Mace's shield. The force was redirected without changing Iron Mace's angle of motion. Iron Mace twisted as they passed each other like two freight trains, and blasted the ground ahead of Oilcan. A great crater appeared.

Oilcan ignored the oncoming disaster to keep Iron Mace focused tightly on him and not on where he was heading. A childhood of racing go-karts on the island had taught Oilcan to never lose track of the river's edge. It was a lesson Iron Mace learned the hard way when he flew off the end of the parking lot and out over the water. Like a flat stone, he skipped three times before sinking.

It turned out that tumbling into a massive crater

at twenty miles per hour wasn't painful when Oilcan had his shield spell up. He scrambled quickly back up to the edge of the crater. Iron Mace's shield was still active under the muddy water, drifting downriver like a massive hamster ball. It was possible that the elf could save himself, but he was against a ticking clock—there was only so much air trapped in the shell with him. Iron Mace cast a scry spell. The river and its currents were mapped out, bisected by the Emsworth Dam and the powerful undertow beyond it.

"Yes, bastard," Oilcan whispered. "You need to get out before you hit that."

The current was going to sweep Iron Mace across the river and up against the high walls of the lock on the far bank. Annoyingly, there was even a ladder there for someone to scramble up from a boat. It would be impossible for a human to climb it with one hand, but an elf's longer reach meant Iron Mace could do it and maintain his shield.

Oilcan slid to the edge of the parking lot and took off running for the dam. Tommy was right about needing the strength to do the hard thing, because this fight was to the death. Iron Mace had to kill Oilcan and anyone else that might know about what he'd done. He had dug a deep, deep hole, and the only way out was to fill it with bodies. Oilcan had to be sure that the elf never got out of the river. He held close to the anger thrumming through him, hot and heady. So, how did he kill this bastard?

There was no way Iron Mace could go near the sluicegates without being swept over the dam. Beyond the gates was a dangerous undertow that would pin Iron Mace under water. The only safe way out was the ladder. It was the same heavy steel as the catwalk, bolted solid into the cement wall of the lock. If Oilcan hit it with a force strike, it would blast the entire ladder to shards.

He could mark Iron Mace's position by the circling jumpfish. Oilcan reached the end of the catwalk and scrambled down to the lock's wall. At the top of the ladder, he cocked his fingers, brought his hand to his mouth, and then paused. If he blasted the ladder now, Iron Mace might just find another way out of the water. As long as the male maintained his shield, he was safe to find another way. If Oilcan waited and cast the spell while Iron Mace was holding on to the ladder . . .

The result would be awful and utterly necessary. It went against everything Oilcan tried to be, but he wouldn't have a second chance to take Iron Mace while vulnerable. So he waited, hating himself, trying to hold tight to his anger. This male had attacked him in his home. Had left his kids defenseless. Had come to Neville Island to kill Tinker.

The last brought the rage he needed.

Iron Mace surged up out of the water and caught hold of the lowest rung. Jumpfish were bouncing off the elf's shield, trying to snatch him off the wall. Oilcan waited until the male had heaved himself up, swearing and grunting with effort, and got a foot onto the rung and grabbed the second rung tight.

Oilcan tapped the Spell Stones. Iron Mace looked up, eyes going wide in surprise. Oilcan closed his fist tight in the force strike. Iron Mace's hand and foot shattered along with the steel of the ladder. The male screamed, falling backward, his shield vanishing as he flailed in pain, and the jumpfish took him.

45: IMPATIENCE

For reasons that weren't clear to Tinker until much later, Oilcan, Tommy Chang, and Riki Shoji all showed up after the fireworks were over. Thankfully, they had Oilcan's kids, minus Rustle, safe among them.

"Hey," Oilcan called as he scrambled through the wreckage of what had been their home. She whimpered at the sight of him, his eyes and ears proof that he wasn't human anymore. He looked young and haunted, but at least he was alive. She caught hold of him and hugged him despite his efforts to check her for new cuts and bruises.

"You had me worried with that last explosion." His voice was his own, rough with emotion. "I'm sorry about the hotel."

She closed her eyes and focused on his voice and the hammering of his heart, like he had just run a race. "It's just a thing. All things wear out eventually."

"Usually not so spectacularly." He unknowingly echoed her thoughts about Ginger Wine's.

She clutched him tighter, giggling. "Well, you're finally showing the family destructive gene."

He head-butted her gently. "One occurrence doesn't indicate a trait."

"We'll see. Time will tell." Tears filled her eyes as she realized that they had forever to see. How could something be in theory a good thing and yet feel so awful?

"Hey, don't." Oilcan wiped at her tears. "Or I'll sic Pony on you."

"No fair." She scrubbed at her eyes with the back of her good hand. "I'm fine."

"Is—is this Chloe Polanski?" Riki had discovered the body that Tinker had covered up with a deflated seahorse float.

"She's a Skin Clan *intanyai seyosa*," Tinker said. "She engineered all this so I would figure how the kids tapped their ability and God knows what else. Oh, Oilcan, I've screwed up bad. I've lost Rustle." Tinker waved a hand at the gleaming spell shell. "Well—sort of lost him. I think he's still right here—but I don't know how to get him out. Yet."

Oilcan stalked around the spell, eyeing the gleaming runes. "It's just a two-layered spell? The divination spell from before and a focusing array?"

Tinker sighed. "Yeah. The weirdness is all Rustle. Look at this." She knelt beside the gleaming spell to point out the earbuds and the pinpoints of blues and greens. "It's reacting to the music. Really, it's resonance that I think is key. Providence spoke of worlds in harmony. If you think of each world represented by a single note, then the linked worlds will . . ." Tinker's knowledge hit a void, and she looked at Oilcan to fill in the words.

"The next note in the chord."

"Yeah, something like that. String theory states that subatomic particles behave like vibrating strings. Subatomic particles make atoms; atoms build into molecules, which form our DNA. If each world has one grand note, then every living creature would have that note built into its DNA. We resonate to the world of our DNA, so the kids, having dragon DNA, have at least two different 'notes.' They might have a 'chord' structure. Heck, since the dragons can travel between matter and worlds, the dragons might even start with a chord structure. I think applying a large amount of magic to Rustle allows him to change notes, sliding to the next world in harmony."

"He's on Onihida?" Oilcan said with alarm.

Tinker made calming motions. "It's possible that he's on all the worlds at once. It depends on how diffused he is."

"What?"

"I don't think it's hurting him. The iPod is still playing!"

"How do we free him?" Oilcan asked.

Tinker blew out her breath and tugged at her hair. Yeah—how? "Just need to figure out what this world's note is . . . and tell it to him . . . somehow . . . and . . . something."

"*Quiee*," Baby Duck said.

They glanced in unison at the other children, huddled close together.

She really hated to say it aloud, but there was no other logical choice. "Since the other kids have the same ability, they might be able to figure out the note."

"No!" Oilcan snapped.

"I didn't say I was going to experiment on them!" Tinker cried. "Not directly. We could see if they recognize the note, and then tell it to Rustle."

"Can he even hear us?" Blue Sky asked.

This was how it always went, and there was comfort in the familiar. "We'll tackle that after we figure out the note. By now you should know the steps of the scientific method. Ask a question, do background research . . ."

"Now I know we're in trouble," Blue grumbled. "You only say that when the shit is about to hit the fan."

Tinker forged on. "Construct a hypothesis, test your hypothesis by doing an experiment, analyze your data, and draw a conclusion."

"And communicate your results," Oilcan added as always.

"But we never tell anyone anything," Blue mumbled.

"*Sama.*" Merry was holding her bulky *olianuni* case to her chest. "I can tell Rustle."

They blinked at her in surprise, and finally Oilcan sputtered out, "How—how exactly would you tell him?" as Tinker murmured, "I thought you said they weren't telepathic."

"I'll join him inside the spell." Merry edged closer to the spell.

"No, no, no, no, definitely not." Oilcan reached out for her, and she flinched away.

"It should have been me!" Merry circled the spell, keeping away from Oilcan's outstretched hand. "He's hurt! He can't even drum! And he has nothing to drum with. I love him and I couldn't bear it if I never saw him again and I know I might have been able to save him."

"Merry," Tinker said. "I don't want to lose both of you, because I don't know if I'm right. I might be totally wrong on this whole resonance thing. Music might not have anything to do with it. I probably am wrong."

"Doesn't matter," Merry said. "I'd be with him. I'll be where he is."

"You should let her go," Blue said. "It would be right to let her go."

Tinker stared at him, surprised and a little horrified. Even worse, when she looked to Pony, he nodded sadly.

"What is the worth of your life if you can't protect the ones you love the most?" Pony said.

Of course the bodyguards would think that way. They were lucky to see the world in black and white. The world was so clear-cut to them. If it was her, yes, she'd throw herself into the spell in a heartbeat to save Oilcan, or Windwolf, or Pony, or Stormsong, or Blue Sky . . . Gods, the list kept getting longer and longer the more she thought about it—which probably only proved their point.

Yes, she would chance it. That wasn't the point here. She was the adult, and Merry was just a child of approximately thirteen. Although some people would say eighteen wasn't an adult. And to be fair, at thirteen she had started her own business and lived by herself.

And had risked her life to save a total stranger from a saurus.

If it had been Oilcan on the ground unconscious, she wouldn't have even done a hit-and-run on the saurus. She would have beat on it with everything she had. She hadn't known Windwolf, had no reason to think that saving him was her responsibility, and yet she'd felt like she *had* to do something, and that hitting and running would be an acceptable risk. That it would be best to strike once, strike hard, and flee.

Stormsong said that her mother's talent made Tinker ruthless on the racetrack. Maybe her talent had guided her that day. Maybe she knew deep inside that Windwolf would someday be someone that she would risk everything to save.

How sure did she *feel* that she was right now? If she had nothing but a hunch, how strong was that gut feeling? "Okay."

"Tink!" Oilcan cried.

"I think it will be okay," Tinker said. "It feels right."

While the tengu and the *laedin* set up a new perimeter, her Hand stayed close, keeping her shielded so she could focus on saving Rustle. She was glad that Thorne Scratch shadowed Oilcan, keeping him safe. Merry played all the tones the *olianuni* could make, starting with the deep rumbling notes, while the other children listened intently.

"Do it again?" Barley suggested after Merry finished hitting the highest chime-like notes that the instrument produced. "None of them seemed special."

"They're just sound," Cattail Reeds grumbled.

Baby Duck quacked nervously.

"I don't think they can recognize it," Oilcan murmured, and behind him Thorne Scratch nodded, agreeing with his assessment.

"If we could recognize it normally, then Rustle and I would already know it." Merry had been stoically silent up to now. "We've studied music our whole life. Really! Whole summers just practicing chord progressions!"

"She has a point." Tinker considered the problem. "Here's what we know. None of the other kids had the problem of losing stuff like Rustle did. Right? The enclaves are on a strong ley line, but none of the other kids' powers activated. And Merry didn't do this"—she waved toward the gleaming spell—"when we just did a divination spell."

"We established those as given." Oilcan pinched the bridge of his nose.

"Could we just null all magic in the area?" Riki asked.

"That might destroy the only link we have with him." Tinker's comment made Merry meep and Baby Duck quack in distress. "Providence exists elsewhere without a body? He needs a combination of magic, what's left of his body, and Jin to manifest?" Riki nodded to this, so Tinker plunged on. "If the kids have the duality of intelligence, there might be information they can only access while connected to large amounts of magic."

"That's a huge leap in logic." Oilcan gave a sad smile to Thorne Scratch, who had laid her hand on his shoulder.

"I know," Tinker said unhappily. "The gut feeling is still there, but I don't like risking Merry's life just on a hunch." She paused to look around, suddenly aware that her test subject had vanished. "Where's Merry?"

Everyone pointed at the spell.

Thorne tightened her grip on Oilcan to keep him from leaping after Merry. "She earned the right to choose her path when she walked away from all that was safe and ventured out into the unknown."

"Why didn't you stop her?" Tinker cried to Blue Sky, who had been standing closest to Merry.

"You said it was okay for her to try!" Blue Sky backed up, holding up his hands to fend Tinker off.

"I—I—no! That was before!" Tinker cried.

The spell started to flash colors all up and down the spectrum as music suddenly started to play loud enough to hear.

"She's with him." Thorne Scratch still held tight to Oilcan.

"How do you know?" Oilcan asked.

"That's an *olianuni* duet. It needs two people to perform it," Thorne Scratch explained. "They're played often at court."

"I dress people for court," Cattail Reeds said as the other children looked to her for confirmation. "I don't actually attend court."

Stormsong breathed out a laugh. "It is a duet. 'Mating Dance of the Dragons.'"

The light flared within the spell shell fast and brilliant. Deep violets rumbling and pale yellows shimmering with reds and oranges trilling around and around each other. Once Tinker considered the speed of the notes, it was clear that more than one person had to be playing the song.

"This means that both Merry and Rustle are in the same location," she said. "Wherever that may be. They are able to communicate with each other and exist in a manner that allows them to create music."

Tommy gave her an odd look. "And?"

Tinker tugged at her hair. "I'm still analyzing data to draw a conclusion."

There was a sudden flare of power from the spell, an overwhelming sense of falling without actually moving.

Tinker cursed softly. "Was that Startup?"

"Sure the hell felt like it," Oilcan said.

The spell collapsed to reveal Merry standing in front of her *olianuni* with Rustle pressed against her back. Both kids had mallets in hand, sweating and panting heavily.

Merry yipped triumphantly and brandished her mallets, nearly smacking Rustle in the nose. "We did it!"

"Well," Tinker said. "At least that part of the plan worked."

The entire hotel, including the frictionless parking lot, had been transferred to another world. They stood in the doorway of the casting room and studied it with fear. Tall trees shrouded the island and something gave an echoing call.

"Well . . . at least we now know why the Skin Clan wanted the kids so bad," Tinker finally managed. "They're a portable large-scale gate system to multiple worlds. It's quite possible that the more power you feed into them, the bigger the area they can shift."

"*Quiee*," Baby Duck said. "*Quiee. Quiee.*"

"Which planet is this?" Blue Sky asked.

"It's not Onihida, is it?" Barley asked with fear.

"We can get back home?" Cattail Reeds asked.

"I'm sorry," Rustle said. "This is all my fault."

"Actually, it's mine," Tinker said. "And this isn't Onihida. This section of Onihida is overpopulated. Actually, much of Onihida is overpopulated."

"That's what those of the flock that were born on Onihida report," Riki said while Tommy nodded in agreement.

"Earth?" Oilcan guessed. "This area would be virgin Elfhome forest where Pittsburgh should have been on Earth."

"I think this is Ryuu," Riki said. "Home of the dragons."

Was this why Providence and Impatience had gotten involved with protecting the children? Was the Skin Clan trying to find a way to conquer Ryuu after it took Elfhome? Tinker thought about the emperor "distilling down the essence of a god" and shuddered.

"We can get back?" Cattail Reeds repeated.

"I want to go home," Baby Duck added in quietly.

So did Tinker.

Something moved in the shadows. It wove closer through the massive tree trunks.

"Incoming," Tinker cried and tried to set up a link to the Spell Stones. Nothing happened. "Oh, not good."

Oilcan did a call on the Stones and shook his head. "I'm getting nothing, too."

The *sekasha* triggered their shields, and anyone with a weapon pointed it toward the shape.

"Wait!" Riki cried. "It's Impatience!"

"What is he doing here?" Tinker had thought the dragon had been stranded on Elfhome. Then again, if the kids had a dragon's ability, then he should be able to come and go as he pleased. Why had he stayed in Pittsburgh? Just to be close to the kids? The little dragon butted up against Oilcan, talking nonstop, patting him over and over. "What is he saying, Riki?"

Riki's eyes went wide at the question, and he scrambled to answer. "Ah, he's saying . . . um . . . it is you but not you. All the little pieces are the same and yet different. Why would they do this? Oh, I see, they made you more like the little princess."

Was Impatience talking about the small changes in Oilcan's ears and eyes, or was he talking smaller, as in DNA?

"Ask him why he's here," Tinker said.

Riki spoke in dragon. Impatience cocked his head, his eyebrows jumping up in very human surprise, and then he gave a rumbling "huuhuuhuuhuu" of a dragon laugh and answered.

"To help you to return from whence you came, of course," Riki translated Impatience's reply. "Why else would I be here? It is not like our little ones know what they are doing. Babies must be taught, despite what others might say. What is ours is ours. We have duty to those who are no longer able to do for themselves."

"Huh?" Tinker said.

"Providence has implied that the dragons loosely cooperate but are territorial. The tengu are Providence's, and he will allow no other dragons to tamper with what is his. I believe Impatience is bucking someone's authority to help out Oilcan's kids."

Weird that no matter what their shape, they were all alike enough to share the concept of politics.

Impatience looked expectantly at Tinker, and she looked expectantly at the dragon until she finally growled to Riki, "Ask him how do we get back."

After a few minutes of talking, Riki said slowly, "Everyone does the same as they did before. But this time . . ." He paused to apparently ask Impatience for clarification. "This time the babies are to tune to home."

Tinker managed not to scream in frustration. "Tell him that was what they were trying for in the first place!"

"Huuhuuhuuhuuhuu." Impatience laughed and patted Oilcan gently on the chest and said something at length.

"What did he say?" Tinker asked.

Riki looked confused. "They know the truth when they hear it. They must remember the sound that touched their soul and made them know that they were home."

"Oh!" Merry gasped. "I know what it is!"

Tinker checked the inscription of the spell. It was no longer active but still drawn on the only clear spot in the bomb-blasted casting room. Having been out of phase with Elfhome's reality, that section of the pool had been spared. Reassured that it had taken no damage, Tinker waved Merry and Rustle into position with the *olianuni*. She made sure that they hadn't stepped on any of the glyphs and blurred them. Oilcan double-checked all her work.

Reassured that the spell was perfect, she spoke the command that brought it to life. The kids vanished into brilliance.

"That's what happened before." Tinker took Oilcan's hand. "They'll be okay. If nothing else, they'll come back to here again. Probably."

Oilcan snorted and leaned close to whisper, "You hate not being able to lie."

"Yes!"

Music started inside the shell. Judging by the heavy driving beat, it was a human song. It sounded familiar, but Tinker couldn't place it. Oilcan laughed as he recognized it.

"What is it?" Tinker asked.

"'We are Pittsburgh,'" Oilcan said.

She recognized the song then. Oilcan had created it during the impromptu concert in the gym. A defiant anthem to the city, it snarled their fierce independence and unity to all those that would try to beat them down and divide them.

"Blood on the pavement," Oilcan sang along with the music. "Blood on the blade, blood flows through common veins. Three worlds bridged by a single span, steel that climbs from earth to sky. Freedom to create, freedom to fly—one world, one people, one kind. We are Pittsburgh."

Yeah, that's home, Tinker thought.

The universe dropped out from under their feet and reality shifted and they were home.

46: KNIGHT ERRANT

Tommy had always hated the legend of King Arthur, a boy yanking a sword out of a stone and suddenly he was the king. He realized now that the boy had always been a king—the sword was just an outward symbol of what was inside. The sword was more than just a weapon, it was a crown.

Oilcan always had that quiet power of command. Even when Tinker was princess of the track, he kept order in her wake. He had never reached out, took hold of the weapon, and gone to war before. Now that he had, the power crowned him.

Tommy could see the news of Oilcan's fight with Iron Mace move through the Wind Clan elves. They stared at the black-mirror parking lot and then looked across the river at the hole blasted into the side of the lock. Iron Mace had been a Stone Clan warlord during the clan wars. He had been one of their enemies' best. And Oilcan faced him down and killed him. The elves bowed low to Oilcan, awe and respect clear on their faces.

Obviously, Tommy's part in the day's win was being ignored because he wasn't "one of us." The elves were still looking at him with open suspicion. It was starting to really piss him off. He drifted into the shadows of a rusting Tilt-A-Whirl carnival ride as the elves did the messy work of cleaning up dead oni. He was thinking it was time to disappear when Oilcan showed up with two wicker baskets of *mauzouan*.

"Dumpling?" Oilcan held out one of the wicker baskets. He took the full glare of Tommy's anger without flinching. "You saved my life today. I can at least make sure you get some of the free food that's showing up."

Tommy's stomach reminded him that he hadn't a decent meal for days. He jerked the basket out of Oilcan's hand and stuffed one into his mouth. "Elves don't use enough ginger."

"I used to think that." Oilcan waved his hand to take in his elf-pointed ears and elf-screwed-up taste buds. "Royally ticked off that beer is going to taste like piss from now on."

Tommy laughed and settled on the railing that encircled the Tilt-A-Whirl. Oilcan tucked himself into a rusting car of the carnival ride. They ate in companionable silence. When he was done with the dumplings, Oilcan licked clean his fingers and produced a flask from his back pocket.

Oilcan tasted the contents tentatively and raised eyebrows at the result. "It's good, but it's not beer." Oilcan held out the flask to Tommy. "Ouzo?"

What Tommy needed was a cigarette, but he settled for the sweet hard kick of the liquor.

"Thanks for everything." Oilcan took the flask back

and winced through another taste test. "The elves are all impressed, but I couldn't have done any of it without you. You did more than save my life. You—you helped me be strong enough to do what I had to do." Oilcan studied the river from the shadows, sorrow filling his eyes.

The kid had never killed anyone before, and everyone is acting like he's a big hero for it.

Tommy laughed bitterly, shaking his head. "You do what you have to do because the other person is more than willing to rip your throat out if you don't. Doesn't make you a monster. It makes you a survivor."

"I went through this with beer." Oilcan sipped again. "One beer doesn't make you a drunk. One killing doesn't make you a murderer—just doesn't have the same truth."

"He picked the game, not you."

A half-dozen *laedin* soldiers spotted Tommy in the shadows and closed on him, hands on weapons. This "not one of them" was really getting to be a pain.

"What are you doing here, oni spawn?" the tallest of them asked.

Oilcan leaned out of the Tilt-A-Whirl car and chased the elves off with a look and a quiet "He's with me."

Tommy knew true words when he heard them. "Yeah, I'm with you."

Oilcan tilted his head, catching that there was more to the words. "You are?"

"It took me a while to figure out, but I need to make the world I want to live in. It's going to be more than just stopping the oni. The elves are locked into this stupid mental straightjacket of us versus them."

"Stone Clan versus Wind Clan."

"Any of them. It's one clan against all the rest. I know how that works—or I should say, how badly that works. 'Them' is always everyone else that isn't us, when it really isn't, and doesn't need to be." If he hadn't turned to Team Big Sky when Kajo used the tengu against him, he would have lost everything. Up to that day, John Montana, Blue Sky, and Oilcan had been "them" despite years of working with them.

"I'm really sick of all this us against them," Oilcan growled. Tommy realized it was because the cousins never saw the world that way. It explained why they had gone to extraordinary lengths to save Windwolf when Lord Tomtom had tried to assassinate him. Why Oilcan had helped Tommy even though he knew Tommy was half-oni. And why Oilcan took in the young elf female and turned the city upside down looking for the others.

By concerning themselves with everyone, Tinker and Oilcan had managed to keep the city strong enough to defend itself against the likes of Kajo. They raised people up to their standards and made them part of that strength. It was their code of chivalry. Be compassionate. Be honorable. Be good.

"I realize I can't hide in my little corner and hope that it all works out to my liking. I need to sit at the table where decisions are being made and make myself heard and fight for the world I want."

Oilcan grinned. "Good. Pittsburgh needs you. It needs places where everyone can come together as a whole instead of sticking to their own little neighborhood, isolated by the rivers and hills and their culture. We need places where we can meet each other as just common everyday people."

Tommy hadn't even considered the racetrack to be anything more than a way to make money. Put that way, it made sense why Jin had asked him to drop his ban. The tengu wanted access to the common meeting grounds. It was important that they weren't the monsters hiding in the woods. And he would drop the ban; he didn't want Kajo controlling him. Besides, it gave him a better leverage on the tengu if he gave them access to his businesses.

"What I hate about this Beholden bullshit is the word. Beholden." Tommy spat his disgust. "Too much like 'owned.'"

And "I want to be your knight in shining armor" would sound like he was hitting on Oilcan.

"Yeah," Oilcan said. "It should be more like 'team,' like at the racetrack. The guy on the hoverbike is worthless without a good crew in the pit. And a good pit crew doesn't stand a chance without a good rider."

Put that way, it was easy to say, "I want to be on your team."

"Mine?"

"Team Oilcan."

Oilcan backed up, waving him off. "Team Tinker is the only team I have."

"The elves made you a team captain, like it or not. They gave you the power to be a force at the table."

"There's Tinker."

"No offense, but your cousin is like a boy scout on crack. Squeaky clean, trying to do a month's worth of good deeds in one day, and bouncing off the walls at the speed of light."

Oilcan grinned. "Yeah, that's her."

"You and I are a lot alike."

"Ah, secretly you're a bohemian artist?"

"We both watched the one thing we loved most in the world get beaten to death in front of us. I know how it makes you feel weak and helpless. And you swear to yourself that you'd eat broken glass before ever going through that again. But the one thing you won't let yourself do is become your father."

Oilcan winced and looked away. "It's that obvious?"

"I've seen you with your cousin, and I recognized all the signs," Tommy said. "I understand you. I trust you. I want to be on your team."

"I don't know what the hell I would do with a team."

"We would make peace and live in it."

Oilcan studied the river and the distant lock. He took another swallow of ouzo and passed the flask to Tommy. "Okay, let's team up."

47: COMMITMENT

Sacred Heart had unofficially become "the orphan house" as all the various shattered Stone Clan households drifted into Oilcan's care. Jewel Tear took up residence on the third floor as Iron Mace's newly orphaned warriors shifted down to the second floor along with the remains of Earth Son's household. Again and again, the elves mentioned that the front door needed to be painted. By that, they meant "should be Stone Clan black."

He'd been haunted all night by his conversation with Tommy. Just as the half-oni recognized himself in Oilcan, he could see his reflection in Tommy. They both had been lone wolves while surrounded by people. They had perfected being apart even while crowded by others. They clung to the status quo because it was safe and comfortable.

Oilcan could have taken Tinker's sponsorship days ago—should have taken it the minute he realized that he needed to provide for five kids. He was afraid if he forced the issue, the kids would walk away from him. He had taken the easy way out by not choosing. He had even drifted along in whatever he had with Thorne Scratch—silently accepting whatever she gave him because if he asked her to clarify, he might not like the answer.

In fact, wasn't that his whole life, drifting behind Tinker, letting her choose the path? He had one-night stands with women who couldn't stay on Elfhome, did nothing to discourage the one night becoming one month, and then watched as the relationship ironically imploded under his fear that if he put demands on the other person, he would lose them. The pattern was there, clear to see, if he only made himself look.

Much as the possibility of losing the kids and Thorne Scratch scared the shit out of him, he couldn't drift along anymore. He had to take a stand. He had to make his choice of clan clear as the color of his front door. A household of Stone Clan members and a city full of Wind Clan wouldn't let him be apathetic any longer.

He knew that he couldn't be Stone Clan. It would be like walking away from everything that was him. But if changing clans would slowly drive him insane, wouldn't it be even more so for the kids? Avoiding the issue, though, wasn't the answer.

Talking to all the kids at once seemed like a bad idea. They were very good at joining forces, and he doubted his resolution could withstand their combined will. He decided to start with Baby Duck. She only had scattered memories from before Pittsburgh. In theory, she had the least attachment to the Stone Clan.

"*Quiee*," Baby Duck quacked after Oilcan finished.

They were sitting in the grass out before the anchor rocks. The *indi* leapt from stone to stone with the bells on their collars tinkling with each jump.

He waited for her to say something else. After a few minutes, he realized that she wasn't going to say anything else. He felt like he'd broken her.

"I'll be your *sama* as long as you want me to." It scared him a little to know that now it meant forever.

She climbed into his lap and buried her face against his chest. "*Quiee.*"

He'd take that as a yes.

Fields of Barley was practically chained to the kitchen now that he was cooking for an army. It delighted him to no end. "I'm going to bake these carrots with honey glaze and sprinkled with chopped walnuts. The peas I'm just going to blanch quickly—it would be a crime to do more to them than a dab of butter and pepper. Wish I could do a presentation piece with the rabbits—but we need to stretch the meat. I'm going to make a pie with shallots, mushrooms, and apples. I need to do something other than pie with the peaches that cousin sent over."

Apparently "cousin" was now going the other way.

"That sounds good." Oilcan hated to break Barley's good mood with bad news, but there was no way around it. He explained what he planned to do.

Barley carefully wiped down his knife and slid it into the butcher-block holder. "*Sama*—my first *sama*—said never use a knife when you're upset."

"I'm sorry."

Barley attacked the bread dough. "We have the advantage of being the only Stone Clan enclave. The incoming clan members would come to us first and only go to the others if we have no room. If we become Wind Clan, we're the smallest and most crudely furnished enclave. We don't even have beds—we have cots. Our bathing room is still unfinished and our courtyard is paved and being used as a laundry."

"Yes, we have rough edges. We'll smooth those out. I think, though, that much of our business will come from humans. They'll come for the music."

Barley laughed, punching the dough. "You cannot make money from music."

"We'll charge . . ." There wasn't an Elvish word for it, so he used the English. "A cover."

"A cover? What is a cover?"

Oilcan explained the idea. He'd already talked to Tommy Chang about using the gym as a nightclub. It was going to be their first joint effort.

"They'll pay for not sleeping the night?" Clearly the concept mystified Barley. He pondered it as he shaped loafs and covered them to rise again. "We would not have to wash so many sheets if they do not spend the night."

Currently, their laundry was very makeshift, with one industrial washer that amazed the kids and a maze of clotheslines in the backyard. It was taking up lots of time from everyone's life to help keep up with the sheets.

"It frightens me, *Sama*. I walked away from my enclave and got so lost. I'm afraid to walk away from my clan."

"Even if something happens to me, Tinker and Wolf Who Rules will take care of you."

"I know," he whispered. His bottom lip started to

tremble, and he went to scrub at his tear-filled eyes with flour-covered hands.

"Hey." Oilcan caught Barley's hands before he could rub flour into his eyes. "It will be okay."

"I hate being so weak."

"You'll get stronger." Oilcan pulled him into a hug and let him cry. It was only fair, since he was the one rocking the children's world.

Cattail Reeds was attempting to achieve the maximum effect of the paint and fabric on the extremely sparsely furnished second-floor bedrooms. "This is so beautiful." She held out a rich Waverly floral print of reds and greens and blues. "But we have so little of it, I'll have to be careful with it. Can we not get more?"

"I bought all that they had." He cleared whole sections of the little fabric store knowing that what didn't become curtains would become clothes. "Perhaps we can arrange for fabric to be brought from Easternlands."

"Not like this." She laid it aside to pick up the white broadcloth he'd found cheap and plentiful. "This, though, this is boring. I will have to see if I can dye it. If I can match the green, then the print can be an accent to it. If I can't, maybe the walls will have to be green instead."

Cautiously, Oilcan explained his decision.

"Cousin will take us if something happens to you?" Cattail asked.

That was one thing he was sure of even though he hadn't talked to Tinker yet. "Yes."

"Fine." She took hold of a hunk of fabric and ripped it.

That didn't sound like fine.

"Are you okay?" he asked.

"I was dismayed when I learned that Earth Son was dead. I had been at court with a chance—slim as it may be—of catching the eye of the queen with my designs." She grabbed another section of fabric and ripped it. "It had been my choice, though, to leave court and come to Pittsburgh, because I was chasing a dream that had nothing to do with the queen's favor.

"I had been alarmed when no one could honor his offer." She ripped another section. "But—but—but—" She clenched the fabric tight. "These new *domana*: Darkness, Sunder, and Cana Lily. They come straight from Diamond, the bitch who not only gave birth to that sniveling rat Earth Son but also sent him to Pittsburgh."

Clearly in Cattail's mind, Diamond was still in full command of the Stone Clan. After all that Oilcan and Tinker had learned in the last few days, it was possible, though, that Diamond was just an unknowing puppet for the Skin Clan.

"Not a single fucking one of these newly arrived Stone Clan *domana* carries an explanation—an offer of compensation—or even so much as an apology from Diamond. We—the children that her son lured out into the wilderness and gave to the oni to torture, rape, kill, and eat—are beneath her notice. Another clan has to rescue the living, give the dead up to the sky, and see to all our needs? Well, fuck the Stone Clan. I'm more than fine to be Wind Clan. I'm happy."

She was right. No matter who had been behind the children's betrayal—the Stone Clan had continued to fail them.

He reached out to hug her, but she flinched away angrily and tore another length of the broadcloth.

"You'll have your dream," he promised. "With the extra money of sponsorship, we'll turn the library into a boutique where you can sell clothes."

He started to turn toward the door, and she lunged and caught hold of him in a fierce hug.

"I am happy," she whispered. "I'm just too mad at them to show it."

Letting him go, she stalked away, the strips of fabric still tight in her hand, fluttering in her storm wind.

Rustle of Leaves and Merry were in one of the little back rooms patiently crafting a hunk of ironwood into an *olianuni* for Rustle. Apparently a fifty-year apprenticeship included how to build instruments from scratch. Considering that an *olianuni* would wear out in a dozen years from constant use and that elves lived forever, it probably was a good thing. Luckily Merry still had all her tools that she had brought with her to Pittsburgh.

Halfway through his explanation, Merry reached out for Rustle, and he took her hand. Oilcan pushed on even though his stomach was doing sickening flip-flops.

The doubles glanced at each other.

"If Moser had taken me in, I would have been Wind Clan," Rustle said to Merry.

"My home is Pittsburgh," Merry said. "Where you are."

Rustle grinned and wrapped his arms around her. "We are Pittsburgh."

That left only one person, the one he was most afraid of losing. He was worried he might have already lost her by not speaking his heart.

Thorne Scratch hadn't come to his room the night before. He had been painfully aware of her absence.

And like an idiot, he'd done what he'd always done and not gone after the female he had come to love. Jewel Tear was just down the hall, battered and needy, and without a Hand. Had Thorne Scratch assumed he didn't want her and offered to Jewel Tear instead?

He found her among the sheets in the backyard, practicing alone like the first time he'd seen her. Unlike that time, she was barefoot, wearing only glove-tight pants and a camisole, hair unbraided. Her ponytail formed a wonderful exclamation point over perfection in snug cotton.

He watched her move, serenely fierce, and ached with the possibility that she might never be his again.

She turned, sword in attack position, and saw Oilcan. Her lips turned upward into a Mona Lisa smile as she gazed over the blade at him. Behind her the brilliant white sheets rose to snap in the wind. He would paint that moment so he would always have her.

She blushed slightly and sheathed her *ejae*. In her wonderfully husky voice, she said, "You always look at me as if I'm the most beautiful thing you've ever seen."

"You are."

Her blush deepened. "No, no, I'm not."

Oilcan reached out and caught her callused hand.

She stared down at their joined hands in horror. "How awful I am," Thorne whispered. "I looked at your face and was secretly glad that I would not lose you so soon, but this is not your hand."

He brought her hand up to rest on his chest. "This is my heart; it has not changed." She curled her fingers until she gripped his shirt tight. He forced himself to finish. "I am Wind Clan."

She laughed in surprise and then leaned her forehead

against his to look deep into his eyes. "Oh, yes, there you are. I see you now."

"Be my First."

Her eyes went wide, but then she looked away, shaking her head. "You should ask a Wind Clan *sekasha* to be your First. You will need a full Hand, and the Wind Clan *sekasha* will not accept a Stone Clan First."

He took joy in that she had not said "No." He wrapped his arms around her and pulled her tight against him. "If they will not accept you, I do not want them."

Her emotions warred on her. He was afraid to press her, because she would take it wrongly, but also afraid that he wasn't pushing because he was falling into the same old habit. So he put it out, cold and frank, all that he felt.

"I'm scared that I'm going to lose you. I love you. I want you to be with me. Always."

She dropped her head to his shoulder, and they stood twined together, pressed close. "I love you, too, you idiot," she finally whispered. "It makes me weak. I shouldn't let you be so stupid as to bind yourself to one like me."

"I won't let you talk me out of it."

She lifted her hand to smack him lightly on the chest but then kissed him as if he was the thing she needed most to live.

48: KNIGHT IN SHINING ARMOR

Sacred Heart was a humming beehive of activity but in a happy, peaceful way. There were *sekasha* laughing in the gym as they taught Blue Sky some wicked looking moves. The young lovers were in the dining room, practicing music with Moser's band. The smell of something rich and spicy wreathed the whole place with bounty.

Tommy had brought his younger cousins to help with the rebuilding on the stated theory that it was better for them to meet people outside his family instead of being hidden away like something shameful. And yeah, that was one reason. But it gave him a good excuse to be in the building.

Once he was sure his cousins were under Cattail Reeds' artistic supervision, Tommy slipped unnoticed upstairs to the third floor and moved cautiously down the hall to the end room where he knew Jewel Tear was staying. The door stood open, seeming to welcome all comers, but he had heard that Jewel Tear had been quiet and withdrawn. The elves were giving her space to put her ordeal behind her.

He wasn't sure of how she would react to him, but he wanted to see her again. He told himself that he was a fool—that she had made herself clear days ago—but want was eating at him.

She was at the window, looking down into the backyard. She wore a dress obviously by Cattail Reeds. It was a flirty splash of bright yellow that only came to midthigh in the front but trained down in the back nearly to her bare feet. Seeing her there in the light did all sorts of strange and painful things to his insides.

She put her hand to the glass and smiled radiantly at someone in the backyard. Tommy's insides twisted hard with jealous anger. He ghosted forward, needing to know whom she was waving at.

Spot was in the backyard with Baby Duck. The little elf female had crowned him with dandelions as brilliant yellow as Jewel Tear's dress against his black fur. They had the chickens in their laps and were hand-feeding them while Baby Duck talked earnestly to Spot.

Tommy breathed out as surprise and relief punched him hard in the gut.

Jewel Tear turned and saw him. Her eyes went wide. She glanced to the door standing open.

"It was open." He really hoped she wasn't going to scream. Things could get messy if she did. He tried not to think of all the *sekasha* down on the first floor.

Jewel Tear ran to the door and shut it.

He had expected her to run out into the hall and stood there confused as she locked the door quietly.

"Stupid," she hissed as she hurried back to him

and pulled him away from the window. "We have to be careful not to be seen together."

"Gods forbid we be seen," Tommy sneered.

"They'll kill us both if they catch us." She caught his head and pulled him down to a hard desperate kiss.

For several minutes Tommy couldn't think coherently as his hands discovered that the dress rode up when she wrapped her arms about his shoulders and his fingers had access to bare skin.

"Who—who will kill us?" he finally managed.

"The *sekasha*. The *domana* are forbidden to take lovers outside of their Hands."

At the faire grounds they had been surrounded by nearly fifty Wyverns. She had acted so distant and dismissive that even he believed there was nothing between them. He breathed out a laugh at his own naïvety.

His fingertips brushed higher, and his brain stopped working again. "You're not wearing any . . ."

"They said your cousins were coming to help. I knew you would be brave enough to seek me out."

"Oh," he said and then realized what that meant. "Oh! We'll have to be quiet."

She smothered her laughter against his mouth.

49: ELF PRINCESS

The meeting was Tinker's first real official *planned* function as an elf princess. Everything else really didn't count because she had charged ahead without a full thought of the political implications. This time she calculated out maximum strategic impact of every possible detail. She decided on a casual afternoon tea in the courtyard under the peach trees. She would wear the new yellow baby-doll shirt that Cattail Reeds had made her with the shorts she had permanently borrowed off Stormsong. She drilled all morning on the etiquette of pouring tea, not so much so she could do it exactly right but so she could humanize the activity without delivering any grave insult. She talked Lemonseed into creating finger sandwiches using human condiments such as mayonnaise, bread and butter pickles, and Dijon mustard. She wanted to deliver a strong message of "This is Pittsburgh, not the Easternlands."

And then there was nothing to do but wait on the elfin vagueness of time for "afternoon" to roll around.

She should have made it "morning" tea. Luckily, her guest was impossibly early by elf standards.

Apparently Forge's Hand was taking their unintentional complicity with the Skin Clan hard. His First bowed slightly to Pony without the normal cold stare-down. Forge echoed the humility in his bow to Tinker. It made it a little easier to bow back.

Forge settled uneasily on the cushion. He had the invitation she had sent up the road to him. She had spent an entire hour crafting it. He turned it over and over, as if confused by it.

"You sent this?" He held it out reluctantly, as if he didn't want her to take it from him. After great deliberation, she had written: *Grandpa Forge, come see me this afternoon, your granddaughter, Beloved Tinker of Wind.*

She clamped down on the first three snarky things that wanted to come out of her mouth. This was politics. Keeping your mouth shut was part of being smart. "Yes," she said once she got the impulse for sarcasm under control. "I wanted to talk with you."

"What do you want of me, Beloved?"

It was weird having someone other than Windwolf, Pony, and Stormsong use that part of her name. It was kind of creepy to have some old guy using it.

"Please, call me Granddaughter." He looked so hopeful that she had to focus on pouring out the tea. "For most of my life, my cousin was all that I had. There are no words to describe how important he is to me, but I know you understand how I feel about him."

He bowed his head over his teacup. "I am stunned that you can even speak civilly to me. I would not be able to forgive . . ."

She didn't want to get into a discussion of forgive and forget. Not with the elves demanding truth. "Our family has the capability to love without reservation. The Skin Clan knew that—maybe even bred it into us—and reached out and tried to use it to control us. Both of us. You to take Oilcan, and me to launch a war against the Stone Clan to get him back."

"You did not fall to them." Forge's voice was thick with shame. "I betrayed a child that trusted me."

She controlled the urge to smack Forge for still thinking of Oilcan as a child. *Be happy that he's ashamed.* "It was a close thing. Prince True Flame begged me on bended knee not to throw us into a war, and it made me realize how we were being used. That we've been manipulated again and again since the day that Unbounded Brilliance fled Elfhome. We face an ancient enemy who would have us ignore all that is good and reasonable to destroy each other."

She reached out and took his hand. "We are family. Not Wind Clan and Stone Clan, but family. Do not let the Skin Clan destroy that."

Forge's eyes widened as he gazed at her small hand in his large one.

"I know your heart," she said. "I know that you will be true to it. I want to be able to trust you."

"I will never betray my grandchildren's trust again," Forge promised.

"Thank you, Grandfather."

After Forge left, Tinker was warned by the sudden appearance of traditional teacakes and fresh tea that Windwolf was returning. The rest of the universe vanished as he swept into the courtyard, his joy at seeing her blazing on his face. They were sprawled on the blanket, her one good hand tangled in his hair, kissing, before she remembered that they had a fairly large audience.

Of course most of their audience was probably overjoyed that their lord and lady were going at it like teenagers. Domestic bliss and all that.

"Tea?" she managed, pushing at Windwolf's chest.

He gave a warm chuckle but rolled off her to sprawl lazily beside her. Somehow most of the nearly eighty people in their joint household and the extra thirty-some of Poppymeadow's staff were making themselves invisible. Only their Firsts and Seconds were nearby, standing guard as Shields.

Windwolf stole a teacake and nibbled on it as he watched her pour out tea. "You spoke with Forge?"

"I don't want Pittsburgh swamped by old hatreds. If you look at who was sent—an old rival, a desperate ex-lover, and an insane mobile howitzer—it's like someone loaded the dice for war. I'm not going to let them do that to my city. I want Forge as an ally, not an enemy. And I think we should do something with Forest Moss—like find him a sex therapist."

Windwolf smiled so wide that she wondered if she had said something funny.

"What?" Perhaps it was the sex therapist part; it was kind of weird, but the elf desperately needed something.

"Elfhome dragons are spawned in the roots of mountains. They grow to adult with their wings folded back, out of the way in the tight spaces of their nursery caves. Then one day, they climb out and spread wide their wings and take flight to rule the sky."

"Huh?"

"You've spread your wings, Beloved. I'm enjoying seeing you take flight to rule."

"So that's how it is?" Tinker asked when Oilcan came and settled beside her and Thorne Scratch did the *sekasha* cold-eyed stare-off with Pony. Odd how she hadn't noticed that little tradition had been missing—until today.

Oilcan grinned sheepishly and then admitted, "I figured she would hit me if I asked her to be my *domi*."

"Smart man." Tinker bumped shoulders with him lightly. "We still good?"

"Always," Oilcan said.

She wanted to ask him how he felt about the change, but she knew how long it had taken her to just get over plain mad. She'd let him deal with it without having to drag how she felt into the mess. What was important was that no matter how he looked on the outside, he was still mentally the same. He tapped his thigh to some inner rhythm, obviously stringing words together to a song she may never hear.

"Loan me some money," he said out of the blue.

"Okay." Normally they swapped money back and forth like it was joint property, but things had changed. "Do you want it on the sly, no strings attached?"

"Nah, I want the strings. Make it all official."

"Sponsorship?"

He nodded and grinned again. "I need so much to get my enclave up and running—again."

"Thorne and the kids?" she asked.

"They seem to see it as 'cousin' and not 'the Wind Clan,' but they're signed up for the whole shebang."

She wasn't sure how things worked between *domana*, but she didn't care. Whatever he needed, she was going to see he got it. It turned out ridiculously easy to give it to him, too. It only took one phone call to the president of their bank and bludgeoning the man with her vicereine title, and the money was transferred from her account to Oilcan's. All the while Oilcan silently laughed at her. "If you need more, let me know. I'll put the squeeze on Windwolf." She'd been ignoring how the whole money thing worked—enjoying the opportunity to get whatever she wanted without thinking where the funds were coming from—but she really should start paying attention to that whole mess.

They talked for a while, making plans, just like they always had. Giant plans sketched out with the barest details and a hell of a lot of trust that they both understood what had to be done and would do their part. She couldn't have done half the things in her life without him beside her. This time, it was his dreams that they were making true.

The following is an excerpt from:

WEN SPENCER

Available from Baen Books
June 2013
hardcover

1

BOUNCE

"Your mission, if you choose to accept it, is escape your powerful, control-freak mother," Nikki whispered to the mirror hung on the back of the apartment's door.

"Miss Delany," the policeman said on the other side of the door. "I have a court order for your commitment to a psychiatric center for evaluation. Please open the door."

Considering Nikki was in a flannel Hello Kitty sleeping shirt, her hair looked like a rat's nest, and her roommate's fox terriers were barking up a storm, escaping was truly going to be mission impossible. Taking off nearly naked was not an option; she was going to have to be clever. She grabbed a hair tie from the hall closet doorknob and stalled as she fought with her long blonde hair. "Under the New York State Mental Hygiene Law, Article Nine, Hospitalization of the Mentally Ill, I have the right to appropriate personal clothing and safe storage of personal property. Do you understand my rights?"

For some weird reason, quoting law to some policemen was like hitting Superman with kryptonite. They just couldn't cope with material from their home planet. She totally lucked out—there was complete silence from the other side of the door. Score!

She did a mad loop around the tiny living room that currently doubled as her bedroom, snatching up clothing. Bra. Sweater. Blue jeans. She dashed back to the door, dropped the clothes on the floor, and stripped quickly. Over Yip and Yap, she could hear her mother arguing with the policeman—probably telling him to grow a pair of balls and just break down the door. It was a really good thing that the officer was waffling before he even got in the door.

"Please, miss, open the door or I'm going to have to break it down."

Nikki had learned young that escalation to force was a bad thing; it led to restraints. She had taught herself how to escape a straightjacket, but it involved dislocating a shoulder. She *really* wanted to avoid that if possible. Opening the door while nude, however, would be very bad.

"Okay, okay!" she cried to give herself more time. "There's lots of locks and they stick, so be patient!"

Luckily, like any good New York City apartment, the door did have multiple locks. She fumbled loudly with them between yanking on pieces of clothing. Of course her bra ended up inside out, but she could just suffer. At least the sweater pulled on without a problem. The jeans attempted to be an octopus of alternating reverse and right-side-out legs. Panic was trying to set in, which would be very bad. While she wasn't dangerously insane like her mother would like the legal system to believe, to the causal observer her hypergraphia certainly made her seem crazy. If she didn't have pen and paper in hand, her compulsion would make her write on walls with anything available. Time to go to her happy place. She took a deep breath and imagined ocean waves against white sand. Wind through palm trees. Colorful drinks with paper umbrellas.

"Miss Delany?" The officer knocked again.

"I'm opening the door!" She hopped in the foyer, tugging on the jeans one leg at time. "This last lock is sticking!" She gave the top lock a half twist, zipped up her jeans, and looked into the mirror. A Ford model at a fashion shoot she wasn't, but she'd pass as a normal, *sane* coed about to head out to class. "As always," she whispered, "this message will self-destruct in five minutes. Cue the *Mission Impossible* theme music."

She jerked open the door.

The policeman seemed impossibly young, although that could be because he was only about five-six. The clean shave, buzz cut, and wide eyes did not help either, effectively rendering him about twelve years old in appearance. His name badge identified him as H. Russell.

Behind him, her mother was trying to gracefully shove him aside.

"Officer Russell." Nikki backed away from the door, heading for Sheila's bedroom as fast as she could, hands in plain sight. She still needed something on her feet, her wallet, and something warm, since it was freezing cold for early May. "I need a minute to get shoes on and gather my things."

Yip and Yap decided that her coming down the hallway meant that they were getting out of their crate and fell silent.

"Nikki, I don't have time for you to get your things." Her mother was in full queen-warrior-senator mode in a black Chanel business skirt suit, more diamonds than some African nations, and Prada three-inch heels. "I've got a limo outside. Just put on some slippers and come quietly."

Nikki locked down on the first ten things that wanted out. She focused on the policeman instead. *Look, Officer Russell, I'm cooperating. I'm sane. You can just stand there and be embarrassed for me.*

"Let me pack one bag of my clothes," she pleaded aloud. "I'm crashing here. My name isn't on the lease. If I just walk out, my roommate doesn't have to let anyone back in to collect my stuff."

The truth was she didn't truly "own" anything. Somewhere far back in her childhood, she had a faint memory of having a bedroom full of things that were hers and hers alone, an entire room full of privacy. Currently everything "hers" was actually stuff she permanently borrowed from her roommate, Sheila.

"I will buy you new stuff." Her mother closed fast, her heels clicking menacingly on the hardwood floor.

They hit the bedroom door at the same time, and Yip and Yap went ballistic at the sight of a brand-new person to play with. Instantly Nikki was alone in the room. The fox terriers were the main reasons she was crashing with Sheila instead of other friends; her mother was terrified of dogs. She wanted every advantage she could use against her mother, just in case of days like this. Nikki hurriedly yanked open "her" drawer in Sheila's dresser and grabbed her wallet and passport.

A quick check confirmed her wallet had everything she needed to start life over. Again. Next time in Japan. That had been her plan since she was fifteen, only she wasn't supposed to leave for another six months. This wouldn't be the first time, though, that her mother had screwed up her plans. Nikki shoved her wallet and passport into her jeans' back pocket and grabbed a pair of socks.

Officer Russell appeared in the door as she sat on Sheila's bed to put on her shoes. Sheila's perfume still hung in the air, making Nikki aware that she was about to vanish out of her roommate's life without a decent good-bye. *This is so fucking unfair!*

Fair or not, it was what she had to work with. How was she going to get out of this? She pulled on her running shoes. She needed time to think, so she grabbed Sheila's gym bag and made a show of stuffing clothing into it. Yip and Yap would make sure that her mother stayed as far as possible from the bedroom, but Officer Russell was firmly anchored in the doorway.

"This is for your own good," her mother called from the living room, nearly shouting to be heard over the barking. "You're not stable enough to live alone."

Nikki breathed out a laugh. This was going to be one of those conversations where the whole point was to influence the interloper, not the person actually addressed. Her mother realized that Officer Russell was the main thing blocking Nikki now and was trying to shift him to her mother's side. Nikki hadn't been totally aware of winning him over but trusted her mother's judgment.

"I don't live alone," Nikki pointed out to both her mother and Officer Russell. "I have a roommate."

"She posts homosexual erotica on the Internet," her mother countered. "Some of it involves underage boys."

Nikki heart leapt slightly in fear. "You did a background check on Sheila?"

"My teenage daughter disappears to go live with a complete stranger she met on the Internet. Yes, I had a background check done on the woman."

"I turned twenty last month, Mother." Nikki picked up her lip balm and used it on her lips one last time. Her hypergraphia begged her to scribble an entire random scene onto the dresser mirror. She controlled the urge and only wrote "Bounce" onto the glass.

There, this time she let her roommate know that she hadn't been murdered in a back alley. Poor Julie had actually reported her missing before the FBI let her know that Nikki had been involuntarily committed to a mental hospital. *And wasn't that fun to escape from*?

Did her mother know about her plans to flee to Japan? The biggest problem with her plan was how easy it was for a senator to track a US citizen via a passport. Provided, of course, they knew to look. Up to now, Nikki been careful not to cross any borders. She had used a spy level of caution in getting a copy of her birth certificate and applying for her passport. She had researched methods of getting out the country quietly and how movements of citizens were reported. If her mother didn't have her flagged, then she could hopscotch to Japan. If she did . . .

Nikki closed her eyes. *Breath deep. Happy place.* A desert island, far, far away from her mother. Away from the closed-in spaces of a mental hospital. Nikki, a laptop, Internet connection, and nothing but white sand, shifting shadows, and the dazzle of sun off the ocean.

"Are you okay?" Officer Russell stepped closer, and Yip and Yap howled their disappointment that the second new person wasn't letting them out of their crate.

Nikki nodded, opening her eyes. "Just trying to remember if I'd forgotten anything." *Like getting out of this apartment a free woman.* Still, she needed to find out first what her mother knew. She made a show of opening drawers and going through the contents.

"Sheila writes stories based on Twilight," Nikki called to her mother. "You know—vampires and werewolves? They're not real people. It's called fan fiction, and it's all on a password-protected forum. You have to register with a valid e-mail account and verify you're over eighteen to read the stories."

"And you think this makes a site secure?"

She knew it didn't. The question was, in digging through Sheila's private websites, did her mother's people find Nikki's? Did it matter? If Sheila broadcasted Nikki's "Bounce" command, everything would be abandoned and everyone would move to the new site.

Nikki took a deep breath and tightened her hands against taking out the lip balm and this time writing on the walls. Fighting with her mother would get her into more trouble. She needed to run, not stand and try to win this argument she had no hope of winning. She never won. Right now, she needed to be clever and quick.

There was a fire escape outside the window. She had tested it out—once. The open steelwork triggered her mild fear of heights. If she could get a head start, the subway station before Officer ught her. She needed him out of the room.

ere.” She pushed the gym bag into his hands. “Oh, my pills. Can you grab them from the medicine cabinet?” She pointed toward the bathroom and scooped up coins from the dresser top. The one time she attended high school, she lived in dorms. There was a prank that involved the heavy room doors and coins. She had never tried it out on the apartment doors.

“Pills?” Officer Russell’s eyes went a little wider.

“Medicine. Mental patient. I know you guys are all a little jumpy about mixing the two. My birth control is in the medicine cabinet with some of my roommate’s prescriptions.”

“Y-y-yeah.”

She followed him across the hall.

“Birth control?” her mother cried from living room—as far as possible from the dogs as she could get while staying within supervision range of the bathroom.

“Trust me,” Nikki said. “None of us want you to be a grandmother.”

Officer Russell snickered and opened up the crowded cabinet. “Whoa.”

“It’s in the back,” she said unhelpfully, pulled shut the door, and pushed coins into the space between the wood and the jamb.

“Hey!” Officer Russell yelped as he found the door wedged shut tight.

“Nikki!” her mother shouted.

Three steps and Nikki was in Shiela’s bedroom. She hit the latch on the dog kennel even as her mother cried, “You stupid idiot! I told you that she was dangerous!”

Yip and Yap came bounding out, nearly levitating with their excitement. They ignored Nikki; she was familiar and thus boring. Barking madly, they charged toward the living room. Nikki slammed shut the bedroom door and flicked the lock. Two more steps and she was to the window and then out onto the fire escape.

Nikki's heart lurched as she forced herself out onto the steel catwalk and then down the rickety ladder. She couldn't let her fear of heights slow her down. She hit the street and started to run. She didn't stop running until she was in Japan.

2

THE OMG BASEBALL BAT

She was living in Japan. Osaka, Japan, to be exact. Two months and it still startled her in a way she found weirdly uncomfortable. She had moved dozens of times before in the States, from suburban mental hospitals, to a dormitory at a private high school in the middle of nowhere, to walk-up apartments in gritty inner-city neighborhoods. Never before had she constantly felt like she was being hit in the head with a baseball bat labeled "OMG."

Some days it seemed like everything triggered the feeling. Waking up lying on a futon on the floor. *Whack!* Going pee at a public restroom by squatting over a ceramic trough. *Whack!* Wandering up and down the levels of a bookstore with thousands of interesting-looking books without being able to read a single word. *Whack!* Walking through an entire shopping district, surrounded by people, and unable to guess or even ask where to buy a basic cooking knife. *Whack!* One minute she would be steaming along, enjoying the adventure of living on her own, and then the "OMG" baseball bat of cultural shock would catch her smack between the eyes.

By lunchtime, she was slightly punch-drunk by the number of hits she'd taken. The only reason she didn't suggest meeting at KFC or McDonald's was somehow the combination of familiar and uniquely Japanese that the two food chains represented would have been more unsettling than the little hole-in-the-wall traditional *okonomiyaki* shop. At least the act of taking off her sandals in the restaurant's foyer, putting them in one of the many cubbyholes, bowing to the waitress, and stepping down into the sitting area around a grill-topped table was now comfortingly familiar despite being totally foreign.

Nikki waved off the menu that the waitress was trying to offer her. "*Sumimasen,*" Nikki tried to remember the Japanese word for "menu." "English—English . . ."

"Ah!" The waitress smiled as she realized what Nikki was trying for. "English menu. *Hai*! One minute."

The waitress disappeared into the impossibly small kitchen hidden behind a half-wall where a cook was already standing.

Her best friend, Miriam Frydman, laughed in greeting. "One of those kinds of days?"

"God, yes." Nikki tossed her backpack onto the seat beside her. "There are days I could just kill my mother. All this would be easier if I'd been able to stick to our plan and learn Japanese."

Nikki had met Miriam the only time she attended "normal" high school. Not that you could really call Foxcroft "normal" as it was an expensive private boarding school. Miriam always had a fascination for all things Japanese. Nikki just wanted to have half the planet between her and her mother. She and Miriam had come up with the detailed plan that would have had both of them fluent in Japanese, employed by the same company, and sharing an apartment together. Her mother, though, had yanked Nikki out of school in her senior year and ruined every later attempt to keep to the plan.

Miriam tilted her head and squinted in deep thought. Her bright pink-dyed hair, gathered into quirky pigtails, and her high-school outfit were both part of her own battle with all things Japanese. She'd confessed that she had come to the conclusion that as a *gaijin*—an "outsider"—she would never fully fit in, so she had decided to stand out. Nikki would never have the courage to dye her hair or wear anything as short as Miriam's miniskirt, but Miriam was fearless. "Nah, I think you'd still be reeling even if you'd learned Japanese first. I felt the same way for the first six months. Really? The toilets alone break all language barriers when it comes to cultural shock." She slid her glass slightly closer to Nikki's side. "A stiff drink does help."

Nikki snorted. "I'm actually tempted. Much as a drug addiction scares the willies out of me, knowing that something like valium would make it—make it *seem* better—for a while . . ."

Miriam dragged the glass back to her side of the table. "My bad. Sorry."

The waitress came back with a sketchily translated menu and slightly better phrased "What do you want?"

They picked their *okonomiyaki* toppings, Nikki pointing to her selection on the English menu and Miriam ordering from the Japanese one.

Nikki tentatively added her drink order. "*Mazu*?"

The word got a muffled giggle from Miriam and a blank stare from the waitress.

From behind the hand covering her mouth, Miriam murmured, "Water is *mizu*."

Nikki winced, wondering what she had actually said to the waitress. Hopefully nothing obscene. "*Mizu kudasai*."

The waitress smiled. "Ah, yes, water!"

"*Mizu. Mizu*." Nikki repeated softly after the waitress left. Miriam might be right and being fluent might not stop the cultural shock, but she was tired of being clueless of what was being said around her. Her whole life had been a series of being completely helpless and at her mother's mercy or heavily dependent on the kindness of friends. "The plan" was for them to live together, but Miriam was locked into a lease for another four months at a place where she couldn't have a roommate. For the first time, Nikki was living alone, buying her own clothes, and cooking her own food. She loved being independent, but constantly being lost and confused the moment she ventured out of her apartment was frustrating the hell out of her.

The waitress returned with their drinks and two mixing bowls with the ingredients for the *okonomiyaki*. They watched as the waitress mixed up the batter and poured it onto the hot grill. She used a large steel spatula to round the batter into a thick pancake.

Why *okonomiyaki* was considered Japanese "pizza" still mystified Nikki; it was shredded cabbage mixed with flour and topped with barbeque sauce and mayonnaise. The only similarity was that it was circular and came with countless toppings. Personally she thought of them as very weird pancakes. She had discovered early on that the shrimp came with their heads still attached and she couldn't quite deal with having her dinner stare at her with accusing eyes. The other thing that slightly creeped her out was the fact that the shaved *bonito* on top wriggled as if still alive.

Once the waitress had both "pizzas" in place, she motioned that they weren't to fiddle with the dough with the little spatulas that were in lieu of forks and spoons. "Ah—cook—don't touch."

The *shoji*-style front door slid open, triggering a call of "*Irasshaimase*" from the two employees. The new customer was one of the impossibly slender *salary-men*, looking like he would only weigh over hundred pounds if you dipped him and his two-piece suit in one of Osaka's many waterways. It still freaked Nikki out that, at five foot three, she could look down at a goodly number of the Japanese men, the newest customer included.

He took off his shoes and tucked them into a cubbyhole next to her sandals as the waitress hurried across the twenty feet between the kitchen and the foyer to greet him properly. Waitress bowed, *salary-man* bowed back. It was like watching anime come to life; a good, happy moment that Nikki desperately needed at this point.

The *salaryman* was installed in the booth beside theirs and the grill-top of his table fired up to get ready for cooking.

"So?" Miriam nudged at Nikki with her socking clad foot. "Who's dead?"

"Hmm?" Nikki studied the *salaryman* in the guise

of cleaning her hands with the wet wipe. He was thin and delicate like a sparrow. She couldn't tell how old he was; he was so tiny he seemed like he should be only thirteen, but most likely he was a college graduate and in his twenties. Certainly, he made many manga storylines about boys passing as girls more believable.

Miriam nudged her hard, forcing Nikki to give up her study of the *salaryman*. "You're wearing your shirt of mourning. You only wear that after you kill someone. Who's dead?"

Nikki tented out her Goth Lolita shirt. It was the most beautiful thing she ever owned, all black silk with long sleeves, and lace everywhere. She'd bought it to cheer herself up after the Brit vanished out of the novel. Did she really only wear it after a murder? "I blogged it. Didn't you read it?"

Miriam covered her mouth as she yawned. "I had an *nomikai* Friday night. God, only the Japanese would require employees get hammered together on a regular basis. I spent most of yesterday in zombie mode. I did see your blog on doing your laundry but nothing on you killing someone off."

"I posted the murder later."

"Who did you kill?"

"The expatriate, George Wilson," Nikki told her glumly. "The idiot pervert."

Miriam laughed. "What does this make? Three love interests you've killed before even getting to the sex? You have to stop killing people."

"I've tried! I just can't stop myself. One minute George is drinking sake in his Umeda apartment, getting ready to go out, and the next he's taking an eight-hundred-dollar Blendtec blender to the guts."

"A blender?"

"Yeah, ever notice how sharp the blades are on a blender? I broke the glass container against George's head and set the blender on puree." Nikki made the sound of the blades spinning and twirled her index finger in a tight circle. "Blood all over the white countertop."

"Cool. I approve."

Nikki laughed. "I thought you would. The color contrast was stunning."

"Where did he get the blender?" Miriam pointed out the one thing that worried Nikki about the murder.

"I think he brought it from the United States. Does it really matter? It's not like it's a sword or firearm." It still geeked her out that the Japanese had more laws controlling swords than guns.

The waitress returned to flip over their pancakes. They were nice and golden on the cooked side. As Miriam asked the waitress something in Japanese, Nikki realized that the office worker was staring at her in utter horror.

Oops.

It was something she kept forgetting; since English was taught in Japanese schools from first grade up, Japanese people normally understood a lot more English than she understood Japanese. She played back their conversation and winced. How was she going to explain?

"I didn't really kill anyone. I'm a writer." Was that what the Japanese called authors? "I write books. Novels? Miriam, help."

Miriam laughed and said something that made the man bolt from the booth, grab his shoes, and run still in his stocking feet out of the store.

"What did you say?" Nikki cried.

"I told him you don't kill nice little *uke* like him, only big bad *seme.*"

"Miriam! I don't kill people—real people."

The waitress returned with the *salaryman*'s drink order and eyed the empty booth with confusion.

"Ix-nay on the urder-may," Nikki said. "I don't want a burned *okonomiyaki.*"

"You know, you could just delete the scene. George had real promise as a hero. Rich. Handsome. Alive."

"No, I couldn't," Nikki grumbled. "You know that. George is now dead to my hypergraphia. When characters are alive, everything just flows. All I have to do is occasionally nudge things into place with a little research on the details. Once they're dead, it's blank-page time. I don't have time to be staring at blank pages. Besides, he was turning out to be a completely sick bastard."

It had been the sale of her first novel that allowed her to continue on with their plan despite the fact she couldn't speak the language, hadn't gone to college, and had no work experience. Her advance on royalties arrived two days before her mother. It had gotten her to Japan and into an apartment, paid for a laptop and all the things she needed day-to-day, like clothes, with enough left over for her to survive for over a year. Even better, her publishers asked her to write a second novel. Unfortunately, they wanted the book within a year's time. She needed to deliver it on time because she would run out of money shortly after her deadline. It was a race to see if she could finish writing before her funds ran out.

The problem was that the novel had to meet certain standards. Because her first book was being marketed as a romantic thriller, she needed a heroine and a hero who meet, fall in love, and survive to the end. So far, all her possible romantic leads had been killed—except the one that mysteriously vanished in mid-sentence. But she suspected that he was dead, too.

"Don't worry, we'll work through it," Miriam said. "Do what you do best, and I'll fill in any missing pieces. Team Banzai go!"

Which was why Miriam was her best friend. She had always protected Nikki and gave her hope when life went to hell.

"Thanks," Nikki said.

"Okay, so we need a new romantic hero. A stud muffin for your little dormouse artist."

"She's not a dormouse; she's just emotionally scarred. George would have completely freaked her out. Him and his school girls in bondage fetish."

The *shoji* door slid open again and two more *salarymen* in dark suits ducked into the shop. These two were tall and sturdy looking.

"*Irasshaimase,*" the waitress and the cook called, welcoming the new customers.

The men scanned the shop, said something to each other as they noticed Miriam with her pink ponytails, and then focused on Nikki. There was something decidedly unfriendly about their faces.

One slipped off his shoes and headed for them like a very polite avenging angel.

"Miriam." Nikki indicated the man.

"Tanaka *desu*." He introduced himself as Mr. Tanaka. Make that Detective Tanaka as he produced a police badge and flashed it. He continued talking.

"What's he saying?" Nikki turned to Miriam for a translation.

"Oh my God, Nikki," Miriam gasped. "He's arresting you for murder."

—end excerpt—

from *Eight Million Gods*
available in hardcover,
June 2013, from Baen Books

Wen Spencer's Tinker:
A Heck of a Gal In a Whole Lot of Trouble

TINKER

0-7434-9871-2 • $6.99

Move over, Buffy! Tinker not only kicks supernatural elven butt—she's a techie genius, too! Armed with an intelligence the size of a planet, steel-toed boots, and a junkyard dog attitude, Tinker is ready for anything—except her first kiss.
"Wit and intelligence inform this off-beat, tongue-in-cheek fantasy . . . Furious action . . . good characterization . . . Buffy fans should find a lot to like in the book's resourceful heroine."—*Publishers Weekly*

WOLF WHO RULES

1-4165-7381-X • $7.99

Tinker and her noble elven lover, Wolf Who Rules, find themselves stranded in the land of the elves—and half of human Pittsburgh with them. Wolf struggles to keep the peace between humans, oni dragons, the tengu trying to escape oni enslavement, and a horde of others, including his own elven brethren. For her part, Tinker strives to solve the mystery of the growing discontinuity that could unstabilize everybody's world—all the while trying to figure out just what being married means to an elven lord with a past hundreds of years long. . . .

ELFHOME

Coming in July 2012

Available in bookstores everywhere.
Or order ebooks online at www.baen.com.

If You Like... You Should Try...

DAVID DRAKE
David Weber

DAVID WEBER
John Ringo

JOHN RINGO
Michael Z. Williamson
Tom Kratman

ANNE MCCAFFREY
Mercedes Lackey
Liaden Universe® by Sharon Lee & Steve Miller

MERCEDES LACKEY
Wen Spencer, Andre Norton
Andre Norton
James H. Schmitz

LARRY NIVEN
Tony Daniel
James P. Hogan
Travis S. Taylor

ROBERT A. HEINLEIN
Jerry Pournelle
Lois McMaster Bujold
Michael Z. Williamson

HEINLEIN'S "JUVENILES"

Rats, Bats & Vats series by Eric Flint & Dave Freer

HORATIO HORNBLOWER OR PATRICK O'BRIAN

David Weber's Honor Harrington series

David Drake's RCN series

HARRY POTTER

Mercedes Lackey's Urban Fantasy series

THE LORD OF THE RINGS

Elizabeth Moon's *The Deed of Paksenarrion*

H.P. LOVECRAFT

Larry Correia's Monster Hunter series

P.C. Hodgell's Kencyrath series

Princess of Wands by John Ringo

GEORGETTE HEYER

Lois McMaster Bujold

Catherine Asaro

Liaden Universe® by Sharon Lee & Steve Miller

GREEK MYTHOLOGY

Pyramid Scheme by Eric Flint & Dave Freer

Forge of the Titans by Steve White

Blood of the Heroes by Steve White

NORSE MYTHOLOGY

Northworld Trilogy by David Drake

URBAN FANTASY

Darkship Thieves by Sarah A. Hoyt
Gentleman Takes a Chance by Sarah A. Hoyt
Carousel Tides by Sharon Lee
The Wild Side ed. by Mark L. Van Name

SCA/HISTORICAL REENACTMENT

John Ringo's "After the Fall" series

FILM NOIR

Larry Correia's The Grimnoir Chronicles

CATS

Sarah A. Hoyt's *Darkship Thieves*
Larry Niven's Man-Kzin Wars series

PUNS

Rick Cook
Spider Robinson
Wm. Mark Simmons

VAMPIRES & WEREWOLVES

Larry Correia
Wm. Mark Simmons

NONFICTION

Hank Reinhardt
Tax Payer's Tea Party
by Sharon Cooper & Chuck Asay
The Science Behind The Secret by Travis Taylor
Alien Invasion by Travis Taylor & Bob Boan